THE DRAGON NEXT DOOR

A FIREBORN SERIES SIDE QUEST

VANESSA RICCI-THODE

THODESTOOL FICTION

Publisher: Vanessa Ricci-Thode
Editors: Kristopher Mielke, Sydnee Thompson, Kaya Skovdatter
Cover art: Leesha Hannigan
Cover design: GetCovers

Library and Archives Canada Cataloguing in Publication

This is a first edition of *The Dragon Next Door.*

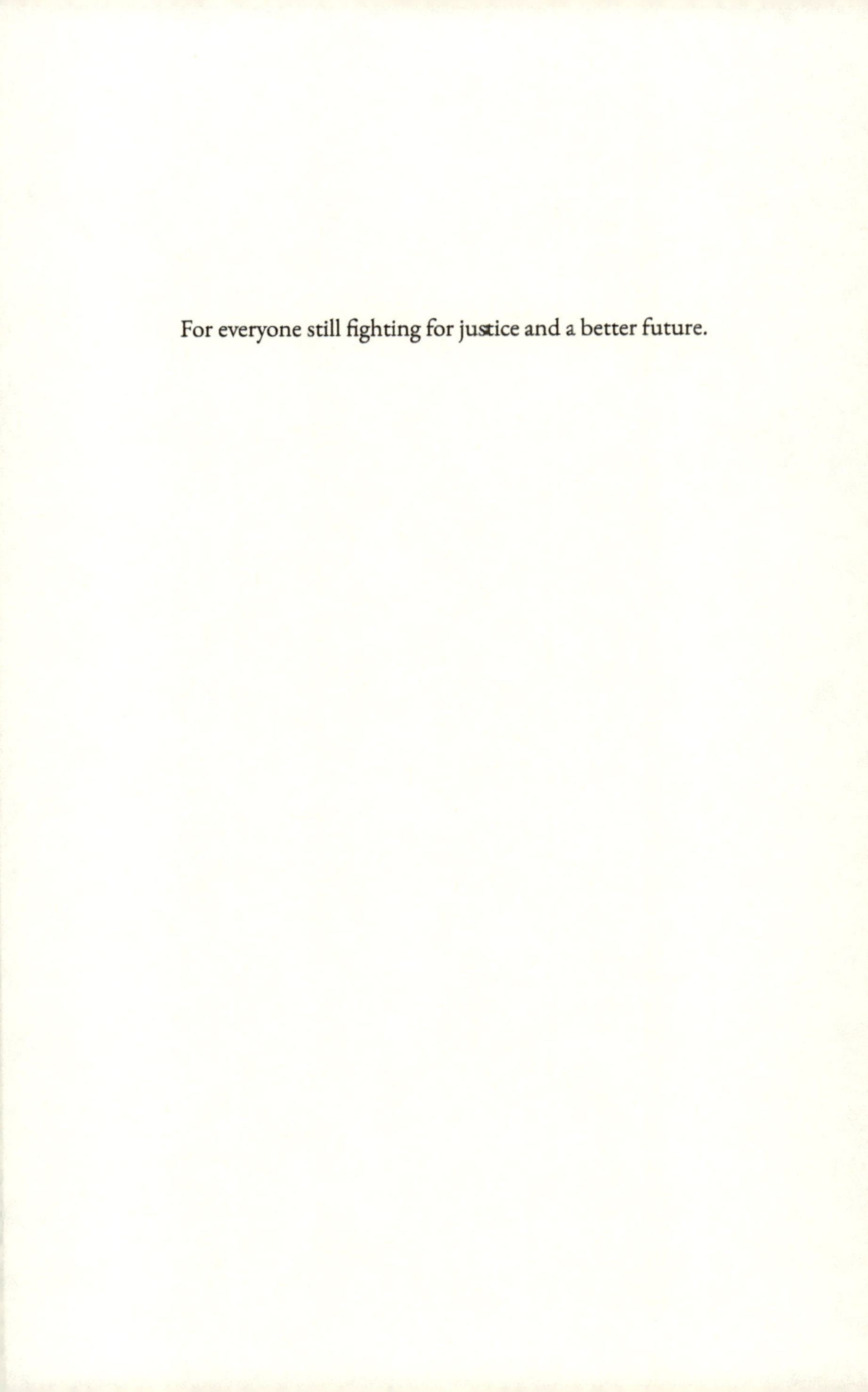

For everyone still fighting for justice and a better future.

AUTHOR'S NOTE

Hello reader! While this book takes place in the Fireborn universe, it is a standalone so you don't have to read any of my other books to read this one. The identities I don't share with the characters have been read for authenticity by people who do share those identities, so if something seems off or wrong to you, please remember that identity isn't a monolith and we all experience it a little differently, though this isn't meant to dismiss any accidental, real harm.

Also note that Canadian spelling is being used throughout the book. It's not American, it's not British. It's its own thing, it's weird, and I'm proud of it, especially right now when a certain orange buffoon seeks to erase my entire country and the many cultures it nurtures.

Content warnings: anxiety, bones/skeletons, drowning (implied), exsanguination, the dog lives.

YESTERDAY

Tollar could make water do anything she wanted, but she never expected to have to boil it under a stolen dragon egg while rafting upriver for five days straight. Her feet shifted on the water's surface as she balanced behind the egg, steam billowing warm on her face, the rapids propelling them both down the river and closer to safety. Tollar was safe enough anywhere she had a decent sized body of water to work with. But this egg? It needed fire. And it needed to stay hidden until Tollar could come to grips with the enormity of what she'd done.

She inhaled the cool night air, closed her eyes, and focused on the rush of water beneath her. The roar through the canyon drowned out the sizzle around the egg, but the sound pitched to thundering fury ahead.

"Wait, what?"

Even leaning way out, Tollar couldn't see around the enormous egg. Only the dim shape of rock walls loomed high in the darkness at her sides, so she crouched on the water, submerging her fingers to extend her senses into the river.

To where it dropped.

"Shit, already?"

She kept her hand in the water, feeling the river like an extension of herself—another long, meandering limb—feeling when the water under her tipped over the edge of the rock shelf like sliding one leg over the edge of the bed. She bent her hand level with the horizon and splayed her fingers, holding the water stable under her and the egg, letting gravity do the rest.

Like she had once already. Like she'd have to do once more after this. And never mind the two sodding waterfalls she'd had to go *up*.

"Another drop," she called to the egg. "But I've got it."

While she and the egg plummeted on her little half-boiling water shelf, the rush of air lifting her long dark braid to stream above her, Tollar extended her senses to the river below. Making a fist in her mind, she held the water, stopping it from flowing away so that it piled up beneath, defying the riverbanks. Until her water shelf hit the surface below, and she unclenched, letting the river flow naturally.

Like that time she and her oldest brother, Jarku—back when they'd still believed he was a girl—had piled every last cushion against the side of the house and jumped off the roof.

A corner of Tollar's mouth curled up at the memory. So few of her memories were good ones when it came to her family that she cherished them when they surfaced.

But the water under her feet lurched and sagged, like some exhausted beast collapsing. Tollar's brain buzzed behind her eyes, and she closed them until it stopped. She gasped as she lost her balance and nearly tumbled into the river. Again. The water around her calmed and the egg sank.

"Gah!"

Her thoughts skipped along the surface of her mind like a stone across a pond. This was too much and it was too late. Gritting her teeth, she solidified the water under her feet, pushed more water under the egg to get it on the surface, and began the painstaking process of heating that water up through absolute stubbornness. Flapping her hands like she fanned a fire.

As the river glided around her stationary water island, Tollar scanned for a place to stop. Jumbled boulders loomed out of the dark on both banks, the silhouette of the viny jungle canopy reaching across the gap to obscure the night sky. Ahead, on the inside curve of the river, the land flattened out, looked grassy.

"It'll have to do," Tollar muttered to the egg, rubbing her hands over her face. She'd never heard a dragon talk, but she knew they listened.

The current carried her little water barge to the bend, and she stepped off the water, her boots thudding over solid ground. Dead and boring and unmoving. When she focused, the water moving between grains of sand sang out to her like her people sang on the solstice to welcome the rains and a cycle continued.

Tonight she did not have that kind of focus and was glad she wouldn't sink into the ground if she didn't think hard enough about it. Not having to think about sinking for the moment freed up some brain space so she could strongarm the river's current, using wide stirring gestures to guide her focus, and use it to hollow out part of the bank where she left the egg sizzling in a boiling pond.

"We're almost there, little friend." Tollar glanced at the egg and then stared downriver. "One more waterfall. A couple more hours. But not tonight."

She considered lying down with her gear and longsword strapped to her back.

"Never get any rest that way," she groaned, unbuckling everything and dropping it to the ground. She sprawled on the grass, not bothering with her sleep mat, and used her gear as a pillow.

She had to keep the water boiling to keep the egg's inhabitant warm. She'd done it for four nights. But she really didn't think she could do it for very many more. Spending the first two days going against the current had taken far more out of her than she'd anticipated.

"I don't know what those raiders wanted with you, but I'll keep you safe."

In reply, the egg sat silently in its gurgling, steamy puddle. Whether the egg—or more specifically the baby it contained—heard and understood her, it seemed right to reassure it the best she could. Hopefully her efforts and the boiling water were enough.

It was a far cry from where she'd found it, in a lake of fire with a half dozen other dragon eggs next to a pen of chained and captive dragons, all inside a guarded compound. Keeping dragons captive was something she hadn't thought possible, much less by the people she'd gone there to fight—the raiders who'd taken over the port and laid waste to half the harbour.

Tollar had friends in the port, ones she hadn't been able to locate. It was probably too much to hope that they were still alive.

The gurgling pond rolled to a furious boil as Tollar's pulse throbbed in her ears. She pressed her fists against her forehead and took a long, slow breath before raking her fingers down her face and exhaling a groan.

"What a sodding mess."

She hated that she hadn't been able to do more. Dragons didn't belong in chains. Port Sawulxo and her friends deserved better. She'd have taken all of the eggs and freed all the dragons if she could. Would have stolen every last grain of salt those raiders had if that would have actually done some good. Instead she'd done the only thing she could—taken this one egg and run.

There was only one safe place to go. Only one place where she could trust people until she made sense out of what she'd seen in the port four days ago. That was, if being stuck exposed on this stupid plateau didn't doom them both. Tollar was half asleep despite the cool air but watching the night sky all the same, waiting to see if any dragons would spot her with this egg she wasn't supposed to have.

So far the night was full of the usual chatter of monkeys and birds, the buzz of insects. Nothing indicated something was lurking, waiting to pounce. No mountain cat lurking nearby to make a meal of her in her sleep.

But the quiet in the skies was odd. She really had expected to encounter dragons by now. There was a whole blaze of them living in these mountains.

Sleeping in the wild again hadn't been part of her plan. She'd meant to sneak into the farm a little later in the night and be tucked away somewhere safe. Safe and next door to her best friend. Tollar smiled up at the sky.

Stars glittered overhead, sharper and clearer than she'd seen in nearly a year, and the moons either hadn't risen yet or were both set. She never paid much attention to their phases. This trip, she'd spent most of her time in damp, turbulent places where the stars were blurred if not totally obscured. And they were different stars than the last time she'd bothered looking up at the night sky. She wasn't entirely sure how long it had been since she'd crossed the equator, heading south and not far inside the borders of Upalint, her home nation, but these were the constellations of her childhood.

She tried not to think too much about that.

But Beenala would be home—she was rarely anywhere else—and that was something to look forward to. And Tollar would have somewhere quiet and out of the way to stash this egg until the right sort of dragons got her message and came for it.

Hopefully it wouldn't take long. Tollar rarely stayed home long, and Beenala wouldn't be thrilled about having a dragon egg around.

Tollar sighed. Dropping in out of nowhere like this—she always dropped in out of nowhere, but it was the part about the dragon egg that would be interesting—had all sorts of potential to go very wrong. Tollar didn't like the idea of disrupting the carefully cultivated routine of the only proper friend she had.

"Nothing for it."

Couldn't go back and didn't have the energy to get much further.

She shifted closer to the riverbank, as close to the heat of the boiling water as she could—the water itself wouldn't hurt her if she fell in, it was the boiling part that worried her—and let the warmth of it lull her.

Just a bit of rest and then she'd finish the trip home, away from raiders or big animals sneaking up on her, where she'd be safe.

I

A growing roar came through the kitchen windows from the direction of the river—but Beenala ignored it and finished her breakfast, using the last morsel of pan bread to sop up the grease on her plate and pop it in her mouth. She dropped the scraps of fish to the dog, whose name was Ash (even if she was a shade of brown that true ashes never were), and set her plate on the tottering stack in the sink. The morning mist had burned away from between the trees on her farm, and it would be a perfect day to get her mulching done.

As long as whatever that noise was rumbling from near the river and out across the jungle wasn't some kind of trouble.

"Is that thunder?" she asked the dog. "I hope not, it's mulch day."

She should have finished mulching the bean vines three days ago, but it had been a market day and then she'd had linen to finish dyeing for Per Graza and then yesterday had been a lovely painting day so she'd taken her easel halfway up Mount Acrintaga to capture the early summer's vibrant hues. She couldn't very well put it off to tomorrow because she'd promised to bring some of the fresh crop of strawberries to her parents in their new apartment in the city.

"Ready, Ash?"

Beenala unhooked her machete from its place next to the door, surprised the dog wasn't pushing her nose impatiently into the jamb, waiting to be let out like usual.

Ash whuffed, sitting next to the table where Beenala had left the other half of her breakfast wrapped in banana leaf to bring with her out to work.

"Oh, right."

She tucked the snack into the pocket of her faded grey linen shorts and pushed away thoughts about dyeing them a more interesting colour. The grey was dowdy but didn't wash out her tawny skin and make her look pale like some kind of ghost. Beenala brushed a lock of her light brown hair off her forehead only for it to spring back into place. She sighed and pushed open the door.

The roaring sound, louder now, rolled out over the jungle as she stepped down the front ramp and to the humid warmth of the kitchen garden. Not thunder. Sounded more like a waterfall. But the nearest waterfall was seven leagues up the Arazow, and the river itself was far enough out at the edge of her farm that she couldn't normally hear it. And she didn't like the way the mist roiled through the trees toward her when it should be just about gone.

Ash hadn't come down into the yard with her, growling softly from the doorway to the cottage, ears alert.

The noise echoed off the hills, hissing and gurgling like the whole river was one big teakettle. Mist bubbled out from between two patches of trees on the northern edge of Beenala's forest, right between her trees and the Lipraxo family's farm next door.

Not mist. Water.

Beenala froze as it tumbled toward her. Had the power dam burst? But her farm was uphill from the river.

There was something in the water. No. . *On* the water. A boulder?

Beenala blinked and gripped the handle of her machete.

Yes, Bee, just machete the floodwaters.

She glanced around, considered climbing up onto the roof of the house. She didn't think the pillars supporting the house raised it off the jungle floor high enough. It was solid stoneworks and she had enough skill in terramancy she could probably hold it against the flood. Probably. Her pyromancy would be useless though. She doubted there was a pyromancer in existence who could stop flash flooding with fire.

Running wouldn't do any good. And she was more likely to fall than actually make it onto the roof. Beenala stood in her garden and trembled. Dropped her blade and watched the deluge approach.

Ash pressed her shoulder against Beenala's leg and Beenala remembered to breathe. Each breath wheezing and ragged as the water raged toward her.

Until it slowed, veered east toward the Lipraxos' abandoned farm, and settled into their side yard where a kitchen garden would have been if the farm itself hadn't sat empty for over a year.

The river stopped like it hit a wall and sank into the ground, roiling and hissing, until the boulder sat in the mud with water bubbling—no, *boiling*—around it. The water was stationary, boiling around the strange black rock marbled with amethyst. As Beenala stood, trying to process how this great rock ended up next door, a wave rolled around the side, bearing a familiar aquamancer along its crest.

Beenala grinned.

Even from across the field and over the shoulder-height berry hedge separating the two farms, Beenala recognized that form. Her body relaxed. Beenala's sometimes-neighbour, Tollar Lipraxo, stepped lithely off the water and onto the ground. Tollar wasn't light on her feet in the same busy way as Beenala, but every movement was graceful and intentional.

Tollar stood with her back to Beenala, staring up at the smooth, shiny rock she'd floated into the middle of the yard, and went through the complicated gestures of a summoning spell. Her long, dark arms moving gracefully through the magic that was more complicated for Tollar since she could use only aquamancy to achieve results. Beenala's heart fluttered. She was torn between retreating into the house and running over to greet Tollar.

She finished the spell, a tight vortex of water shot into the sky. Tollar took a step back and shielded her eyes against the sun to watch the spell's progress as it vanished, but she swayed, stumbled and dropped to one knee. Ash barked and ran over.

"Tollar!" Beenala dashed through one of the gaps in the hedges, reaching Tollar as her friend shoved to her feet, swayed again, but found her footing.

"What happened? Are you all right?"

"Bee!" Tollar grinned, her unusual silver irises sparkling, bright like the afternoon sun on the surface of the Arazow. "It's great to see you! I was worried you wouldn't be home."

Beenala squeaked out something that was meant to be a greeting, her face grew hot, but she couldn't stop grinning.

Up close, Tollar's little white tattoos stood out even more against her umber skin with the strange blue undertones—not the cool jewel undertones many of Beenala's neighbours had, but real blue like in the cenotes at the far edge of the city. Tollar had a few new tattoos since she'd last been home, more of the white symbols across her left shoulder and a pair of thin diagonal white lines at her cheekbones.

Beenala, holding her breath since greeting Tollar, worried her heart may have stopped as well. Tollar stepped closer, her arms twitching up as though she meant to sweep Beenala into an embrace, but then she halted and held her hands palm up in greeting instead.

Of course Tollar would come swooping in after all this time and offer such openness, like it had only been yesterday she last saw Beenala. Beenala was inclined to react as she normally did to people's greetings, a polite bow to welcome the openness but not to reciprocate.

But it was Tollar.

She was more than a neighbour even if it had been nearly two years since Tollar had last been in the city, and they'd both been fifteen when she'd last lived next door—and Beenala had just turned thirty-three. Yet Tollar still wore that wristband Beenala had woven for her an age ago, though it was faded almost to nothing and nearly threadbare.

What sorts of wondrous tales will she have this time?

Beenala only realized her hesitation in returning the greeting when something in Tollar's face shifted. Something like panic flashed in Tollar's eyes. Feeling her face warming, Beenala reached up, a little too quickly, to give Tollar's hands a squeeze of greeting and reciprocation.

Tollar's grin returned and she held Beenala's hands for a moment. Then Tollar released her, bending to scratch Ash behind the ears.

"That's a good dog." Tollar crouched down to knead her fingers into Ash's squishy cheeks. "Been keeping our Bee safe while I'm gone? I brought you a good bone, just you wait!"

Tollar gave Ash a final pat and stood, but staggered before catching herself and straightening. She was a head taller than Beenala, and Beenala noticed the dark circles under her friend's eyes and the way the other woman's hair, usually plaited neatly or in long smooth curls like eddies in the river, was a frizzy mess half escaped from a battle braid. Tollar was in full gear, longsword at her back and dagger at her hip, thin mud-streaked armour plating over her torso, upper arms, and thighs.

"What's going on? You're not yourself."

Tollar shrugged and stared at the boulder. "Been a long trip, is all. So glad I made it."

"You... came straight here this time? Are you just getting in?"

"Yes, thought I'd stop in and see my best friend." Tollar grinned.

"But, you never..."

"Ah, well, seems that farm is mine now?" She gestured toward the abandoned house. "No need to avoid it if it's empty. Good thing too, I needed a quiet place to land this time. And you're always on me to come visit."

"Oh. Right. It's wonderful to have you back!" Beenala glanced at the empty house. Tollar never said as much before, but Beenala suspected it was her family she'd been avoiding. Still, it warmed her to know Tollar hadn't been avoiding her.

"It's good to be back, good to see you." Tollar's smile faltered and her gaze drifted to the boulder as she stifled a yawn with the back of her hand. "Listen, I'll be here a few days at least and we can get caught up, but right now I've got a spot of trouble to take care of. I need your help keeping this thing warm." She gestured at the massive boulder, several handspans taller than Tollar, nestled in its boiling pond.

"Wait, how are you doing that?" Beenala stood straighter. "You haven't got fire magic."

"Tell me about it! Do you know how hard it is to boil water without it? I could borrow from a pyromancer, but they'd have to be close enough to touch for it to work."

"You're making that up!"

"I can show you sometime." Tollar paced around the side to where her kit lay on the ground, all of it sucked dry by Tollar's aquamancy except for the little puddle of water gurgling under the boulder. Tollar's kit, while dry, was as mud-caked as the rest of Tollar's things.

As promised, Tollar pulled out a monster of a bone, nearly as long as the dog, and tossed it to Ash, who immediately pranced off through the berry hedge and around the far side of Beenala's cottage, probably to bury it somewhere inconvenient, like in the herbs again.

Beenala stood before the boulder, heat rising from the boiling water, the air thick with the smell of hot mud.

"Sorry, Bee, nothing for you this time." Tollar was slow and unsteady getting back to her feet. "I thought to get you more of that orange pigment, but didn't get quite that far north. I know I missed your birthday and the solstice, but I wanted to bring you something. I thought I'd look for some nice fabrics in the port, maybe something you could make a new dress with? But anyway, business didn't go quite like I'd expected and now..." She shrugged and flicked her hands toward the boulder, then paced away.

Beenala gave it another look, something about it unnerving her, but before she could give it much thought, her mind seized on a piece of what Tollar had said.

"Wait, the port, do you mean Port Sawulxo? Is that where you brought this from?"

"Bee, I need your help. I can't keep that water boiling forever—it's been five days as it is!"

Tollar stilled, no more pacing, her arms hanging placidly at her sides with her cool silver gaze focused intensely on Beenala. Beenala's heartrate danced away, and she had to trace the purple veins in the boulder until her heart calmed.

"I need to keep it safe until I can figure out exactly what I've gotten myself into," Tollar said. She winced and pressed her hands over her face. "I need your help."

"I've got work to do or the corn will never get planted." And she'd never meet her quota to the city and that entire building full of people her farm was responsible for feeding would starve and— She inhaled deeply. It had been so much easier when her brother the floramancer had still lived here. But it wasn't unmanageable as long as she stayed focused. Right. Focus.

"It's always wonderful to see you, but it's mulch day." Beenala half turned to go to her cottage and find the machete she'd dropped.

"Just an hour!" Tollar's tone was desperate. Beenala stopped to watch her.

Tollar stifled another yawn and staggered sideways before catching herself.

"Toll! Are you all right?"

"I need to not have my attention divided. I just want to stop using magic for a bit."

Beenala blinked slowly and met Tollar's tired gaze, heat rising to her cheeks at the thought of her friend using some impressive feats of magic for five days straight. That she'd kept the water boiling *in her sleep*. Though she clearly hadn't had much of that.

Beenala took Tollar by the shoulders and led her toward the house. "Let's get you out of the sun."

"I just need to rest, just an hour." Tollar slumped on the ground against one of the stilts elevating the house. "Wake me up then and I'll explain everything."

"Yes, all right, I suppose I can spare an hour." Beenala held her hand up to the sky, measuring the time through the sun's height.

This won Beenala one of Tollar's magnificent grins, and she sincerely hoped her friend planned on keeping the farm because Per Graza was pleasant and all, but Beenala couldn't talk to anyone quite like Tollar. It was always so nice to have Tollar around.

"I'll help you with your chores," Tollar said through another huge yawn.

"That would be lovely. Now how do you need me to help?"

Tollar gestured at the boulder and toppled right over. Cold jolted down Beenala's spine, her stomach tightening.

"Blessed ancestors, Tollar, are you all right?" Beenala crouched next to Tollar and grabbed her arm to help her up, but Tollar was suddenly deadweight. "Toll? Toll!"

Beenala's limbs went watery, like she'd melt into the ground the way all that river water had. She clutched Tollar's wrist. Warmth returned to her body when she felt a strong pulse, Tollar's chest rising and falling with each long, slow breath. Beenala shook her, trying to wake her, but Tollar didn't stir.

Beenala glanced at the big rock. Five days. Tollar had been hauling this thing around, boiling water without fire magic, for five days.

"Okay, she's burned out, needs a nap. Fair enough."

Beenala dragged over Tollar's kit and wedged the bag under her friend's head, getting her better positioned to rest so she wouldn't wake up with a cramp in her neck. Then she sat on the bottom step of the abandoned house and stared at the large rock Tollar claimed to need help with.

A feeling of unease returned. The rock was too smooth, too shiny, even if it was stunning with its glittering amethyst veins. What kind of rock was it? Obsidian maybe? Onyx? Beenala placed her palm flat against the ground and focused her terramancy through the dirt and steaming mud, trying to get a sense of the rock.

But there was nothing.

"Wait, what? That's impossible!"

She tried again, getting a sense of the shape of the mud under the rock, but not being able to feel with her magic the thing she could see with her eyes. Glaring, she stood up and got closer, tried again. Still nothing. Leaned across the hot muddy mess of the former garden to put one hand against the rock, drawing back immediately because of the heat.

But still not feeling the rock with her magic.

"How is that..." Her eyes widened. "It's not a rock."

She stepped back, taking in the full view of the thing. Sidled around it until the shape grew recognizable. Beenala bunched her hands into fists and pressed them against her mouth, sucking a ragged breath through her nose.

"Oh... Oh no. Oh, blasted ancestors, Toll, what have you *done*?"

Beenala closed her eyes and held her breath, trembling despite the heat radiating off the egg. The dragon egg. No wonder Tollar needed to keep it warm.

Beenala stared up at the rock-like dragon egg and fought down the urge to run back into her house. Or out into the garden to mulch like she was supposed to. Dragon eggs? She was not qualified for this sort of nonsense. What was Tollar thinking? Tollar probably wasn't qualified to deal with dragon eggs either, and they would all end up eaten.

And this was more than stories, more than the safe comfort of hearing about the wild world Tollar ventured into from the familiar bubble of home. This was a dragon egg in the yard.

Where had she gotten it from? Who in the port would have a dragon egg? Surely, Tollar wasn't so reckless as to steal a dragon egg from an actual dragon? Beenala shook her head, no that didn't make any sense.

"Oh no, the summoning..."

Had Tollar summoned dragons? Beenala glanced around the pair of yards as though a whole blaze of dragons were descending already. Was a time, around when Tollar had last been home, that dragons had been a regular sight over the Naldes Mountains, especially near dawn and dusk when they hunted the gezars—giant mountain cats coming down into the jungle from the peaks.

Since then, the dragons had all gone off, and Beenala had grown used to the empty skies. The idea of it being filled with beasts made her head spin. Ash, back from digging, bopped her muddy nose against Beenala's hand, and she took a deep breath and stopped fidgeting with the hem of her shirt.

"Right, keep it warm..."

The water, while steaming, was no longer bubbling and there was a lot less of it, already seeping into the ground without Tollar's magic to make it stay put.

"Fire, Bee, you're a sodding pyromancer."

She took her flint off her belt to make a spark, ballooning it into a fire with her magic and pushing it into a ring around the dragon egg, the air around her growing cool with the effort. Could she use magic for the entire hour? Probably, but Tollar using boiling water to keep the egg warm was purely ridiculous, and Beenala simply couldn't expect her to start doing it again when she woke up.

"We'll have to build a fire," she said to Ash, who woofed in agreement.

Beenala fetched a stack of wood from the pile near her cottage, but stopped short of building a fire. Setting the logs in all the soggy muck was only going to make more work for her. Beenala sighed and went back to Tollar, shaking her shoulder.

"Tollar? Come on, I just need you for a minute. I'll even restart the hour."

But nothing, Tollar dreamed on.

Ash sat in front of her, staring expectantly.

"Now what?"

The dog cocked her head to one side.

Beenala blinked. "Yes, you're right! Just need to get the egg over a bit, don't I?"

Beenala pressed her palm against the dirt again, but not seeking this time. The ground rose up a few inches and the egg rolled onto a patch of dry ground, the fire still orbiting around it. The ground under Beenala softened from the effort. Ash barked and scurried away. Beenala hurried to push the wood in around the egg and bring the ring of fire down to get it started.

Before heading back to her house to get more wood, Beenala stopped to check on Tollar, where the morning sun was already encroaching on her friend's nap. Tollar would be better off inside the boarded up house and the boards would have to come off eventually—might as well be sooner rather than later. So Beenala set to prying them away and carrying them to the fire.

She looked at the dragon egg, her breath stilling at the sheer size of it and what it contained.

Ash leaned against Beenala's leg and she inhaled deeply. Just an hour. She could do this.

2

Tollar woke to darkness, heavy like all the depths of the ocean pressed against her. Like her joints burned with the fury of a fire demon. And no wonder. She'd fallen asleep in her armour, sword hilt pressing into her back. She groaned her way to unsteady feet and rubbed at the stiffness in her neck, wrinkling her nose at the cool, musty air. Tollar had fallen asleep without spreading out her sleep mat, just lying flat on the dusty stones, her kit as a pillow. Blinking into the gloom, walls loomed up and she remembered she was home.

Whatever home meant.

This place had only ever been four angry walls. And Auntie's place in Nytaltek had only ever been a dry place to sleep. Was that home? Tollar was certain home meant more to most people.

People like Beenala had a feeling for home, in Beenala's case to the point she clung to walls no longer meant for her. Beenala really needed a cozy little apartment in the city. Something like Auntie had. With bright light and space enough for Beenala's paints and textiles where she could make pretty things and not have to worry about mulch.

"Oh shit. It's mulch day!"

Tollar winced. She should know better than to impose like this. Should have stayed out in the mountains until the dragons came for the egg. But it just hadn't been safe enough.

And it had been two sodding years. Tollar *wanted* to see Beenala. She'd have to be more careful if she didn't want to send her friend spiralling.

Tollar stumbled around until she got her bearings, sinking into the familiarity of the house like sinking into a pit. But why was it dark? And when did the boards come off the windows?

"What is going on?"

Tollar propelled herself out the front door and down the ramp perpendicular to the stairs. Stars blinked through the mist, though it wasn't utterly dark, with a brush of grey to the east and the orange glow of a fire nearby. She skidded to a halt, staring around at the dark. Shook her head and got going. Had to find Beenala.

She rounded the corner and found the hulking form of the dragon egg in the yard where she'd left it in Beenala's care, surrounded by gentle firelight. Beenala had come through, ancestors bless her.

Tollar circled around the egg as she headed for Beenala's cottage.

"Ah, there you are." Beenala came through the hedge with logs stacked in her arms. "Are you up for good this time?"

"This time?"

"You were up at dusk to eat."

"I was?"

"And again after midnight to relieve yourself."

"What?"

Tollar stared at Beenala, trying to make sense of what she'd said. How long had it been?

Beenala set down the cords of wood and came closer, looking Tollar in the eyes. The tension in Tollar's shoulders melted away under the gaze of Beenala's warm brown eyes like firelight Tollar could just about drown in.

"Ah, good. You look awake this time. Tollar, I daresay you may want to consider never again using the boiling river raft trick."

"Err... Maybe five days was a bit much." Tollar rubbed the back of her neck. "Did I really sleep all day?"

"And all night, it would seem. So much for 'just an hour' but I'm glad you're here now. Help me get some new wood on the fire, will you? I ran out of pyromancy about three hours ago."

"Bee!" Tollar gathered up the logs. "Go to bed. I'm so sorry."

"Couldn't be helped. I don't like this," she gestured toward the egg, "but I'm not about to let the poor creature die. And it was clear you would sleep until you no longer needed to."

"Thank you. And I'm sorry about this. Go get some rest."

"Just an hour?" Beenala's eyes twinkled in the dark.

"Off with you!" Tollar chuckled.

She set to work adding logs to the fire, using her magic to coax the water out of them when they took too long to catch. And why hadn't the dragons come for the egg yet? They had homes all through the mountain range and should have got her message via the Guild by now. She came around the egg and stopped when she found Beenala standing there, a faraway smile on her face as she watched Tollar work.

It only made Tollar feel worse, Beenala standing there with great dark circles under her epicanthic eyes and her sepia hair that was short and straight and usually standing on end like a pale flame, more dishevelled than normal, like each strand insisted on getting back to the cottage to sleep, but not one could agree on the direction. And that machete hanging at one wide hip like she thought she'd get her mulching done yet.

It was all so very Bee. Her extensive routines and the baffling way she loved this tiny corner of the world. Tollar dropped the last log into the fire, confident it would be fine for an hour or two, and sidled over to Beenala.

"Bee, at least go have a nap. I can fetch more firewood if I need it. I can't believe you drained your magic over this!"

"I didn't think to use normal fire like a swib until I'd just about run out of juice."

"All the more reason for you to rest now." Tollar tried to gently shoo her away, but Beenala crossed her arms, glanced at the egg, and gave Tollar a pointed look.

"At this point a few more minutes isn't really going to matter. Tollar, where did you get a dragon egg? And *why*?"

"What a mess!" Tollar threw her hands into the air and paced around the egg as she spoke. "I couldn't just leave it there, now, could I? What kind of raiders keep dragons? No one keeps dragons! Dragons keep themselves! So it couldn't be anything good, could it? Can't leave something like a dragon with bad people, now, could I?"

Beenala stared at her, eyes wide, mouth pulled down.

"Look, those dragons I summoned will be here soon enough."

"You summoned them *here*?"

"Well it's not like the egg can trundle off on its own to meet them. I expect they'll just swoop in and pick it up and be off."

"But with only a summoning, are they going to know why you've got a dragon egg? Tollar, you're going to get us both eaten!"

Tollar waved a hand and looked over at the egg. "I sent a message to the Wizards Guild earlier, but there's no way one of them will make it up here any time soon. They keep talking about building a southern Guild centre up here but, well, you know how they are." Tollar shrugged. "Anyway, they should have gotten a message to whichever dragons are coming."

Beenala closed her eyes and gripped the hem of her shirt, shaking her head very slowly. "Tollar, you can't just—"

"It's not going to bother your family too much will it? What did you tell them?"

"Oh, no. My parents went with Erxo when he moved into Nytaltek proper just after you were last home. He's at the school, wants to be a scholar, and Mammi's knees don't tolerate the work like they used to."

Tollar stopped and stared at her. "Wait, you've got all this on your own?"

"The harvesters come regularly for the city's share, and Per Graza and her boys help when I need it. They've been helping make sure your place didn't go to weeds and the harvest gets delivered since your ma moved into the city."

Tollar exhaled noisily and glanced back at the empty house. She could think about the farm and what she was going to do with it (how she was going to get rid of it) after she got this egg back to the dragons.

"Well, that's three less people to bother with this." Tollar looked at Beenala and forced a smile. "But it's bothered you enough for one night. Go, rest."

Beenala continued shaking her head, but her stance softened. "Ash has been snoring in the cottage since the last time you were up. The only one of us with any sense is the dog!"

Tollar laughed and Beenala looked quite pleased with herself. Beenala turned toward her cottage. And froze. Hands trembling at her side. Tollar looked over Beenala's shoulder and a cold wave prickled over her skin when she saw the gezar, a mountain cat bigger than a horse, slinking through the shadows next to the hedge like an inky black pool.

"Ash...!" Beenala whispered, her voice cut off.

"Your door closed?" Tollar slid closer to Beenala, barely breathing out the words, her mouth next to Beenala's ear.

Beenala nodded but otherwise remained still.

"Dog can't get out, gezar can't get in. It's us you need to worry about."

Tollar glanced at the dragon egg, safe in the bonfire. She considered her house, but Beenala had pulled off all the boards and opened everything to air it out. They'd never get in and get it all shut up quickly enough. They were better off in the open where the big cat couldn't corner them.

The gezar stopped, its eyes flashing in the firelight as it lifted its head, scenting the air.

Tollar's hands twitched with the need to pull out her longsword, but one sword wasn't enough against a jungle cat with tusks as long as Tollar's forearm. Beenala was out of fire magic, which would be very handy right now, and Tollar wasn't sure yet how much water magic she could muster.

Only one way to find out.

She concentrated on the ground, feeling for the water, before pulling it up—but not too much or she'd trap them both in a sinkhole—and launching a spear of it at the big cat. The hit flipped the gezar end over end, crashing through the hedge, and it roared out its displeasure.

But then it was back on its feet, prowling their way.

"We need to run." Tollar half turned, but Beenala stared at the approaching beast. "Bee! Run!"

Tollar tugged on Beenala's arm and got her moving. But they were too slow. There was no outrunning this killing machine.

So Tollar reached for the groundwater again, syphoning it up and solidifying it under their feet as they went. She gripped Beenala's arm above the elbow to get her to stop running and help her keep her balance on the water platform.

Then she propelled them on a chute of water out away from the houses and deeper into the orchard. Up rows of crops between rows of trees, down the narrow paths joining rows, always heading for the river. It was complicated magic, especially when groundwater was her only available source at the moment, but it was far easier than keeping a dragon egg afloat on a boiling wave.

Not that she could keep this up for anything near five days. She was already getting foggy brained. She needed to deal with this before it drained her. Again.

First order of business had been to draw the cat away from the houses before it got the idea they were a good area to hunt. Now she needed to actually lose the cursed thing.

She continued sliding them up rows and down paths, worried her memory had failed her or the pre-dawn gloom betrayed them. But she heard the river growing closer and spotted what she was looking for.

The sentinel.

A whole row of sentinel trees edged the river between its bank and the road that ran alongside the farm. The neighbours across the river farmed fish and kept their banks swampy, but here Beenala's family focused on crops. The sentinel trees held the ground in place when the water was high to keep the river from encroaching.

And near the middle of the row was the biggest of the sentinels.

The sheet of water skidded to a halt underneath the sentinel's boughs, the nearest of them more than fifty feet up—lost in the shadow of the canopy, even as the deep, pre-dawn blue continued to brighten.

"Why did we stop?" Beenala asked, her voice shaky and eyes wide, staring out into the forest.

"We can't run forever. We need to lose it."

"I can't— We don't— But how—" Beenala's gaze roved everywhere and nowhere.

"Broken moons, you're awful at this," Tollar said, not unkindly, and lay a hand on Beenala's shoulder to make the woman look at her. "I know what to do. So you need to listen to me, all right?"

Eyes wide and frantic, Beenala nodded.

"Take a deep breath."

Beenala did.

"You're going up the tree."

"What?"

Something rustled in the foliage down the road, and Beenala squeaked in terror.

"Sit down, trust me, and call down when you've got a firm hold on a branch."

"What!"

The sentinels, with their thick but brittle bark, were unclimbable for anything heavier than a monkey. Most gezars knew better than to try. Tollar just had to get Beenala up there.

At least Beenala listened to her and sat on the ground. Tollar was close enough to the river to draw water from it, and she pulled away a wave and slid it under Beenala. Then she funnelled the water into a column and pushed it up and up, her friend perched on the top and voicing a little "Eep!" before disappearing into the dark. Tollar pushed the water up rapidly before slowing it so she didn't smash Beenala into any branches or fling her past them too fast to catch hold.

But she watched the forest around her, not the canopy above. A pool of shadow at the end of the row looked unnaturally dark.

"Gah! Toll, I'm up!"

Tollar stopped the water's advance and let the column sink down slowly. Beenala would cry out if she didn't really have a grip, but everything stayed silent so Tollar let the whole column rain down at once.

Then Tollar ran.

She was swifter without Beenala, who was sturdy in her own way but had her mother's knees and generous curves and only moved so quickly. The padding of feet on grass behind her confirmed the beast gave chase. The skin across her shoulders tingled. She would never outrun a gezar, not without more magic.

And right now, she didn't intend to outrun it. She left the stand of sentinels and ran along the riverbank until she got to the head of the rapids upstream of the tree keeping Beenala safe.

Tollar launched herself off one of the riverside boulders and parted the current around her descent until she landed on the riverbed between the two biggest rocks at the head of the rapids. She glanced up at the riverbank to make sure the cat wasn't ready to pounce. It wasn't, and she widened the part in the water until she found what she was looking for.

Smooth old wood tangled up against the boulders. She climbed into the gaps between trunks and branches, braced securely, and then closed the water around her.

She let out one long breath, releasing all the air in bubbles that rushed away, before slowly drawing in another, this one all water. The river wasn't too silty today so it filled her lungs smoothly, no different from air except for the cold. She coughed, but her body adjusted.

A smile played across her face. She didn't care how weird it was, submerging in the water and letting the river run through her was like coming home.

Could she live at the bottom of the river forever?

It was cool against her skin, refreshing like a cold drink on a hot day and comforting like a favourite blanket, even as it drove her against the snarl of wood on rock. But at least she didn't have to use magic anymore. Not having to focus on it lifted a weight from her thoughts.

Tollar settled in and watched the riverbank from below, the surface a dark silvery blue in the growing light. The waiting wore on her like ice pellets driven by a fierce wind.

What if it didn't work? What if the fool beast fixated on Beenala's scent up the tree rather than going after the moving target?

Tollar scowled at the bank and resisted the urge to climb out of her little nest and pace the riverbed. The whole point of sitting in this pile of debris was to save her energy. Swanning off in a fit would defeat the purpose.

Come on, where are you? Ancestors curse your stupid hide.

Her hands ached to hold her sword, and she gripped the branch in front of her instead.

And then there it was, great big stupid head silhouetted against the sky.

With barely a thought, Tollar pushed a wave out of the river to knock the big cat from the bank and into the rapids. She held her breath, hoping it wouldn't start swimming, but its dark shape rushed away on the current. It was someone else's problem, if it survived the battering it would get from the boulders.

She winced.

Cat dealt with, Tollar climbed from her perch and pushed herself through the river on a column of water much like the one she'd used to propel Beenala up the sentinel. She breathed out the water, using a bit of magic to get it all out in one go, then breached the surface and took in a deep breath of air. She set herself down on the waterside boulder and drained the excess water from her hair and clothes. Her armour had been crafted by an elemental blacksmith who knew how to protect the metal from rust, but that was no reason to go around like a swampy mess all the time.

A column of water trailed lazily along the ground behind Tollar as she approached the big sentinel where she'd left Beenala. She lifted it all in a big spout.

"Hop on, I'll bring you back down!"

It had grown light enough that Tollar barely made out the shape of her friend on one of the branches. But even once the waterspout sat flush with Beenala's branch, the woman didn't move.

"Soggy ancestors," Tollar muttered. She pulsed out a glob of water to engulf Beenala and pull her down with the column.

Once on the ground, Beenala sputtered and smoothed her rumpled clothing like she was trying to wipe away water, but Tollar had already drained it and sent it back to the river. Beenala raked her fingers through her hair, managing to make an even bigger mess of it. Then she dug her fingers into the hem of her shirt, though Tollar saw the way they trembled, and she took several breaths, each one slower and deeper than the last.

Beenala fixed her with a burning glare.

"Up a tree?" Beenala snapped. "Really? That was your brilliant plan?"

"It worked. You're welcome."

"You put me up a tree and used yourself as bait! What if it had caught you? I'd be trapped up in that tree for days. Probably die up there!"

"Someone would have come along in a few hours, down the road from the dam or maybe even Graza herself. And it wasn't going to catch me! I had control of the water all along. I could have rerouted the whole river at it but wanted to take the path of least risk to you and your farm. Come on now, Bee, it wasn't that bad."

"Says the one who wasn't stuck in a tree!"

"No, I was stuck at the bottom of the river. That's much better."

"How did you stay down there so long?"

Tollar went colder than the river could ever make her. She couldn't tell Beenala the truth, couldn't risk anyone knowing. People didn't like her as it was.

"Just used an air pocket." She shrugged and turned down the row of sentinels, heading toward the house. "Honestly, Bee, I had it under control. I knew you wouldn't be able to help, so I did what I could. If you'd practice a bit more, you'd have had some energy left over to help me with the gezar. You probably still can't light a spark, can you?"

Beenala scowled. "I've gotten by fine with my skill the way it is. I didn't learn the way you did. I didn't have to."

"Well. Looks like maybe you do now. Come on, let's get back so you can rest now that we've dealt with our bitey friend. You get many of those cursed things around?"

Beenala stared downriver and tapped her fingers against her thighs. "Probably had one a season for the last year."

"What!" Tollar stopped and stared at her. "I saw maybe three in my whole life before this! What're they doing out in the farmland?"

"I suppose there's more of them now that there aren't any dragons around."

Tollar tilted her head, taking in the words. That's what seemed so different. So quiet. Only the birds and monkeys to make any noise, and a whole jungle's worth of monkeys couldn't compare to the racket from a blaze of dragons.

"Is that why that egg is still sitting in my yard? I thought they'd have come for it hours ago."

"You didn't know?"

"There's been dragons in these mountains as long as there's been dragons," Tollar said. "Where the rotting moons did they go?"

Beenala crossed her arms around her middle. "I don't know, wherever dragons go. People didn't really want them around, some lot in the city convinced enough people they were a menace, and I guess the dragons took offence and left."

"I'm gone for two years and you all let the place fall to ruin!"

"It really hasn't been so bad. Quieter for a start. And all my past gezar encounters, I've had fire to chase them off."

Tollar paced over to a sentinel and drummed her fingers against its springy bark before she paced to Beenala. This was all wrong. Who knew when the dragons would get here for the egg? They could be coming from anywhere since she hadn't seen dragons since the captive ones on the coast. It could be a whole week! After the message she'd had the Wizards Guild forward to the dragons, she'd expected the Upalintan blaze to be waiting for her. Would they come at all?

This was approximately twelve times the mess she'd thought it was. And she needed about twelve times the intel.

"No one bothered asking the necromancers to do anything about the cats?" Tollar asked.

Beenala shrugged. "Oh, you know they never come out of their hills."

"But why chase off the dragons? They've always done such a good job keeping the gezar numbers in check. It's only going to get worse with no other predators to combat those monsters."

Beenala shook her head and kept walking. "We've had monsters fighting monsters. But what happens when it's time to fight the dragons?"

Tollar inhaled sharply and stopped dead, blinked at the back of Beenala's head. Had coming home been the wrong choice? Was it safe here at all? Tollar's limbs jangled and she quickened her pace to catch up.

"Why in the name of every ancestor there ever was would you fight a dragon? No one needs to fight dragons! Make sure they've got enough wild game to eat and mind your manners and they make the perfect neighbours! Bee, what is going on around here?"

Beenala stopped and glared at her. "You can't just frog off for years at a time and then swoop back in thinking you have all the answers just because you're some fancy soldier."

Tollar's mind stumbled like she'd stepped in some particularly foul mud, anger buzzing through her limbs. She bunched her hands into fists, gripping the emotion like she could physically hold it back, and chose to believe Beenala was not growing cruel and was only tired and scared and letting her mouth get away from her better judgement.

But Tollar's mouth went and did the same.

"I'm not some fancy soldier," Tollar said. "Thought you knew that."

"Not a soldier?" Beenala made a point of eyeing Tollar's sword and armour.

Tollar rolled her eyes and smiled, getting moving. "I'm not a real soldier anymore—those belong to proper armies."

"Then where have you been the last two years? And all the ones before?"

"Bee, every time I go, it's somewhere different and with different people. I trained here with the army, but it really wasn't a good fit. I'm a sell-sword."

Beenala stared at her like she'd said something particularly stupid, and Tollar's stomach went cold as she braced herself for the judgement, wishing she'd kept better control of her traitor mouth.

"But you're not a blacksmith," Beenala said slowly, uncertain.

Tollar grinned. "No, I don't make swords to sell." She patted the edge of her sword's scabbard. "I sell this sword."

"Do you have to buy it back?"

Tollar bit her lips together to keep from laughing. "I don't literally sell my sword. I sell my sword's service. It stays attached to me." Beenala squinted at her, and Tollar stopped walking and sighed. "Look, what I really mean is that I sell my services with the sword."

Beenala's mouth fell open and the cold feeling sharpened to a spike and drove through Tollar's insides. She leaned against a tree and stared down the row.

"So you go around cutting people for the highest bidder?"

Tollar swallowed. "Not the highest bidder, no." She crossed her arms and looked up at the cover of the fruit trees. "Just the most interesting one."

"Oh." Beenala coughed nervously and shuffled her feet. Tollar kept focused on the canopy. "Tollar... Does it bother you?"

"What?"

"It's just, you're upset now. Does being a sell-sword bother you?"

"No. Seems to bother other people plenty." One of her former comrades from training—one with a powerful position here—was especially bothered, but she pushed thoughts of Saivyn aside.

"Oh. Well then. It's just, if it bothered you, you shouldn't do it. But if it's just that it bothers other people... Maybe you should spend time with better people."

Tollar turned slowly but Beenala blushed furiously at her feet.

"Maybe I should." Then she sighed, pushed away from the tree, and continued down the row. "But it's the same everywhere I go. People don't really like me."

"You don't stick around long enough to give them a chance." Beenala met Tollar's gaze. "I'm sorry, I didn't mean to upset you, it's just I don't know much about what you do or where you go when you're not here. All I know is the stories you bring back, and those are highlights, not the whole picture. Is this what your normal days look like? Hiding in rivers to out-clever predators?"

"In a fashion, yes. Doing real battle like I did in Port Sawulxo is rarer for me. Mostly I join merchant caravans and follow them up one side of the world and down the other, keeping them safe and seeing what there is to see. Some days keeping them safe means standing around where people can see my sword and not get ideas. Some days it means out-clevering things as bad as gezars. Sometimes it means fighting bandits or raiders."

Beenala smiled and stopped to pull a weed, leaving it in the middle of the path before catching up to Tollar.

"Well, that doesn't seem so bad," she said.

"Thank you, Bee. Now let's get back so you can get some rest."

The cold spike melted out of Tollar's gut, replaced by warm light, like she was filled with sunshine. She remembered exactly why she was always so pleased to see Beenala whenever she came back to Nytaltek. There was a tragic dearth of constants in the company Tollar kept while she was away. Most of the time it was exciting, but being in Beenala's easy company reminded her how lonely being away could be.

But there was still the matter with the dragons and getting the egg safely returned to them. Tollar examined the canopy, green and vibrant in the growing light, and clenched her jaw against a groan. She didn't have a sense yet of how bad things were with the local dragons. Gentle Beenala didn't pay much attention to politics beyond what would affect her farming and her access to art supplies, so it could be much worse than she'd let on. Beenala, like a lot of Upalintans, didn't pay much attention to the wider world and had little understanding of how safe and lucky they were.

The cold spike drove through Tollar as she thought of the egg being in danger. If anyone found out about it, would *she* be in danger?

If the rift between humans and dragons was ugly enough, it didn't take much to imagine the worst that could happen. Egg destroyed, farm burned down, Tollar maybe in chains. Or worse. And what about Beenala?

If I have to flee on another boiling wave, I'm going to drown the entire sodding world.

She needed more information. Not just about what was going on at home, either. Everything in Port Sawulxo was wrong—the enslaved dragons were the worst of it, but there was more to it she couldn't quite see. Surely someone here would know something? And of those in Nytaltek she knew she could trust, only one of them could give her insight; only one of them held a position with the sort of power to keep Tollar and the egg safe if coming home really was the colossal mistake it had the potential to be.

"Bee, I need to go talk to Solia. Will the egg be safe while you rest?"

"Tollar, I need to go into the city to see my parents—I promised. If I'm not there on time, they'll come here."

Tollar squeezed her eyes shut and exhaled loudly.

Would a couple more hours really make much difference? No one was going to stop by, except maybe those dragons and that would be quick and solve the matter anyway. Let Beenala see her parents and try to catch Solia before she went on shift.

"Let's get back to your place before we run into more trouble and I've got to geyser you up a tree again."

"What does geyser mean?"

"Bee, old friend, I think I have an excellent story for you." Tollar grinned and, while she told Beenala about that steamy basin she'd been through four years back, she tried not to think too much about how things had changed since she'd last been in Nytaltek. Was bringing the egg here a mistake? Hopefully Solia would have some answers.

3

Tollar tossed another plank onto the fire and stared down the lane toward the city. Again. Beenala was gone, having taken some strawberries for breakfast with her parents—some new routine since they'd moved out of the cottage.

And Tollar wanted to get going. If she was fast, maybe took the river instead of walking, she could catch Solia before she started work. And maybe this was big enough to interrupt work?

Tollar growled to herself and looked up at the egg.

She *should* get into the city to talk to Solia, but she didn't like the idea of leaving the egg alone. Not without a better idea of the level of hostility locals had toward dragons. Send a message to Solia to meet her here? But Solia would lose her mind when she saw the egg and not give Tollar a chance to explain things.

"Ugh, that'll never work," she murmured to the egg before going to the house.

Some chocolate remained in the mug Beenala left for her, and Tollar sipped the last of it and gathered the last of the planks Beenala had pulled off her windows to bring to the fire.

Good sense said she should go see Solia and probably stop at Auntie's on the way back to pick up some normal clothes. All she took with her when she left was travel gear, and everything actually fashionable stayed at Auntie's house. The travel gear was fine and all, but it was utilitarian and ugly—green that had faded into something colourless and dull, plain trousers and shirt. Honestly, she preferred wearing her armour because at least it had some flair, and the lengths of armoured leather that protected her hips and thighs made a cute enough skirt.

She could have a nice visit with Auntie, bring her some of whatever grew out in the forest for a nice breakfast. Right after she popped into the guard house, see about getting on the roster for a week or two, and talk to Solia about... Well, everything.

She should go. And yet... Something kept her rooted here, a mild sense of distress over leaving the egg alone. Like some invisible band snapped her back into place if she tried to go too far.

The egg gleamed in the sunlight peeking over the mountains, the amethyst-coloured bits sparkling. Tollar walked its perimeter, dropping planks anywhere the flames were low, and noticed a long, deep crack in the exterior.

Had it somehow been damaged by the gezar? Or...?

As she watched, the crack lengthened, and new ones spiderwebbed out from it, crackling softly.

"Oh no."

Tollar dropped her planks and retreated, pulling water from the ground and pooling it at her feet to bring up in a quick shield if needed. Did dragons hatch angry? Or hungry?

"Oh shit."

What did a baby dragon eat? Would it know better than to eat her?

Yes, well, maybe should have thought of that before bringing a dragon egg home, eh?

"Ancestors be damned, I hope Bee left Ash in the house!"

Tollar caught glimpses of deep black and bright amethyst scales sliding past the gaps in the egg. And then the shell split in half, two great chunks rolling away while smaller flecks rained down, an ashy scent filling the air.

The baby dragon, and there was no mistaking it for anything else—leathery wings, four scaly legs, and spiky armoured body like the adults, but smaller, only about twice the size of the gezar—had its back to her and for that Tollar was profoundly grateful. It was beautiful, though, coloured like its egg with a glossy black body streaked with glittering amethyst, wing membranes of pure purple, and horns, spikes, and talons the deepest midnight black. It was a clumsy thing, coltish on spindly legs, flapping wet wings about ineffectually. Could it fly already?

It was the dragon's fire Tollar worried about, but there didn't appear to be any of that either.

When was Beenala coming back? Best person to have around with dragons of uncertain temperament was a pyromancer. Stronger the better. Having a dragon whisperer around didn't hurt, but first and foremost, Tollar wanted a pyromancer. And she had one. Usually.

All right, water shield will help some. It can't move fast yet so running is probably a safe bet.

Tollar didn't fancy hiding at the bottom of the river again, but she also didn't fancy being burned alive or eaten. So.

Thankfully, the creature hadn't noticed her, quite content to flail about and eat its own eggshell. Well, that made some sense, didn't it? Made for a convenient food supply. But with dawning horror she realized the eggshell wouldn't last more than another minute, and she needed something to feed the dragon that wasn't herself.

Tollar had met some dragon scholars in her time, though she paid minimal attention to what they said. Always talked about adult dragons. Tollar got the impression humans didn't have much opportunity to interact with younglings.

"If my farm gets overrun with scholars..."

But Tollar hadn't planned on telling anyone beyond Beenala, Solia, and that message to the Guild about what she had in her yard. Doubly so, now.

The baby dragon turned and spotted her. Its glittering black eyes were full of sentient intelligence, and Tollar had never felt so much like a cricket before a tarantula. All of its teeth were long as her forearm, and the pair of spiralling horns on its head were about as long as Tollar's legs.

"Good morning," she said, voice shaky and feeling stupid. What did you say to something born smart? Did it understand human language? Ugh. "Fine day to make your debut, good work! My name's Tollar. Do you come with names? Afraid I don't know much about your lot."

"Tollar!" the baby squeaked in a voice that reminded her of that sizzling wave they'd spent five days travelling on. Something in the tone spoke to curiosity rather than aggression and Tollar relaxed.

"Just so you know, since I don't think anyone's had the chance to tell you, I am not for eating. People are not for eating, all right? And my friend Beenala has a little brown dog named Ash that might look like she's for eating but she's not. All right? You can't eat Beenala or Ash. You understand?"

"Eating!"

"Oh shit."

Tollar glanced at Beenala's cottage, wishing her friend was home but equally glad she was out.

Tollar snapped her fingers and pointed at the dragon. "All right, you're probably hungry and you can't eat me or Beenala or Ash. But you know what you can eat? Monkeys! We've got so many monkeys, cheeky little demons always stealing the things that *I* like to eat. So you can help me and I can help you. Want to follow me? I'll show you the best spot to find some tasty monkeys."

"Monkeys!"

"Yes, excellent. Just this way, we'll head into the jungle. Sound good?"

"Eating!"

"Just so. Eating monkeys in the jungle and *not* eating me or Beenala or Ash."

Tollar sidled sideways to keep an eye on where she was going and watch the dragon too, in case it misunderstood that she was definitely not for eating. The dragon shoved itself up on its thin little legs, took a shaky step and promptly flopped over, scattering bits of the bonfire's remains everywhere.

Tollar put out a dozen little fires from the scattered burning planks and used some strategically placed columns of water to get the dragon on its feet. Where it promptly fell over and made a horrific screeching noise that she highly suspected was crying.

"Oh. Shit."

So abandoning anything even resembling good sense, Tollar walked right up to the dragon. "Is it okay if I touch you?"

The dragon responded by stretching out its long neck to nuzzle its barrel-sized snout against her and knocked her down.

"Right then." She patted its deceptively soft nose, used some water to ease it back so she could stand. "Look, you can't walk just yet, and I can't feed you anything just standing here. Maybe you want to have a nap while I go fetch you some monkeys to eat?"

"Monkeys!"

Tollar sighed. What if someone came by while she was gone? What if Per Graza heard the screeching and came poking her nose around? Tollar really could have used another couple of hours to suss out the situation in the city before having to deal with a baby dragon. Of course, she couldn't stand around until it got hungry enough to decide that she was, in fact, for eating.

"All right. Just stay here. Don't go anywhere if you figure out how, and I'll be back in a snap with some food."

The dragon lay down in the dirt that had at one point been a kitchen garden. It watched Tollar leave with such a pitiful expression she almost wanted to stay and let it just gnaw on her arm. But she got to the treeline and followed the shrieks of the screecher monkeys, little monsters always ripping down the bananas and smashing coconuts before they could be harvested. Made a mess out of everything. And if it wasn't cleaned up fast enough, the rotting fruit attracted the daggerflies and *no one* wanted that.

Not far from one of the old irrigation canals on what Tollar supposed was now her farm, she found a whole colony of monkeys. Little shrieking grey blurs darting through the foliage, about half the size of Ash. They'd always been the thing she missed the least when she was gone. But this was far worse than she remembered. Was it because the farm had been abandoned so long and they'd moved in? Or did it have to do with the dragons being gone? With the dragons gone and more gezars around, the monkeys would be looking for new, safer habitat, wouldn't they?

"Oh, but no one thought of that before chasing out the dragons, did they?"

Tollar sighed.

Beenala always talked to the farm when she tended to it. Tollar had been to so many places, and no one else talked to their food before harvest. She gripped the pendant made of her granny's finger bone—only other family member who'd cared about Tollar besides Auntie, who'd cared enough to gift Tollar the bone on her death—and took a deep breath.

No, other places didn't talk to the trees and the shrubs or the animals. But other places could be barbaric. Stripping the good out of everything around them without seeing. Tollar couldn't ever stay in Nytaltek for long, or any part of Upalint for that matter, but she couldn't stop coming back, either. It was the only place they did things right. Was that what home meant?

While they harvested nearly constantly, major harvest times each season involved a lot of ceremony. The last one she'd been part of, she'd been out here with her family and Beenala's and some harvesters from the city, and they'd been between the rows performing a whole song and dance. Keeping time with the drumming meant to evoke the sombreness of the year's final harvest. Some of the more traditional families came out in full costume, often feather adorned to mimic the plants they tended, and with symbolic offerings.

Tollar was not singing and didn't have time for costumes and offerings. She needed to get this over with and get back to the dragon before Beenala came home and got herself eaten. Or one of the neighbours stopped by.

This had been such a bad idea.

She'd never trapped or hunted before. Was the ritual different from the harvest? There was no getting out of harvest duty, except in leaving entirely. She groaned and pressed her fingertips to her forehead.

"All right then, what am I supposed to do?" she said, feeling ridiculous.

Food was food, regardless of where it came from, it all deserved respect. There was tradition, even if she couldn't remember what it was.

Well, there was fishing, she'd done plenty of that. This was close enough, wasn't it?

Giving Granny's bone a final squeeze, Tollar took a deep breath and opened her eyes, walking closer to the canal. The monkeys screamed at her and darted farther away, to the opposite bank. Some of them fought, the bigger males tearing at each other's fur.

She said as much of the fisher's prayer as she remembered, adapting it on the fly.

"Okay, look, I'm sorry about this," she said to the monkeys. "It's not for me, nothing personal, all right? Circle of life and all that."

They ignored her and went on fighting and screeching, but she had a clearer conscience when she washed a wave over a pair of males and pulled them down into the murky canal water. Waited. Focused on the ones fighting obliviously in an attempt to not think about what she was doing. Drew the now-dead monkeys out on another wave that followed her back to the dragon lying with its chin in the dirt, whistling mournfully.

"Okay, look. Here, monkeys! For eating!"

She deposited the corpses in front of the dragon's nose, being sure to drain away all the water. The dragon lunged forward, snapping its jaws around both monkeys at once and swallowing them whole.

"Sweet merciful ancestors give me strength and protect me." Tollar gripped the bone pendant. She hoped Granny's spirit was listening. And could do anything about dragons.

The little dragon lifted its head, which in retrospect was not actually that little, and fixed Tollar with its terrifyingly intelligent gaze. "Monkeys!"

"Yes, all right, those were a snack I guess? Merciful ancestors, how many of these things are you going to eat in a day?"

The dragon tilted its head, gaze fixed on her, and Tollar decided to assume the creature understood everything she said.

"Right, fine, you probably can't count yet. But that was two monkeys." She held up two fingers. "I'll see if I can fetch you—oh, how about six more?" Now she held up six fingers.

"Six monkeys," the dragon said.

"All right, fine."

And so it went, Tollar apologizing and drowning monkeys half a dozen at a time and hauling them out of the jungle on miniature waves much like the one she'd used to get the dragon here in the first place. She'd bring it monkeys like offerings to one of the old gods who dealt in blood, and the dragon devoured them in an instant and then stared at her until she went back into the jungle for more.

At least the monkey supply was endless.

Or was it? And did she really want to test that theory? What would she feed it if she ran out of monkeys? Should she feed it more than monkeys? She tried not to wince at what a phenomenally bad idea it had been to bring the dragon egg home. Of course, leaving it would have been far worse. Dragons did not belong in chains. But how was she supposed to know her foolish kin had driven away the dragons and she'd have to wait like this for help?

She really needed more support. Really needed to get to Solia, not that she could leave now.

After the dragon ate its twentieth monkey and stared expectantly at Tollar, who was resigned to her fate as monkey slayer and feeder of dragons, Ash started barking from somewhere near the direction of the city.

"Oh shit."

The dragon whipped its head around to follow the sound, and Tollar immediately threw herself between it and Ash's approach.

"That's Ash! She's a dog. Not for eating."

"Dog."

"Yes. You eat monkeys, not dogs."

"Monkeys."

The dragon craned its neck to peer around Tollar, and she turned to see Ash, hackles fully deployed, barking furiously from the end of the lane that sloped down to join the main road along the river into the city. Beenala came around the bend and stopped dead. Her lovely brown eyes widened and she nearly fell off her bike.

"Oh good, you're back! I could use your help," Tollar called.

"Get lit!" Beenala shrieked. "I did not sign up for this!"

"Oh shit," the dragon said solemnly.

And despite her guilt at heaping more on Beenala and her desperation over how rapidly the situation got away from her, Tollar nearly died laughing.

4

Draminedes was late again. Every day he got up earlier to make sure his robes were immaculate and his notes in order, but every day the unfamiliar garment in lovely sea foam refused to cooperate. It took forever to get it to hang right, and he felt shapeless, his soft middle and round belly—proof of his wealth and prowess—hidden beneath all that fabric. At least it was a stunning contrast to his terracotta skin tone.

That was why Karthiry said she bought it for him, one of many gifts she claimed a virile young man like him simply had to have. His father expressed concern over the woman lavishing gifts on her employees, but it wasn't like she paid him in fancy clothes.

Of course, Draminedes was too embarrassed to admit to his father that two days ago, while going over reports in her office, he'd realized she gave him these gifts in an attempt to seduce him. When he told her he was flattered but only attracted to men—and never mind she was older than his mother, though he knew better than to mention that—something dark flickered in her eyes before she smiled, readjusted her robes to reveal less of her lean form, and told him he could have the rest of the day off.

She'd been brisk yesterday, and Draminedes was determined to make a better impression.

But this morning he'd noticed dirt on the hem on his way out the door and had to stop to clean it. He'd held the robes up out of the dirt all the way to the manor and down the hall to Karthiry's counsel chamber, but now he let them fall around his feet. He readjusted his lenses and smoothed down his dark brown hair, which always stood at embarrassing angles as he tried to grow it out to match the new custom of his employer. Taking a steadying breath and lifting his chin, Draminedes gripped the strap on the satchel containing his papers, inkwell, and best quill, and pushed open the door.

"—Master Loch will not be pleased if we don't—" Karthiry said to Hollen, stopping short as Draminedes came in.

"Sorry I'm late." He slid into his seat at the little table off to the side.

"Not at all." Karthiry's pale pink face lit up in a flashing white smile. He looked down at the tabletop in front of him, never able to hold her rich green gaze for long.

Draminedes left her to her conversation as he pulled out his supplies and laid them out before him on the table. He glanced at the timepiece over the door and saw that, while he was the last one here, he was five minutes early. He let out a slow breath.

Karthiry continued talking to Hollen in low tones. Draminedes knew better than to write down anything said before Karthiry called the meeting to order, so he made a point of not listening in. But Draminedes did wish he could sit closer to Hollen and have a word with her before things got under way. She was the only other brown-skinned person in the room, even if she was a lighter shade than him, and all those pale faces around the table always made the back of his neck itch.

The fact that they were all sorcerers and he was the only swib only made the itch worse. But he was a professional, godsdamnit, and he needed this job.

So he set his supplies at the ready, polished his lenses out of habit, and let the conversations wash over him as he faded into the background.

"All right then, let's get down to business." Karthiry smiled her overbright smile and gestured toward the pitcher at the centre of the table. Spouts of water sprayed from its opening into the cups of everyone sitting at the main table with her.

Everyone else always ignored this display, so Draminedes pretended it was natural as rain. But Karthiry was unquestionably the strongest aquamancer at this table, probably in this manor, and possibly on the island and Biterna's entire archipelago. He'd seen plenty of strong aquamancers in his day, of course, there was no living on a string of tiny islands without them, but Karthiry was something special.

For starters, she wasn't merely an aquamancer, but a powerful elemental, though water was her strongest suit. She had a lyrical way of speaking, her voice clear and bright and full of jest, with her lovely accent from the far north. And she was so immaculate all the time, how she kept her flowing white outfits so clean out in the dust of the port and how her long flaxen hair was always so intricately braided and looped around her head like a crown. Draminedes was convinced she used magic to achieve the effect, but he didn't dare ask her. It was bad enough he was trying to work up the courage to ask what kind of jewels she wore, so clear and sparkling like nothing he'd ever seen.

It made him think of the way his family's life once sparkled and why he needed this job.

Well, the job was a means to an end. Karthiry promised to restore Biterna's prominence, promised to bring them the best goods through trade so none of them would have to toil in the dust anymore, and anyone from a kingdom made of gold must know the path to greatness. Draminedes would work hard with the northerners as an architect of the nation's revival.

He smiled at the thought of the port bustling with activity again.

"All right, Breon, report? Are we having success with the new acquisition?"

"Yes, m'lady," Breon said. He sat directly to the right of her, pale and beige as anyone Draminedes had ever seen, with strange rust-coloured hair. "There was some minor resistance, but the locals are realizing the benefits of the change. One asset was lost in the final kerfuffle, but the rest have been secured. Prospecting has begun, with limited success so far, but as our agents on the ground win over the locals, we expect their help in the matter to yield better results."

Draminedes let the words wash over him, barely understanding the code Karthiry and her inner circle chose to use, even around him. But Draminedes didn't need to understand, only to transcribe. Breon went into detail about supplies and resources and Draminedes zoned out and took notes.

"Excellent, Breon, this is exactly what we need for the expansion to be successful. Your implementation, as always, is brilliant. Master Loch will be pleased when I deliver my next report. Now, Crendin, how are our agents making out with the new target?"

Draminedes sat perfectly straight in the chair as he wrote, but poured in more focus. He didn't know much about the new target, but it sounded like a bountiful prospect, and Karthiry promised fresh trade and marvellous riches unheard of.

"Yes, m'lady, our agents are doing well. The dragon threat has been neutralized, and our agents have managed some favourable weather patterns. Unfortunately, the local elementals are a greater challenge than we anticipated, so we've had to move to the auxiliary plan and push our efforts back by as much as two years."

Draminedes hazarded a glance at the counsel. Karthiry's eyes flashed darkly while she drummed her fingers on the tabletop.

"Well, that will never do," she said, her voice crisp. "Do you think I spent my lifetime outwitting my three older brothers to allow for setbacks now? Perhaps we need to consider further alternatives."

"M'lady," Hollen said softly. She was a tiny woman who shrank even more next to Karthiry's splendour. "What if you sent a delegation and invited them? Biterna welcomed you, certainly these people will as well?"

"Hollen, really. Have you seen these people? Filthy savages, barely understood the prime of the first agent I sent there. We cannot work with them, there's barely anything to work with. They are not our equals and have done nothing to deserve our respect. They've none of the same ambition that made the good people of Biterna worthy of cooperation."

Draminedes shifted in his seat, but quickly stilled himself before anyone noticed.

"No, they must be saved from themselves." Karthiry's tone left no room for argument. "Master Loch has great plans for the land there. Do you not trust his judgement?"

The others shifted uncomfortably. Draminedes had heard of this mysterious benefactor before but knew nothing about him except that he was a man of great power. Even Karthiry deferred to his wisdom.

"We need to teach those beasts how to improve their land," she said. "The widespread famine must be dealt with before we can hope to stage our operations there. And the famine isn't going anywhere until they give up their ridiculous tree worship."

"And I've heard locals here say the forests are filled with demons and reanimated dead controlled by deranged witches." Crendin gave Hollen a withering look.

"Exactly. And they don't even have marriages, for star's sake! Just rutting in the dirt like animals, children left to drift with no notion of lineage." Karthiry shook her head. "They've got a long way to go to be nearly modernized enough for us to work with them. No, we must bring them around to the light and make room for proper farmland like we have been in our latest acquisition."

"M'lady has something in mind?" Breon asked.

"We need more agents, new ones, directly in their midst. And we need someone competent to organize them."

Draminedes nodded along and kept taking notes, until there was nothing left to write and silence stretched on. He looked up and everyone was looking at him. Tensing, he shifted.

"What do you think, Dram?" Karthiry held his gaze until sweat trickled down the back of his neck.

"I am always pleased to serve you, m'lady. But am I not better suited to taking notes?"

Her smile widened. "Nonsense, dear boy, you're perfectly suited for what I have in mind, don't be so modest."

He inclined his head politely, though he wished she'd stop calling him a boy just because he was the youngest in the room by more than a decade. He was twenty-three and not a child. Did he perhaps remind her of one of her own adult children back in Golden Hill?

But good work was his only hope of proving his worth.

"Of course, m'lady. What do you wish of me?"

"Go there and do what you do best—take notes. Connect with my other agents and see how best to help the locals get out of their own way so we can start trading with them. And find out who the biggest resisters are. We'll need to bring them around to the right way of thinking so they can help us with the rest."

Draminedes gave a shallow bow. "As you wish, m'lady."

He turned back to his notes, doing his best to take down further instruction and a final report on estimated resources held by the new target.

But his hands moved too fast for what was said and not fast enough to keep up with his thoughts.

When the meeting ended and the others filed out of the room, Karthiry had him remain behind.

"You'll do excellent work, Dram, you really shouldn't worry so much. You're like my middle daughter. She's a soft thing too, always needs reassuring, needs to be pushed out of her comfort zone to achieve greatness."

"Thank you, m'lady." Was that the right response? He tried to breathe evenly and keep his expression neutral.

She leaned closer, her floral scent dizzying.

"Are you sure you don't want to reconsider my proposition?" She ran her fingers over the sleeve of his robes, watching his gaze with the expression of a barracuda closing in on a floundering shrimp.

He swallowed and pressed his palms against the desk to hide how they shook. Maybe he should give it a try? She was so insistent and he owed her so much. It was such a small thing. But he couldn't hold her gaze anymore. It would be awful, he would be terrible at it and somehow that seemed worse than refusing.

"M'lady flatters me." He barely held his voice steady. "But I fear I would not meet your expectations in this matter. It's best I stick to my notes."

She sniffed. "Pity. Well, if you're sure."

She pulled a bell from her robes, the clear bright ringing echoing off the polished walls, and she stood and moved back to the large table. A side door opened a moment later and a servant came in bowing low. She was thick and round with smooth brown skin a touch lighter than his and long black hair pulled back into a neat braid. It took a moment for him to place her as one of his school friends, Peniope, who he hadn't seen since he'd started working with his father. She must have come to work for the chief straight after school, now working for Karthiry, as everyone who served the chief now did.

"M'lady, how may I serve you."

"Draminedes is leaving us on a new mission. See to it that he has everything he needs. Lord Crendin has the relevant details. And be quick, the boat leaves in the morning."

Draminedes blinked and his eyes widened. So soon? Had she known he would accept? What if he hadn't? Who would she find to go in his stead? He'd never seen Karthiry misstep, so she must have believed in his ability and his loyalty all along.

Peniope gave Draminedes a stony look but smiled brightly for Karthiry, bowing again. "Of course, m'lady."

Karthiry left the room without another word, and Peniope gestured for Draminedes to follow her.

"Let's get you outfitted, note boy."

He took a deep breath, a light feeling swelling inside him.

Karthiry had been in Biterna only two years and already she was expanding their influence.

Draminedes exhaled deeply. He had never left the archipelago before but was relieved by the prospect of going somewhere new. It would be dangerous, of course, especially if the local residents were as uncouth as Karthiry suggested, but it was exactly the sort of opportunity he'd worked so hard for.

See, Father? She's elevating us, just like I said she would. No more smuggling, we'll be back at the centre of island life where we belong.

Draminedes smiled and raised his chin. He'd bring back truly impressive information and move the timeline for acquisition back up where it belonged.

BEFORE

Beenala sat in the shade at the southern edge of the banana grove with a clear view of the family cottage, her easel set up before her, paint smudged all up her arms and no doubt all over her face. It was such a lovely spring day, the most perfect of spring days, and it had been far too long since anyone had let her have a painting day. But winter crops had been harvested and the spring planting done and there wasn't a whole lot to do for now.

Finally.

Beenala breathed in the rich smell of warm earth and damp leaves, all of it alive with the buzz of insects, the twittering birds, the distant calls of the dragon blaze, and picked up her brush, trying to put the feeling onto her canvas.

Except it wasn't turning out quite right.

Even from this distance she heard the shouting. Just indecipherable noise coming from the neighbours' house. Again. She tried ignoring it, but it was an especially frantic pitch today.

Beenala took a deep breath and scrunched up her face, trying to focus on how glorious it all smelled and channel that into her paint.

"Frog you! I hope a dragon eats you!" This was Tollar, the girl next door, screaming at someone, ancestors only knew who, and screaming loud enough for Beenala to hear clearly from across the long yards on the other side of the cottage.

Tollar sounded especially angry. Which really said something.

Beenala set down her paints and crept around the side of her family's cottage to see Tollar storming along the hedge, headed for the lane that joined this little cluster of farms with the main road into Nytaltek. Beenala's heartbeat sped up, and she stepped around the side of the house toward the hedge and the fleeing girl. Beenala had seen less and less of Tollar over the last two years. She barely showed up to school and was seldom home. Beenala's mother had mentioned something about Tollar spending a lot of time with an aunt in the city.

Today Tollar wore her hair in a tight battle braid and carried the largest pack Beenala had ever seen. How Tollar didn't collapse under the size of it was astounding.

Then again, rage as powerful as Tollar's could probably move mountains.

"Tollar!" Beenala picked up her pace to intercept. "Toll! What's going on?"

Tollar glanced back at her house, not that there was anyone to see, though Tollar seemed especially disappointed about that—there were plenty of raised voices coming from within. Tollar sagged, like she finally felt the weight of her pack, and dipped through the next gap in the berry hedge between farms to come stand before Beenala.

Beenala grinned up at her, always pleased to see her, but something was off about Tollar today. She seemed less angry and more defeated, her face slack and expression faraway.

"What's going on?" Beenala asked.

Tollar blinked once, looked directly at Beenala, dropped her pack, and crumpled, gasping great sobs of air and hiding her face in her hands.

Beenala tensed, her stomach feeling heavy as a moon. She couldn't remember the last time she'd seen Tollar cry, but was certain they'd been about five years old. She looked at Tollar's house and back at her own, up and down the hedge, before crouching down next to Tollar.

Now what?

She held her hand up to touch Tollar's shoulder, to try to offer some reassurance. But Beenala seldom liked to be touched, even for comfort, so her hand hovered over Tollar's trembling shoulder. What did Tollar like? Beenala rarely saw her with the rest of her family—Tollar's two oldest siblings left home seasons ago—and hadn't ever paid attention to how they interacted.

Instead, Beenala held her hand out, palm up, where Tollar could see it, like a half greeting, an offering.

Tollar gripped her hand. Leaned closer.

Beenala slipped her other arm around Tollar, rubbing her back and making the sorts of soothing noises her own mother made when one of the younger kids was upset.

Some of that heaviness eased out of Beenala's stomach and warmth spread back to her limbs.

"Tollar, what's happening?"

Tollar took a deep, shuddering breath and let go of Beenala's hand to wipe the tears from her face.

"I'm leaving."

"I see that. Where are you going? What about school?"

"Who cares? None of it matters anymore."

Beenala kept her hand on Tollar's shoulder, but shifted to look at her directly. The heaviness didn't return to her gut, but cold tightness crept across her chest.

"Well, I care. School matters, Tollar. Where you're going matters."

Tollar sobbed once, but no more tears fell. She looked down at her hands, shaking her head vehemently as she spoke.

"I don't know, okay? I'm just going. If Auntie won't take me in, I'll just go, but I'm never coming back here."

"You're just going to leave your parents?"

"Mum won't stand up for me, and *he* is not my father even if he sure likes to act like he is."

Beenala nodded. It had been six years since Zarro moved in with the family and became Tollar's subfather, her actual father having died before her mum knew she had one more baby on the way.

"But what about the farm?"

"That's not my problem anymore. And I'm not their problem anymore."

"Tollar! You're not a problem."

"You tell them that!" She flung a hand toward her house. "I am who I am and he just won't accept it and he just won't let Mum accept it and I have to go now."

Tollar stood and hoisted her pack, tears welling up in her eyes, though now she clenched her jaw and balled her hands into fists. If Tollar had been a pyromancer, Beenala expected sparks would shower down around her. As it was, the air grew thick and damp.

"I'm sorry, Tollar. This isn't right. This is your home."

"Not anymore, and it's not your fault. Maybe I'll see you around?"

Tollar headed along the hedge, staying on this side, and Beenala's heart raced with the need to go after her. She glanced at Tollar's house. Were they really letting this happen?

Beenala stayed rooted to the spot, watching Tollar go, the perfect spring day shattered and tightness growing across her chest. Tollar stopped at the bend in the road at the bottom of the slope and turned back. Beenala waved and Tollar waved back, a smile touching one corner of her mouth, though the rest of her expression remained sad. Then she was gone, around the bend and just gone.

Beenala stood there, watching the road for uncounted minutes before retreating back to her canvas to paint a very different day than the one she'd begun.

5

Beenala sat at the long kitchen table where she'd once eaten with her large family—the table now strewn with half-finished projects—and stared at the empty sink. She'd planned on cleaning today, but Tollar beat her to it. Every time Beenala went out to tend to the fires around the dragon, which had no fire of its own and got cold easily despite the summer heat, Tollar would come into the cottage and clean something.

Penance for disrupting Beenala's life and keeping a monster in the garden. At least the dragon was uninterested in eating her or Ash. Ash was currently under the table, curled up on Beenala's feet when she'd normally be out in the garden keeping the chickens from wandering off or chasing away anything that wanted to eat the chickens.

At least the dragon had stopped trying to eat the chickens after Tollar gave it a stern talking to.

Beenala sighed and Ash sat up to rest her chin in Beenala's lap.

Her eye caught the gleam of her machete hanging by the door, waiting for the mulch day she kept putting off, and if she could just get through her normal chores at her normal pace and in the normal order, the hot feeling in her gut would go away.

But the dragon's schedule was erratic. They couldn't predict when it would get up to hunt monkeys on the farms—at least it could walk on its own—and Beenala didn't want to be out there when the dragon could interrupt her. When it could further disrupt the proper order of things. She also needed to be available to help Tollar build fires for the creature whenever it napped, which was frequently.

"This is madness."

Ash whimpered and nosed Beenala's hands. The dog had been doing a lot of whimpering the last two days. Just as Beenala heard Tollar's voice and the dragon's hissing squeak, indicating they'd returned from their latest hunting session, the dog started growling.

Beenala sighed and got up. The dragon always napped after it ate, so it was time for her to light a fire.

Oh sure, Tollar could light a fire just fine, but she didn't have the magic to do it quickly or make it hot enough to keep the dragon comfortable, and it took Beenala's pyromancy to keep the fire burning clean so the neighbours wouldn't notice the extra smoke and come poking around. It had only been two days since the dragon hatched, but Beenala couldn't remember ever feeling so tired.

Gripping the hem of her shirt, Beenala went out into the side yard, half wanting to stay safe in her house and not encourage this folly. But Tollar had set her mind to it. And it wasn't like Beenala would be able to live with herself if the poor creature died because she didn't help.

"Bee!" the dragon said, always pleased to see her. It only made Beenala feel guilty for wishing the other dragons would come for this one quickly.

"Yes, it's me. Naptime?"

"Sleep," the dragon agreed.

It settled in on the stack of wood Tollar brought in from the jungle and tucked its nose under a wing while Beenala lit a fire around it. When she finished, Tollar came out of the cottage with a fish roll in each hand.

"Oh, is it lunchtime already?" Beenala asked.

Tollar offered Beenala one of the rolls and somehow looked even guiltier. Beenala needed to stop letting on how disoriented it all made her because Tollar's guilt over the disruption only made Beenala feel guiltier for not doing a better job coping, and then Tollar felt guiltier for making Beenala feel guilty. They kept out-guilting each other in the worst sort of spiral.

Beenala ate the roll without really noticing and headed for the cottage while Tollar approached the dragon.

"This is fish," Tollar said.

Beenala stopped on her side of the hedge to watch the dragon sniffing at Tollar's lunch. Just because she didn't like having a dragon around didn't make it any less fascinating.

"Would you like to try some?"

"Fish!"

Tollar tossed a chunk, which the dragon snapped out of the air.

"Fish."

"All right, I'll bring you some after your nap. They come from the river, but you can't go to the river, remember? Don't want the neighbours to see you."

The dragon snorted, a blast of hot air but no fire yet, and curled in on itself, wings folded over like a big purple blanket. While it hadn't gotten taller or longer, necessarily, the dragon was certainly bigger. Rounder, fuller. All those monkeys were doing it good.

What happens if it flies away before the adults come for it?

Beenala shrugged to herself and went inside. If the dragon flew off, that was someone else's problem, and that would be just fine because then she could stop being so concerned with everything it did. With keeping it hidden from anyone who might want to hurt it.

It would probably sleep for at least an hour. Beenala could get a good start on her work before she'd have to worry about the dragon awake and nosing around. Sometimes the dragon slept two or three hours at a stretch. But there was no telling from one nap to the next how much time Beenala would get, and the very idea of being interrupted made her want to go back to bed for the rest of the day. Tollar, on the other hand, had no problems keeping herself busy while the dragon slept—cleaning up the house and tending to the crops. Tollar had even been down to the river to fish, making sure she and Beenala had enough to eat. Her farm was approaching functional again, and it gave Beenala hope that Tollar might stick around for once.

How did Tollar make managing chaos look so effortless?

She glanced out the side window, catching a glimpse of Tollar turning toward the forest, very likely to go get some work done.

A piercing cry rang out over the mountains and Beenala startled, shrieking. Ash was at the front door, barking ferociously and clawing at it. Tollar stopped dead in the yard. The cry came again and Beenala curled in on herself, pressing her palms over her ears. Ash came over and barked in her face.

"Yes, thank you, you're so helpful," Beenala groaned.

When she looked out the window, Tollar was with the dragon, both of them watching something out toward the mountains.

"Oh good! Looks like your kin has come for you!" Tollar said.

The dragon, for its part, flapped its wings and wiggled like Ash did when it was time for fetch. Beenala wished Ash would wiggle more and bark less right about now.

"Yes, yes, dragons are coming. I hear them, thank you very much. Hush now!"

The dog ran to the door and barked some more.

When the call came again, Beenala understood why the dog was especially worked up.

"Oh no." Eyes wide and heart pounding, she glanced out the window where Tollar had gone still. "Tollar—!"

Beenala wanted to shout for Tollar to get inside or hide or anything but stand there, but her chest constricted around the words.

Ash, still barking, pawed the side of Beenala's leg, startling her and getting her moving. She rushed to the door, managing to squeeze through it without letting the dog out. That was the last thing she needed.

Then she ran down the ramp on numb legs, halted in the gap in the hedge when she saw the pair of dragons swooping straight for Tollar. One was larger than the other, so likely a dragoness, emerald green with a lacework pattern of lemon yellow scales across her body, while her companion, who was much smaller and likely male, was light grey like an overcast day had up and decided it ought to be a dragon.

Both of them had claws extended and all their very long, pointy teeth bared.

And Tollar stood there, hands twitching, probably wanting to grab her sword. Not that it would work against a dragon. Probably make them angrier than they already were. They'd see it as an insult.

But what did that leave her? Did Tollar have enough water magic to counter dragonfire?

Feeling like a ball of ice dropped into her gut, Beenala got her wobbly legs moving.

The dragoness came down in the yard like some great winged house a dozen paces away from Tollar, the male landing somewhere behind her. She bent down and screeched at Tollar.

Beenala cringed at the way the sound of it tried to cleave her head in two. She kept moving, trying to get close enough before it was too late.

"Greetings, Mistress." Tollar bowed deep. "I—"

Beenala gasped when the fire came, Tollar disappearing behind the wall of it. Time slowed down, the instant stretched out, but Beenala had been ready, all her will and all her power focused on where Tollar stood. The fire magic was a warm rush in Beenala's bones as she parted it around her friend like a blade through wheat.

She felt slow and sluggish even though little more than a second had passed, and then, hand out and against all better judgement, Beenala plunged into that blaze, bending the fire to her will and parting it around her, just as she parted it around Tollar somewhere ahead.

The heat of it made her skin hot and tight, but she kept shielded enough to prevent real harm. Her heartbeat hammered and if it wasn't for the heat she doubted she'd feel her body at all.

Her hand shook so much she worried she'd lose control of the magic and be incinerated. A subjective eternity later that was probably only a couple of seconds, she came through the fire to where Tollar crouched, a shield of ice in front of her, not melting despite the heat. Tollar held Beenala's gaze a beat, her mouth hanging open, the two of them an eddy in a river of fire, and Beenala shivered and turned away before she lost her concentration.

When the blast of fire receded a moment later, Beenala crouched at Tollar's side, ready to part the flame again if she had to. Easier now that she wouldn't have to part the flame in two different places and divide her focus. Hopefully.

"Mistress, forgive me, I don't understand—"

The dragoness roared and lunged, talons out and teeth bared.

Beenala inhaled sharply and clenched, eyes wide as the dragon bore down on them. Tollar's ice shield rapidly expanded and thickened. How would a sheet of ice stop a living volcano?

An instant before the angry dragoness reached them, they were enveloped in purple and yanked out of her path, clutched against something soft and hot.

"My friends!" the little dragon squeaked in its bubbling teakettle hiss, the words vibrating against the back of Beenala's head.

"Didn't see that one coming," Beenala wheezed, the dragon squeezing too tightly in its effort to keep the pair of humans safe.

"I mean, we have basically been its mothers for three days."

Beenala blinked and tried to look up at the little dragon's face. It was more like tending a particularly troublesome pet than rearing a child. She went cold, like rocks filled her lungs, and her heart beat against her ribs like it was trying to escape.

Tollar pulled down a fold of wing and craned her neck to peek out. "Mistress, may I have a word?"

The dragoness hulked nearby, teeth bared and smoke billowing from her nostrils, looking so angry Beenala was shocked she hadn't combusted. She was grateful Tollar had any idea of what to do. If the baby dragon wasn't securely pinning them both, Beenala would have run. Or collapsed.

"Look, I'm not sure what's going on here, and it's possible I phrased my message to the Guild poorly? Or they relayed it to you poorly? Can I have just a moment to speak with you before you decide to shred me?"

Still baring her teeth, the dragoness crouched, her head hovering above where the little dragon kept both women in a protective embrace. Tollar must have taken it as a good sign because she launched into explaining exactly the circumstances under which the little dragon's egg had been recovered.

"I'd have brought it to the Guild, of course, if that wasn't half a world away. This was much closer. I'm sure you understand?"

The dragoness narrowed her eyes but otherwise nothing about her countenance changed.

Tollar glanced at Beenala. What on earth did she think Beenala could do about any of this? Beenala shook her head and held her hands up helplessly. Tollar pressed her lips together, then continued.

"Okay. So I don't know what message actually reached you, but I meant only to keep this youngling safe until you came for it. And honestly, I didn't expect it to hatch before you got here. I've been gone a while and had no idea there were no dragons here anymore. I'm no dragon whisperer, barely know any scholars, but I've done the best I could."

While she never stopped snarling at them, the dragoness took a step back and sat on her great haunches.

The little dragon let the two of them go, and Beenala pitched forward, bracing her hands on her knees and forgot about running. Instead, she was breathing too fast while her mind sorted out what it ought to do next but couldn't come up with anything, so her stomach acted first, completely emptying itself into the dirt. Beenala gasped, sucking the air in deep, trying to breathe evenly, hoping her heartrate would slow down before she passed out.

"Bee?" Tollar leaned at her side, watching the dragons, with one hand stretched out like she meant to pat Beenala's back and remembered at the last moment that wouldn't make anything better.

Beenala took a couple more deep breaths and managed to say "I'm fine," in a nearly convincing tone.

Tollar, calm and poised as ever, cast Beenala a quick appraising look before stepping cautiously toward the dragoness.

"Right, good. So anyway, here you go! Baby dragon!" Tollar's arms moved in wide, graceful arcs as she spoke. "Safe and sound and well-fed. You perhaps noticed my friend is a pyromancer, so we've kept your kin adequately warm. We have no idea what we're doing and we are delighted you're here."

The dragoness stared. Beenala stood, almost feeling better. Tollar cast her another glance.

"Um, you've come to take the dragon, haven't you?" Beenala asked, surprised by how calm she sounded when she was certain she would tremble herself right over.

The dragoness hissed something teakettle-ish that resulted in the baby dragon squawking and clutching Beenala and Tollar again.

"Oof," Tollar groaned.

"Friends," the dragon said.

"Why is this one talking but the big one isn't?" Beenala asked.

"I think the dragoness *is* talking, just not a language we understand."

The dragoness growled.

"What's she saying?" Beenala asked.

"Eat you!" the baby said.

"Um..."

"No need for any of that," Tollar said.

How was she so bloody calm!

"Little friend, it's time for you to let us go and join your kin. They'll take far better care of you than we have."

"Staying."

Tollar's eyes grew wide, and she slowly turned, staring at the little dragon.

"Can it do that?" Beenala asked.

"I have no idea." Tollar tried to catch the baby's eye. "Look, we don't know much about your kind and frankly it's kind of a miracle we didn't accidently kill you. You need to go with your kin. You're safer with them. I mean, we can't teach you how to fly or anything."

It let them go and crept far enough away to see the two women properly. The dragoness had not stopped growling, the sound rumbling out of her like thunder to end the world. But the little dragon drooped in every way, staring intently at Tollar.

Beenala held her breath, afraid she knew where this was going.

"Look, you're welcome here any time, but you're safer with your kin." Tollar gestured at the dragoness. "I'm sending you away for your own—"

Tollar snapped her mouth shut and went still, her expression darkening. Beenala didn't know what she'd worked herself up over when it was perfectly reasonable to expect the dragon to go with its kin. The two of them simply couldn't look after it.

"No, you know what, you can stay."

Beenala's mouth fell open and she bunched her hands around the hem of her shirt. What on earth was Tollar thinking? How could she not take the briefest moment to consult Beenala before making a decision like that? Beenala took a step in her direction to protest, but the dragoness was on the move as well.

Tollar turned to the dragoness and held up a hand. "It can stay, but only if you can help us figure out how to get it to adulthood properly."

"Toll, what are you doing?"

"Oh, just look at the poor thing! It doesn't want to go. Why should we make it?"

"Tollar, we cannot look after a dragon." Beenala shook her head, the rest of her body shaking right along with it.

"You don't have to. You've coped with the disruption long enough, and I know that's hard for you. I'll figure it out on my own. Hadn't put any thought into it because I assumed it was going when this lot came for it. I'll sort it."

Beenala couldn't stop shaking her head, standing there with her mouth open but unable to get any more words out. This couldn't be happening. How did Tollar possibly think she would suddenly be able to manage this dragon, that could somehow freeze to death in the summer heat, without Beenala's help? When Tollar didn't have a scrap of furniture in that husk she called a house? This would mean more adult dragons, perhaps these two, coming around more frequently, and even if Beenala wasn't expected to help care for it, it would always be around. Would it keep ignoring her chickens, or Ash, as it grew?

The baby dragon hissed that strange language Beenala could never hope to understand, speaking to the dragoness who looked ready to erupt.

"Mistress, if I may?" Tollar said.

The dragoness lowered her head, scowling at Tollar.

"I know enough not to turn someone away. Is there any precedent to this? To a human taking care of a dragon? Properly, I mean, not like whatever's happening to the dragons on the coast. That's an abomination."

The dragoness looked like she was about to devour all three of them whole and be done with it, but then the tension drained out of her and she leaned forward, scratching in the dirt with one long talon.

Beenala stared. She glanced at Tollar who looked as perplexed as Beenala felt, brow furrowed and leaning forward. Tollar sidled sideways, closer to the dragoness, who was done. Beenala tilted her head and the lines in the dirt sorted themselves into letters.

The dragoness wrote a message in prime.

Not a pet.

Seeing it, Tollar gasped and turned slowly to meet the gaze of the furious creature behind her.

"No, of course not," Tollar said. "More like... A child? Like a child that could shred or devour us on a whim."

Beenala glanced at the baby dragon, who crouched beside her and leaned forward to watch while Tollar negotiated with the dragoness. Beenala shook her head some more. How was this not like having a pet? Or raising livestock? How could this possibly end without the dragons being furiously insulted and burning down the entire farm? Both farms.

"All right, how does this work?" Tollar asked. "What do I do? We've succeeded this far but that feels more like luck. Do I need a scholar? Does it need a name? Soggy moons, here I am calling it an it when surely...?"

The dragoness blew out hot air, and gestured between herself, her overcast companion and the baby. Pantomime. Great.

"I..." Tollar looked at Beenala. Beenala shrugged.

"Like her," the baby said.

"She means you're like her?" Tollar ventured, turning to the dragoness. "The baby is female?"

The dragoness settled back down.

"All right, so what do we feed her?"

The dragoness hissed something new.

"Whatever I want!" the baby declared, but the hissing out of the dragoness begged to differ.

"Little friend, I really need you to be honest with your translations right now." Tollar inclined her head toward the dragoness. "And 'little friend' is going to get tiresome, what do we call her? How do names work?"

The dragoness snarled, hissed something at her companion and sprang into the air. Beenala stumbled under the force of the wing gale and shielded her face from the dust and debris it kicked up. The dragoness skimmed low over the farmland, heading toward Nytaltek.

"What...?" Tollar looked at the cloudy male who did not move or make any kind of sound. Then she turned her perplexed gaze on Beenala.

"How should I know?" Beenala snapped.

Tollar kept looking between Beenala and the silent male.

"But why did she...? How do I...? Gah!" Tollar turned to the baby. "What's going on?"

"Getting help."

"Help to eat us? Help to sort this out? What kind of help?"

The baby dragon continued staring. Tollar glanced at Beenala.

Beenala shook her head and threw her hands into the air. The danger had passed and the longer she stayed out here, the more she encouraged this. It would never work. She glanced at the cloudy male and her stomach tightened. Dragons, right here in the yard.

Tollar looked between her and the dragons, giving Beenala the distinct impression she was somehow letting Tollar down. Beenala ran her fingers through her hair and swallowed the thickness in her throat at the notion she couldn't handle this like Tollar could.

"I'm sorry, Tollar, I can't do this. I've got a farm to keep."

And she turned abruptly, fleeing to her cottage without looking back.

"Bee!" Tollar called.

Beenala shut the door and let out a long breath. This was a fine mess Tollar had them both in, no matter how she insisted Beenala didn't need to be involved. There was a *dragon* next door. How was she not supposed to get involved?

"Ugh, what is she thinking?" Beenala said to Ash as she nudged the dog out of the way so she could get further into the kitchen. "Does she really think it's not going to affect me?"

Since Tollar showed up on a boiling river, Beenala had hoped she would stick around like a proper neighbour, but there was nothing proper or normal about raising a dragon. A few days was bad enough, but this was... What was it? How long could the dragon stay? How long *would* it? And what if something went wrong and it died? Or worse yet, was killed?

Tollar would be heartbroken. And would she be in danger? Would the dragons blame her? Blame them both?

Beenala wiped her damp palms on the front of her shirt and picked up the linen she needed to dye, before setting it back down and shuffling her paints around. She went to the door, unhooked her machete and hung it back up, and stared at it. She couldn't see how, but there had to be a way to get Tollar acting sensibly and reclaim a sense of normalcy from all this.

6

Tollar nearly had all the chokevines out of the banana trees on the edge of her garden when the overcast dragon whistled. The dragoness was returning, so Tollar ran to where the baby napped in the yard and the male sat vigilantly nearby. Tollar reached the pair of dragons as the large dragoness angled in to land.

She was carrying someone.

The region's dragon whisperer, though Tollar couldn't remember their name. She'd seen them down at the guard house a time or two. They were stunning with their thick black hair, umber skin so dark it was nearly charcoal, and mysterious grey eyes. Proper grey, not like Tollar's weird silver nonsense. The last time Tollar had seen them, they'd had their hair out in a great black cloud around their head, wearing plain trousers and bare-chested in a simple vest, but today they looked far more put together with their hair up in thick knots and wearing a black ankle-length smock that was high collared, sleeveless to show off rippling muscles, and tailored to fit snuggly to their wiry form but that elegantly flared at their narrow waist. It was richly embroidered in turquoise and orange. Official garb for a dragon whisperer? Tollar had never really paid attention.

"Praise the ancestors," Tollar muttered, kissing her thumb and pressing it to her forehead. Maybe things would make sense.

"Ah yes, I see the urgency." The dragon whisperer came toward Tollar but watched the sleeping baby. Everything about the way they moved was light and fluid, like a dancer, though their brow was furrowed in concern.

"Can you explain this to me? The Mistress has been flustered and conveyed only that it was urgent."

"Sorry, who are you again?" Tollar asked. "I mean, I know you're the dragon whisperer but what's your name?"

"Balipar." They rolled their eyes.

"Yes, right, sorry."

"Tollar, what's going on? Why is there a baby dragon on your farm?"

Tollar sighed and explained. "And now it doesn't want to go with them, and I'll be damned if I force it to leave."

While listening, Balipar first steepled their fingers, then tapped them against their pursed lips. Now they dropped their hands and gave her a direct look.

"Ancestors' bane, you're lucky the Mistress didn't eat you."

"Oh, am I?" Tollar clenched her fists and bared her teeth, blood pounding in her ears. "I should be grateful they didn't eat me in my own home? Well, isn't that lovely."

"Tollar, weren't you the one extolling on the virtue of manners?" Beenala strode toward them with her gaze fixed on the still-angry dragoness, and Ash trotting along beside her, also fixated on the dragons.

"Oh, manners, yes. Why can't *they* have some frogging manners!" She gestured at the pair of dragons and paced away. She'd had about enough being painted as the problem here. She should have known coming back to this place would be like this. Why should it change now?

"This is a rather delicate situation," Balipar said.

"They're the ones trying to set my cursed life on fire!" Tollar stomped back to Beenala and Balipar. "Coming into my home being the rudest guests, after I've done everything in my power—including dragging you into this mess—to keep their kin safe and thriving when I have absolutely no duty to. I don't expect thanks, but could they at least not try to kill me!"

The dragoness leapt at Tollar.

Beenala had her hands up like she might try for some fire magic and Ash was barking and the baby dragon lunged to intercept. But Tollar was quicker than all of them, ripping the water out of the ground under both adult dragons. The dragoness got halfway through her leap when the destabilized ground gave way beneath her hind legs.

The sinkhole that opened up was enough to contain both dragons, and Tollar had half a lake's worth of water spiralling up in a column next to her.

"This is my home and you can act like the distinguished guests you are or you can frogging leave!"

The dragoness, scrabbling at the soft edges of the pit, opened her mouth, bright with flame. Tollar was ready for her this time and dropped that entire column of water on her.

"Toll!" Beenala gasped.

"I warned her."

"And now I'm warning you." Balipar moved in front of Tollar. "Get back and let me see if I can do anything to fix this."

Beenala gave Tollar a wounded look as she moved next to Balipar, muttering assurances she could help keep the dragon whisperer safe until they could calm the situation.

Tollar didn't know why Beenala kept coming out when she so clearly wanted to get on with her farming, but it made her inordinately happy to have her friend back out here with her. And then immediately guilty for being the reason Beenala couldn't get on with her farming.

Both dragons floundered in the sinkhole, snarling and snapping, steam rising around them. Tollar solidified the water under their feet to help them climb out.

Balipar approached the struggling dragons, bowing so low their forehead nearly touched the ground, murmuring whatever platitudes the dragoness needed to hear. The baby dragon moved in around Tollar, tail and one wing wrapped protectively around her.

Tollar smiled and stroked the dragon's soft nose.

"You really should go with them," she whispered.

"Staying."

"I want you to be safe."

"Staying!" The dragon nuzzled her nose into Tollar's side hard enough that Tollar would have fallen if the tail and wing weren't there to keep her propped up.

Tollar stroked the baby's nose some more, feeling light and warm.

The adult dragons were out of the hole, and Tollar dried the water from their scales. See? She could have some frogging manners if they'd stop trying to vaporize her! They didn't look like they wanted to vaporize anyone anymore, though the dragoness didn't exactly look happy. Though Tollar had no idea what happy looked like on that one because she'd never seen it.

"Everyone is tired and confused and possibly hungry," Beenala said. "Would our new dragon guests like something to eat after their long journey here? Tollar can bring in some fish from the river or maybe some monkeys? Failing that, you're welcome to hunt all the gezars you want."

Tollar crossed her arms and leaned back. She was absolutely not fetching any monkeys, and they could rot if they thought she might.

But the dragoness hissed something and then both dragons flew off, Ash barking in their wake.

Beenala gave Tollar a sharp glance. "You're welcome. Again."

"Really, Bee, I've got the dragon whisperer here to help—"

"More like get killed right along with you, but fine."

Balipar snorted a laugh.

Tollar rolled her eyes. "Fine, but you don't have to keep getting involved like this."

"Tollar, this involves me whether you like it to or not. If that dragon decides to light some impressive fires, do you think it will only burn your yard or your trees?"

"You maybe noticed the part where I handled the fire?"

"You can't keep making cenotes in the yard!"

"Why not?"

Beenala growled.

"I'll get it put back. I can handle this."

"Even when my family comes to visit? Twice a week."

"What?"

Beenala gave her a hard look. Ash booped her nose into Beenala's hand.

"Just because they don't live here anymore doesn't mean they've abandoned the farm like your family. I'm not turning them away to help you keep a ridiculous and dangerous secret. They're coming for dinner tomorrow."

"What!"

"Just so you know." Then Beenala bowed politely to Balipar, gave Tollar one last look, and left again. Ash remained where she was for a moment, watching the baby dragon curl up to resume her nap, before trotting after Beenala.

Tollar watched her disappear into her cottage, the light feeling of seeing her sinking away.

"Right. Balipar. What the rotting moons is going on here?"

Balipar grasped their hands behind their back, the very picture of poise, and watched the baby dragon.

"Picking a fight with the dragons you want help from isn't the best way to lead."

"She started it."

"They're rightfully furious about you having a dragon egg. Not you specifically, but the situation broadly. They understand you were and are acting on the hatchling's best interests. But this is a bad situation. It's not something they would have ever been pleased about, but in the last nearly two decades or so, relations between dragons and humans have grown more strained."

"In the north," Tollar said. "But things have always been a mess down there."

"Says the woman who dropped a pair of dragons into a cenote."

"Pfft."

"The dragons are less than pleased with Upalint these days, and this is honestly the first time I've seen any dragons in almost three seasons. It will be better for all parties if we convince the hatchling to go."

"I know what it's like to be pushed out of places you'd rather remain, so I'm not doing that to her. She wants to stay. I'd like to find a way for her to thrive here."

Balipar closed their eyes but otherwise remained still.

"It's not safe here," Tollar said.

"There are safer places for a baby dragon. I will find out if it's this place," they gestured at the jungle, "or you specifically the baby has become attached to. Perhaps if you go with them..."

Tollar glanced at the mountains where the dragons had disappeared, the urge to go calling to her.

"You'll need to stop picking fights."

Tollar rolled her eyes. "So why can I understand what the baby says but not the adults?"

"Something to do with an attack on the dragons, their city and a particularly potent family of pyromancers. And when the dust settled, the dragons had all gone silent. Something's changed in the last season or so that has some of them talking again, mostly the younger ones. Before I was born, all a dragon whisperer needed was to be lovely to look at and someone the dragons could be fond of. Or fireproof. I've heard certain pyromancers do well in this role."

Tollar snorted. She supposed what Balipar lacked physically—which wasn't much—they made up for with their outrageous outfits.

"So they understand us just fine but mostly won't talk to us?"

"That's correct. They pick up languages quickly."

"Well, it's been two days but that one seems to know everything I say." She gestured to the baby. "So I've been talking to her like she's a person."

Balipar nodded. "If you've treated her like more than a beast, it could explain why she's so fond of you. Look, I'm not a scholar so I don't know the intricacies of dragon parenting."

"Wait, you're a dragon whisperer but not a scholar?"

"You don't need to know everything about their ways to talk to them. Some dragon whisperers are both but I am not, even if I pick up lore here and there. So I can't speak to raising a hatchling—not sure even the dragon whisperer who lives in the dragon city and *is* a scholar knows much about that—but it's likely she sees you in a motherly fashion. You and your friend both."

Tollar paced a semicircle around the sleeping dragon and the pretty dragon whisperer. "If those dragons insist this one should go with them—I expect she's got parents somewhere—I'm not going to fight them. But if you think they'll have me along, that might be the best option."

"They'll want to leave immediately. Will you have time to prepare?"

"I'll need to say goodbye to Bee, but I haven't unpacked. I can go now."

Beenala wouldn't like that, and Auntie wouldn't let her forget she'd come and gone without so much as a hello. But going with dragons, seeing the world they saw... She couldn't pass that up.

Balipar looked up, the pair of dragons glided in from somewhere out over the mountains.

"I will talk to them. Stay here and be quiet if you truly want this to work. I'll call you over if your input is needed."

The pair of dragons landed nearby, and Balipar bowed deeply to them.

Tollar groaned and resumed pacing. Balipar said little and the dragoness said nothing, though she did a lot of scratching in the dirt—more messages in prime.

"This is ridiculous."

The baby lifted her head. "Ridiculous."

"You sure you don't want to go with them?"

"Staying."

Tollar shrugged and kept pacing, ready to crawl out of her own skin when Balipar returned to her side.

"They don't like this, but tell me the hatchling is quite insistent about staying with you," they said. "Her mother is dead and father missing and presumed also dead. Her egg was one of nearly a dozen stolen recently by a particularly foul group of northerners."

"They sound delightful."

"You've displayed a surprising amount of competence in addition to your luck with this hatchling so far. I trust you understand this isn't a game."

"Of course it isn't. She's a different species, but still someone's child. I know enough about dragons to know they're a lot like people. So are we doing this here or should I get my pack?"

"They will not allow humans near their homes in the mountains."

Tollar nodded, keeping her face neutral even while her body grew heavy as a moon. "How's this going to work then?"

Balipar watched her. "I'll provide you with some information—there's one scholar in particular I can contact."

"Can those two stay long enough to teach her to fly and hunt?" Tollar asked. "We can keep her warm and out of trouble. No one knows she's here. I can bring her into the jungle easily enough when visitors come calling."

"You won't be able to keep her hidden long."

"I'll do what I can." She put her hands on her hips and faced them. "How dangerous is it? What's changed here that she's not safe?"

"I only really know the details from the dragon side of it, but they rather took offence."

"I should talk to Solia. Or the chief? Who even is the chief these days?—never mind, Solia can talk to the chief. Ugh, I might have to talk to Saivyn, even if he is a great load of llama pucks."

"Nice to see you still haven't gotten over that." Balipar smiled wryly.

Tollar rolled her eyes. "He started it. I'll talk to Solia first. She can talk to Saivyn. Whatever. He can rot."

"He's not that bad and you need to stop isolating yourself. Everyone needs allies."

"Pfft! No one needs a toad's wart on the ass like him!" Tollar crossed her arms.

"Probably best you talk to Solia first, you can trust her. The less people know the dragon is here, the better. And I really don't think you'll keep this secret for as long as you think you will. The dragon will grow. And fast."

"Well, maybe she'll get bored and go off to seek her kin. I want her to feel at home here for as long as she wants to."

Balipar took a long breath and went back to the dragoness, talking with her for a shorter time before calling Tollar over.

"The dragons will remain in their home in the Naldes for the time being so they can check in with me frequently. I will check in with you constantly. At the first sign of trouble, they take the hatchling to their home beyond our lands, no matter how much of a fuss she raises."

So much for keeping her business in Upalint short—she'd be lucky to get back out into the world before winter, and she couldn't remember the last time she'd stayed put for more than a season. Tollar pressed her lips together to suppress the urge to sigh. Going with the dragons would have been so much better.

"Fair enough." She shrugged. "But the thing that sent the dragoness into a fit and off to fetch you was my question about names."

"Dragons don't have names. Not ones we can understand, at least. They name their own in community naming ceremonies, typically after the hatchling has survived a full year."

"So do we just call her 'dragon' all the time or what?"

"You really should." Balipar leaned in closer, a gleam in their eyes and whispered, "You're probably going to come up with something that's easier to call her, and as long as she doesn't object, just don't let these two hear about it. There's plenty of precedent for humans, particularly riders, giving human-like names to dragons they have a special bond with."

"Well, does practically being its mother count?"

Balipar flashed her a grin full of bright white teeth.

"Can she travel?"

"Not for months. It will be weeks before she can fly at all. Until she can fly well, she's extremely vulnerable."

Tollar groaned and nearly called the whole thing off, but the dragon gave Tollar the absolute most adorable look. Her heart swelled. And that dragoness watched Tollar way too closely. Working with Balipar and these adult dragons was in the hatchling's best interest and picking any more fights with them wouldn't help.

Not when they would apparently be around so much.

But maybe Tollar could win them over and get them to change their minds about taking her with them? Staying on this farm where so many of the memories gnawed her insides was going to be worse than daily battles with a dragoness. Not to mention she had to clean the farm up and find a new family for it. But it would give her more time to visit with Beenala, provided she ever got over the whole dragon thing.

And she needed to keep the dragon a secret. Who knew what the locals would do if they found out, and what if those northerners wanted it back? Tollar sighed and watched the little dragon sleep. Beenala was right that Tollar was out of her depth. There were so many ways this could go wrong, even with the dragon whisperer's help.

7

Beenala set out into the pre-dawn jungle mist, Ash trotting along beside her, and her machete thumping against her thigh. The blade wouldn't do much good if she ran into a gezar, but she had energy for fire magic this time.

"You're watching for the cats, right?" The dog's ears went up, nose to the wind. "Good enough, I suppose."

It was the worst time of day to be out in the forest, but she wasn't missing another mulch day, especially when she had to get the gourds planted on her next planting day. Dragon baby or not, crops couldn't wait.

Bale—Tollar announced out of the blue two days ago that they were calling the dragon Bale. So that sealed it, they were mothers to a dragon.

Beenala sighed.

With barely enough light to see by, Beenala found the last garden plot to mulch up, and hefted the machete in her hand. Her tired muscles warmed, and her storming thoughts spun themselves out as the swinging blade filled her ears with the satisfying *thwack* of it hitting home. Her brother Ballow liked to extoll on the virtues of meditating, but Beenala didn't know where he found the time to sit around listening to himself breathe.

Beenala listened to the blade do its work, breaking up the vines, all harvested of beans, and lost herself to it. Surrounded by crops, she could forget about dragons and faraway ports and the way certain neighbours made her head spin and her heart dance.

The garden made sense.

Ash whuffed softly, staring back the way they'd come. Beenala's grip tightened on the blade, and she stood alert, eyes scanning the morning gloom. It would be nearly an hour yet before the sun crept over the mountains.

"Eh, what are you doing up this early?" Tollar called from deep in the mist.

Beenala winced.

Tollar materialized, carelessly nimble in the poor light as she picked her way over roots and between banana trees to come to Beenala's side.

"Ah right, mulch day. I'm sorry, I forgot. I said I'd help."

"Really, Toll, I just want some—"

"I help!" the grumbly little teakettle shout came from the next row over, and before Beenala could shout Noooooooooo! Bale sprang into the plot and raked at the bean vines with her long talons. Ash barked once and sprinted off into the trees.

"Ack!" Beenala managed.

"Bale, come away!"

The baby dragon paid no mind, rolling gleefully through Beenala's garden bed, grinding up the vines and scattering debris across the jungle.

"Monkeys, Bale! Focus!" Tollar called, lobbing a ball of water at the dragon's snout, catching her attention.

"Why are—?" Beenala started.

"It's breakfast time. I try to get it out of the way before you get your day started. And those two dragons are coming here later to teach Bale how to dragon, so I need her presentable so they don't try to eat us."

Beenala groaned.

"Sorry about that. Can you give me a little fireball to distract her? Get it going down the row and I'll get her off."

Beenala sighed, unclipped the flint from her belt for a spark, growing it into a ball to fill her palm. She blew it out toward the dragon, sent it spiralling around Bale's snout until the little dragon stopped making an absolute disaster of mulch day and chased the ball of light into the gloom.

"There's those screecher monkeys been stealing your fish over by the western canal," Tollar offered, and Beenala concentrated on the little ball of light, dragon hot behind it, and sent it off that way.

Much as Bale made a mess of things, at least she kept the damned monkey population down. Maybe she'd be big enough to eat the gezars soon.

The machete hung limp in Beenala's hand, and she stared at the muddy mess of her field in the growing light.

"Sorry," Tollar said. "Can I help clean it up?"

Beenala tugged at the hem of her shirt and tried to stop her face from pinching up the way it liked to.

"Look, I can clean this up in a flash." Tollar pulled water from the ground to do just that. A churning wave rose from the soil, collected the mulch and let sediments sink to the bottom, and then the water trickled back into the ground, leaving the mulch spread evenly across the field.

"Yes, well. Thank you."

Beenala hooked the machete onto her belt and smoothed down the front of her shirt, whistling for Ash to come back. She shouldn't be angry with Bale and Tollar, but she'd planned on spending most of the morning out here working and now...

"Can I help with anything else?"

"Find me something to do with the rest of my morning," Beenala blurted, her cheeks growing hot. Ash burst through the undergrowth and trotted over, sniffing the new mulch.

"Well you can come with me to fetch Bale from wherever she's run off to. If you really want more work, the eastern end of my coconut grove is overrun with vines. You can put your blade to good use. Or fire. Fancy burning something down today?"

Tollar grinned and her liquid silver irises sparkled like sunlight on waves. Beenala rolled her eyes and followed Tollar into the forest toward the western canal while Ash trailed along behind them, sniffing the plants as they passed.

"You'd love to be a pyromancer, wouldn't you?"

"It'd be fun. Wish I were a full elemental. You get two elements, why can't I have another?"

"If only we could pick our skills."

"You don't want to be a pyromancer?"

"Oh, it's convenient enough and certainly saved my life with that gezar over the winter. I like terramancy, it's nice and slow and quiet. If I could trade fire, though, I'd take aeromancy."

"But that's just as chaotic as pyromancy."

"Can be. Or it can be perfectly still." Beenala sighed.

Tollar gave her a knowing look, one corner of her mouth pulled up. It drew Beenala's attention to the white lines on Tollar's cheekbones.

"Do those mean something?" Beenala asked, pointing.

Tollar blinked and stared.

"The tattoos. You've got new ones since you were last home."

"Ah! Right. Yes, the rank lines. They're new. Got them because someone finally noticed my brilliance." Tollar's grin was full of teeth. "All of my tattoos are part of warrior culture and the rank lines show leadership. Means I get to be in charge now and then. That business on the coast, there was a rank three and she called the shots. But when I'm working with merchants, they all listen to me when things go wrong."

"How many rank lines does Saivyn have?" Beenala asked innocently, trying not to smile at the way the question made Tollar sputter. Ash trotted over and gave her a concerned look.

"Frogging goat-jumper's got five. He'll be cursing the ancestors when he sees I've got any at all though." Tollar's little half-grin returned, her eyes shining.

"Mind you, being in charge all the time does have disadvantages. I'd have never had the freedom to slink around behind enemy lines if I'd been calling the shots down on the coast. Never would have found Bale's egg if I'd had to stay at the front and keep the rest of them in line. Course, I'd have called retreat a lot earlier."

"How'd you slink around?"

"Waterways," Tollar said slyly. "Aqueducts and canals everywhere in Port Sawulxo. It was magnificent. Five more aquamancers with my talents down there and things might have gone differently. But we were outmatched and too late."

"It bothers you, doesn't it."

Tollar kept walking.

"What about your other tattoos? You've got more of those little white ones on your arm than last time."

Another half-grin, Tollar watching her askance. "Been counting, have you?"

Beenala coughed nervously and drummed her fingers against her thighs.

Tollar stopped walking and pulled off her faded green shirt, leaving the top of her body covered only by the fabric sling she used to support her breasts. Beenala held her breath as she took in the extent of the design, seeing it for what it was and not merely random white dots on Tollar's arm. There were some spiral shapes too, little whirlpools on Tollar's dark skin.

"It's beautiful," Beenala said in an exhale.

"Thank you. The Keepers have done well."

"Keepers?"

"These specific tattoos are warrior class and spiritually sanctioned. They can only be given by a Keeper of the Markings. I've had a few of them work on mine, obviously, because I'm so frequently somewhere new."

Beenala shoved her hands into her pockets to resist the rude urge to touch them.

"The Keepers are guided by the ancestors, and in my case I suspect Granny's been advising them."

"Ah, because of the finger bone?"

"It helps me stay connected to her when I'm away."

"So the marks mean something? Like your rank lines?"

"These ones are for bragging. The small ones are for individuals, and the smallest of those for children. These bigger dots," she pointed to one on her shoulder, "are for families, and these whorls are for communities, size of community corresponds with size of the spirals."

"Oh, so these represent people you've helped?"

"They're close to my heart for a reason."

Beenala studied the pattern more closely. It branched out from the left side of Tollar's chest, marching its way over her shoulder and starting down her left arm. A couple of spirals peeked out from the bottom of the sling, starting down her side.

"Goodness! There's a lot of them."

"I've been busy," Tollar said softly. "Like I said, they're for bragging. They're white so they stand out." She pulled her shirt on, but then slipped off the bracer on her right arm and gingerly held her inner forearm out to Beenala. "These ones are just for me. Reminders. Failures."

At first Beenala wasn't certain what Tollar meant. But then she saw the dark ink nearly camouflaged against Tollar's skin. She opened her mouth to ask what they meant when she recognized they were all the same symbol.

The one that meant death.

So small they were barely recognizable, but little butterflies, like the coronatail that old myths said ushered the spirits across the veil. That was before people stopped being too afraid of necromancers to know better.

"Oh..." What else could she say? Of course Tollar would be responsible for deaths—killed people—even if she didn't want to.

"But there aren't very many," she ventured. "Not compared to the white ones. What are they supposed to remind you of? What failures?"

Tollar pulled the bracer on and looked out into the jungle, absently patting Ash's head after the dog bopped her nose against Tollar's leg. "To be cautious. To keep training. A true warrior should be able to help those in need without killing anyone. My bracer covers them easily right now. If I get careless or bloodthirsty... Well, everyone will know. Everyone who knows what to look for anyway."

"I'm sorry, maybe I shouldn't have asked."

Tollar met Beenala's gaze. "You didn't notice these ones, and I wouldn't have told you about them if I didn't trust you with it."

Beenala's cheeks warmed and her insides felt light. Tollar held her gaze for a beat before gliding off in search of Bale, moving with long liquid strides. Beenala scritched Ash behind the ears before trailing along behind Tollar, floating along like she was on one of Tollar's waves.

When the two of them caught up to Bale, the little dragon splashed through the western canal as she chased monkeys. Tollar used whips of water to knock the critters out of nearby trees, making it easier for Bale to catch them. Were there enough monkeys in the jungle to keep the dragon fed? Of course, as Tollar kept hoping, Bale should be big enough before much longer that she could hunt gezars as her kin had until recently and as Minty and Cloudy were again—not that Beenala was about to let anyone know she was just as bad as Tollar for giving dragons names. Of course, she knew better than to use those names out loud.

Bale sprang out of the water, snapped up one final monkey, and tried to shake herself off with little luck. Beenala stayed back while Tollar laughed and used some magic to dry off the dragon, who ducked her head to nuzzle Tollar.

Watching Tollar stroke Bale's snout filled Beenala with warm light almost to bursting.

The warm feeling carried her back through the fields and rows of trees, across the narrow lane dividing the farms. Where it crumpled like a delicate flower in driving rain. Tollar's aunt was on the veranda, peeking in the farmhouse windows, one hand on wide hip, the other braced against her cane, and muttering to herself.

"Oh shit," Tollar gasped.

Ash barked and galloped over to Per Dirondi—or DiDi as she insisted most call her. She turned at the sound, grinning and reaching down to pet Ash, waving at them with one hand.

"Thought the trouble up this way might be you," DiDi called to Tollar, who whispered a rapid string of curses under her breath.

"Auntie, what—"

Bale came crashing out of the trees. "Auntie!"

DiDi's brown skin, dark like Tollar's, went ashy grey as she stopped petting the dog and stood up straight so fast she lost her balance and stumbled, Beenala going cold as she thought the old woman would tumble right down the ramp, before she caught herself with the cane. Ash barked at Bale.

"What—" DiDi gasped, her voice choked, one hand pressed to her chest.

"Bale, to me!" Tollar shouted, barely audible over the racket.

Beenala froze to the spot, both hands twisting the hem of her shirt, and stared with her mouth agape. She felt sweaty and like her skin was trying to hide from the unfolding disaster.

Bale, for her part, skidded to a halt and looked imploringly at Tollar who was trying to get between the dragon and her aunt. Ash kept barking and moved to get between Tollar and the dragon.

"Ash!" Beenala gasped.

Fear that the dog would get herself eaten jolted Beenala into action. She intercepted Ash before she reached Tollar and Bale and grabbed her by the scruff of the neck. With a panicked look to Tollar, Beenala dragged the dog back to the cottage before anyone could make a bad situation worse.

"Stay." Beenala gave the dog a piece of fish jerky before shutting the door despite her whines of protest.

When Beenala returned to Tollar's yard, DiDi sat on the front steps, less grey but breathing unevenly and fanning herself, her lenses knocked askew, while Bale crouched off to the edge of the yard, her head drooping, and Tollar's hands wove through the air as she explained.

"—more coming for this one to train her any minute now."

DiDi shook her head, eyes on Bale. And then she caught her breath, pushed her lenses back into place, and chuckled.

"Girl of mine, I knew it was you when Graza said Beenala was acting strange and dragons coming and going out this way. Thought maybe you'd come see me, but I guess you have your own place."

Tollar's expression pinched. "I've been trying to come, Auntie, but I can't exactly leave this to Bee to manage on her own."

"No, I suppose not."

"Do you want to come say hello to her?" Tollar gestured toward the dragon. "I've told her all about you, and she seems delighted that you're here."

DiDi's eyes widened and she shook her head, glancing at the dragon. "I am not prepared for anything like that."

"Well, she's confused and I need to go explain to her."

Tollar gave Beenala a pleading look and headed over to Bale. Beenala wiped her cold palms on her shirt and offered DiDi a hand up.

"Best to be out of sight when those other two dragons get here." Beenala ushered DiDi inside.

DiDi was a head shorter than Beenala and a good measure heavier with rich amber brown eyes and black hair in a fuzzy cloud around her head. DiDi was Tollar's father's sister and short and round like he had been. Tollar got her height from her mother. DiDi staggered in the door, leaning on Beenala, and huffed indignantly once they were inside.

"Not a scrap of furniture!"

"She spends most of her time outside with the dragon or over at my place. I tried to give her some of Mammi and Da's extras but she won't have it."

"It's just a place to sleep," Tollar said from the doorway.

"This is no way to live."

"Auntie, this is how I live when I'm not here, which is the vast majority of my life. That's not going to change just because my mother got it in her head to leave me this place." Tollar kept looking out the window, out toward the mountains probably for Minty and Cloudy, so she missed the way DiDi's expression sagged.

"I don't suppose you heard why Mum gave the place up?" Tollar asked. "Why Zarro didn't keep it or give it to his kin? I know he's got a younger sister over in Sentinel Bend."

All of Tollar's siblings, all of them older, had left the farm years ago. Tollar's middle sister left the region entirely, going to the southern coast to take up an apprenticeship as a healer.

"Well, yes, I didn't exactly expect your mother to leave it to you, but your granny told her she ought to. This was at solstice after Zarro left."

"Granny wanted me to have this? I thought she'd know better."

DiDi's eyes sparkled behind her lenses, and a smile danced across her lips. "Oh, I suspect Granny *did* know better, and it will make sense to you in time."

Tollar shrugged. "I'm here for now, but I'm no farmer. If you know someone who can take it off my hands, I'd like to see it go to a good family."

"You could stay," DiDi said.

Tollar rolled her eyes, squashing the warm feeling trying to creep back into Beenala's chest.

"Auntie, I'm sorry I didn't visit you, or at least send a message to warn you. I'll come visit you as soon as Bale has fire—she'll be able to defend herself better if she needs to. I promise, instant she shoots flames, I'll come see you. But there's no sign of those two dragons yet, so it's probably safest for everyone if Bee helps you back down the lane to your bike."

Tollar gave Beenala an apologetic look, but Beenala let out a long breath and held out her elbow to DiDi, ready for some fresh air and more space between her and the impending arrival of dragons.

"Thank you, Bee. What would I do without you?"

Beenala pressed her lips together to keep from blurting "Get eaten by dragons," and guided DiDi out the door and down the ramp. Once they were at the end of the lane where DiDi collected her bicycle, DiDi stopped at the edge of the main road leading into the city and patted Beenala's hand, giving her a smile that was a little sad.

"She'll come around one day, don't you worry."

"What?" Beenala tilted her head.

DiDi's smile widened. "I suppose you will too."

Beenala blinked at her, but DiDi gave her hand a final pat, sturdier on her feet now that she was over the initial shock. She stood there watching the older woman put her cane in the bicycle's large basket and head off, until the hiss of dragons in conversation pulled her out of it. She looked up the lane, not quite able to see the farms from around the bend.

And kept standing there.

Beenala hoped Bale would seem less burdensome as she grew and became more self-sufficient. The dragon wasn't a sometimes chore like mulching or planting, and she was far needier than Ash or any of Beenala's six younger siblings had been.

Or perhaps it wasn't that they were less needy, but that Beenala hadn't had to do much of the mothering. She'd barely been ten when Erxo, the youngest, was born.

It was so much to get used to. Especially with Tollar around all the time. Usually, Beenala saw Tollar infrequently when she was home, especially since she had, until now, stayed with DiDi in the city when she was back. Having Tollar around would be more than enough, but the constant presence of both Tollar and Bale weighed on her.

She'd shaped her days around the arrival of each of her siblings, but they'd been permanent fixtures in her life, changing gradually as they grew older. And each of them had left slowly, so that their absence was easy to adjust to. Getting used to her parents and Erxo not being around had been a chore but she'd managed.

How could Beenala shape her days around someone who could leave at a moment's notice? And never mind trying to get used to the dragon. Beenala had tried to withdraw and stick to her chores, but that meant standing by and watching Tollar nearly get incinerated.

She sighed and started up the lane.

"What's on your mind?" Tollar called, once the houses came into view.

Beenala shook her head and didn't look up. Where to begin? How to explain? It would be so much easier if Tollar would stay put. She stopped next to Tollar, who leaned against one of the house's stilts, the dragons around the other side, preferring not to have humans around as they spoke with Bale.

"That place is yours now, you can make it whatever you want," Beenala gestured to the house behind Tollar. "What are you out in the world looking for?"

Tollar watched her. "I hope I'll know when I see it."

Beenala stared down the lane so Tollar couldn't see the way she blushed. She wanted to be the thing missing from Tollar's life. But if Tollar did stay... she couldn't be idle. How could she stay? It didn't seem to be in Tollar's nature and adjusting to chaos was certainly not in Beenala's. They were too different for Beenala to be the answer. But she also didn't want to be the reason Tollar left.

Yet she couldn't abandon Tollar to whatever demons kept chasing her away from Nytaltek, no matter how exposed Beenala felt in the process.

Whether or not she saw it, Tollar needed help, and Beenala would keep doing what she could to see that Tollar got it. Beenala hoped she could keep herself together while Tollar needed her.

8

ollar strode down the wide main avenue of Nytaltek with her kit
heavier and her heart lighter. She'd been able to visit Auntie, who'd
sent Tollar off with a hammock, in addition to the clothes she'd come for, so
she had somewhere real to sleep. Auntie talked her ear off half the day and
didn't miss the opportunity for a good lecture about Tollar's interesting
life choices with regard to dragons. Or about how Tollar was always in a
hurry to get somewhere else.

Right now, she needed to get to the guard house to catch Solia coming
off her shift but not quite gone home yet. She'd been delayed enough
having to check in with Balipar at their apartment on the edge of the chief's
compound before heading in to have dinner with Auntie.

Bale had sneezed her first fireball yesterday and kept herself warm
through the night. Which was information Balipar needed. It put the
dragon one step closer to being self-sufficient, which brought Tollar one
step closer to leaving.

It wasn't that she hated Nytaltek. It was one of the better cities she'd
been to, with its white limestone buildings all draped with strings of little
flags and ancestor banners in a bold rainbow of colour, and bright tile
mosaics over the streets and the occasional wall in crisp geometric patterns
or sunbursts and starbursts, moonscapes and floral blooms, lizards, birds,
and lush cenotes. All of it checkered in green by rooftop gardens and
clusters of banobi trees. Then there were the twinkle lights at night that
made it look like a field of glitterbugs when seen from the foothills. And

she'd taken those lights for granted in her early years, surprised as she travelled by how so few places had figured out how they worked.

It wasn't the most advanced place she'd been, though it was close, and definitely not the friendliest (or maybe it was that no one really liked her, no matter what Bee thought). The local guilds loved bickering with each other, but it was... bickering like a close family bickered. Well, there was Saivyn, and she certainly did more than bicker with him, but he generally got along with the city and guild leaders—and he had to or he wouldn't keep getting re-elected. No, it was just Tollar he didn't like because he couldn't see past Upalint's borders and didn't think anyone else should either.

But generally there were so few problems that needed solving here that it left Tollar with nothing to do, no sense of purpose. Tollar had been to so many places, but she never stayed long, and she returned to this place the most. Maybe that made it home? It was simple and solid. No wonder Beenala loved it so much.

She shrugged mentally and focused on the familiar path between Auntie's and the compound that served the city watch.

The loudbirds from the banobi trees lining one edge of the street distracted her from her task, reminding her that she was near the central market. She hadn't been there in two years.

"No, now is not the time, you'll just want to buy a book and then upset yourself when you can't."

It wasn't that she couldn't afford the books. But where would she keep them? Couldn't bring them with her, and Auntie's place was already brimming with books and plants and soft things without Tollar adding more than she already had.

But artisans streaming away from the market with laden pack llamas and overstuffed bike wagons let her know it was too late for the market anyway. Tollar gave the loudbirds a look and kept going, leaving the squat, wide, hollow trees behind. These banobis were full of shops (and loudbirds) but there were clusters of them throughout the city serving as family compounds. Nearly as wide as they were tall, and with a flattened canopy, the trees reminded Tollar of large tables.

Solia had lived in one with her parents and subparents and grandparents and siblings and their lovers and children the last time Tollar had been home.

The guard house was pure chaos with the shift change when Tollar followed a few night watch stragglers into the tall stone building and barely got a second glance from the duty guard at the door. The cool air hit her immediately, with the smell of beer and frying fish.

"Tollar! Didn't know you were back in town," Solia said out of nowhere, materializing out of the crowd.

Solia came toward her with that slow rolling gait of hers, otherwise easy to overlook because she was average in every way—medium height and medium build and medium brown skin and plain brown eyes in a hard square face and dull brown hair cropped short. And Solia leaned hard into that, disappearing into the background to connect dots and size people up. She had four rank lines already.

And she didn't let Tollar forget that she was five years younger.

"So, you going to stick around this time? Put your competency to good use?"

"Who says I don't."

Solia grunted and smiled in her knowing way, having already taken in Tollar's new rank lines, and came over to greet her, hands out, palms up. Tollar took them briefly before pulling Solia into a quick embrace.

"Really, though, I could use you here," Solia said. And a lack of the usual jest in her tone made Tollar take note.

"You know I can't stay."

Solia put a hand on Tollar's shoulder and nodded toward the stairs that led up to the offices. "Come have a word."

"Well, I came for more than a word anyway."

Solia glanced over her shoulder, giving Tollar another of her assessing looks.

"What happened with that millwright you had your eye on right before I left?" Tollar asked.

"Nolly. I moved in with her a year ago."

"Well done!"

"Well, her and Arvanin—the chocolatier on Hark Street. Nolly was already with him when I took interest in her, and she didn't want to choose between us and why should she?"

"Ah, sounds complicated."

Solia shrugged. "It's not, though. We share a cozy bed, and he and I share Nolly but don't have much to do with each other. I started on the tincture anyway, to be safe. Nolly's pregnant, a season left to go, and that's about as close as I want to get to that."

"I've heard good things about the tincture. Never needed it myself."

"Look, the fact that I never have to deal with monthlies again is worth it on its own."

Tollar grunted noncommittally as reply and glanced into the locker room on the way to Solia's office. Tollar didn't need the tincture for monthlies, either. Not that she would admit to using blood magic, even to Solia and even if she only used it on herself to make her monthlies efficient, compressed into one uncomfortable moment.

And besides, they'd reached Solia's office and had no more need to fill the silence with trifles. Her office hadn't changed much, maybe a few more papers scattered across the desk and stuffed onto shelves, still the same plush green chair across from the plain wooden desk. And while Solia only ever smoked her cigars in here under the greatest of stress, the rich smell still permeated the room. As soon as Solia's office door closed, Solia got straight to business.

"You been home long?" Solia sat in the chair and folded her hands in her lap, feet up on the desk. Tollar had been sitting on a pile of cushions at Auntie's all day and needed to move.

"Little over a week. It's a bit of a disaster. Did Balipar mention?"

"Bali? What have you got them involved in?"

"A dragon. I've got a dragon—a baby—"

"You what?"

"Up at the farm. You maybe noticed those two adult dragons, a green one and a grey one? They're checking in with Bali and helping me keep the baby alive."

Solia put her feet on the floor and leaned forward. "Where in the name of the ancestors did you get a baby dragon and not get eaten?"

"I mean they tried, but I opened a cenote under them until they calmed down."

Solia closed her eyes, and she pressed her lips into such a tight line they nearly disappeared.

"I stole a dragon egg from raiders in Sawulxo."

"Raging ancestors, Toll, what were you thinking?"

"The cursed thing hatched before her kin came for her, and now I can't get her to leave."

Solia sat with her hands on her desk, one finger tapping, and staring at Tollar with an indecipherable look.

"You have a dragon."

"Yeah, Bale. She—"

"Bale? You named it?"

Tollar shrugged. "Bali thought I should tell you. But Sol, the thing in the port is weird, I've never seen anything like it. And there's a lot I don't know about what's gone on here the last two years. Why all the dragons are gone. Even Bee was being tetchy about them. So I need to keep Bale secret."

"You're damned right you do."

"How bad is it?"

"Depends on the day. Mostly I don't think anyone will hurt your dragon, but some days I just really don't know this city anymore."

Tollar stopped pacing and stared at Solia. This city was in Solia's blood, it was part of her soul. Was Solia losing her touch?

"Anyway, the dragon's only part of the reason I came to talk to you. Those raiders—"

"Tollar, something's happening here and I can't see what."

"Maybe you need a break to see things from a fresh perspective. Come with me next time. I know you want to see what's out there."

Solia had, right before Tollar last left, clawed out an election win to move from the night watch to the head of the day watch. Night watch saw all the drama but day watch got all the glory, on account of people generally being asleep while night watch did their thing. Being head of the day watch also put her at the head of the entire guard. Tollar had tried convincing Solia to come with her before, get her need for glory out of the way, and then return where she could be satisfied with the night watch where she did the most good.

Maybe this time?

"The worst thing I can do for this city right now is leave it." Solia leaned back in her chair and watched Tollar pace. "But I do need a fresh perspective, and that's what I need you for. Before they go and do worse things than drive out the dragons."

Tollar stalked over to the desk and plunked down in the chair across from Solia, sprawled sideways with one leg up over the armrest. "Worse things?"

"We've had some disasters. Mostly flooding rains, bad enough to destroy crops."

"Have your elementals been sleeping through it or something?"

"That's the thing. They've had a hard time controlling the worst of the weather, especially the flooding. Some of them have raised concerns that this doesn't feel like natural weather."

"That's odd and unpleasant but how does that cause so much tension?"

"Planting has been disrupted, sometimes by a month. Crops destroyed right at harvest. And it's been going on six seasons. Supplies are getting low and that's when swibs start to take notice. First they complained that the dragons around were a tax to our dwindling resources. Of course, that offended the dragons and they up and left."

"What a load of swamp slime! What resources can the dragons possibly drain? They mostly eat the frogging gezars!"

Solia grunted. "I know. But people get mighty irrational when their way of life gets threatened. And the dragons leaving wasn't enough. Now I catch word here and there of swibs grumbling about the elementals being dead weight on society if they can't do their one job and keep the farmland secure."

Tollar stared. "When has anyone ever been dead weight? What..." She shook her head. "I can't with this nonsense."

"I know." Solia let out a long, slow breath. "This has been my life for the last year. There's some undercurrent driving all this."

Tollar nodded slowly and stared at the desktop between them.

"You've got an outside perspective that fascinates the folks who know about you," Solia said. "You bring in stories like the traders do, but you anchor those stories because you're one of us, no matter how much you leave and try to be the outsider."

Tollar leaned back in her chair. A few stories before she left again wasn't too bad. "All right, we can talk about those details, but my most recent campaign in Port Sawulxo was weird and not just because I brought back—"

The door pushed open, not even a knock, and there was Saivyn, not much taller than Solia but about as wide as he was tall like some great brown muscle-brick, standing like his spine had been fused together. He had a bit more grey in his short dark hair than last time Tollar had been home.

"Solia, they said you were—" He spotted Tollar and scowled, pointing at her with the adjustable multipurpose tool that served for a hand at the end of his prosthetic arm. "Thought we'd finally seen the last of you."

Tollar smirked and scratched her cheek, her smile growing as his eyes widened when he noticed her rank lines and sputtered. "Thought I'd come home and see if you're up for re-election yet. Get me a couple more rank lines and see about giving Solia a hand keeping this city together. Sounds like she needs it."

"You— I—" He growled in wordless frustration.

"How can I help you, Saivyn?" Solia leaned back in her chair, watching him closely.

Tollar stood and paced to the far side of the room where she leaned against the wall. She could go to the other side of the world—and she had—and not be far enough away from Saivyn. Maybe she could go to one of the moons?

"I need to talk to you," he said to Solia, then glared at Tollar.

Heat rose in her, that he thought he could storm in and make her leave. Tollar wore her uniform minus the armour plating, had left her longsword at home, but dropped one hand to the blade at her hip.

"I was here first."

"City business. Don't expect you to understand."

Tollar rolled her eyes. "I'm here on city business too. Probably more important than yours, even. So run along." She shooed him with her other hand.

"Tollar," Solia warned.

Tollar shrugged and crossed her arms. Saivyn could get cursed for all she cared.

"Sai, she's right, it's some bad news she's got."

"Isn't she always bad news?"

Solia leaned on her desk, cutting him with a hard look. "You can act like the professional you are, or you can get your ass out of my office until I'm done talking to Tollar. I'm technically off duty and don't need to listen to either of you right now."

Saivyn's face scrunched in on itself like he'd licked a sour toad, but he stopped flapping his lips, so that was a start.

"There's trouble in the north. Port Sawulxo's got a problem with raiders."

"Monkey shit."

So much for his silence. Tollar pushed away from the wall and resumed pacing.

"You've heard from our contacts in the port in the last few weeks?" Solia asked him. "Because I haven't heard from any of them in a season. Everyone's noticed the scarcity of merchant caravans, and that's not helping anyone feel better about the fouled crops. I've been too focused on the mess here to think much of it until Tollar brought it up just now."

Saivyn managed to look even more puckered.

"Tollar, you were about to expand on what you saw down north?"

Tollar gave Saivyn a final glance and focused on Solia. "Right. The city was overrun with these raiders, I couldn't find any of my contacts, not that there was time. They've got dragons."

"Bullshit, no one's got dragons," Saivyn snapped.

Tollar had never wished so much in her life that he was somewhere else. There were a lot of unbelievable things she'd seen in the port and trying to make sense of them with him around would be that much more the challenge.

"I don't know what they've got them for, kept them all in pens, some dragon eggs too." Tollar gave Solia a significant look but pressed on before Saivyn noticed. "Roads in and out were blocked, so there's your caravan mystery solved. No merchants in port, only raider ships. And..." She pressed her lips together. "Most of these raiders were aquamancers."

"Water raiders! That's not a thing."

Solia had looked pensive, leaning her chin on tented fingers, but now she cut Saivyn with a look before Tollar could.

"What do you think we should do about it?" Tollar asked. "If you've got a few wizards to spare, I can guide them down there and free those dragons. Let them run off the raiders so the trade ships can land and get the caravans through here properly. Maybe it'll win some points with the dragons you've all managed to isolate while I was gone."

She spoke generally, but looked directly at Saivyn with her last comment.

"Oh yes, think you've got all the answers? What do you know!"

"They don't just give these out to anyone," she snapped, pointing at her rank lines.

"Apparently they do."

"When was the last time you got your hands dirty helping anyone, Sai?" Tollar snarled. "What good has lying idle in your barracks done for this city?"

Saivyn opened his mouth and closed it again. And again, repeatedly, like some gasping fish while his face darkened, brown-purple like some overripe berry close to bursting.

"One more word out of either of you, and you'll spend the night cooling it in the holding cells, I swear," Solia growled, standing up. "Saivyn, I'm sending a bird to my contacts, and I suggest you do the same."

Her tone was both a command and a dismissal. Saivyn's face got darker, he scowled at Tollar even more severely, but he turned and walked out again, slamming the door behind him.

Tollar nearly commented on what a frogging child he was, remembered Solia's threats, and stood on the other side of the desk.

"You bring out the worst in him without trying," Solia said. "So could you stop trying?"

"Pfft."

Solia braced her hands on her desk and glared.

"It's not my fault he can't handle that I'm a better fighter than he is."

"Yes, you're a better warrior than him by a longshot, even without your magic, and you could be elected to his position if you'd stick around you know."

"Pfft."

"But that's no excuse for the way you taunt him with it."

Tollar crossed her arms but didn't see the point in arguing. Saivyn was the one with the grudge, and that wasn't Tollar's fault.

Solia sat down and rubbed her hands over her face. "You're sure about the raiders and trade?"

"Weren't many boats in port, barely any traffic on the road when my campaign was on its way in. It was all frogging weird."

Solia nodded. "We'll get to the bottom of it."

"You'll mention it to the chief? I have no idea who the chief even is."

"You're conveniently never here for elections." Solia's tone was dry. "I'll let Metar—she's chief this term—I'll let her know."

Tollar shrugged and sat down. "You're more worried about home. Is Sai wearing off on you? You're not worried about raiders keeping dragons?"

"Course I am, but I'm more worried about swibs looking for a reason to stop seeing the humanity in my elementals."

"And you think my travel stories are going to make any sort of difference?"

"You're never here long enough to see what people think of your stories, but they matter, Toll. People still talk about what you did with those water demons in Singsi."

"It's been seven years!"

"Exactly. You summoned *five* of them, Tollar. I've never heard of anyone summoning more than two demons at a time. And most people barely get beyond Nytaltek's farmland or Upalint's borders, never mind off the continent entirely. They barely think of the poles or the other side of the world or even much further than the Nishram territories or the Tinitan Plains until you come home full of stories. And if your stories include trouble close to home, they're going to notice. Sawulxo is a nation close enough for them to take note. If you can bend those stories to include communities embracing each other like we always have, they'll listen. It makes it easier for me to break down walls later."

"Me telling the rest of the guard about nonsense with water demons half a world away really gets that far?"

"Most of the guilds have their own circulars now, in addition to the city's weekly. Started with the students, spread to the artists, athletics and military. And again, the students started the trend asking to see circulars from other guilds. Now they're all printing off enough to share. I'm trying to get the inventors guild to stop being quite so secretive and join in."

"And my travels fit into this how?"

"I need to ease the tensions, and fostering some fresh empathy seems to be the best place to start. We need to remind everyone that community matters. I need you for this, Toll."

Tollar sighed. "All right, shouldn't be hard to get a few words done in the evening while I get the farm ready for new occupants. I assume you'll want it sooner than right before I leave?"

"Tollar, put real consideration into staying longer this time. Give me your log for the circular, but then stick around and talk to people about it. *Listen* to them. I need someone new on this to see what I can't."

"I'll give it some thought."

She always left a log of her travels with Solia each time she was back in the city, and writing one with an agenda wouldn't be that different. She'd seen plenty of what Solia wanted in the last two years. And plenty where people had forgotten the value of their neighbours and been swallowed whole by disaster and adversaries.

And maybe doing something conventionally useful to directly benefit the city would get Saivyn to shut it for once.

But staying put? Even for a couple of seasons? What if she stayed and made it worse? Or stayed and couldn't help Solia. The idea of no longer being welcome in Nytaltek coiled up her insides. Of course, being seen helping Solia might help keep her from wearing out her welcome.

9

Tollar sat on the edge of her sleep mat—which had become more of a chair now that she had the hammock to sleep in—frowning down at the pages in front of her, trying to get the details right. Her mind kept coming around to negative examples of community—especially that place suffering from an earthquake and didn't have any terramancers to help sort it because they'd driven away all the wizards, each family only looking out for itself. She hadn't stayed there long, even if managing to hide her abilities. But she wanted something uplifting to start with.

Child, why are you such a miserable thing? Her mother's voice. Tollar couldn't remember what she'd done to earn that one, but echoes of Zarro's words followed close, *Leave your mother alone with your nonsense.*

"Maybe this isn't the best place to be productive."

It never had been, why should now be different?

She hadn't seen her mother in years, wondered if she knew when Tollar was in town. Auntie didn't get along with Janda anymore than Tollar did, so she wouldn't be the one letting her know. Did her mother travel in any of the gossipy circles that would know what Tollar was up to?

Footsteps plodded up the ramp a moment before the knock came at the door, followed swiftly be Beenala's voice.

"Tollar! I'm so sorry, I forgot to tell you my parents are on their way for breakfast and—"

"Oh shit, Bale."

Tollar launched to her feet and threw open the door, Beenala first startling and then her mouth falling open. Right, it was the first time

Tollar had been out of uniform and travel gear, her hair out of a braid, and properly washed since she'd shown up on Beenala's doorstep. Today's dress was flowy but simple enough, sleeveless and shin length, made from glacier blue linen, with bright green, yellow, and orange beadwork and embroidery at the square neckline and hem.

Beenala's face went pink. She coughed and looked down at her feet while holding up a mug of chocolate and a breakfast wrap packed in banana leaf.

"You don't have much time before they get here."

Tollar sighed, managing to drink the chocolate while she stuffed her feet into her boots. Not the best pairing with the dress, but it wasn't like anyone would see her, hiding out in the jungle with the dragon.

"Wait, where *is* Bale?"

"Um... She's not with you?"

"Bee, she doesn't exactly fit in my house."

Beenala blinked at her, fidgeting with the hem of her shirt.

"Right, I'll find her. Thank you for breakfast." Tollar slipped the meal into a pocket and called a disk of groundwater to take her out into the forest, searching Bale's favourite hunting grounds. It didn't take long to hear some sizzling splashes and teakettle groaning that could only be caused by one thing.

Bale was at the western canal, her favourite place to hunt monkeys, but instead of hunting she rolled around in the water.

"Bale?"

"Itchy!"

The little dragon slunk out of the water, her head drooping and talons clawing at her chest. Greying flecks of black and purple skin drifted in the water and fell to the ground around Bale.

Tollar pressed her hands over her face and let out a long breath.

"You're moulting. Today. Of course you're moulting today. Why in the name of the bleeding moons didn't anyone think to mention to me that you would moult."

"Itchy. Don't like it."

"No, I don't imagine so. But you'll like it even less if Bee's family notices you out here. Come on, we've got to go hide."

They couldn't get very far what with Bale constantly stopping to tear at her own skin.

"Here, I've got an idea."

Tollar pulled water from the nearby canal, froze it in much the same—but opposite—way that she'd boiled that wave, making little ice pellets, and then set it to rotating tightly over the dragon's skin, giving her a cool scrub. And to add speed, she brought more water from the canal to act as a platform to swiftly carry the both of them off the farm entirely and up the side of nearby Mount Acrintaga. A nice little shelf overlooked the valley and was difficult to reach on foot. Tollar geysered them both up.

Sitting on the edge of the shelf, she ate the wrap from Beenala and watched out over the jungle. From this far away, Tollar could only spot the general vicinity of Beenala's farm, but she imagined she could see the cottage through the trees and Beenala's family arriving for a nice visit that wouldn't involve any shouting at all. What was that even like? She'd only ever known her own family's hostility wasn't normal because she'd lived next door to such lovely people.

"Itchy," Bale whispered.

"What? I didn't tell the water to stop."

Tollar pulled her attention away from Beenala's farm in time to see the last of the water droplets evaporate from around Bale.

"What...?"

The air felt light and electric, suddenly so dry it stung her nose.

"It doesn't get this dry this fast on its own," she said to Bale.

The dragon was already back to tearing at her own skin, growling softly as she did. Tollar extended her senses, looking for more water. There was plenty in the soil beneath her feet, so she pulled some of that up into a blob in the air in front of her and waited, all her focus on it. It evaporated instantly, but water couldn't wink out of existence, and she followed its course.

"Around the mountain. Let's go, quickly!"

"Itchy!" Bale roared.

"Hush! I don't know what's out here doing this. Here, have more ice pellets. Now let's go!"

A little groundwater to exfoliate Bale and a little more to whip them up the mountain and over its shoulder, following the evaporating water. Now that she knew what was happening—well, sort of—she blocked it from stealing her water or Bale's ice.

She cleared some trees and found another outcropping to get a good look and stopped. Forgot to hold onto her water and dropped onto the stone as it vanished. Barely noticed Bale hissing and scraping herself along the stones.

The storm on the far side of Mount Acrintaga was dark and vast, an angry ocean turned open in the skies. It poured down into the valley. A mountain of water crashing down into the farmland below.

"Shit," she gasped.

And got to work.

Tollar lifted herself on a wave and plunged into the midst of it, seeing nothing but grey sheets all around her, hearing nothing but the roar of it. The water raged around her, none of it actually touching her though the wind tugged at her hair and dress, while she stared unseeing, trying to feel the shape of this storm. Trying to get the originating point.

It was too far off, somewhere to the east. Probably.

Didn't matter. She had to stop this.

She pushed her senses deeper into the water, the cold rush of it electrifying her bones. Taking hold of it like a blanket, she lifted the water up out of the valley and its fields, pushing that sheet of water up under the clouds. Extended out so the torrent passed above the farmland like a skyborne river, coming out of the mountains and straight into the air to waterfall into the Arazow.

Downriver of the power dam or the entire city would be without electricity.

And she drew it out, piling water up above her head, one arm extended out to guide it, another out toward the river. Like the candy makers pulling taffy in that cute little seaside town way down to the northwest.

Didn't want to add more water than the riverbanks could handle.

Despite the cold rush of water and magic, Tollar grew warm, breathing heavy with the effort of concentration, trying to find the source of all this water while keeping it away from the farms. Trying to redirect some of it back to the air where it belonged, back into the ground on the other side of the mountain, back to wherever it came from. All this water magic was going to have dire consequences beyond the flooding, and Tollar's head ached from the focus required to not pull too much magic from any one place and risk turning Bale into jerky.

Noise like a rockslide shattered her concentration, and it was all she could do to keep the water from slamming back down into the valley.

Bale roared from behind her and Tollar groaned.

"Hush, you! Something very wrong is happening. I need to focus."

"The itches burn!"

Tollar sighed, kept her focus on the water above but made some new ice pellets for Bale.

"Back into the jungle before someone sees you. Go, now!"

Bale slunk away in her swirling cloud of scouring ice.

"What the cursed Pit is going on out here...?"

She scanned the skies, dizziness reeling her from the motion of looking up, but her sheet of water had mostly dissipated, some of it into the river, the rest of it returned to humidity and proper clouds. The clouds themselves were clearing out and the warm nudge of nearby magic brushed against her. More elementals, but these ones working to the same end she had been. Tollar closed her eyes and focused on the mountains to the east, but there was no sign of magic that way anymore. But she didn't know who had enough power to conjure a storm like that, unless there was a group. Even still, they'd have to link power with each other.

She would have to get those two adult dragons to communicate with Balipar a whole lot more. She couldn't have a moulting dragon bringing the attention of the entire city down on them. Or distracting her at another critical moment. She'd learned the hard way how catastrophic mistakes with power like hers could be.

More magic brushed against her, searching the same way she had been to the east. Shouts carried on the wind.

"Wait, the locals weren't flooding this valley on purpose, were they?"

That didn't make any sense. None of this made any sense. But Upalint had changed in ways she still didn't understand. Despite the weariness settling into her limbs, she solidified the puddle under her boots and whisked herself into the jungle, hoping she hadn't shown too much of her power or somehow mucked something up.

Solia was the only one who would have the sorts of answers she needed, and not try to end her for messing up an intentional flood.

10

Tollar scowled at the little patch of road ahead, the only part revealed through the pre-dawn gloom by the lantern Beenala maintained. Talking to Solia again had done nothing but net more questions, and Tollar was running out of places to seek answers. This was a long shot, but if it didn't work, she didn't know what she'd do. Beenala stopped nattering, and Tollar realized the ensuing silence was an expectant one. Beenala watched her.

"Sorry, Bee. What was that?"

"It doesn't matter what order everyone shows up. You don't have to be the first one there."

"I know. It's the principle. I really need to talk to her."

"The spirits will see that or they won't. Skipping breakfast and not getting enough sleep won't change that."

Tollar gripped the fingerbone pendant, running the pad of her thumb over the familiar bumps. Even Bale was still asleep—or gone back to sleep after being reminded to stay on the farm. She was big enough, doing well enough, that those two adult dragons recently left the Naldes range to go wherever it was the local dragon blaze had gone. Balipar could probably summon them back in an emergency, but Tollar didn't like her odds if an emergency came up.

"I need this reading."

"Then I'm sure your granny will be there."

"What if the old woman ignores Granny?"

Beenala sighed and gave her a hard look. Tollar would love to have the kind of faith in the necromancers that Beenala did, but the fact they left the dead cities at all amazed her. And Tollar discovered it was the Wise Mother, Toresona herself, who would be doing the readings today.

The necromancers weren't supposed to ignore the will of the ancestors, and Granny was pretty stubborn, but Toresona was a hard woman who disliked Tollar almost as much as Saivyn did. Tollar always maintained proper respect for the entire necromancers' guild, she just wasn't afraid of them—or didn't revere them like gods?—the way everyone else did or the way the necromancers thought everyone ought to.

Tollar scowled ahead, the silence trailing along behind them like a ghost. The city streets were quiet, only a few merchants getting an early start to the day. Gentle pink alpenglow brushed the mountaintops to the east as they reached the central market where a semicircle of benches were set up around a large, soft chair on a dais.

Tollar hated the way the necromancers held court like the self-important nobles of distant lands.

Her best chance of getting answers, and good answers, would be to go to counsel in the Dead City around the winter solstice, but she didn't think this could wait that long. Not with that flood—worst one they'd seen according to Solia, or almost seen since Tollar had stopped it in time. Whatever was happening was escalating and that the damage was so minor was a complete fluke. If Tollar had been even a few minutes later getting into the valley...

She sighed.

So her second best option was to sit around all day for a bone reading and hope Granny's spirit had something to say and that Toresona would be willing to pass along the message.

"Here, save a seat for me and I'll find us some breakfast." Tollar gestured Beenala onto one of the benches in the second row. Eager but not too eager.

While the market was far quieter than normal this early in the morning, there were a few vendors set up to attend the growing crowd come to receive a bone reading, or just listen in on them because half the city were insufferable gossips. Tollar got a pair of halved and roasted coconut shells filled with sweet rice, pineapple chunks, and moon ants fried in coconut bread, topped with a plantain wrap. And a pair of halved nolanut shells filled with steaming chocolate. Extra spice in Tollar's.

All balanced on a disc of water held in one hand because she was nothing if not a show-off.

When Tollar offered the tray to Beenala with a flourish, Beenala gave her a playfully longsuffering look before taking her share of breakfast. The look turned horrified when Tollar started dipping the bites of fried ant in her chocolate.

"I'll have you know, this is the customary way to eat basically everything with your morning chocolate up on the south coast."

Beenala bristled. "We're not on the south coast."

"It's lovely there, why don't you come with me some time?"

Beenala's cheeks flushed pink, but she covered it by huffing indignantly. Tollar grinned and popped another chocolate-dipped, coconut-fried ant into her mouth.

Beenala gripped her arm and pointed to the east side of the square where the procession headed toward them, Toresona up front, flanked and followed by her acolytes, all of them in black, mostly robes though some in plain shirts and pants or dresses, many with silver and gold embroidery along hemlines. Except for Toresona, whose robes were more gold and silver than black. Her black eyes flashed in her heavily wrinkled face, her black hair gone mostly white, though her skin remained an almost youthful rich umber. She walked with a staff made from an elongated femur. Tollar had heard rumours that the femur belonged to a bitter enemy. She'd also heard it belonged to a beloved child, lost far too soon.

Either story could be true. Both could be lies.

It was always hard to tell with the necromancers, but Toresona especially.

In her prime, the woman had been taller than Tollar, though she was now stooped in a permanent bow. Given her particular gift with magic, Tollar was surprised the woman hadn't corrected her own posture. Unless she could only work with dead bones?

Tollar was quicker than Beenala in setting her breakfast on the bench and kneeling, keeping her head down until one of the acolytes spoke something in their dead language, signifying the beginning of the reading. All but one of the acolytes left again, Toresona settled into the big chair with the bone staff shrunk and balanced across her lap. Everyone in the crowd stayed in their seats, whispering softly to each other if they said anything at all, and waited for Toresona to call on them.

Of course Tollar wanted to be first, but wasn't surprised when her breakfast was long gone, the sun bright overhead, and her stomach starting to think about a second breakfast and she still hadn't been called upon. The old woman hadn't so much as glanced in her direction.

Beenala sat politely next to her, feigning interest, neither of them speaking though others carried on hushed conversations while Toresona doled out wisdom from the ancestors, who were not bound by corporeal limitations and could see what their descendants could not. Tollar tried not to tap her feet.

"Bee, you don't have to stay," Tollar whispered.

"I promised I would."

"Yes, but this could take all day. You've got chores. And our mutual guest might be getting bored. That could get dangerous."

Beenala's eyes widened slightly, just remembering that they'd left a dragon alone on their farms. She nodded once, picked up her bag and their discarded shells to add to the compost wagon down the lane, and then sidled quietly out of the square. Tollar watched her go, legs twitching to follow. She ground her teeth and glared in Toresona's direction.

It wasn't until she was on her way back from another food vendor, her fingers greasy from the fish wrap, that Toresona looked her way and gestured for her to come up.

Tollar tried not to take it personally.

She stuffed the last of the wrap into her mouth and wiped her fingers on the leaf as she approached the dais, stuffing the leaf into her pocket as she knelt before the old necromancer.

Who tsked at her.

"Never quite prepared, are you?" Toresona said.

Okay so now she was definitely taking it personally. She bit back her immediate response of pointing out that she'd been sitting here literally *all frogging morning*.

"That's why I hope to confer with the ancestors," Tollar managed.

"All right, girl, let's see the bone."

As Tollar stood, she wondered how many other thirty-three-year-olds the woman referred to as children. But she needed this. Needed Granny's advice. She forced a polite smile, thumb worrying over the bone again. Toresona scowled at the hesitation, and Tollar remembered how the woman hadn't wanted to deliver the bone in the first place. Thought Granny was mistaken in giving it to her. Tollar had taken it down off its safe shelf for this and if she didn't get it back...

She unclasped it and placed it in the woman's gnarled waiting palm.

"What wisdom do you seek?"

Tollar's mouth got away from her brain's need for answers about the storms. "Everyone else seems to know what I should do with my life, like all the people I've helped somehow isn't enough. What's Granny got to say?"

Toresona tsked again, the expression on her face darkening as her fingers closed around Granny's bone. Tollar maintained eye contact but pressed her lips together to keep her traitor mouth from making things worse.

The old necromancer's gaze unfocused for a moment, her head tilting to listen to a voice only she could hear.

"Go back with your eyes open," Toresona pronounced, dropping the fingerbone into Tollar's hand.

"What? Back where? I've been—"

Toresona called on the next person, her acolyte shooing Tollar away.

"Well that was worse than useless," Tollar muttered, taking long swift strides out of the market. She paused at the edge, torn between going to the farm or maybe further into the city to see if Solia or Auntie could help with the puzzle. Solia wouldn't be off duty for hours yet and she'd bothered Bee enough already, so she opted to head for Auntie's.

How much easier would that have been if the old woman liked you? Was that even Granny's message? Would Toresona lie?

She shouldn't have sent Beenala away. Toresona liked Beenala and probably would have given her a straight answer.

Go back? Last place she'd been was that flooded valley, which she'd been back to *twice* with Solia. If she kept her eyes anymore open while there they'd fall right out of her head. Assuming Granny understood what Tollar was up against, going back must mean Port Sawulxo, right? Maybe it had something to do with the dragons she'd left behind. Someone needed do something about that mess, it might as well be her.

II

Beenala met Tollar in the lane, Bale already tucked around the side of the house for her afternoon nap. Tollar came out of her house in a cheery yellow sundress with fuchsia and moss-green embroidery at the neck and hemlines, her curls towering out of a sunset-coloured head wrap, and Beenala stopped short. Tollar's eyes glittered and her lips twitched up at the corners.

"Are you sure you don't want to come with me?" Beenala said. She was standing with her bicycle, off to have dinner with her family, and Tollar hadn't seen them yet, always busy with Bale.

"I expect I'll be a while with Solia, especially if she can get me outfitted right away. You go ahead, I'll come another time."

"Outfitted?"

"Yes. I can go with what I've got, but Solia's supplies are better."

The words *go* and *supplies* lodged in Beenala's mind, and she stopped in the lane. Tollar had been here so long now that Beenala thought it was for good this time. Had Beenala failed her somehow? She exhaled only to take another breath to speak.

"You're leaving again?"

"I'm sorry, Bee, but I need to go north."

Beenala crossed her arms and looked at her feet. "Just running away again, then? You've been running away for eighteen years. Where does it end?"

Tollar went rigid, breathing shallow.

"I didn't run away that first time."

Beenala's eyes widened. She swallowed the lump in her throat, but Tollar had already propelled ahead on one of her water chariots so that Beenala had to stand on the pedals to catch up. The silence on the trip into the city proper was like a blanket of broken glass over Beenala's thoughts. When Tollar paused at the intersection where they should part, Beenala shook her head and took a fortifying breath.

"I'll come with you to see Solia."

"You sure? It'll be boring."

Beenala shrugged. She wanted to know more about Tollar leaving but didn't want to outright ask how long she'd be gone, not when she'd already overstepped and Tollar wasn't volunteering details. So she trailed after Tollar to the guard house, startled to see the dragon whisperer outside the building, waiting for Tollar.

Balipar stood calmly, hands clasped behind their back, with their hair in a crown of braids and wearing a vest and flared ankle-length skirt in such a rich scarlet that Beenala nearly wept with envy. She had no idea where they found that colour, but she had questions.

The three of them greeted each other with polite bows, and then Tollar got straight to it, apparently giving them a report on Bale.

"She's started hoarding!" Tollar beamed.

It was a small pile of treasure—most of which was little more than shiny refuse like a tarnished mirror and broken knife. But Balipar was enthusiastic. Beenala zoned out as the trio entered the building, already knowing everything about the little dragon.

The guard house was quiet inside, Beenala guessed because it was mid-shift and everyone was out on patrol, but she'd never actually been inside, only ever passed by it, usually on her way to the market. Tollar talked enough about it that she felt like she'd been here before, and they walked through the main room full of tables with stacks of mead casks at one end next to a small kitchen. The air was cooler than out on the streets, but stale, like no one ever opened the windows. It was the social club, where the watch coming off duty could unwind before going home. It seemed wrong for it to be so empty.

Tollar moved straight across the room to a stairway at the other end.

"Are we all going up to see Solia?" Beenala glanced at Balipar.

"I've been invited to offer my opinion," they said.

They passed a door on the landing and, from what Beenala understood, it led to locker rooms where the watch kept their gear. There were a couple of them like Tollar, who had training and their own weapons but weren't steadily part of the guard, but most of them used communal gear that stayed on site.

Up one more flight of stairs to the administrative area where Solia's office was at the end of the hall. The door was open, which Beenala took to mean she was available. Did they need an appointment? Or was it fine to walk in because Tollar was friends with her?

Regardless, Tollar tended to do what she wanted, and walked in either way.

"Ah, Toll, you're early." Solia narrowed her eyes at Tollar's entourage but nodded a greeting. "Per Balipar, Per Beenala. Toll, what's going on?"

Balipar shut the door behind them and stood calmly in front of it, hands folded at their front. Tollar gestured for Beenala to take the seat across from Solia while Tollar pulled a rolled sheaf of papers from her pocket and spread it on Solia's desk.

"What you asked for. Hope it does what you think it will." Then Tollar began pacing.

Solia grunted. "Toll, what have you got yourself into now? I'm going to start charging you a bottle of rum per visit. And not that piss they serve downstairs. Something dark."

"Look, I'll bring you a whole frogging cask of rum. From the islands even. No finer rum in the entire world."

"You'd know."

"I have become a rum connoisseur. But rum later, plans now."

"Plans?" Solia looked from one face to another and sagged further into her seat. "You're leaving."

"It's only temporary."

Balipar sighed. "And I suppose I'm here either to advise you on finding a babysitter for your dragon, or to devise some way to bring her with you."

"Well..."

"You're a fool," they said calmly.

Tollar threw a dismissive wave their way, stopped pacing behind Beenala and leaned on the back of her chair to stare directly at Solia.

"It's the ancestors' will. Message from Granny. She says I've got to go back."

Beenala crossed her arms and looked straight ahead at Solia's desk. Tollar hadn't mentioned what the message had been, only that she'd received one. No wonder she'd been cagey since returning home yesterday evening. Though she knew it was silly, Beenala felt Granny had somehow betrayed her by sending Tollar away again.

"It's not just the message," Solia said. "You're urgent to get back there, why?"

"I want to see if I can slip back into their ranks and maybe sabotage the dragon pens and get them out."

"You're just going to let the dragons go free?"

"Dragons don't belong in chains."

"Ever the bleeding heart." Solia smiled fondly.

"Yeah, yeah. Keep it to yourself, I've got a reputation to maintain."

"All right, Tollar, I assume you want a squad on this fool's errand of yours, but—"

Someone pounded on Solia's office door, and Beenala jumped when it swung open a moment later, giving Balipar barely enough time to dodge being hit. Beenala couldn't see their new guest around Tollar but could guess by the way Tollar groaned and clenched her fists.

Beenala was not surprised when Saivyn shouted, "What the demon's corpse are you doing here again?"

"That's my business. Do you ever use manners or do you just barge in on everyone? Bali, maybe you should introduce him to some dragons."

Balipar rolled their eyes. "Leave me out of this."

"I will not be brushed off twice because of her!" Saivyn snarled.

"Tollar will be out of your hair soon enough, Sai. And if it's really that important you can make an appointment."

"I happen to have an appointment," Tollar said.

"Solia, you're not actually listening to her foolishness again, are you?"

"Heard back from your friends in the port yet?" Tollar snarled.

"I know you haven't," Solia said to him. "Neither have I."

"It hasn't been that long—"

"Long enough for a bird to get there and back again."

"And if there's nothing going on, they've no reason to rush a bird back out," he countered. "We can stand to wait another span of days."

Tollar rolled her eyes. "You could get some wizards to send a message for you. Oh wait, they all hate you, not that I could imagine why."

"Tollar."

Beenala released a shaky breath, impressed that the tone of Solia's voice cut through the argument and actually got Tollar to shut up, though Saivyn was growling. Actually growling like some kind of animal. It was remarkable the effect Tollar had on him. Beenala hugged her arms around herself and sank deeper into the chair, her eye on the door. Would it be rude if she left? Dinner didn't start for an hour, but surely Tollar would understand? Beenala hadn't come here to watch Tollar fight with Saivyn, and she could find out Tollar's plans later.

But Saivyn was between her and the doorway, and she wasn't keen on trying to get past him.

"This solves nothing," Solia snapped. "Tollar's right about the dragons. No force should be keeping them or using them against their will."

"I'm not doing anything based on her word alone." He jabbed a finger at Tollar.

"Stop being a coward and send some people with me to verify for you."

"That's always your answer, isn't it? Just run off without a plan. I'm not sending good soldiers with you to get eaten by dragons."

"Dragons typically don't eat people," Balipar interjected.

He growled in frustration and turned to Solia, who only sat in her chair, watching the pair of them.

"Anyway, who says I don't have a plan? It would go better if I had some soldiers with me though. So what'll it be, Sai, you going to spare me a few of your finest? Send your favourite rank three if that'll make you happy."

"No one is sending anyone north," he snapped, glancing at Solia.

"Frog him." Tollar appealed to Solia. "Send me a few of yours then, they know their way around a battle well enough."

Solia grunted. "He outranks me, Toll. Looks like you're on your own with this."

Tollar groaned and spun away to pace the room some more. "What about the necromancers?" she asked.

"Leave the necromancers out of this," Saivyn said.

"Toll, if you want the necromancers to help you, you're going to have to talk to them yourself."

Tollar threw her hands into the air. "Come on, Sol, at least put a good word in for me first, will you? You know Toresona hates me."

"I can't imagine why." Saivyn rolled his eyes.

"Sai!" Solia shot to her feet.

Beenala sank deeper into the chair.

Balipar stood next to the door, their grey eyes shining, expression caught somewhere been appalled and amused.

Solia blinked a lot. And scowled through the blinking. And tapped one finger against the desktop. "Two casks of rum, Tollar. The finest you've ever tasted."

"Sol, I expect you'll want three or four casks before you get Tollar out of here," Balipar said lightly.

Solia slumped back in her chair and stared up at the ceiling.

"Look, Bali's right, you know why they're here." Tollar glared at Saivyn for a moment, then gave Solia a significant look.

"Sai, I need a minute with Tollar—"

"You're going to help her aren't—"

"That's my business. Five minutes, Saivyn."

He stormed out, Beenala startling as he slammed the door behind him. Should she go now or would he be right outside waiting like a bear? She exhaled her pent-up breath and sucked in another.

"You're bringing the dragon." Solia gave Tollar a longsuffering look.

"Is Sai really not trustworthy?"

"If the dragon was living on any other farm in the nation, it would probably be fine," Solia's voice was very dry, leaning forward on her desk. "Why can't you and Bali work out the dragon's needs without me?"

"Well, I was going to try to get a squad out of you." Tollar scowled at the door Saivyn had just gone through. "Wanted trustworthy ones, but that plan's been dashed into the Pit."

"You should leave the dragon here," Balipar said.

"Who's going to keep her safe?" Tollar asked.

"How do they survive in the wild?" Beenala asked.

"Used to be, they didn't have much to worry about, and their homes in the mountains were safe enough. Now they take eggs and hatchlings to the dragon city, unreachable by humans."

"There's a dragon city?" Beenala blurted.

"It's supposed to be stunning."

"Maybe we can go with Bale sometime," Tollar said. "But let's focus on here and now, shall we?"

Beenala blinked her way through thoughts of buildings big enough for dragons, and how massive a whole city of them must be. Following the conversation after that took all her focus.

"So if I've got this right," Solia said, "you're going back to Port Sawulxo because you think that's what your granny wants, and you thought I would give you a squad to go with you and your dragon."

"She's not *my* dragon, she's her own dragon. And that was the hope. Fine, I'll go with Bale on my own."

"Can this dragon even fly or breathe fire."

"Fire, yes," Balipar said.

"She's gliding." Tollar was only ever so testy when anyone questioned the dragon's development. "Bet we can get her flying before we get to the port."

Solia winced and groaned. "Tollar. Five casks, just for today's headache alone."

Tollar rubbed her face. "This is hopeless. You really can't sneak a few out to come with me? Three or four even?"

Solia gave her a dark look.

And that was when Saivyn barged back in, grumbling, "Honestly, Solia, I just need five minutes of your time."

"Tollar made an appointment and this time is hers, and I don't give a witch's backside what you think of her or her concerns. *Something* is going on in the north."

Beenala gripped the arms of her chair and stared at Tollar, both lovely in her bright colours and wretched in her hopelessness and desperate need to put things right. Her stomach tightened and her head threatened to float away. Tollar would go back on her own. Or on her own with Bale. Beenala could practically hear that plan forming in her mind.

"I've been thinking about it, and I worry it might have to do with the raiders," Solia said. "What if they've got those dragons to guard the trade routes? Or to be more efficient at their raiding?"

Silence descended over them like a deluge, cold and prickly and stifling.

"All right, yes," Saivyn conceded. "We need to send someone to bring back information. Someone *trustworthy*."

Tollar spun toward him, fists clenched. "Run along and find someone then, see if they can beat me there!"

"I'll go with you," Beenala said with numb lips.

An even deeper silence fell over the room, Beenala's cheeks burned, and she stared down at her lap. She had to focus on stillness to keep from twitching. Now that she'd spoken them, she couldn't very well take the words back.

But she didn't want to.

She couldn't let Tollar go alone. If Beenala went, and was useful, maybe it would convince Tollar to see the value in staying home more. That she didn't need the chaos. That she could find comfort in a routine. And Beenala wouldn't have to spend the entire time Tollar was gone worrying that this time she wouldn't return.

And it was high time Beenala pushed herself out of her comfort zone. She'd already adjusted to the chaos of Bale and Tollar around all the time, surely she could improve more. If she could, it came with the added bonus of seeing more of Tollar.

Something electric buzzed through her at the prospect of pulling off something so unwise.

"You want to come with me?"

"Of course I don't *want* to, don't be foolish." Beenala dug her fingers into the plush chair and kept her gaze on her lap. "But if you're really set on going north, you shouldn't do it alone. I'm a pyromancer, I could help you."

"That's the stupidest thing I've ever heard." This was from Solia, shocking Beenala. Solia tilted her head, pinning Tollar with her glare.

"Why?" Beenala demanded, sitting up straight.

"Bee, it's too dangerous." Tollar's tone had all the gentleness of her mother reassuring her after a nightmare.

"I kept that dragoness from incinerating you."

She hazarded a glance at Tollar, that silver gaze too intense to hold for long. Tollar's mouth was open to argue, but then she closed it and tilted her head. Her face started to crumple, but she clenched her jaw to harden against it.

Tollar glanced around and let out a long breath.

"Bee, you did well with the dragon, but you'd have to do that again and again with no breaks, no retreats, no routine. When we get to the port, we will need to react, again and again, without hesitation. And you freeze when you're scared, Bee. I know you can't help it, but it's true."

"I didn't freeze with the dragon."

Tollar groaned and dragged her fingers down her face, getting her feet moving.

"And I listened to you with the gezar. I could do that again. You just need to say, 'Bee, shoot a fireball that way' and I could do it."

"You can shoot fireballs?"

"I'm sure I could figure it out."

"This is absurd," Saivyn muttered.

"Well if you were any help at all, Beenala wouldn't be out here risking her safety!"

"Two of you isn't enough," Solia said softly.

"Can't Bali come with us?"

"No," Balipar said without hesitation. "There are not enough casks of rum in the world to convince me to come with you."

"Not even if it means you'll get to meet some new and interesting dragons?"

"More like exhausted and angry dragons. I will be shocked if you're not eaten or incinerated by the first dragon you encounter."

"Well, that's what Bee's for. She does great work against dragonfire."

Balipar sighed audibly.

"Anyway, it won't be the two of us," Tollar turned to Solia. "I'll free those dragons, and I'll find out more about those raiders. Bee can be my eyes, she's got excellent attention to detail. I'll bring you six frogging casks of the finest rum any human has ever made if we can drop this right now."

"All right, fine." Solia leaned even farther back into her chair. She folded her hands in her lap and rested her feet up on the desktop, staring over them at Tollar.

"Can I finally—" Saivyn started.

"No," Solia said. "Tollar, I'll make sure she's outfitted with a wilderness kit. You'll both need rations, I suppose?"

"I'll bring you seven casks of rum if you give me the good rations for once."

"There are no good rations. Why do you think I got a desk job that keeps me in the city? I never want to live off rations, not even for a single day, for the rest of my life, may it be long and blessed by the ancestors."

Tollar leaned around the side of Beenala's chair. "You sure you want to come?"

"Solia, please, if we're done allowing private citizens to volunteer to join an idiot's suicide mission, I'd—"

"Commander, I'm afraid I've had about enough unexpected visitors today, and I really must ask all of you to leave so I can finish my business and get home at a reasonable hour. Or do I need to charge you nine casks of rum and a box of the world's best cigars?" Solia directed the last comment at Tollar.

"I thought we were on eight?"

"Out now or it will be ten!"

"But I made an appointment," Tollar protested.

"As did I," said a new voice from the doorway.

Solia winced and Beenala craned her neck to try to see around everyone.

"Wise Mother," Tollar said with a deep bow, curls from her wrap spilling around her face.

Beenala scrambled out of her chair to join Tollar in a bow, looking up through her eyelashes to see Balipar doing the same. Saivyn merely moved aside to let Toresona into the room.

Tollar and Beenala scattered in opposite directions to provide her with respectful space.

"My apologies, Wise Mother," Solia said from where she stood behind her desk, bowing. "As I said earlier, tensions are high and there is much work to be done. Tollar has an... interesting mission that we are trying to finalize. And Saivyn enjoys interrupting."

His face pinched up like he'd stepped on an arrowhead.

"Wise Mother, would any of your rank join me in my impossible task?" Tollar asked.

Toresona tsked. "Your grandmother always warned me of your careless tongue. It will be your undoing."

"Oh, quite likely. But before it is, I'd love some help with the situation in the north. This was Granny's idea, if you recall."

"I care very little for what happens in the north."

"Yes, well, it involves dragons and I care very much."

Toresona only stared. Beenala eyed the door.

"You are crass and disrespectful," Saivyn snapped at Tollar.

"Says the man who couldn't even bother to bow to the Wise Mother," Tollar snarled.

"My ancestors have little to say to me," he said, dismissive.

Beenala's mouth fell open. Tollar didn't miss a beat.

"Can you blame them?"

"Tollar!" Solia again.

"Captain, this is most tiresome. I am pulled from my duties for this?"

Solia gestured for Toresona to take the seat Beenala recently vacated. "I hope to keep this brief, just give me a moment, I beg you."

Toresona eased into the chair, and Solia came around her desk, brown eyes gleaming and her mouth pressed into a hard line. "Out. All four of you. Now."

Balipar was already halfway down the hall, and Beenala slipped past Saivyn, who still thought he would gain an audience with Solia today. But Tollar stopped in the doorway, speaking in low tones to Solia but watching Toresona.

"I'm serious about their help, if you can swing it."

"Go. Now."

Tollar wordlessly joined Beenala in the hallway and they started off. Solia shoved Saivyn out and shut her door, the lock clicking home to leave no room for argument.

Saivyn stormed after them.

"You think you can pull necromancers away from their work over your nonsense?" he snarled. "You're nothing but a distraction when the rest of us have real work to do."

Beenala's head spun with all the shouting and accusations and the sheer lack of support for Tollar's trip to the north, which Solia thought was important but not important enough to actually outfit properly. Saivyn was an ass, Tollar had him there, but he was also head of the military for a reason. Was he right about this? Was it too dangerous?

What have I got myself into?

Tollar kept going down the hallway like Saivyn wasn't there shouting after them at all, and Beenala had no idea how she did it. How she could ignore the shouting, especially after the way she'd been goading him in Solia's office. Tollar ignored him, but Beenala flinched and looked his way every time his shouting rose in pitch.

"Come on, Bee, let's get you to your family. Maybe I have time to visit after all."

The tension in Beenala's stomach uncoiled at the prospect of the peace and quiet of her parents' apartment. And at the promise of her father's wonderful cooking.

Tollar always knew the right thing to say, at least when it wasn't Saivyn she was talking to. At last, they made it out onto the street.

"You said it would be boring." Beenala gave Tollar a sidelong glance.

Tollar sputtered a laugh. Then hurried to catch up to Balipar and arrange with them to talk more later about Bale joining in on her little adventure.

"It seems like an unfathomably bad idea to leave the dragon here without us. She'll probably follow us if we don't include her," Tollar said as Beenala caught up.

Balipar sighed, but agreed to come around tomorrow to talk to them.

Beenala brushed her damp palms against her shorts and tried not to think too hard about what she'd volunteered herself for. Tollar knew what she was doing, and Beenala had to trust in her friend's competence.

12

Tollar stood on the bank of the Arazow, blanketed with roiling mist in the early morning light, and tried to tell herself leaving was a good idea. Sure, she'd wanted to go, but not quite so soon and not back to Port Sawulxo. Maybe Granny was mistaken?

"Breakfast?" came the low burble of Bale's whispering voice from the cover of the treeline behind Tollar.

"Yes, yes."

She crouched, poking one finger into the water to get a sense of it—cold and rushing and lazy and welcoming all at once—and immediately found a pocket of fish. With a small water funnel, she syphoned off a few of the biggest, pushing them in a column into the trees behind her for the dragon.

"All right, that's enough, off to the jungle for some monkeys now. And leave Bee's chickens alone!"

"Too small." The petulance in Bale's tone suggested that they were not, in fact, too small, and maybe Tollar would like to forget how tasty Bale thought they looked. The foliage rustled as the dragon crept away.

Tollar caught a couple more fish in her funnel and kept them in a globe of water that rolled along behind her, keeping them alive and fresh, as she headed toward Beenala's cottage.

She hadn't spoken much to Beenala since returning from her parents' house last night, Beenala very deliberately not talking about what happened in Solia's office. Tollar knew Beenala was nervous, no matter how determined she acted, and Tollar didn't want her friend to regret the clearly impulsive choice she'd made.

Beenala seemed to think that because she'd been useful against a dragoness exactly once that it meant she could handle whatever it was they would find in Port Sawulxo. Granted, Beenala had been utterly magnificent in that moment, and thinking about it filled Tollar with warmth and gave her the chills at the same time. It was a side of Beenala that Tollar hadn't known existed, but it also made her more protective of her friend. Yes, Beenala held her own against an angry dragoness. But then she'd spent the rest of the day hiding in her cottage. And she'd utterly frozen when the gezar showed up on her doorstep.

But Tollar really needed some help. On her own she might be able to steal another dragon egg or two. Or maybe free an adult. But she needed to free them all. And while it was within the realm of possibility, it would require using some terrifyingly dangerous magic that could destroy what remained of the city if she lost control.

Yes, she could do it on her own. But she really really shouldn't.

And it would be nice to have some company. But it would also be ten days of travelling and who knew how long it would take to, at minimum, get the information Solia wanted. That was a long time for Beenala to see things Tollar didn't want anyone to see. A long time for Beenala to get tired of Tollar's presence. Having Beenala around for days on end would make Tollar vulnerable in so many ways.

The loneliness was awful, but rejection was so much worse.

Ash barked from up the lane, and Tollar spotted Beenala and her dog coming toward her, Beenala with her fishing pole over one shoulder.

"Morning, Tollar," Beenala said with a polite nod.

Yeah, she was avoiding the subject.

"Morning, Bee. Just coming back from feeding fish to Bale. Kept some extras."

Beenala's gaze went to the ball of fishy water trailing after Tollar like a soggy puppy. She opened her mouth, closed it. Then said, "I could cook it up for you."

"That would be excellent. I brought enough for both of us. Got a sack of rice that's more than I need."

Ash trotted along next to the ball of water as Tollar followed Beenala toward the farms. The dog pawed at the water, trying to get the fish, and even snapped at the little ball, getting nothing but a wet snoot for her efforts.

Tollar pushed the ball of fish to Beenala's front door and went to fetch the bag of rice. She barely used any of it, not doing a lot of cooking in her own place when it had no furniture except the hammock. The house was large enough to have comfortably held her whole family, including Auntie and the grandparents, if the grandparents were alive. But Tollar didn't need so much space and set up her things in the main room right inside the front door, like she had a small apartment like Auntie's. Too many ghosts in the rest of the house, and Tollar kept the doors shut against them.

When she got to Beenala's cottage, Beenala had all her focus on cleaning the fish, dropping the odd bit to Ash while setting the rest aside for compost. Her deft hands stilled only when Tollar started preparing the rice.

"That's, um, not enough water," Beenala said gently, trying her very best not to imply that Tollar had made it to adulthood without learning how to cook rice.

"Says you."

"You're not boiling it?"

"Don't need to."

Beenala had all her attention on what Tollar was doing, her fish knife set aside, and Ash giving her the very best "Why have you stopped feeding me?" look, so it was probably the best chance Tollar would get.

"I'm sorry I didn't tell you about Granny's message sooner. But I know how it upsets you when I leave. I just didn't realize it would upset you into wanting to come with me."

"Yes, well."

"Going north won't be some kind of adventure."

Beenala stiffened. "So you said yesterday."

"You'll have to sleep on the ground and piss in the jungle and eat whatever rubbish rations Solia sends with us."

Beenala gripped the hem of her shirt. The dog trotted over, leaning against Beenala's legs the way she did to remind Beenala to keep breathing.

"And who's going to look after Ash? And worry about planting day? Or do the mulching? And what about your art? Can't bring it with you."

Beenala absently patted the dog and pressed her lips together. And then she stood up straight.

"If you don't want me to come with you, just say so."

And Tollar crumbled. "I *do* want you to come with me."

"But." Beenala sighed. "But it will be dangerous and uncomfortable? Well, I suppose I will have to adjust. But we'll be gone a while? Perhaps as long as a month? I'll have to see if Per Graza can look after Ash and the farm. Or see if my parents can stay for a few days, I can ask them at breakfast."

"Bee, it's not that simple."

"Isn't it? You don't always travel on your own. You're not some constantly solitary wandering rogue. If you can travel with others, why can't you travel with me?"

The truth burbled up to the tip of her tongue, and she had to bite it back to keep Beenala from seeing her cowardice. And the reason behind it.

And hadn't Beenala been understanding about the tattoos? And what if Beenala managed this as well as she thought she could? The idea of Beenala coming with her on other campaigns, of having a constant in her life without having to always return to a place that was haunted...

But the truth was Beenala was soft. She belonged somewhere safe with her books and her art and her dog. The dog in question was at the table, nosing the edge.

Tollar turned her attention to the pot, encouraging the water and the rice to become one, watching it grow fatter and fluffier. Beenala set the fish in a pan on top of the oven and used her flint to get it started and used her magic to keep it going, pulling heat from the air to cool the kitchen and heat the pan. Then she started making chocolate to drink with breakfast.

Tollar set the pot on the edge of the stove to warm it. She caught Beenala staring at the fully fluffed rice and smiled.

"Cooking rice is really just rehydrating it. I was rehydrating and dehydrating things before I could walk."

"It's a good thing your mother is an aquamancer too or you'd have probably turned the entire neighbourhood into jerky without even realizing."

Tollar's stomach clenched and she didn't know what her face showed but Beenala's eyes went wide.

"Toll... what happened?"

Tollar clenched and unclenched her fists, then sighed. The memory had come out of nowhere, but she supposed she couldn't leave it to Beenala's imagination.

"It was one of the first things I did after I left home for good. I was on my way to the western archipelago to see where my ancestors came from and there was a rogue wave coming right for the boat. I didn't even think about it and just jumped straight into the water and propelled myself into the middle of it and honestly it's a good thing I did because if I'd stayed on the boat to stop the wave, I might have killed everyone on board."

Beenala gasped.

"You know how when you use a lot of pyromancy, the air gets colder? And with aquamancy the air gets dryer? Well, when I'm using really big magic, the power comes from whatever source. In this case, since I'd jumped in the ocean, it was a league's worth of sea life that got turned into brittle husks."

Beenala's eyes managed to go even wider.

"So anyway, that's how I found out my magic could do that. And that's why I used all those demons in Singsi. The demons draw from their realm for magic, not ours."

"Bleeding ancestors, Toll, that's terrible! I've never heard of anything like that. It would be like if I used too much pyromancy and froze someone solid."

"A strong enough pyromancer could. In a lot of ways you're lucky your power is what it is." Tollar chuckled. "Would have been worse if I were a pyromancer. You're a dangerous lot to raise."

"I'll have you know, I've never set anything or anyone on fire I didn't want to."

Tollar laughed and left the pot of rice to warm on the stovetop while Beenala added some herbs to the fish and sliced up tomatoes. It was hard to imagine Beenala setting anything on fire out of anything other than necessity.

"Please, Tollar. Let me try."

Beenala stood stiff again, fists stuffed in her pocket, actually meeting Tollar's gaze. Tollar turned away, making a circuit of the room.

"Bee, if something happens to you..."

Tollar's roving gaze fell on a machete on the side table with a particular design on the blade and her thoughts started wading through slush. She gasped and picked it up for a closer look. Ash trotted over to her, ears and tail raised in alarm.

"Bee, isn't this the same design as on my longsword?"

The city's best blacksmith, Abilerit, was a full elemental, a powerful one, and had used all four elements at the height of their power—working with elemental demons—to craft Tollar's blade. Her sword had this very same braided vine pattern etched into the blade at the hilt.

"I hadn't noticed," Beenala said. Her tone said otherwise.

Tollar looked at her, but she turned back to making breakfast, putting the corn wraps on the stove to heat up. Tollar caught a glimpse of the bright pink on Beenala's cheeks.

"I just spent an evening cleaning that blade and everything else, and it definitely is the same pattern. Looks an awful lot like that braided chain your Mammi always wears. Bee, did Abilerit steal your design?"

Tollar said that last bit with more force than she meant to, though her blood rose, her fist clenched around the machete's handle. Ash whined. Beenala startled and met her gaze.

"No." Beenala sounded horrified, wiping her palms on her shorts. "Abi would never."

Tollar blinked, her cheeks grew hot, trying not to notice the way Beenala's own cheeks were even redder as her friend turned back to making breakfast. She set the machete down and paced away from it.

"It's a lovely design," Tollar said softly.

Beenala gripped the panhandle and spoon so tight her knuckles were white, so still it was clear she was holding her breath. Ash had been following Tollar around but went over to Beenala, booping her leg.

Tollar's gaze cast around the room, looking for other traces of the design.

Despite Ash's best efforts, Beenala was frazzled, her movements jerky, hasty, as she scraped the fish onto the wraps, spooned in some rice and brought the meal to the long table in the middle of the room. Once meant for Beenala's entire family, half of it was cluttered with textiles and half-finished art projects. The other half was cleared for food prep with enough room left for one person to sit.

Or two.

Yes, having companionship was wonderful and no one kept her company quite like Beenala. But that wouldn't make the trip north less dangerous. Tollar leaned against the sink and closed her eyes. She wanted to be wrong that Beenala coming with her might leave Bee in a constant state of terror. Tollar couldn't bear that. Or the idea Beenala might get hurt. She wanted Beenala to be right. She wanted the possibilities that opened up.

But her thoughts were snarled up in that vine pattern.

Ash growled softly and both women turned to glance out the window, where Tollar spotted Bale returning and settling in behind Tollar's house to nap. It hadn't been long, but the little dragon was not so little anymore and wouldn't be able to hide behind the house much longer. She had fire and was almost flying. That had to change things. A dragon helping with the travel and whatever dangers they might find would make the trip safer.

And Tollar had been head of small campaigns in the past that involved warriors of unknown skill and bearing. Everyone had survived. If she kept thinking of it like that, like some brand new campaign, maybe she could keep it all together. And when they returned, if Saivyn didn't believe Tollar, he would probably still believe Beenala about what they saw.

She took a deep, fortifying breath and leaned on the table next to where Beenala sat, catching her gaze and holding it.

"You don't complain about how uncomfortable it is. You practice making fireballs—maybe with Bale? And you listen to me." She gave Beenala a hard look, gesturing to her rank lines. "These mean something. If the time comes to fight, you listen to me. Even if I'm telling you to stay behind or to turn around and go home. Because if you disregard my words, I absolutely *will* send you home."

"Yes, of course!" Beenala clapped her hands once and held them against her chest, smiling wide and brown eyes bright. "Where do we start?"

"With breakfast." Tollar grinned when Beenala rolled her eyes. "But as soon as we're done breakfast, we'll take stock of our collective supplies. Then talk to Balipar."

Tollar poured herself into the other chair and accepted her breakfast wrap with a smile, holding Beenala's gaze for a moment.

Tollar was already taking a mental inventory of what she had, what she knew Beenala had, trying to take the dragon into account, and to assess Beenala's skill. Just like any other campaign. She could make this work.

13

Draminedes was certain his backside would be sore for the rest of his life after spending what felt like all eternity on a donkey to get here. He'd wanted an oxcart, but his role was supposed to be that of a new merchant, one just making his way. So less people would ask questions or try to recognize him.

Blend in with the background, he'd been told.

And he'd spent enough time around merchants of all stripes, back when there'd been any still coming to Biterna and working with his father, that he felt confident in mimicking their ways. He'd had no trouble on the endless journey south.

But now that he had arrived, he was expected to act the part of a scholar. Draminedes had met scholars, but they were a dim memory. One he failed to recall as he took in his absolutely unexpected surroundings.

He was in the new target's main city, and it was stunning. Lush and green so that it was often hard to tell where the city ended and the jungle began, but not in the muddy hut kind of way Karthiry had led him to believe. There were mosaic-covered stone buildings that likely had a terramancer's hand in raising, and he'd passed at least one neighbourhood where all the homes were trees. Just live hollow trees. And the people were friendly and kind. He hadn't yet run into someone who didn't know a passable amount of prime.

The city was alive and bustling, with clean streets of bright tiles, lined with unusual drainage like nothing Draminedes had seen before. Well, it was similar to the aqueducts used on Biterna's big island, but clearly not being used the same way.

And it smelled so wonderful, fresh and green, a hint of damp earth, and every time he passed a market district, he got a whiff of homey spices.

These were not dirty savages in need of civilizing. This was not a struggling nation that needed to be saved.

Had he taken a wrong turn somewhere? The caravan mistress insisted this was his destination, and there was no reason she'd lie.

Had Karthiry been misinformed? Or was the city the only part of the country that functioned? He'd have to venture out into some of the surrounding villages and see if he could find the turmoil Karthiry insisted her people needed to put right before there was any hope of meaningful trade.

Or was this some kind of test?

Draminedes's insides went cold and watery. He took off his lenses and gave them a quick polish. Karthiry did so love to test the loyalty of those around her. Draminedes thought he'd performed well beyond expectations, but maybe no one was free from scrutiny.

What was she testing him on? To see if he'd challenge her? She certainly couldn't stand the way Hollen questioned her actions.

He shook his head and continued fumbling his way through the city, looking for the university. It had taken too long to understand that that was where Karthiry's instructions were sending him. She'd told him to find the elders and tell them he'd come to learn their ways and take their wisdom back to his homeland.

Draminedes hadn't especially liked the tone Karthiry used to emphasize elders and wisdom. Like she expected him to encounter wizened school children.

The city didn't have the sorts of elders Karthiry had indicated. No kings or chiefs, as far as he saw. Well, if he translated the prime correctly, there was a chief of some kind, but one who served for a short period and was drawn from the local population at random. That probably wasn't right. He'd have to learn more of the local language and suss it out properly.

He was told about the necromancers and their leader the Wise Mother, but Karthiry had most certainly not mentioned anything about him talking to necromancers. She hadn't addressed the issue of them at all, except to indicate in previous discussions with her counsel that the necromancers needed to be "dealt with."

So, the locals told him, if he sought wisdom, but not from the Wise Mother, then he probably wanted the university. He was to find a person named Rasson, at the university compound at the far edge of the city from where the caravan had left him. They would help him.

The closer he drew to the university, the less he liked the situation.

Convincing a bunch of bumpkins he was some important scholar had seemed like a simple enough ruse. Convincing other scholars, proper ones, that Draminedes knew anything about academic pursuits, was a tall order that had him gripping the straps of his pack to keep his hands from visibly shaking.

But he couldn't screw this up. There would be no restoring the family name if he couldn't perform as expected.

He lifted his chin, squared his shoulders, and marched along the stone streets, staying on the pedestrian half to avoid the carts on the other side of the road. While he'd been given good directions, he couldn't read any of the local signage, and had to stop to ask for directions. Again.

At least he wasn't far.

The university stood on a slope with a lovely view of the river. He knew from taking Karthiry's notes that this river was a major access point deeper into the continent's interior. It wasn't considered a trade route between this city and the northern coast, where the steep terrain made it impassable to all but skilled aquamancers.

But it was nestled between the foothills and a vast limestone shelf that spread deep into the jungle, and to apparent riches. Karthiry had been silent on what, specifically, those riches were.

The university itself was a series of stone buildings, more elaborate than some of the others he'd passed, with mosaics on the polished white limestone walls and wide arch doorways and airy colonnades. A sign on the wall of the building along the main road gave its name in prime.

He stopped twice more for directions that finally brought him to the lead administrative offices where he was pleased to discover Rasson was free, so he wouldn't have to make an appointment and return later. Rasson stood from their desk, tall and thick but somehow delicate with bushy grey hair, rich brown eyes, and light sepia skin under an immaculate turquoise short-suit, and greeted him warmly, smiling and giving him a polite bow.

Draminedes had been able to put together that these people had a complicated greeting structure, but that a bow was fairly standard. So he bowed slightly in return, never going wrong by mirroring his hosts. He introduced himself as Nedrim, the cover name Karthiry had provided him with, and was aghast when Rasson immediately began calling him Ned.

"Well met, Ned. How may I serve you?"

"I've come to study."

"Well, yes. This is a university. Where did you say you're from?"

"Um." Draminedes strained to remember. Karthiry hadn't mentioned this part and probably expected him to know the name of his own godsdamned university, though he'd never actually attended. "Biterna... of the Faithful Pursuit."

Rasson gave him a look.

"Forgive me, it's been a long journey. I never want to see another donkey as long as I live."

Rasson chuckled and switched to a dialect Draminedes was more familiar with. "No, they're not my favourite way to travel either. So what can we teach you in your Faithful Pursuit?"

"Um." Shit. Karthiry hadn't covered this either. "Faithful is a bit misleading these days. Only the faith division is devout anymore."

They smiled and waited.

Godsdamnit, what more did they want? "Architecture," Draminedes blurted. "I've heard so much about your tree buildings and stonework."

They watched him for a moment, nodding slowly. "Yes, the banobi trees are popular. Not easy to grow, especially out of their natural climate, not even for floramancers. As for the stonework, you don't have terramancers in Biterna?"

"Plenty, though the aquamancers get all the glory."

Shit, shit, shit, you're screwing this up, they don't believe you for an instant.

"I'm doing a comparative study of technique and design, as part of my apprenticeship. I'm not actually a full scholar yet."

Was that how the apprenticeships worked? He'd never really paid attention, just naturally falling into his father's business like breathing.

Draminedes didn't sigh with relief when Rasson smiled at this information, but it was a near thing.

"Ah yes, the big test, is it? Send you away to see if you sink or swim on your own?"

Draminedes smiled nervously and sincerely hoped they were wrong.

"Well, as you say, you've had a long journey. We have a special dorm for visiting academics such as yourself. I'm about to break for my lunch, so why don't I show you around?"

Draminedes waited politely while Rasson gathered their things and escorted him out onto the main campus square. There was a kitchen where the students and staff ate, and they let him know he was welcome to join them. He could pay for his meals, or sign up for harvest duty.

They passed the library on the way, and then Rasson brought him into a low stone building in the shade of some large ferny trees that were close enough to the palms of home to be comforting and different enough to unsettle. It was dim in the narrow hall, lined with doors. Rasson stopped at one that stood open and gestured for Draminedes to go in. It was small and dim, but not crowded.

"I hope you'll find this comfortable. They're simple accommodations, but we do our best to cover the basics." Then they reached in the door and pulled a lever on the wall, making the room explode with light.

Thankfully he had his back to them and they couldn't see the way his mouth fell open. He pasted on a grateful smile before they left him to it.

Simple.

The furniture was well-crafted from some dark, gleaming wood and the small bed covered in fine linens. When he sat on it, his eyes widened at how soft it was. Feather bed? And then there was whatever Rasson had done to light the room. Draminedes studied the lever a moment before pulling it, plunging the space back into gloom. He pushed it up and the light brightened. Little glass lanterns hung from the ceiling like tiny suns.

He didn't think it was magic. And if it was... He shook his head, that cold watery feeling returning to his gut.

He left his bags at the foot of the bed but decided maybe he wasn't so tired after all. He took the key on the bedside table, along with his satchel, and set out back into the city. Karthiry had given him instructions on how to find one of her contacts, and while this was someone he was to report to sparingly, Draminedes hadn't felt this unmoored since his father shuttered the family business.

Draminedes knocked on the non-descript door in the non-descript building located off the eastern riverside market district. Karthiry's instructions said to find the place near *the* market district, implying only one, yet the city had nearly a dozen. There was a central market district that was the biggest and most diverse, but almost every neighbourhood had its own. It had taken him longer than he'd have liked to figure that out.

He knocked and waited. It was late, nearly dark, and he was exhausted like he'd been wandering the city for a week.

A small, shrivelled elderly man like a human walnut opened the door and squinted aggressively at Draminedes.

"I'm here to see Norli."

The squint turned into a scowl, and the man barked something in the local language. Draminedes repeated his inquiry more slowly in prime and was met with the same result but louder.

Finally, a local who didn't know how to speak prime. Wonderful.

"Norli?" He spoke the name slow and clearly, hoping.

"Ach." The man opened the door wider and started down the hall, waving for Draminedes to follow when he stood dumbfounded on the threshold.

The old man stopped outside a door and pointed, waited, then walked away. Draminedes sighed and knocked on the door. It was opened by a short round woman with the same light brown complexion as Hollen and a mound of black curly hair orbiting her head like her own personal galaxy.

"Norli?"

She watched him expectantly. Draminedes wanted to run.

"Oh, right. I'm here for the golden hour." Stupid passphrase.

She opened her door further and let him in. "You one of the new guys?"

"Our Shining Lady didn't tell me if there were others coming and only hinted at how many others are here. Your name was the only one she gave me, though I assume your name isn't actually Norli anymore than mine's Nedrim."

Norli nodded. "I'm in charge here. At least for another moon cycle, but I understand someone's coming to replace me soon."

"Oh, that's likely me then."

"Sure. What do you need?"

"I just don't think I understand what I'm supposed to be doing here."

"You do whatever our Shining Lady sent you to do."

"Well, she wanted information, but none of it makes sense now that I'm here. She told me to find out how best to help the locals, but everyone seems clean and fed and content."

Norli stared at him.

"Did you just get here?" she asked. "Don't waste my time with this. Have a look around and you'll see it."

"Yes, all right. She told me to find who the biggest resisters are. Have you seen much?"

"Not yet. The elementals in general have been a problem, and the head of the city guard is sharp even though she doesn't look like much. Haven't narrowed it down more than that."

City guard? That seemed like the sort of leadership position that could rally the locals.

"All right, she seems like a good start."

Norli told him how to find the building. "They've got a social club, it's where she's easiest to find when she's not working. Lots of social clubs, starting to talk to each other, especially with the elementals getting loud. Might be a good place for you to start. Oh, and go see Borlu for some lessons on the local language or you'll be arsed."

"Yes, thank you."

He retreated back to the street quickly after that, the watery feeling not going away. He'd make his rounds of the social clubs and find out as much as he could. Something was not right here, and he needed more clarification.

BEFORE

The empty roads suited Tollar just fine. She'd never tried returning to Nytaltek in the winter before, always heeding the warnings about the impassable roads. She'd never thought to ask why.

Water. It was raining. That was it. That was the whole story.

Oh sure, drowned half the jungle. Buried roads under raging rivers. Brought down great slides off the sides of the mountains, shifting the lands around so that the terramancers would have their work cut out for them clearing out the passes once the mountains dried out mid-spring.

Tollar only wished all of her travels gave her this much to work with. She was like a stone skipping across a pond. Safe in her little bubble of dry air, not that she really needed that either. But it was nice to keep her supplies dry.

Especially since she didn't know how this trip's gift for Beenala was going to hold up. She didn't know anything about art supplies, but they seemed finicky and fragile, especially things that weren't forged in steel. But she didn't think Beenala was learning any metalwork.

Well, she'd find out soon enough.

Provided Beenala was even in the market. Tollar glanced down at the wristband Beenala had woven her the last time she'd been home. It was dirty. Tollar pulled some rain out of the air and washed it through the fabric, funnelling away as much of the dirt as she could.

A quartet of dragons, half the local blaze, dived and spiralled through the rainclouds, occasionally calling out to each other. Of course the rain didn't slow them down anymore than it did her. If she hailed them, would they give her a lift home? That'd be something!

Leaving a long wake through the sodden valley, Tollar did her best to follow the road, but it was so much easier to make a beeline toward the final pass.

It went far quicker than she expected and still took nearly an eternity to round the mountain and come down into the foothills, the Arazow a swollen grey ribbon in the distance, and Nytaltek hugging its northern shore. Out where the land got increasingly flatter but for the little hills covered in sparse vegetation that marked the larger buildings of the dead cities.

But Tollar never gave much thought to the necromancers, even if they had delivered Granny's fingerbone.

Little dots among the pattern in the city represented all the market squares. And it was far enough out of the mountains and their ground-hugging clouds that she saw a good distance without having to artificially part the gloom.

It might not be raining all the way down in Nytaltek. That meant there was an even better chance of finding Beenala in the market.

Tollar's stomach swished around like her own little personal whirlpool, and she couldn't stop grinning like a frogging fool.

But Beenala would love what she had this time.

And while Tollar really should slow down and walk now that she was out of the deluge and onto a road that wasn't utterly mud, she just wanted to get back into the city. Sleep on a proper bed and eat some proper food and visit with Auntie until the passes opened up properly and there'd be a new caravan to carry her off somewhere else new and exciting.

There was enough excitement ahead of her. As long as she could find Beenala. Of course, she knew where to really find Beenala, but she didn't want to have to go out to the farm to do it, because then she'd probably be obligated to visit her mother and subfather or some nonsense.

All of her siblings had moved out, and Tollar would have to see from Auntie where they'd all gone off to. She was pretty sure Jarku, her oldest brother, was in the city.

He was never especially interested in talking to her though. None of them were.

But it didn't matter. Auntie was always delighted to have Tollar around. And Beenala always lit up like a firecracker whenever she first spotted Tollar after a long absence. It warmed her with her own personal blaze.

She couldn't stop grinning.

Once she reached the first stone streets, she let go of the water, let it drain naturally away, and walked. She wanted to skip like a girl, or run like a dragon chased her, but she needed to calm down and temper her disappointment in case Beenala wasn't around today.

Tollar passed the guard house on her way south to the main market square. Thought about stopping to see Solia, but maybe later, when Solia was going on shift. It would be a few hours yet. Time enough to look for Beenala, stop in on Auntie and get cleaned up and out of her travel gear.

Tollar loved her gear, but she didn't have to live in it. And her clothes always felt so much more natural anyway. Obviously they looked better, swirling around her like little eddies.

And then she was around the corner and the market opened up before her, row upon row of vendors—tables and tents and wagons. It was damp but not raining, overcast but not gloomy, and busier than she'd expected. Tollar gave the clouds a nudge, they were water after all, and brightened it all a little more.

Nothing like a bit of dramatic flair.

A bright flash of the most vibrant yellow Tollar had ever seen, dazzling in the new sunlight Tollar brought. It was a streak of yellow fabric woven into a basket, of all things. Few textile artists went in for that sort of thing. Tollar grinned.

Be cool. Don't frog it up.

So she hitched her bag up higher on her shoulder and sauntered across the stones. A familiar plume of pale hair bobbing over something out of sight.

Tollar's face hurt she was smiling so wide. She squished her cheeks. How obvious could she be? So she took a deep breath and picked up the saunter a bit, but trying not to get too eager. Beenala was always happy to see her, so far, but that was likely to change, wasn't it?

Everyone in Nytaltek kept going on with their lives while Tollar was away. Even Auntie went through gradual shifts, though she always kept space in her life for Tollar.

Tollar made it right up to Beenala's table without her looking up from... whatever it was she was doing. Tollar craned her neck to see that Beenala had something spread out across her lap that looked like a canvass had grown a rainbow sheep. The rainbow sheep resolved itself into many bits of brightly coloured fuzzy fabric, though the design didn't make any more sense.

"So, still making art then?" Tollar tried not to cringe too hard when Beenala startled and shrieked, nearly dropping her work onto the mucky stones.

"Tollar! Bleeding moons, you scared me!"

Tollar cleared her throat. "Er, sorry..."

"Did you just get in? Or did you fall in a ditch on the way here?"

Tollar's cheeks grew hot. "I just got into town."

Beenala tilted her head to one side. "Have the rains stopped? That's early."

"Oh no, it's an absolute disaster. No one but a duck or an aquamancer is getting through that for at least another month."

"Ah, right. Well, it's wonderful to see you." Beenala smiled, her cheeks still flushed. She bit her lips and looked down at her... whatever.

"It's excellent to be home. What are you making?" Tollar barely kept the rainbow sheep comment to herself.

"Oh, it's going to be a sunset over the Arazow when I'm done."

"It looks like a painting. But fuzzy."

Beenala laughed. "Yes. Like a painting but made out of scraps of wool I dyed."

"Ah." So she hadn't been too far off in her rainbow sheep assessment. "It looks lovely. Very bright. And cozy."

Beenala beamed.

"Well, I just got in and haven't even been to see Auntie yet, but I found something for you."

"How far away did this one come from?"

Tollar let out a long breath. She hated to feel like she was bragging, but at the same time, Beenala always seemed genuinely curious about the things Tollar saw and the places she visited.

"Just about as far away from Upalint as you can go without heading for the moons."

"Really? What was it like? What was the place called?"

"It was called Laminala on the caravan map, but the locals called the place Bettar. It was a mountainous place, but nothing like home. Much bigger mountains, very little greenery, and cold. The mountains were all jagged steep peaks, but there were lots of plateaus too, and that's where the locals lived."

"You found me something way up in the middle of nowhere?"

"Yes! It was amazing! All this dull and grey everywhere, and then the people wore the brightest colours. And I found out they made it from this lichen on the rocks."

Tollar set down her pack and dug around until she found the sealed wax pouch in the spice box that had been empty for half the trip. She held it out to Beenala, cupped in her palms. Beenala's eyes shone as she pulled out one of her little paring knives and slit the seal on the wax.

"Careful with it, I don't know when I'll find you more like that."

Beenala didn't quite roll her eyes at Tollar, but it was a near thing. Then she peeled back the layers and gasped, sitting up straighter. Her mouth fell open and she looked up at Tollar.

"So you like it? I thought of you as soon as I saw it. Never saw a colour quite like that, but it's fiery. Reminded me of your magic."

Tollar pinched her lips together and tried not to cringe.

Shut up, stupid!

"Tollar, thank you! I've never seen a shade of crimson quite like this."

Tollar grinned, feeling as airy as mist in the morning light. The only time she'd seen a colour remotely like this pigment was one evening, far west of here in distant lands when the air had been full of smoke from a massive forest blaze and the large orb of the sun passed through it.

She'd thought of Beenala then as well.

"If you ever want to come collect more of it, I'd be happy to take you."

"To the other side of the world?" Beenala's eyes grew wide.

"Or you can make me a list of the colours you'd most like to see and I'll bring them for you. I can bring you a whole vibrant rainbow, I'm sure."

Beenala kept smiling as she folded the wax up and tucked the pouch away into her bag.

"You bring me the most wonderful things, Tollar. Why don't you come by and tell me more about those mountains?"

Tollar froze for an instant, but Beenala continued.

"Or if Auntie doesn't mind a visit, I can come by some day soon. Will you be home long this time?"

"At least until the caravans are getting through again."

Beenala clapped her hands. "Excellent. I'll find something exquisite to make with some of this pigment and bring it to Auntie's for you both to enjoy."

"That sounds like a perfect way to pass an afternoon."

Tollar leaned against the table, smiling and watching Beenala get back to work on her rainbow sheep sunset thing. Sometimes she never wanted to come home again, but then she'd find something perfect for Beenala and not be able to get back fast enough. The urge to go would return, but for now, it was the perfect welcome home to spend some time with her best friend.

14

Beenala stood on the little water platform next to Tollar, Bale crouched behind them, and only half-listened to another of Tollar's wild tales about her travels—something about moving walls of snow?—while her gaze darted from one rugged snow-capped peak to another. They glided across a long, narrow glacial lake between mountains, the far end of the lake disappearing behind a curtain of grey ahead of them. She wasn't keen on the idea of more rain. Even though Tollar kept the water off them, she couldn't do much about how it cooled the air.

Beenala also resented that more rain would obscure her view of the mountains. She wanted to slow down and get a better look. To paint them. To capture the secrets of every crevasse and canyon. These towering crags were imposing, powerful, older than ancestors. The mountains near Nytaltek were mere hills in comparison, and far cheerier with the bright jungle foliage marching most of the way up their slopes.

Of course, they weren't in Upalint anymore, apparently most of the way across the Nishram territories and coming up on the nation of Sawulxo, though there were no permanent villages along this route.

Tollar told her that morning they'd crossed into a new watershed. The word itself was new to Beenala, having never really considered where other rivers flowed to or from. She'd grown up on the Arazow and hadn't considered anything beyond it, including where it began (a giant glacial lake they'd crossed yesterday) or where it ended (the Azure Sea, which she'd barely known existed).

They'd already crossed one alpine lake earlier that day and then skidded along on one of Tollar's little water shelves through the forest between some mountains, down an icy slope and to the current lake.

Crosswinds buffeted them and Beenala stumbled, Bale reaching out to steady her.

"We'll stop to rest at the other end of the lake," Tollar said.

Beenala drew her cloak tighter around her and tried to huddle closer to Bale, whose furnace-like body heat radiated away from her on the wind.

Tollar's water platform propelled them passed the tallest mountain along the lake, one with a sharp, jagged peak, dropping off into a sheer cliff lakeside. Beenala turned her whole body to watch it recede, leaning to see around Bale. And that was the only reason she saw the two dragons come around the far shoulder of the mountain straight toward them. One green and one grey and both looking very familiar.

"Um. Toll..."

Tollar slowed and then stopped, the three of them resting on an island of water, which made Beenala's stomach lurch even more than the whooshing water chariot did. At least when it was moving, it was easier to pretend it wasn't just water keeping them afloat simply because Tollar wanted it to.

The dragons angled toward them, coming in low over the water, and Beenala tried not to clench, noting that they weren't making any noise. Then the dragoness, Minty, shrieked once, a low, truncated sound different from what Beenala had previously heard out of her.

And then Bale responded in kind.

Beenala screamed and flinched so hard that Tollar's tight grip was the only thing that kept her from careening into the lake.

"It's safe," Bale said, her hissing tone hushed. "That was hello. To me."

"Does she want to eat us?" Tollar asked in a tone like she was remarking on the weather.

"Didn't say."

"Ugh," Beenala groaned.

Minty banked around them, Cloudy not far behind. Water sprayed up in her wake, trickling down off the invisible dome of Tollar's will.

"Greetings, Mistress," Tollar called, bowing deeply. "What a pleasant surprise to meet you on our journey."

Minty's tail came down on the water as she circled, sending a wave up at them that Tollar parted much as Beenala had done with the fire. Then she hissed something and flew higher, Cloudy following and nearly disappearing as the rain approached. They circled overhead, silent.

"Keep going," Bale said. "Stop on the shore."

That had already been their plan, so Tollar shrugged and continued on.

The lake ended at a stream cutting through a boggy area that gave way to a beautiful alpine meadow that made Beenala sorely regret not having brought her paints. Even in the gloom of the rain, it was a riot of colour—rich green grass, flowers in deep purples, bright pinks and yellows, bursts of red.

As soon as Tollar steered them off the stream and into the field, the two adult dragons landed not far off. Beenala frowned at all the crushed flowers under them.

Minty leaned forward and snarled but at least wasn't trying to immediately incinerate anyone so that was an improvement. She hadn't so much as glanced at the humans though, all her focus on Bale as they hissed at each other in dragontalk. Until Bale sat abruptly, head tall, and said, "Staying."

"Oh no, what now?" Tollar asked.

"They want me to stop. She says it's too dangerous because I can't fly."

"You're gliding." Tollar looked from Bale to Minty.

Whenever they stopped for a break, Tollar tried to make sure it was somewhere high. Near the head of a waterfall if one was around. And Bale would leap off and glide down to the water below, and then Tollar would use a column of water to bring the dragon back up and she'd do it all over again. At their last stop, Bale got halfway back up the waterfall under her own power, flapping her wings furiously but not quite making it.

Minty only growled in response.

"All right, Bale, what do we do? It is dangerous in Port Sawulxo. The last thing we need is for them to recapture you. You can't stay by yourself out in the middle of nowhere or go back without us."

Bale glared at Tollar and then spoke to Minty. "Teach me."

Tollar exchanged a look with Beenala.

"Um, isn't that the sort of thing that takes some time?"

But none of the dragons paid attention to her as Minty and Cloudy both sprang into the sky, kicking up debris and slashing rainwater in all directions. And Bale enthusiastically and rather clumsily jumped after them, not getting very far for all her flapping. But Minty sliced back around and caught hold of Bale, bringing her higher up into the air, disappearing above the low cloud deck.

"Now what?" Beenala asked.

There was nowhere to sit but the soggy ground, though it was far less soggy now that Tollar had done her work, pulling the moisture out and directing it to the little stream. Beenala pulled her sleeping mat off her pack and set it on the ground so she wouldn't have to sit directly on the grass and dirt.

Tollar just plunked down wherever, chewing on a bit of fish jerky. She shrugged. "Birds learn to fly sort of all at once. Hopefully this is the same?"

"What if it isn't?"

"Let's see how this goes before we start fretting."

Easy enough for Tollar to say, she had no problems having nothing to do and no idea what came next.

"Do you think you can handle a waiting day?" Tollar asked. "You could make it a sketch day?"

Beenala opened her mouth to argue that it was entirely too wet for that, but realized all at once that she was dry. The rain sprinkled soothingly down around them, pattering against leaves. Just none of it reached Beenala or her gear.

"Tollar... It's not raining. On me. Specifically."

"Oh? I hadn't noticed."

Tollar went on chewing her fish jerky, lucky she hadn't lost any teeth to it, and pointedly ignored the look Beenala gave her.

Beenala considered her pack, where she had some art supplies to lend weight to their cover story that they were travelling artists. Sketching was a good suggestion but it didn't feel right. Before leaving, Tollar told her what to expect of the days of travel, and the two of them had worked to decide on what their routine would look like and what Beenala could do. Sitting in a field for hours hadn't been in any of their planning and now her brain wasn't ready for it.

She let out a long breath and wished Ash was there next to her, soft and warm and grounding. That she was properly dry in her cozy cottage with all the art supplies she'd ever need. Where she always knew what came next.

When she wasn't moon eyed over the scenery, Beenala profoundly missed the comforts of home, but wholly believed that Tollar would send her back if she complained. So she tried to be useful by not getting in the way. By practicing fire magic with Bale.

Her stomach grumbled. She put real thought into going hungry before tearing off a piece of bread to chew on for half the afternoon. Tollar was good at fishing and scouting berries and nuts and fruit, especially in the Nishram territory which was really more like one big orchard carefully tended by the nomadic tribes, so they hadn't had to rely on the rations as much as they might have otherwise.

Beenala had thought Solia was exaggerating about the food.

"Shit!" Tollar jumped to her feet, spinning water up out of the stream and Beenala followed her gaze.

Bale was glide-falling toward them, Minty and Cloudy spiralling around her but not intervening. Would they?

Tollar shot a spout of water that hit Bale on one side and righted her so that the fall turned back into a glide. Minty roared, not sounding especially pleased.

"She can rot if she thinks I'm going to let Bale just fall out of the sky."

"Toll, they know what they're doing."

"Pfft."

Minty dove down, skimming over the field to growl at Tollar.

"I'm not going to stop!"

"Tollar!"

"I didn't ask her to come after us—this is probably Bali's fault." Tollar paced up and down the edge of the stream. "Bale's gliding is good enough. I don't intend to let her get close enough to the port that she'll need to fly to make a quick escape."

"So you have a plan for when we get there?" Beenala sat down and tore off another chunk of the dry, chewy bread that tasted worse than nothing.

"Eh, sort of." Tollar waved her hands in a flicking gesture, like she wanted to brush away the question.

"You're worried about something."

"What's happening in the port is weird. I've never seen anything like it."

Beenala's eyebrows shot up. Tollar had travelled to faraway battles off and on since she was a teen, and she always came home with more stories than books could hold. While a dragon egg was the oddest thing she'd come home with outside of stories, her tales kept Beenala rapt for months—for as long as Tollar stayed home.

"The thing with the captive dragons is just plain bad, but the rest is wrong too. Only time I ever see a battle force favour one element over another, it's been aeromancers or pyromancers. So why aquamancers this time?"

Beenala thought of Tollar roaring in on a boiling wave and shuddered, tamping down her questions before they fully formed.

"So, is that what we're going to find out? Is that part of your plan?"

Tollar shrugged. "I know Bale needs to stay away from the city. And from there I just need to assess what's going on. If we end up in a fight, I think I might summon some water demons to help. Have you done any work with earth or fire demons?"

Beenala felt cold and shook her head. "Only what I needed for the Guild entrance exam."

"Fair enough. It's dangerous, hopefully I won't need it. But I want to find my friend Chalky, she should have good intel for us. She had an inn near the docks, excellent rum. Might be a good place to stay."

Beenala noticed, over the course of the last three days, that most of Tollar's stories began with running into an old friend in such and such a place before some misadventure ensuing.

"Do people know you everywhere you go?"

"Well only the places I've already been. Not everyone knows me, but there's always someone who recognizes me when I go back. Usually someone I've helped."

"Is Chalky one of those people?"

"I suppose. I helped her get home when she was injured, and she tried to convince me to couple with her brother."

Beenala blinked and then stared. "Why... would she do that if you helped her?"

Tollar burst out laughing. "That's what I said! She said her brother wasn't that bad. Ha! Could you imagine?"

Beenala shuddered.

Tollar flung another column of water at a wobbling Bale to right her again as she attempted to bank around the meadow, all the while Tollar glared at Minty as if in challenge. The dragoness growled as she passed overhead.

"I've no interest in coupling," Tollar said firmly. "Especially not like that."

"It just all sounds awful."

Tollar shrugged. "I don't mind a bit of kissing and a good snuggle, but the rest? Not a shred of interest."

"Kissing sounds awful too."

Tollar smiled. "It's not for everyone. I've kissed a few lovely women and one very pretty man, but it's not something I really need, either."

Something about that made Beenala's stomach churn. "Only one man?"

"Just to see if it was any different." She shrugged. "It was fine. I did end up spending the night curled up with him—my mat against his—and that was the first time I'd done that. It was nice to have someone warm nearby. Cozy, I guess."

While Beenala had been borderline horrified at the thought of doing any of that with anyone, the idea of having another person nearby at night didn't seem that terrible. The only time she'd liked sharing a room with her sister was when she was asleep—the reassuring presence of someone else in the loneliest hours. She liked snuggling Ash while she slept. And when she thought about it, snuggling people probably wasn't much different.

Tollar's gaze tracked Bale's progress, but her silver eyes darkened, like storm clouds on the horizon.

"Is something wrong?" Beenala asked.

"Eh?" Tollar blinked and glanced her way. "No, no. Just thinking about that pretty man. He seemed... disappointed we were going separate ways. Got the impression he wanted me to go with him, like, couple—even if on my terms. But no. Just no. Also, I think he was from one of those places where coupling is more formal. Did you know that some places ritualize it? And some of them you need a whole other ritual to break the coupling! Or you can't break it at all until one part of the couple dies."

"You're making that up."

"I swear. I met a northern pair who were coupled like that." She shuddered. "They seemed to enjoy it but... To not be able to just, go your own way without someone's permission?"

Tollar squinted, all three dragons had disappeared above the clouds again.

"What... Who..." Beenala shook her head and wasn't sure she wanted the answers. "How can someone tell you that you're a couple and you can't not be? Where does someone get that kind of power?"

Tollar shrugged. "I hope to never find out."

Beenala drummed her fingers against her chin, trying to put everything Tollar said the entire way out of her mind. Permanent couplings. It wasn't unheard of, people like her parents started families and found it convenient or enjoyable to stay with one partner for all their days. But Beenala's parents were an exception. More were like Tollar's mother. Tollar's oldest sibling had a different father from the other three, and then her mother had coupled with Zarro for years before leaving him and the farm to go live with Piori.

Beenala had never put much thought into romantic partners. Hadn't ever wanted what her parents had with each other, though she hadn't minded the affection they had for her. But like this, what Tollar was talking about—she didn't want someone messing up all her things and touching her all the time.

On the other hand, since her parents had gone with Erxo and left Beenala with the farm, she'd noticed more acutely a sort of emptiness that lurked on the edge of her life like a gezar stalking the shadows. It had always been there, but now it flared, gripping her so tight that sometimes she could barely breathe. She saw her family plenty, the void in her life remained.

Was this what she was missing? Someone who respected what she needed?

Tollar gasped and jumped onto the surface of the stream, pulling a massive wave out of it and rolling it out away from Beenala toward the other side of the meadow. And Beenala gasped too. Bale was diving straight at the ground, Minty and Cloudy just coming through the cloud cover.

Bale spread her wings and angled them, pulling herself out of the dive, but even Beenala could tell she'd waited too long. She clenched both fists around her awful bread and stiffened, unable to look away. Tollar's wave of water was there to buoy the dragon and keep her from skidding across the field. With another burst of water, Bale shot back up in the air, doing a spin as she reached Minty and Cloudy.

Cloudy stayed with Bale, both of them doing some spirals, but Minty dived at Tollar, who had disappeared into a bubble of water. The dragoness gave it a parting shot of flame as she swooped past, Beenala heard the hiss of fire on water from where she was. But Tollar emerged from the water, grinning.

Beenala let out the pent-up air and set down the smushed bread to wipe her palms on her grubby pants.

And so the afternoon went, Bale making progress with some watery nudges from Tollar that resulted in some more anger from Minty, but nothing nearly as bad as the first day they'd met the dragoness. And finally Bale was doing it on her own without near misses and without the wibbling. She was sloppy and clearly putting more effort into it than she needed to, but she was flying.

"That was amazing!" Tollar hugged Bale's big snout once she landed for good.

Minty landed nearby while Cloudy circled lazily overhead, easier to spot with the break in the clouds. Minty hissed some dragontalk at Bale, gave Tollar one last measuring look, and flew off.

"She says I learned quick."

"Course you did. You had excellent teachers."

Beenala rolled her eyes. "Honestly, Tollar, you shouldn't have interfered."

"Who's to say it's not why she learned faster? It always helped me to have someone correct my form mid-mistake."

"Thank you." Bale nuzzled her. "She said if I get caught she'll eat you."

Tollar rolled her eyes. "Of course she will. If you get caught again, I'll let her. Now, you had an excellent day and I bet you're hungry. Go see what you can find."

Beenala had a fire going, and Tollar went to the lake to catch them fish for dinner. While they waited for Bale to return after they finished eating, Beenala stared into the fire and shaped it into different configurations, cooling the air around her as she tried perfecting her rose-bloom blaze.

"Now that she's flying, we'll be able to get there faster," Tollar said.

Beenala looked up. "She can carry us?"

"Don't see why not. It means we'll get there middle of tomorrow instead of two days from now."

"So we don't need to follow the water?"

"I know my way best if we do. This little stream will be fed by other streams and eventually grow into the Black River that we'll follow the rest of the way to Port Sawulxo."

Bale came bounding out of the nearby jungle not long afterward looking quite pleased with herself. She puffed a bit of fire at Beenala, a little game they'd started the first night in the wild. Beenala caught the fire with her magic and pushed the line of it up and over their little camp, spreading it out like a big tent over them before letting it dissipate. Some nights Bale would shoot fire and Beenala would use magic to stretch the range beyond what Bale was capable of. Last night, Tollar had made standing waves out in the lake for Beenala to aim the fire at. She wasn't very good at it yet. But Bale didn't seem interested in practicing more tonight.

The little dragon crept up to Beenala and nudged her big snout into Beenala's side, nearly knocking her over. Beenala gave her a gentle pat on her nose, always marvelling at how soft it was for a creature so covered in sharp bits.

"Sleep," Bale announced, and she eased herself down next to the fire and spread both her wings out on either side of her.

It was earlier than usual, but Beenala wasn't complaining. Wordlessly, Beenala split the fire in half, moving each bit near the openings of the little wing-tents Bale made. Small as she was, her wingspan could house an entire family.

While Beenala moved the fires, Tollar pulled the moisture from the ground around the dragon. Then both women dragged their gear in under Bale's wings, each on either side of her. The fires would burn out soon, even with Tollar keeping them dry and Beenala pulling the maximum efficiency out of them, but Bale was like a massive furnace and would keep them both warm and dry all night.

"Goodnight, Bee; goodnight, Toll."

"Goodnight, Bale," they chimed automatically.

"Goodnight, Bee."

"Goodnight, Toll."

She smiled fondly. It had been the same every night. Ridiculous but comforting.

Beenala leaned her kit against the dragon and spread her sleeping mat out next to it. Then reconsidered and switched things so she slept against Bale's side. It was hot, but not uncomfortably so, and felt a little like being curled up with Ash. She might still be a baby, but Bale was a dragon all the same, one that Beenala felt at ease with. A shocking realization that had crept up on her yesterday. But travelling like this, spending every last moment with Tollar and Bale, had been exhausting in ways she hadn't expected, but also endearing. Like Bale nuzzling her big head into Beenala's side like a child.

Tollar wasn't complaining, and Beenala hoped she wasn't creating extra work by coming along, but she worried she'd made the wrong choice. That she was more burden than help. And this was the easy part, as much as Beenala hated sleeping on the ground. Last night was the first time she'd really slept at all, passing out more than falling asleep. She wanted to go home.

How was she supposed to help Tollar essentially spy when she couldn't even manage some camping?

Then again, Tollar had been doing this for half her life. Beenala had begged, but Tollar had accepted when she didn't need to. Beenala would keep doing what she was told and try not to muck it all up too badly.

15

Tollar caught herself looking out toward the mountains again, making sure Bale wasn't doing some damn fool thing like flying where anyone could see or, worse yet, trying to follow them. But now that they were all the way into the city proper, all the looking around would draw attention.

So far, there'd been no patrols or bandits on the road, no one asked them any sorts of questions. There hadn't been anyone noticing them come down the road from the eastern approach and they were far enough into town before they encountered anyone that they could have easily been normal Port citizens out for a walk. Well, they did have their travel packs, but lighter and smaller since they'd left all weapons and armour in the mountains with Bale.

Port Sawulxo initially sprang up centuries ago because it was the closest port to Biterna, once a major stop on trade routes. The port remained a trade hub even after ships started bypassing the archipelago. The mountains weren't as treacherous along the coast, allowing for a reliable highway running east-west. And another fork of the Black River passed further west with a gentler rise in elevation and a lack of rapids that made it a good trade route further inland.

Descending a slope on the eastern approach gave Tollar a full view of the city and some of the surrounding land. She stopped short.

"What is it?" Beenala asked.

"It's..." But Tollar had no words for what she saw. She bunched her hands into fists and gritted her teeth. The western district along the river running out of the mountains and between the city and a marshy plain was flooded and plenty of areas were mostly rubble. The bridge over the river that connected the city to the western approach was damaged but still standing, but appeared to be barricaded.

"Granny was right. I needed to come back, eyes open. How did I miss all this?"

"You were a bit busy fighting and stealing dragon eggs?"

Tollar's lips twitched in a smile that she didn't really feel.

The swath of jungle that had been cut down and burned partway up the mountainside was concerning. Why would anyone need to cut down that much forest at once?

Especially with the winter rains not far out. It was asking for mudslides.

Unless these raiders had an impressive number of terramancers to go with their aquamancers.

And with the jungle gone she had a clear view of the power dam, or what was left of it anyway. Had it been like that when she was last here?

None of it made a lick of sense.

"Are we far from Chalky's?" Beenala asked.

Tollar looked down into the main port area where there were a lot more people on the streets, but also heavier damage to the buildings. "I don't know if her place is still there."

While Chalky's injuries had never healed properly and had been bad enough to keep her from further campaigns, they hadn't been bad enough that she wouldn't have fought these raiders. She could be dead. Or imprisoned somewhere. Or enslaved and sent back as a spoil of war.

Tollar's skin buzzed. Her blood sang out to the ocean, wanting to pull it into the city and drown every last one of these cursed raiders.

Seeing the port in this light, she re-evaluated her plan to find locals she could rely on. The harbour was the busiest point, but even from here and in the fading light, it was clear most of the people down there were pale raiders. Even if Chalky hadn't fought, or hadn't been caught at it, the likelihood of her inn being there was small.

"This is a mistake."

Beenala didn't reply but sucked in a breath and held it.

"I think I remember where Chalky's brother lives. It's on the edge of that flooded area. Hopefully not actually in it, or he'll have cleared out."

She turned back the way they'd come, backtracking a few blocks before heading down a different, mud-caked avenue. Beenala had been solemn since they reached the edge of the city. The journey had been hard on her, and she'd remained quiet rather than complain, which Tollar admired, but the shine of this had clearly worn off.

Whatever adventure Beenala thought she'd signed up for, she now understood the reality of their situation.

As long as she didn't freeze. Or blurt something weird... And at least she'd finally warmed up to Bale.

And right when Tollar saw the floodwaters spanning the avenue ahead with the smell of stagnant water churning her stomach, she turned down a side street and had to slow, trying to recall the location. She'd been fleeing it, and Chalky's ridiculous suggestion, the only time she'd been to the brother's house.

But things looked familiar, so that had to count for something.

She was tempted to risk asking a stranger for directions when a crooked, narrow windmill stood out. Ah yes, the brother's eccentric neighbour.

"Almost there." She smiled. "Let's hope he stills live here!"

"What do we do if he doesn't?"

"Let's take it one problem at a time."

"Tollar..."

"We find a proper inn. We passed one near the outskirts of town. We keep pretending to be visitors who haven't caught wind of the raiders."

There were also Solia's contacts to consider—many of them city leaders—though they wouldn't be as safe to track down.

Tollar went up to the door, all of it clicking in her memory now, and knocked. Dogs barked from somewhere in the clay home. Someone shouted at them for silence. They kept right on barking.

Tollar glanced at Beenala who smiled, her lovely brown eyes shining.

Good. There hadn't been dogs here last time, but dogs were always a good sign. And they'd help calm Beenala down some more. As long as this was the right house.

And then Chalky's brother opened the door, and his perplexed expression got even more perplexed when he recognized Tollar.

"Well, this can't be good," he said by way of greeting. "Probably best you get in before anyone notices you."

"Why would anyone notice?" Tollar asked once the door was safely closed behind them and the dogs came charging into the foyer, great shaggy water dogs, both of them black as midnight.

Beenala was on the floor wrestling them in an instant, laughing like she was home with Ash, and Tollar grinned while she waited for an answer.

"Everyone notices everything these days. And we haven't figured out which of the neighbours have turned."

"Turned?" Tollar blinked.

"Who is it?" a woman called from deeper in the house.

"Trouble or salvation. Or maybe both."

It was Chalky herself, leaning heavily on a cane, who came in from a side room and stopped like the house was full of ghosts. She was short and stocky, with close-cropped light brown hair, tawny skin, and brown eyes that shone with amusement.

"Trouble," she said immediately, grinning. "Tollar, who's your friend?"

"Beenala. My neighbour."

"Oh right, the artist one? Never thought you'd get her out of her paints!"

Beenala stood and gave Tollar an indignant look.

"Chalky was with me when I found that flame-coloured pigment."

They made proper introductions all around, and Tollar was spared having to guess at Chalky's brother's name. He was Brilly, and cut from the same cloth as Chalky except that he wore lenses and had his brown hair longer and gathered in a knot at the back of his head. Tollar wasn't certain they'd ever been properly introduced, despite what Chalky thought they ought to do with their lives. Not anything to worry about, because Brilly had found himself a partner, and she came in carrying a baby. She was tall and lean, with long black hair, tawny skin, and bright blue eyes. The babe was little more than a brown blobby bundle in her arms.

"And this is Narra and little Trep," Chalky said. "They were good enough to take me in after this mess got started."

"I was here for it. Well, came in with the crew trying to stop it. We were way too late, and I was so distracted by the fighting and the captive dragons, I had no hope of looking for you then."

Chalky waved her hand. "You wouldn't have found me anyway. I had to hide for a bit after I tried to keep them out of my inn and then burned it down to keep them from taking it. Bastards."

Tollar smiled. "That sounds exactly like you. I'm sorry you had to lose everything."

"Oh, I lost a building, didn't say anything about its contents." Chalky's brown eyes gleamed devilishly.

"Well, seems I've come to the right place then. You've been giving these raiders regrets?"

"I did what I could but now we just try to keep our heads down. But if you're here, does that mean Upalint is aware of the problem?"

"Solia knows what I told her, which is only the bit that I saw before I stole a dragon egg and ran off."

Chalky laughed. "You never change, Toll."

"Praise the ancestors." She kissed her thumb and pressed it to her forehead. "Anyway, I'm here to get more information to see how bad it is before we can decide if we can help."

"Nothing's enough for these bastards," Brilly said with a hard look.

"Well, can you give Bee and I somewhere to rest for the night and tell me what happened? As much as you know, anyway."

"That's it? Information and then you're gone again?"

"Well, give me the information first, and I'll see if I can do more with it. I'd like to set the whole lot of their dragons free."

Chalky grinned. "That sounds like a Tollar plan, all right. Come on, we were just sitting down for dinner and we can stretch it for two more."

Tollar and Beenala followed the other three to the back of the house, its main corridors and largest windows aligned with the ocean, allowing big waves and storm surge to pass through the house without taking it. But whatever happened with the flooding nearby hadn't come through here.

Tollar held her questions, even as she noted rooms cramped with supplies, including one stacked full of furniture—mostly beds and tables. And what looked like crates covered in tarps lining the back garden.

"Chalky, you're just waiting to reopen your inn, aren't you?"

"These people won't be here forever. Or their grip will loosen. The only constant is change—and that I rather enjoyed being an innkeep."

Brilly pulled two more chairs around the table and carried out pans of food while the women sat, Narra tucking the baby into the folds of her wrap. He brought out fish baked in seaweed. And a seaweed salad. There were balls of goat cheese, but Tollar suddenly felt guilty taking what little they had.

Chalky caught her exchanging a look with Beenala.

"Oh, it's not as bad as it looks. I've got plenty of stock from the inn, as I'm sure you noticed. But we want to be sure we ride this out and don't have to rely on the, uh, kindness of our overlords in order to eat."

"We could feast like gods for a couple of months, or live by our own means for more than a year," Brilly added.

"It's that bad, is it?" Tollar asked.

Chalky's tight smile didn't reach her eyes. "Eat first, then we'll talk."

Simple as the meal was, it really could have been a feast after endless days of scavenging and rations. Beenala ate with zeal bordering on mania. At least she wasn't using her hands to cram everything into her face. Tollar watched her, grinning like an absolute fool, before she shovelled food into her own mouth.

Brilly cleared away the main dishes and brought out a bowl of berries for them to snack on and a jug of wine. While Beenala nibbled berries, Tollar poured herself a generous cup and longed for a cask of rum.

"So," Tollar began, setting a mug of wine in front of Chalky, "is it really bad enough that you're keeping an inn's worth of supplies to yourself?"

Chalky sagged. "I know how it looks, and we were helping as many as we could at first. But now... we don't know who to trust or what ends our supplies will be used for."

Tollar tilted her head and regarded her friend. "But your neighbours and friends..."

Chalky shook her head, her lips pinched tight in something bordering on despair.

"All right... Help me understand. Where did these raiders come from? How did they run through the city before that team I was part of could have a hope of getting here to help?"

Chalky shook her head in an irritated sort of way and took a drink.

"I don't know that raiders is the right term for them. They were just... there one morning. There were rumours of an armada out in the ocean, but nothing for sure. And then there they were and we were barely prepared. The wizards went out in full force, but the enemy aquamancers kept the boats safe and helped their soldiers to shore. Well, what shore they didn't flood."

"That was all in the first day," Narra said.

"It only got worse from there," Chalky said.

"I'm guessing they used their aquamancers to get their boats in from the middle of nowhere to our harbour overnight," Brilly added.

Tollar gripped her cup. "Seems likely, given what I saw of their aquamancers' power. But still, there should have been some kind of warning sometime in the night. They couldn't have all shown up in an instant."

Her three hosts shared a look.

"We should have had warning, you're right," Chalky said. "We don't know why we didn't. There'd been a shaker wave two days before and everything was in disarray."

"Two days? No way that's a coincidence."

Chalky took another drink. "Looking back, I don't think it was. We didn't feel a shake, just the wave, but what else causes them?"

"Enough powerful aquamancers," Tollar said gravely. "But you've got enough of your own aquamancers here. How did an entire neighbourhood end up submerged. I've seen them disperse waves before."

"Well, we didn't have the shake as warning, only the wave." Chalky stared into her cup. "Parts of the city were shielded, but something failed."

"Failed or was sabotaged?"

Chalky looked to her brother. "I don't know. I'd put stock in sabotage though. The leadership here was a mess and that didn't help."

"The city was incredibly unstable by the time my team got here. What started that? Your leaders have always been solid."

"There was a landslide the terramancers were unable to stop," Narra said.

"And then a drought that lasted more than a year." Chalky focused on her cup again. "Didn't rain a single day. Elementals were hurling all manner of insults and a few physical attacks at our aquamancers and then swibs started attacking all the wizards."

Tollar groaned and stood up, gripping her cup of wine while she paced the room. She took a long drink and rubbed her cheek.

"So it started with a landslide and then a drought? And your wizards started blaming each other and the swibs started blaming the wizards?"

"It got really bad. The blame turned violent. Attacks is... a bit of an understatement. A lot of elementals were murdered."

"Aquamancers?"

"Mostly." Chalky winced.

"And then a great wave right before the armada arrived." Tollar stopped pacing and stared at everyone at the table.

"But what about leadership?" Beenala asked. "They couldn't rally the city once the threat was apparent?"

Chalky raked her hands over her face. "The wave took out the chief's family. She wasn't there, but it may as well have drowned her with them."

"But you have deputy leaders, like we do, for a reason!" Tollar said. "All the heads of all the guilds, the military leaders... How did not one of them step up?"

"We lost one deputy leader in the wave. The rest... I don't know the details, but there was blame and infighting there as well."

"Can you find out?" Tollar asked. "Do any of you have the contacts to poke around for that kind of info? Send me a bird if you learn anything after I leave."

Chalky shared another look with her family. "Do you think you can do anything?"

Tollar shrugged, wanting to hurl her cup at a wall. Or the head of the nearest raider. "I'd hoped there'd be more coherent resistance here."

"There's some," Chalky said. "A lot of people have put together the lack of coincidence leading to this mess, but these northerners, they're brutal. They murdered an entire neighbourhood for one leader. Starved us to the brink. Other things, since arriving, that I won't repeat. Locals who have been tearing each other apart are uniting against a common enemy."

"But it was slow," Brilly said. "The northerners have promised a lot to some key people—food, land, supplies, positions of authority—and those people are turning on their neighbours."

Tollar closed her eyes and let out a long breath. They weren't raiders, they were monsters.

"All right, are they still keeping the dragons near the eastern ridge?" Tollar asked.

"Yes, but the riders are on the prison ship."

"Riders?"

"Dragon riders. Riders probably isn't the best word to describe it. It's almost like the riders are pets for the dragons?" Chalky shrugged.

Tollar thought of being Bale's pet and suppressed a grin.

"These riders, they on the prison ship because they're guarding it or as prisoners?"

"Prisoners." Chalky glanced at Brilly again. "Far as I've been able to tell, they're victims of these northerners, same as the rest of us."

"Okay, so these riders are humans somehow bonded to those dragons?"

"Seems that way."

"And they're on a ship? That's... Perfect." Tollar grinned. "Out in the ocean somewhere? Fantastic. So we get—"

Chalky shook her head. "Narra's got the baby and Brilly has no training and, well..." Chalky gestured to her cane leaning in the corner.

"You're not the only people in this city."

"I told you, we don't know who to trust. And so few people are willing to do anything against these northerners."

Tollar groaned and turned to stare out the window, gripping the frame to still her trembling hands and breathing deep against her need to scream. She turned, hands on hips, to look at Beenala, who was biting her lips together and clutching the edge of the table. She'd have to keep Beenala's role to a minimum and see if she could find a way to do this without involving her at all.

The riders, at least, she could do. And sink that cursed prison ship and every last northerner on it.

"All right. I'll get the riders out, at least. Is there somewhere I can send them where they'll be safe?"

Another exchange of glances.

"Send them here," Chalky said. "They can hide in the old temple in the flood, you can get them there, right? It's on a rise so the main floor is soggy but the second floor is completely dry. At night, they can come here, one at a time and we'll figure it out from there."

"All right. And I'll see if I can't figure out something to get the dragons out too. You think they'll help me? What are the dragon riders like?"

Chalky took a considering drink of wine. "The dragons here, some of them were reared in captivity by these northerners, that's why they have eggs. Easier to break their will when raised from hatching. But the rest were captured in the wild—somewhere in the far west and north, along with their riders."

"All right. The riders will be likely to help me." Tollar paced more, scowling over the facts. But she could do this. She had all night and the walk back to Bale tomorrow to think of more beyond freeing the riders. With such limited numbers, she'd have to plan carefully and strike quickly to have any hope of success.

"I'll do what I can. We will." She glanced at Beenala who was definitely growing pale. "And I'll bring this to Solia. Maybe we can help you flush out these—what did you call them? Northerners?"

Tollar slid into her seat and topped up her cup. They passed the evening on a lighter tone, though Tollar noted they used fire lanterns for light—no power at all with the dam gone—until Chalky brought Tollar and Beenala into one of the less crowded side rooms in the house. There were crates stacked up to the ceiling, but space enough in the centre for the two women to spread out their mats and get some rest.

Beenala's face remained polite but blank, and Tollar felt her disappointment over not getting to sleep in a bed. They sat on their mats, backs against the crates, with Beenala's little lantern between them for light.

"What do we do tomorrow, then?" Beenala asked. "I expected we'd be here a bit, snooping around."

"I thought so too, but I think we've got all the information we will. Safely, at least. We'll go back to Bale, and I'll come up with a plan. Tomorrow will be a walking and planning day. And then... probably a chaos day. Do you think you're ready?"

"I hope so. Do you know what you'll do?"

"Freeing the riders will be easy enough, and I can do it alone. It's the rest I'm not sure about yet. If we can get a better view of the eastern ridge and the dragon pens, that will help."

"You don't plan to stay here long?"

"I don't think that would be wise. Two more days, I think, and we should head back home. Are you ready for all that wilderness?"

"The sooner we get home the better. Even if it means five days of rations." Beenala cracked a smile.

Tollar remained where she was while Beenala settled onto her mat. That Beenala was in better spirits was a good start, but Tollar worried she wouldn't be able to help more—or at all—when the time came. It was nice to have her around, to make the time pass and have a familiar face. While it was true that Tollar knew people everywhere she went, like Chalky, she wasn't especially close to anyone.

Beenala had never liked it when Tollar left, right from that very first time. And every time Tollar left Upalint, she considered going without a goodbye, but that never sat well. She expected Beenala would be upset. Even more upset than *with* the goodbye.

And it was nice to know that someone other than Auntie cared when Tollar came and went.

But that Beenala insisted on coming along this time... It was more than wanting to help. And it was more than simply not liking change. Tollar often recalled how Beenala had been the only one to care the first time Tollar left, always cherishing that image of Beenala waving from the hedge.

It kept Tollar going home. Sometimes made her consider staying. Made her hope that Beenala coming with her could be some kind of regular thing.

Beenala clearly wasn't ready for any of this, but maybe one day she could be?

Tollar shook her head and lay down. She could worry about that nonsense once they were safely home. She had bigger problems to focus on for now. Because these northerners were no ordinary raiders with their barricades and armadas and targeted destruction. This was something worse. And if she hoped to deal with it, she had dragons and their riders to free.

16

Tollar sat with Beenala at the top of the eastern ridge overlooking the port, deep in the foliage and going over the plan. Bale was off hunting, or maybe having her evening nap. Beenala and Bale understood their role, Beenala relieved that it would be small but not liking how long they would be separated. But it couldn't be helped. Tollar couldn't keep Beenala safe or Bale hidden out in the ocean and have a hope of freeing the dragon riders.

And she didn't know how long it would take them to regroup at the temple and figure out how to integrate the rest of Tollar's plan. That part involved Beenala but depended on the skills and willingness of the riders.

"You sure you're okay with not really knowing?" Tollar asked.

"I do know. I know not to expect a time and not to expect a specific order to the events. I know only to watch for your signal. And if it doesn't come by dawn, to flee with Bale and get the information back to Solia. I don't like it, but it's straightforward enough. What I don't understand is all this nonsense you're about to do."

Tollar looked at her askance. "My part is the easiest part! It's all straightforward. I swim out to the boat, tear it apart and float the right people back while leaving the wrong people to whatever the ocean has in store for them."

She balled her hands into fists in her lap, trying to hold back the anger, knowing she couldn't drown all the northerners, no matter how badly she wanted to. From up on the ridge like this, she'd been able to see how the northerners had razed the old Grand Market to use it as a barracks.

"Tollar. I know you're a very good aquamancer, but what you're talking about doesn't seem possible. That boat is a long way out. How will you get there unseen and without drowning."

Tollar sighed and tried coming up with a lie. Decided Bee deserved better.

"I can breathe water."

"Be serious, Tollar. I don't like it when you poke fun at me."

"I'm being serious. I didn't use an air bubble in the river with that gezar. I can breathe water, Bee. I swear."

Beenala pivoted on her knees to face Tollar where she sat among the camouflaging ferns. Tollar kept staring out over the city.

"Tollar... That's not possible."

"Well, it is. Because I can do it."

"That's not a thing."

"It's a thing for me."

Beenala sat back, staring at her silently, drumming her fingers against her thighs.

Something rustled in the jungle behind them, and Tollar pulled out her dagger and got to a half crouch before she caught a glimpse of purple and black.

"It's me," Bale whispered in her burbling voice.

"Good. Did anyone see you?"

Bale shook her head and curled up nearby, tucking her head under her wing to nap. Tollar took another look around, expecting people to come up here, but there was no one else. There was a smooth mound on the ridge south of where they sat that had been a popular spot for sightseeing, but it had been empty every time Tollar checked. That only added to her unease. So many things about the city had changed.

"All right," Beenala said at last. "I don't think you're lying, but I don't understand, Toll. That's not how magic works. I can't breathe fire. No pyromancer can."

"There are a few who can."

More silence save for the sound of Beenala drumming her fingers on her legs. Tollar felt Bale's attention at her back.

"And I suppose you're going to tell me there are terramancers who can breathe dirt?"

"None that I've heard of, but I'm sure it's possible."

Beenala rubbed her hands over her face and let out the breath she'd been holding all day.

"I've heard about all the very most exceptional magical talents. There's no getting into the Guild without learning about all the fancy abilities they hope you'll have," Beenala said. "Breathing water was not one of them. Boiling waves isn't either. Having powerful aquamancers for parents doesn't automatically result in exceptional elemental skill. Please, Tollar, help me understand."

Tollar tapped her foot against the dirt and gripped her hands around her folded knees. She wanted to run. She never should have brought Beenala. She should have known it would come to this.

"I'm part elemental demon. Water demon, clearly."

The silence drew out forever. If it was possible to die of silence, Tollar was about to.

"How?" Beenala's voice came out in a breathy whisper.

"It's incredibly rare. I'm only the fourth person like this that the Guild knows of. The rest are pyromancers. Whole family of 'em."

"Yes!" Bale said. "My auntie's friends."

Tollar and Beenala turned as one to look at her.

"Your auntie?" Tollar asked. "You have an auntie? And she's friends with the half-demon pyromancers?"

"Yes. In the dragon city."

"What...?" Tollar blinked. Beenala's brow furrowed.

"Mistress told me while we flew."

"You didn't tell me."

"You didn't ask."

"I'm asking now. What else did she tell you?"

"How to get to the dragon city. How to hunt in water. How to find safe mountains for sleeping. How my venom works."

"You have venom? What?"

"I can't tell you about that."

Tollar and Beenala exchanged a look.

"Okay. Right, okay. So yes, Bale, I'm like your auntie's friends, but water demon. Anyway, it was caused the same way for all of us. My dad, not Zarro but my actual father, was possessed by a water demon when I was conceived. It burned through him, used him up and that's why he died so young."

"Why would a demon possess a human?"

"For fun." Tollar shook her head. "They sound like arseholes. See humans as toys, especially if we're not careful using them with our magic. So one got my father and left a bit of its power in me."

"The possession killed your father but hasn't harmed you?"

"I don't know a whole lot because neither does the Guild. There's only four of us and I'm the only aquamancer. But no, water demons can't really hurt me. Or at least they haven't so far. It's only a theory, but Dira's top elemental thinks that when demons use people, they use the human's energy instead of their own. But I'm a mix of demon and human, the unique abilities draw directly from their realm—their power source—somehow. My appearance—the blue in my skin, the silver eyes—it's the demon mixing with the human in me. They said the pyromancers have similar sorts of physical attributes."

Beenala stared and swallowed hard. "Why haven't I heard about this before? Not just from you, I mean—why hasn't the Guild said anything to the rest of us?"

"Because we're dangerous." Tollar bunched her fists against her lap, hating to admit this to herself as much as she hated saying it out loud. "We're just so much stronger than normal elementals. The Guild wants to keep an eye on us, make sure we're not being bastards with our power—they don't want more of us."

Beenala's eyes widened and she stared out over the ocean before snapping her attention back to Tollar. "Wait, could someone do this on purpose?"

"As far as I know, the four of us the Guild knows about have been accidents—well, two accidents and two children inheriting it from half-demon mothers. But I don't see why someone couldn't try to use a demon and do it on purpose if they knew."

"But it would kill them, like your father."

"Not if they got someone to help draw out the demon soon enough."

Beenala tilted her head, more questions building. Tollar felt cold.

"Is this why your family drove you away?"

The cold feeling spiked into Tollar's gut and she inhaled sharply. "It's complicated, but that's part of it. I don't know for sure why Zarro didn't like me, but it was easy enough for him to use my power as a wedge. Sometimes I'd get mad and use it on him, kind of like I do to Saivyn. And so he was always making a big deal out of it, painting me as reckless and dangerous. Said it enough I guess my mother started to believe him."

"You... don't seem dangerous. Well." Beenala pressed her lips together and gripped the hem of her shirt. "I mean, your magic is big and can be a bit frightening, but so can mine. So can anyone's."

"I have a unique connection to the water realm. I can... I can open doorways directly to their realm and pull water out of it. Just unlimited water. I could drown the world if I really wanted to."

"And you can make boiling waves for five days straight and breathe water."

"Yes. It's not... As easy as I make it look. It exhausts me. It's different than for normal wizards, but it's still draining. The amount of concentration required is... it's a lot."

Tollar focused on one little patrol boat, a speck on the ocean, and refused to make eye contact with Beenala. Until she felt Bee's warm hand on her shoulder.

"Tollar, that's incredible. Why do you keep it a secret?"

"Those pyromancers? Their entire kingdom turned against them." Tollar kept staring at the ocean. "I don't think it's an accident they're all out in the dragon city. People don't like me as it is, Bee. My *own family* doesn't. I don't need to let everyone know I'm a freak. I don't need to add giving them a reason to really fear me to the list of reasons I'm better off away from people. It *hurts so much* to have people I trusted recoil from me in fear."

"Is this why you run?"

"There are a lot of reasons."

Beenala squeezed her shoulder. "The people who matter will understand, Toll. Anyone who doesn't see the value of your power is a fool."

Tollar smirked. "You going to tell Saivyn that?"

Beenala rolled her eyes. "I won't tell anyone, if that's what you want."

"I appreciate that, thank you."

"No telling." Bale nudged her soft warm snoot against Tollar. Tollar let out a shaky breath, not ready to believe it was this easy.

"So that's how you'll pull this all off? You can breathe the ocean and just, what, drown them all if you need to?"

Tollar glanced down at her right arm. "I always try to avoid that. But I can do things no other aquamancer can. It will take a lot of them to counter what I can do. There are enough of them here to stop me, but not enough of them out at that boat."

Beenala grinned. "Does breathing saltwater sting?"

"Like a cursed ancestor."

Beenala was still squeezing Tollar's shoulder and suddenly withdrew her hand, blushing.

"Thank you for sharing that," Beenala said, breathless again. "I feel better knowing what you can do. I thought you were going on some suicide mission."

"I wouldn't do that to you, Bee. I wouldn't strand you and Bale out here. We'll get those riders out. Ancestors willing, we'll free all those dragons too. There's too many of them down there, Bee. I don't like it."

She scowled at the city, shadows growing in the fading light.

"Too many for you to handle?"

"For me, maybe. For us? Should be okay. No, what I mean is there's more northerners than there should be."

"That sounds bad."

"I don't like having them on our shores. We need to get rid of them. And we'll start by taking their dragons."

It was almost sundown, almost time to get started, and the two of them sat quietly, Bale snoozing behind them, while they watched the sunset turn the ocean to liquid fire. It was beautiful. And sad. Port Sawulxo had always been beautiful and the landscape was still incredible, the ocean views unparalleled, but the ruin of the city and all those warships in the water—it was wrong.

And she would do something about it.

Tollar propelled herself through the water, not far from the sea floor, and tried focusing on her task rather than how refreshing Beenala's devotion was. Beenala had actually come with her, just after dark, to where the eastern ridge ended in a cliff at the ocean. She'd wished Tollar good luck, assured her that she wanted to stay with Bale and the two of them could protect each other, and then stood stolidly by with Bale as Tollar took a running dive off the cliff.

She couldn't shake the giddy feeling. Nothing Tollar told Beenala revolted her, not the way her truths drove away everyone else. She thought Tollar's freakish power was a good thing! It was like nothing she did would drive Beenala away (not that she was interested in testing the theory).

Had she ever felt this? Felt accepted before?

Her anger rose, as it always did, when she thought about her family and how they had categorically rejected her, in large part because she was half demon. Because it was too much. Like she'd asked to be this way. They were the people who should have stood by her but didn't. How she hadn't been able to really be herself even with Auntie and Granny, though they'd cared the most. And she pushed aside her complicated thoughts about Beenala and let her anger drive her toward the job she had to do.

The ocean was dark, she had no light she could bring with her.

She didn't really need it. She sensed where she was, where everything else was—like seeing by feeling the water. Without effort, she could sense every guppy in the ocean within a league of her in all directions. She knew instinctively when to adjust her course over reefs and around forests of kelp that would grasp at her and slow her progress.

If she floated motionlessly and concentrated, she could feel the whole of the ocean and be consumed by its vastness. The ocean challenged her, and she'd only tried it once, preferring to suss out the length of a river or the volume of a lake or inland sea.

And she sensed the prison ship up ahead, the line of its anchor growing nearer. The continental shelf ending not far beyond the ship, dropping away into an abyss. The ship was more of a barge, not that it mattered. It was made out of wood and floated in her domain.

Another coughing fit overtook her as she slowed on her approach to the ship. Her lungs burned with all the salt. It would be a relief to get to the surface and breathe air like a sensible human.

Not long now.

She stopped right at the anchor and stood on the silty seafloor. With more focus now that she wasn't speeding through the water, she filtered out the salt and gave herself something cleaner to breathe. Once she'd rinsed the worst of the ache from her lungs, she set to work.

The barge was hidden by darkness above, the moons not having risen yet, but she sensed its shape in the water. She would have to be quick to avoid a strong counterattack by the aquamancers on board. Hopefully there weren't more than a handful.

Tollar touched the bone pendant, back around her neck for the trip, drew in one final breath of clear water and braced herself. She drove the surface water crashing against the boat with the force of a shaker wave in every direction. The sound of the boat cracking apart distorted by the water.

One of the aquamancers aboard tried to calm the waves and only muted the effects of one of them before Tollar used their magic to hone in on them and encase them in a block of ice. Which she then sent floating away.

She used the battering waves to grind the boat to pieces, careful not to crush the pieces together, before pushing all the water up from underneath to keep everything from sinking.

Now she propelled herself to the surface on a column of water, rising up dry as if she'd been on land this whole time. The night air was warm in her lungs. There were a few lanterns clinging to debris that had survived the disaster and it helped her enemies see her and attack.

That was fine.

An aquamancer made a spear of water, and Tollar encased her in ice before she could so much as aim it. A swib jumped off a chunk of the deck, diving at her with a knife in hand. Tollar swatted him away with a spurt of water. A column of water slammed into her side and she staggered, sinking up to her ankles before getting over the shock and reasserting her will.

She roared as she followed the magic to its source and encased that one in ice too.

Two more coordinated their attacks, one with a water spear and another with a wave. Tollar swept both attacks aside and got both wizards in ice and floating off into the darkness.

"Oh, maybe a whirlpool to hold you? Don't want you floating back here before I'm done."

A league out, she got the ocean churning, a vast whirlpool to hold the floating ice blocks of aquamancers. The effort of it got a headache throbbing behind her eyes, but it was absolutely worth it. Swibs with their sad weapons tried to mount an assault from the floating debris, only to find whatever bit of ship they'd been standing on carry them away to join the iced-in aquamancers.

"What are you?" someone screamed.

"Your doom."

Unfortunately, the dragon riders were all pale northerners, but at least they weren't attacking her. The cages they all floated in made it easier to find them. Though seeing people in cages always put dragonfire through her veins. Scowling out into the dark, she made the whirlpool spin faster, get colder.

She floated herself over to the nearest cage, holding a pair of prisoners.

"Why are you locked up in here?" she asked in prime.

"Loch thinks he can use us ta break our dragons," a large hairy man said.

"*Your* dragons? Really?" Her headache was growing and she did not have the patience for this.

He coughed nervously. "Well, they're their own dragons, of course. Shell is mine in the way my sister is mine—as family or a good friend."

"Ah, you named it?"

"I had to call him something, didn't I?"

"Very good. Which are your people and which do I leave behind?"

"Wait, yer here to rescue us?"

"Secret mission courtesy of Nytaltek. Well, really, most of them think of me as a rogue agent, but if this works out in your favour, do think kindly of those in Upalint. Now, those aquamancers will break free of that ice soon enough. Do tell me who comes with us and who gets left to the ocean's devices."

And the man pointed everyone out, some of the floating cages containing prisoners who were not dragon riders.

"Should I free them?"

"I don't know them," he said. "Hard to say what gets a person bound up on this barge."

Tollar clumped the cages of dragon riders together and inspected the rest. All pale northerners, shouting at her in a dialect of Prairiean she barely recognized and didn't understand. None of them locals. Traitors maybe? But to who? Oh well, their cages floated just fine without Tollar's help. Someone would collect them eventually.

She turned her attention to the riders.

"All right, you lot hold on and stay calm."

She gave the cluster of cages a nudge away from the rest of the barge, let everything that wasn't her prize sink or float away, and got moving, fast as she could, skating along the surface. Even her power wasn't enough to keep those blocks of ice held and that whirlpool spinning all the way from shore. Her limbs grew heavy with the effort. This wasn't anything like rescuing Bale's egg had been, but the strain wore on her and she had to be vigilant against errors. Keeping her focus on the whirlpool and blocks of ice and keeping these cages afloat wasn't particularly difficult, but keeping the magic under control so she didn't accidently desiccate everyone within a league was an entirely different matter.

And she had to slow their approach as the cluster drew closer to the shore and all the patrol boats and searchlights. She sensed each boat, each solitary aquamancer watching the waves. They were easy enough to shield against, inserting the sense of calm ocean in her wake. The shore drew near, her focus on the flooded area of the city when she lost her grip on the carnage she'd left out at sea. The pent-up pressure behind her eyes eased and she let out a long breath.

She put all her focus into getting them quickly and safely through the patrols and the debris littering the flooded areas. The bay near the port was full of what had once been pieces of the city. It was a wonder the northerners could patrol at all. They must have an endless supply of aquamancers to keep all of their boats from running aground.

A wide avenue led from the shore well into the flooded neighbourhood and Tollar steered down that way. It had detritus here and there, but nothing like the bay, all of it easily dodged.

The temple loomed up out of the dark not far from the avenue, and she skimmed the little cages along until they reached it. She pulled the cages up next to the wide entrance.

"Did ye bring the keys?" the man asked.

"I just ripped a barge to shreds without breaking a sweat." Tollar cupped some water in her hands and poured it into the lock. Sensing the shape of the internal workings was a child's task compared to everything else she'd done tonight. The lock clicked open.

"Inside, up to the second floor unless you want wet feet all night."

One cage after another, until she'd freed them all and sent them inside, and then sent the cages floating out to sink into the rest of the rubble at the bottom of the bay.

"Well, that was fun." Tollar reached the second floor, dry as Chalky had promised, and the fourteen dragon riders who huddled there.

"Who are ye?" the large man, who had become their leader—or maybe always had been?—demanded. He was two handspans taller than Tollar and about twice her weight in equal measure muscle and fat with thick treetrunk arms that looked like they'd be comfortable wielding a warhammer. He had wild black hair and a grizzled beard over olive skin crisscrossed with scars and an eyepatch so only one hard brown eye tried to cut through her to look for deceit.

"I'm sure you understand giving you my proper name would be foolish when none of us are friends yet, but you can call me Swampy if you need something other than *hey you*."

"Who sent ye?"

"Upalint, vaguely. More details than that are also probably information best kept to myself for now. I was here when the port first fell, and I've since regrouped and returned to free the dragons. Found out you lot went along with them."

So she explained to them what she'd learned and why she had a problem with people keeping dragons for anything other than as kin. The one who'd been doing all the talking identified himself as Croves. She let them all know they could go to Chalky's for aid or they could come with her and free their dragons.

Croves looked at the rest of the group but barely hesitated before replying. "We're going with ye."

"Excellent. If this doesn't work, you can always go to Chalky to hide and try again later."

"How's this goin' ta work then?"

"Well, I need some distractions. What skills have the lot of you got?"

"I'm an aeromancer," Croves said. "We've got two elementals and a terramancer among us. One powerful wizard with a focus on healing. The rest are what yer lot call swibs."

"And can the swibs among you fight?"

"Aye, some of 'em."

"All right, I can work with that. You saw how handy I am around locks, and anything else water can damage. But I need focus and time. I've got a friend to help as well. Two, if you count the little dragon whose egg I stole from here."

"What colour was it?" one of the women in the back asked.

"Black and amethyst. I understand her parents are dead. Or dead and missing? Would there have been any other eggs near to hatching?"

"That one was closest," Croves said. "There's a turquoise egg and a red and gold egg that're both close to hatching as well. But they should be another season or two, from what I've learned."

"All right. While it would be ideal, obviously, to get every last captive dragon and egg free tonight, we have to be ready for failures. First priority is the dragons belonging to wizards and the two eggs closest to hatching. If we succeed there, we get the rest of the eggs out. And if we succeed there, we get the rest of the dragons."

There was some grumbling from what Tollar assumed were the swibs, but Croves was quick to agree. "Get the young'uns out, aye. They grow up wrong if not cared for properly, if kept captive."

"And wizards teamed with dragons should be enough to free the rest," Tollar said. "Can I trust you to form teams? Swibs supporting wizards? Wizards getting their dragons and the eggs first and then coming to help free the rest of the dragons?"

"And what about you?"

"I get us in, I wash out as many of the guards and enslaved dragons that I can, and I open what locks I can find. I'll signal to my friend and our dragon, and they'll provide air support until we can get more dragons freed."

Croves grinned, shining white teeth beneath the rest of his grime. "All right, Swampy, this sounds like the most fun I've had since these bastards captured us."

17

Tollar peeked out of the canal that ran past the wall circling the dragon enclosure, only her eyes above water and watching for guards. It was more difficult on the ground where she couldn't sense them in the dark. She'd have liked if there'd been an aquamancer or two among the riders, but she could at least get the front gate open for them.

While Tollar had taken a quick nap in a quiet corner of the temple, Croves and his people had come up with some retreat scenarios. Tollar never really thought those through as much as she should. She liked to assume she wouldn't need them. They hadn't had a lot of time, but the spot of rest had taken the edge off her headache and it wasn't like she thought they should dive in here without a plan.

But some of these riders were untested. Beenala and Bale were untested as well. None of them knew how to harness each other's magic, a skill that carried the possibility of exponential increases in power, and it irritated Tollar that the Guild wasn't teaching that to more wizards. Back up plans upon back up plans were only wise, no matter how much she didn't like them. And as much as she wanted to free all the dragons and mash the northerners into the seafloor, releasing even one dragon would be a success. No reason that one dragon couldn't return to help the others later.

And there were a lot of dragons to free. There were the fourteen captives the riders wanted to free most, plus the five remaining eggs. And then there were five enslaved dragons, ones that had likely been born in captivity and never known the wild. They would be unpredictable and dangerous, but couldn't be left behind.

Of course, Tollar had to get the riders all through the gate to the vast, walled-in complex tucked against the eastern ridge. It hadn't been this fortified the last time she'd been here. The walls were higher and watchtowers stood at even intervals, with one right next to the gate. There was dim light at the gate itself and she watched the space under it where one guard stood. There had to be more.

Patrolling? Inside? Stationed at intervals?

She and Beenala hadn't been able to get close enough to tell during daylight hours. So she ran her thumb over the bone pendant. All she could do was wait and watch. And hope.

A second guard appeared out of the gloom and stood with the first. With a flick of her hand, Tollar sent a snake of water slithering through the grass toward them, split it off at their feet and launched the water into their mouths, filling their lungs so they couldn't scream or breathe.

More water up the wall to pull the guard from the tower and fill his mouth as well.

Rising from the canal without a ripple, she rushed as quietly as she could to where the three guards gurgled, eyes wide and pleading.

"Oh relax, I won't kill you. Time for some rest."

She watched them carefully, waiting. It was tricky, waiting for the right moment when they lost consciousness but hadn't died yet. The one she'd pulled from the wall succumbed first. One of the standing guards collapsed before the other, and she crouched to check on him. The other tried kicking Tollar in the face, but she rolled sideways and waited. The extra exertion brought him down to join his comrade.

Tollar drained the water from all of them. Checked that they'd resumed breathing. The one she'd pulled off the wall had broken his arm. But thinking of what they'd done to this city, she couldn't summon any sympathy for him.

That appeared to be all of them. At least in the immediate vicinity.

Excellent.

She bound the first two guards and stuffed a wad of cloth in each mouth. The injured guard took some consideration, but she bound his arms together in the end and gagged him as well. It would keep him still, if nothing else.

Now for the lock. It was more complicated than the ones on the barge cages, but clicked open all the same. She didn't pull the door open, but sent a ripple down the canal to where Croves and his people waited.

She spotted shapes in the gloom before she heard Croves and the riders. The terramancer in his crew softened the ground in such a way that they were all very near to silent when they walked.

"They're patrolling or checking in with each other at least occasionally," Tollar whispered. "So we need to be quick. This will work best if you can get to your dragons before they notice us."

Tollar cracked open the gate, and peeked into the courtyard beyond. Two guards patrolled on the ground, no one within sight on the walls. She brought the two new guards down in the same manner as the first three and ushered the dragon riders inside.

Then she closed the gate behind her. But didn't lock it. The idea was they'd all fly out with dragons, but Croves wanted to be prepared for the worst.

Ha! The worst was they all left there in pieces. Or as ash.

The first of the dragon pens was straight ahead but closer to the ridge. A bonfire burned off to the right, where the dragon eggs were kept. The dragon riders spread out, each wizard paired with a swib, except for Croves who stayed with Tollar, as they searched the pens to see which dragons belonged to which rider.

One of the swibs who had gone ahead to the first pen came jogging back to Croves.

"First pen is Shell. Lucky bastard." Tollar couldn't see her face but heard the smile. Then she was gone into the dark.

"Praise the gods. Let's go, Swampy."

Tollar sent a ball of water ahead and worked the lock as they approached so that the door to the pen swung open by the time they got there. The dragon, a small male but still bigger than a house, was the same green as a sea turtle and watching the door silently. His wings were clamped at his sides, his mouth clamped shut and short chains held each leg to the ground.

"I will tear every last one of these bastards to pieces," Croves growled.

"Well, I think I know where to start to help with that. See if you can find keys, though."

Tollar found the lock binding the chains around the dragon's mouth.

"Have you out in a snap, m'lord. Eat whoever you see fit, though I hope you understand you probably won't get out of here if you eat *me*."

The dragon snorted.

"I think he likes ye," Croves said from the shadows.

Tollar didn't respond with words. She snapped the lock open as promised.

"I suggest silence for now," Tollar said as the dragon stretched his jaws. "The longer it takes them to notice us the—"

"Hey! Who's in there!" That wasn't a voice Tollar recognized.

"Oh shit."

Beenala would get to prove herself after all.

Tollar took a moment's pause from working on the clamps on Shell's wings, squinting in concentration, to turn every last bit of water on the premises, including the surrounding canal, into roaring geysers. She squeezed her eyes against the return of her headache, then gave the magic in the lock a final push. The clamps fell away from Shell's wings and he spread them out, giving them a test flap.

Tollar set to work on his legs, while Croves ran up to his dragon.

"I'm sorry, old friend, but I can't find the gear. We have to do this the ugly way. When Swampy gets us out of here, we try to free the others. But when we go, ye've got to grab the dragon egg next to us, so I've got to be clear of yer hands."

Shell hissed, but lowered his body as Tollar got his forelegs free of chains.

Croves was scaling the side of the dragon when fire rained down from above, and Bale screeched into the night.

"Ah, there's our reinforcements."

"Ach, she's just a wee thing," Croves said.

"Are you kidding me? Do you know how many monkeys she eats in a day?"

Croves chuckled and settled himself between two spikes above the base of Shell's wings, the exact spot Bale decided Beenala should sit for their battle debut. Still working on the locks, Tollar focused on Bale's gentle descent and the not so gentle dragonfire she and Beenala directed into the compound.

In the firelight, Tollar made out the pale shape of Beenala on Bale's dark back. They almost blended into the night. Bale got closer than Tollar would have liked before she adjusted the angle of her wings and swooped overhead, breathing fire at the northerners all the while. As they passed overhead, Beenala screamed, and Tollar paused in her work to track the two of them.

Beenala wasn't falling off and didn't look injured. Probably scared. She was still hanging on and still reinforcing Bale's fire. That was what mattered most.

Tollar focused and freed the last of Shell's legs. The dragon burst into the air, knocking Tollar on her arse with the gale from his wings. Fire exploded from his mouth, and he screeched to shatter the earth. But dived toward the dragon eggs.

Tollar ran out of the pen to see Shell scoop up the turquoise egg and barrel roll back toward the other pens, spitting more fire.

Good. She started toward the next pen over when Bale swooped out of the sky, crouching, and Beenala, still shrieking, leapt from her back and tumbled across the ground. She came to a stop kneeling, and pitched forward, hands braced in the dirt, to vomit.

"Bee!"

"Fly better now," Bale said. She jumped onto the side of the pen and furiously flapped her way up to a better height, chasing after Shell.

Tollar made it to Beenala's side and helped her to stand.

"No." Beenala wiped her mouth on her sleeve. "No. This was a mistake. No, it's time to go home."

"Just a few more minutes, Bee. You did an amazing job. Do you want to wait here, in the shadow, and I'll collect Bale and come back for you when we're done?"

"No."

Tollar stopped and took stock of her friend. She was too pale, shaking so much it was a wonder she could stand, wide eyes darting around, desperate for an escape. This wasn't good.

"Bee. Look at me. We'll go home very soon, all right? Just as soon as Bale comes back. Bee? Try to take a breath, okay? I'm here and we'll be okay. Just a few more minutes."

As Tollar did the mental math of whether to leave Beenala here or drag her from pen to pen, a terrible shriek rose up from the far end of the compound, out toward the shore. A wall of flame erupted, and Shell banked away, aiming his fire at something nearby. The breeze was hot and sulfury, acrid smoke stinging the air.

Bale flew straight through the fire, the heat of it giving her some lift, but then she disappeared from sight.

"Oh no."

The screeching grew louder from that end, and two enslaved dragonesses rose out of the fire, great gouts of flame blazing from their mouths at something on the ground.

"Oh shit."

Tollar had accounted for the northerners using the slave dragons, but she didn't think it would happen so soon. Word of the attack on the prison barge must have reached the pens. Catching them unprepared would have been ideal, but there was nothing for it now. She had to work with what she had. They had to get another dragon free to help Shell and Bale.

They needed more time. She needed more help.

She gathered a small puddle of water in front of her and went through the summoning as quickly as she could, whispering words like rain through the leaves in the demons' strange burbling language. A translucent, vaguely humanoid, glistening shape clambered out of the puddle, growing until it was nearly as big as her. It sloshed around like it was facing her and then froze at her command like it had suddenly turned to ice. As soon as the water demon was clear of the puddle and held by her will, Tollar summoned another and another, holding her focus on them all to keep them from running wild. Beenala gasped. Speaking with the urgency of waves crashing against the shore, Tollar sent the water demons to the far end of the compound.

That would have to be distraction enough. She didn't have time to call any more demons.

"Bee, come on!"

But then the other three slave dragons rose up out of the fire. And the first two went straight for Bale.

"No!" Beenala screamed.

Tollar reached for her hand and Beenala gripped it and they gave each other a startled look. But neither let go. The glance lasted a beat. Then Tollar watched Bale, still clasping Beenala's hand.

Cold fear gripped her stomach even as warmth spread across her chest.

"Bee, is she close enough you can throw some fire to distract those dragonesses?" The demons were fast, but they wouldn't reach the end of the compound in time.

Beenala gripped her hand harder but didn't respond. She was holding her breath.

Shit.

One of the dragonesses darted straight up at Bale, her large jaws wide as if she meant to devour the little dragon whole. Shell swooped close, and Croves sent two blasts of wind—one to knock the dragoness aside and one to give Bale a boost.

Shell and Bale banked, coming back around toward Tollar and Beenala.

The rest of Croves's people rushed toward them, dragons and a host of well-armed guards at their heels. Well, this was part of the reason they'd left the gate open, but Tollar hated that they hadn't freed more dragons.

Without letting go of Beenala's hand, she sent her attention beyond the wall to pull all the water out of the canal and fling it across the courtyard like a river gone wild. It knocked aside some of the guards and then scooped up the thirteen dragon riders and floated them straight past her and out the gate. Into the night. Hopefully they remembered how to find Chalky.

Then she called to the ocean, out on the edge of her reach. The effort of it made her dizzy, and she considered opening a portal to the water realm instead. But the ocean would be less dangerous to her and Bee. She pulled in a wave. It roared up over the exterior wall, washing over everything in its path. She didn't put effort into helping any of those people float.

They could get frogged, every last one of them.

She lashed water from the courtyard up into the air, knocking down one of the enemy dragons and then another and another, taking all of them out of the air and giving Bale and Shell some space to retreat. Bale swooped down for them, arms outstretched, and Tollar realized too late what she meant to do and had no time to brace for it.

Wind knocked out of her, she was tight against the dragon, Beenala too. Bale rose up far too quickly. Unnatural. Tollar thought her mind was going to sink down into her stomach and her vision swam. But then they were level with Shell and Croves.

"What now?" he called.

Heading for the rendezvous point didn't make sense when it was only the two of them.

"Bale, you remember what we talked about?"

"Home!"

"Croves, we go out over the eastern ridge, low over the trees, then follow us."

He dragged Bale up the ridge on a column of air, and then they skimmed the treetops, Bale heading south to the last campsite they'd had before coming into the city. Tollar resisted the urge to rub her face and ignored her headache. She tried not to be disappointed about not freeing more dragons. They had two and a rider and hadn't lost a soul in the process.

Those thirteen remaining riders were free and hiding, to foment discord and to keep trying to free their dragons until they succeeded.

And Tollar had more ammunition to get things rolling at home. This little campaign had gone far better than it had any right to. Hopefully this luck would follow her home and to the task of mobilizing Saivyn and the rest of Upalint.

BALE

B ale watches Toll-mum pace the narrow space on the tall bank of the river, right on the edge of the rocky outcropping where she chose to make camp. She goes back and forth between the man Croves and the dragon he calls Shell but who introduced himself to Bale as Mighty Alpine Evergreen while they were flying. Like Devouring Fogbank and Meadow at World's End, he doesn't speak the human languages. When Bale asked him why, he stopped talking. Devouring Fogbank and Meadow at World's End hadn't wanted to answer that question either. They say she has to wait until her naming in the dragon city.

Bale wants to sleep. The moons are near one horizon and the sun won't be long from the other, and Croves says they leave again at sunrise. But Toll-mum is like the monkeys when Bale hunts. All the humans have been like this all night, but there's something jumpy about Toll-mum now that she's talking to Croves.

Bee-mum is sitting under Bale's wing looking at the little fire sputtering in the drizzle that Toll-mum has become too distracted to stop, but her eyes are empty. She doesn't notice how Toll-mum is upset.

Bale stretches her neck and lifts her head higher to see over Croves, who is between Bale and Toll-mum. He's bigger than Toll-mum and coiled like a gezar waiting at dawn. Bale doesn't like it. Croves and Toll-mum smell like metal, like Bee-mum did until she sat down and went to sleep with her eyes open. But Croves smells like something else. Something hot and musky.

"You're sure it's safe?" Toll-mum asks him.

"Aye, they didn't see which way we went. An' I told ye Shell will keep watch."

Right now, Mighty Alpine Evergreen is spreading venom around the dragon egg he took from the same place Toll-mum found Bale. The venom burns slow and hot, but humans don't know about it so his back blocks their view. He and Croves are coming home with them to help Toll-mum convince her people to help the port. Bale doesn't want to go back to the port.

Toll-mum stops and rubs her face. "I'm just so tired."

"We'll let ye rest, Swampy. Ye earned it." Still coiled and jerky, Croves touches his hand to the side of Toll-mum's face. That hot smell gets stronger. Toll-mum gasps and flinches away from him.

Bale takes a deep breath, fanning her fire, ready to burn Croves to dust.

Mighty Alpine Evergreen looks at her, at the pair of humans, and languidly turns his head back to the egg.

"Where I come from, we ask before we touch someone." Toll-mum's voice is tight and a smell like boiling water fills the air. Bale knows this smell means she's angry. Smoke drifts from Bale's nose.

Croves takes a step back and holds up his hands. "All right, I didn't mean no harm."

Toll-mum shows him the different ways they greet each other at home. Bale didn't know other humans have different greetings. That isn't very practical. She finishes by showing him the greeting that means it's okay to touch someone, and Croves takes her hands and gives her a little bow. His muscles coil up like a ready-to-pounce gezar again, but there's a smile in his voice.

"Does this mean I can touch ye then?"

Toll-mum laughs, "All right fine."

Croves uncoils then, fast but gentle, so Bale keeps her fire ready but doesn't use it just yet. He pulls Toll-mum by her hands until she's closer and touches her face again, touches her waist, slides the first hand behind her head and keeps pulling her close.

"I'd like to kiss ye," he whispers.

They've been too quiet for Bee-mum to hear this whole time, but now he's so quiet Bale almost doesn't hear him. But Toll-mum is bracing her hands on his shoulders and leaning away.

"That's you full of adrenaline with no place to put it." Toll-mum's voice is low. "I need to know someone a lot better than this to do something like that."

Croves lets her go. Bale never sighs like a human but wants to right now. She lowers her head but keeps watching.

"Well, now, I guess it's a good thing I'm headin' yer way. What customs do yer people have for courtin', I'd like to give it a try."

Toll-mum's eyes go wide, flashing silver in the low light. "What, no! I can't—Bee is—we're..." She flails her hands.

"Ah, is she yer lover?"

"No?"

Bale narrows her eyes while Toll-mum shakes her head and goes back to pacing.

Toll-mum and Bee-mum love each other like Bale loves them, like they love Bale.

"What? Yer not sure?" Croves is just as confused as Bale.

"Oh, I'm sure, it's just... not something we've talked about? Not something official?"

"Ah, it's complicated." Croves looks back at them, at Bee-mum wake-sleeping in the dying firelight. "Well, I know yer a worldly lass, but I do have some years on ye, so trust me when I say ye should uncomplicate things quick as ye can." And then he winked. "And if ye've got some space in things after that, do think of me."

Toll-mum's laugh is low, and she paces back to him. She takes his hand and touches his cheek before dipping her head and walking past him, coming Bale's way. Croves watches her until she kneels in front of Bee-mum, and then he goes to settle under Shell's wing.

"He's standing watch," Toll-mum says. "Him and his dragon taking turns, so they can both get some rest. And I can get much, much more rest."

"Oh." Bee-mum's voice is faraway, but her eyes aren't so empty anymore. "Right, all that magic. You make it sound so easy, I forget. Are you all right?"

"It was a lot. It was so easy at the time, like breathing. But the adrenaline is crashing and I feel it now." She glances up at Bale, smiling despite tired eyes. "You both did well tonight. We wouldn't have saved Shell and that egg without your help. Let's rest."

Bale gets a warm feeling inside, like her fire, but all over, the way she always does when Toll-mum tells her she did a good job. Bale spreads out her other wing so Toll-mum can stay dry without magic and then curls up to sleep. It's only three days home now that Bale is flying. Bale likes flying and being in the mountains, but Bee-mum needs to go home. They practiced with fire but not with flying and Bee-mum got too scared.

Bale wants to sleep, but Toll-mum is still awake. Lying still but sighing every few minutes. Bee-mum is still awake too. Rolling over even more than Toll-mum sighs, and giving a sniffy-huff every few rolls.

Mighty Alpine Evergreen is asleep. Croves sits alert under his wing, getting up to wander around the shore now and then, sometimes looking over toward Bale.

Bee-mum sighs like Toll-mum has been doing, and then crawls out from under Bale's wing, carrying her sleep mat. Bale moves her head to watch Bee-mum creep around the front of her to her other wing, where Toll-mum props herself up on one elbow, the white tattoos on her shoulder standing out.

"Everything okay, Bee?"

"Err. Can I put my mat next to yours?"

Toll-mum smiles and Bee-mum holds her breath.

"Of course. Come out of the rain."

Bee-mum has her mat mostly spread out next to Toll-mum before she takes another breath. She lies on her side, facing Toll-mum. Bale tucks in the other wing, curls her tail up around this one and tilts her head so she can watch them. There's a little light from Bee-mum's lantern, and Toll-mum's eyes are tired but shining.

"I'm so jittery," Bee-mum says. "I just want to go home."

"I know, I'm sorry. I was so excited to have you with me that I didn't consider enough how it would affect you. I expected more than you had to give. This was a bad idea. But that's not your fault."

"I let you down."

"I let myself down. You were brilliant."

"I abandoned Bale to fight alone with no one to protect her. She's just a baby!"

"She's a spiky, bitey, fiery baby, and it all worked out in the end. I understand what this has been like for you, I'm truly amazed by all you did out there."

Bee-mum holds her hands out like it's a greeting, and Toll-mum takes them, her cheeks plumping with a smile. They're quiet for long enough that Bale starts to sleep, even though they're both still awake. She opens her eyes again when Bee-mum shifts, the air around her charged like a thunderstorm.

"Tollar... I... I've loved you since we were girls."

Toll-mum smiles with her whole face, and that hot metal smell blows away on the wind, leaving something fresher. Something happy.

"I know. Bee, I say I come home to visit Auntie, but that's not entirely true. I could stop in and visit Auntie for a day here and there between campaigns and be gone again. I don't need guard duty. I don't need to stay at the farm." She tilts her head to look more directly at Bee-mum. "You're why I keep coming back and why I stay as long as I do. You're what anchors me to Upalint."

Bee-mum holds her breath, and this time she might hold it forever. Toll-mum keeps smiling, still holding Bee-mum's hands, squeezing them and pulling them closer to kiss Bee-mum's knuckles like she sometimes kisses the end of Bale's nose.

Bee-mum gets breathing normally again, but they don't say anything else, keep lying next to each other holding hands. Bale's eyelids droop, so do Toll-mum's.

"Goodnight, Bee." She kisses the back of Bee-mum's hand and settles down, still holding on.

"Goodnight, Tollar."

Goodnight Mums. Bale sinks all the way into sleep and dreams of home.

18

Draminedes clutched the strap of his satchel but forced himself to relax his grip. But he didn't want anyone to see the way his hands shook. This was going to be a disaster.

Of course, that was what he thought every single time he came to one of these social clubs to learn what he could of and from the locals. Rasson had been kind enough to find him a tutor to help him learn Upalan, and it shared enough similarities with his mother tongue that he picked it up quickly. But not enough that he always understood what everyone said.

They were always drunk at the social clubs, talking too fast and loud but slurring half of what they said. He needed to wrap this up and get home. But he needed to understand this place and Karthiry's angle—to see how it would benefit his people—before he could go back. Norli had been avoiding him since the first time he saw her, the few others he'd met had nothing to add, and he was running out of sources of information.

This meeting was a big one. Everyone had been talking it up in the last two social clubs he'd been to. Some rabble-rouser, who seemed to be both a local and an outsider, had gotten herself into some impressive trouble. With dragons? None of it made sense.

But this meeting had been advertised in pamphlets at all the social clubs. And this one was in the guard house. Also new. They didn't tend to let just anyone in there.

A group outside the door waited to go in. Some of them knew each other, laughing and joking amongst themselves. Others were like him, standing solitary around the edges. On some cue he didn't pick up on, everyone entered the building, where a few people already gathered. The air was cool and close, thick with the smell of fish grease, sour beer and old smoke. Most of the tables had been shoved to the sides, though there were plenty of chairs. While some people sat, most chose to stand.

A tall, stunning woman with dark blue-brown skin and strange silvery eyes stood near a set of stairs in a tidy soldier's uniform with freshly polished armour plating. Draminedes knew that she was not Captain Solia, but she was very clearly in charge of whatever this was. He glanced around, but didn't notice Solia anywhere.

From what he understood, that was exactly how she liked it.

He stood near the door, not the only dumbstruck loner who didn't know what to do, so at least he didn't stand out. More people trickled in, some taking seats and some standing in clusters. Still no sign of Solia and only one person spoke to the tall woman near the stairs—another woman, not nearly as tall and much rounder, with tawny skin and short pale hair that didn't know what it was doing. But that one bounced on the balls of her feet and tapped her fingers against her thighs, darting glances around the room while she spoke. The first woman stood somehow both relaxed and at attention, listening to her friend but watching everyone else.

Until she stopped and smiled at the round one, briefly taking her hand and running her thumb over the other's knuckles.

Then the round one sat down, and it was like a switch had been flicked in the atmosphere of the room. People rushing to sit down, the clusters of people turning to face the tall one at the stairs. Draminedes scuttled into a seat in the corner where he could see things but wasn't easily observable. And finally noticed Solia, leaning against the table behind him and managing to blend in with all the chairs around it.

He faced forward and tried to put her out of his mind.

You should leave.

Yes, he should, but he couldn't return to Karthiry with what he had. So he leaned forward and focused on what the tall woman said, forgetting about Solia while his mind worked to translate her words.

"All right, let's get this started so we can all get to drinking." The tall woman's voice was crisp, carrying over the crowd, which silenced entirely. "For those of you that don't know, I'm Tollar Lipraxo. Yes, *that* Tollar. My circulars have been entertaining the city for years. Wish I had something entertaining for you this time."

"Shut up with your nonsense and stop wasting our time!" some blocky brown man with absolutely rigid posture shouted from near the door.

"Good to see you, too, Sai. Tell me, you heard back from your contacts in the port yet?"

"Shut it, Sai. You need to hear this." That was from Solia behind Draminedes.

"I was on a campaign on the coast last season," Tollar went on.

The man, Sai, grumbled something followed by snickers, but Tollar spoke over him. What was it with those two?

"I'd been doing security work for a merchant caravan when an elemental came recruiting, looking for help defending her city against attack. It was all over by the time my team got there. Some northerners had come in, with dragons—captive ones fighting against their will—and completely overrun the locals."

"Oxshit!" Sai again.

"Saivyn, don't think I won't throw you out of my building, rank be damned," Solia said.

Wait, was he the commander? Draminedes was getting lost, but Tollar went on.

"The thing with the dragons was concerning enough that Solia sent me back there to take a closer look. Per Beenala came with me. You can talk to her after if you don't want to listen to what I have to say." Tollar gestured toward the round woman, who went utterly still.

"Anyway, we went back and I found one of my contacts and found out more about what's been going on. Because I didn't want to believe that I'd seen Port Sawulxo overrun so easily."

"They held off the siege of Shorsees for three seasons before turning them away entirely!" Saivyn said.

"Absolutely, so keep that in mind when I say they are completely under the control of these raiders from the north. And there's something unsettling about these northerners. Most of them are pale, but I know that northerners come in all different shades. And more than that, most of them are men. I heard tell that their commander is a woman, but the only women

I saw with them were my mother's age. If that weren't enough, they favour aquamancers in battle formation."

"That's not a thing!" Saivyn protested.

Tollar rolled her eyes and took in the crowd. "Everyone here has heard a bit of what I do when I'm not here. Remember Singsi? You get a few talented aquamancers working in concert near something so vast as the ocean? Well."

"But Port Sawulxo has its own aquamancers," said a round, brown woman with a long black braid sitting in the corner near Solia.

Tollar's smile was thin. "I'm getting to that, your excellency. There are pockets of resisters, but they are leaderless and most of the resistance appears to come in the form of simply holding onto dignity. Their power dam is gone. Half of the city has been destroyed. Flooded—yes, Saivyn, even with all those powerful aquamancers they've got. Or had, anyway. Most of them have been killed. And not by the northerners. By local swibs and a few by their fellow wizards."

No one said anything, and Draminedes folded his hands around his knees to stop the shaking. Port Sawulxo. He knew that name.

"The trouble started over a year ago, about the time you fools were chasing off your dragon allies. Same had happened there, but about the time I was last here for a spell. Several seasons ago, they were hit with droughts—yes, even with their aquamancers and all those elementals who hadn't yet been murdered by angry swibs. That came when the drought lasted nearly the whole year. Ended in deluge and landslides with the locals starving, tearing each other apart. And then a shake wave that took out half the city—the leaders' quarter. Two days before an armada arrived on their shores."

Draminedes didn't hear whatever contrary thing Saivyn snarled at Tollar or what she snapped back or what anyone else said because his brain refused to keep translating. He gripped his knees until his knuckles went pale and his fingers dug painfully into his flesh. The pain wasn't enough to distract him from the bile rising in his throat.

He remembered the reports coming through on Port Sawulxo. How pleased Karthiry had been with the progress and then the success. Her recent acquisition, she'd called it, right before sending Draminedes here.

Everything he'd heard about the success in Port Sawulxo indicated that the locals had been shown the errors of their ways and brought around by logic and a bit of strongarm demonstrations about how Karthiry could help them while helping herself. It had sounded perfectly reasonable at the time, and the list of potential gains from trading with them had been impressive—particularly the talk of gold.

This... Destroying the city? An invasion was not what Karthiry had spoken of at all. Did Hollen know? Was that why she was trying to hold Karthiry back?

Or maybe Tollar was lying? That commander seemed to think so.

Tollar shouted a list of atrocities at Saivyn, and Draminedes only picked out a word here and a phrase there, but it painted a grim picture of what the locals in the port faced. They had been invaded, not convinced, and in a brutal, underhanded fashion.

Now, by the sounds of Tollar's list, they were being humiliated and ground down.

Draminedes felt numb, the sour taste in his mouth intensifying, and his chest tightening around each breath. Surely Tollar was mistaken. He couldn't fathom the implications it held for Biterna if she was right.

"If you're not going to listen to me, then listen to him!" Tollar snapped, gesturing to a man at the table with Tollar's round friend. This man was massive, like a bear, and he stood from his seat, nodding grimly. "This is Per Croves, a dragon rider from the north. He and his dragon were taken captive and held like animals, forced to fight battles like the one in Port Sawulxo. There's over a dozen of them—some of them prisoners for years—all been forced under threat of death, to help these northerners overrun everything in their path between Sawulxo's coast all the way down, halfway around the world, to some kingdom called Golden Hill way in the north."

Draminedes closed his eyes. Took off his lenses and rubbed the bridge of his nose, trying not to hear Croves, speaking in prime, confirm Tollar's words. Overrun. Invasion. Captives.

What did I get myself into?

Draminedes had gone along with it because Karthiry came from a place with a flashy name and big promises—more work, more food, new riches. He hadn't seen any of that, had he? Only what Karthiry gifted to her pets.

All the best work went to the people who'd come with her out of the north. An invading force had shown up on his shores, and he'd drummed up the welcome ritual.

What would happen when Karthiry stopped humouring his people? Or stopped finding them useful?

Had she manipulated them into welcoming her?

He tried to think if there had been newcomers on the island before she arrived, anyone who could have brought a false narrative to prepare Biterna for takeover in the guise of rescue. It had been such a long time.

The room had gone silent, and Draminedes looked up. Solia stood next to the dragon rider, staring toward the door where Draminedes presumed Saivyn was standing.

Numb and sick, Draminedes wanted to run. All the way back to Biterna and pretend none of this had ever happened. To forget everything he'd heard tonight. To focus on keeping Biterna safe, restoring his family's honour. But then he considered how hard Karthiry came down on people who'd failed her, how she manipulated everyone around her.

He had blindly followed Karthiry for the promise of glory, none of which any of his people had seen. Was his loyalty so cheaply bought?

He felt watery inside, but clarity came to his thoughts.

Well, he'd got the answers he was looking for, hadn't he? Now, what to do with them? Ignore them and go home? He didn't think he could live with himself. How many lives had he helped Karthiry destroy? How much blood was on his hands?

Tollar was trying to convince everyone they needed to mobilize and help their northern neighbours and free the dragons at the very least, while Saivyn, as far as Draminedes could tell—though his overwrought mind had a hard time following the rapidfire conversation—thought that the port was its own problem and not anything the people of Upalint should get involved in.

"Have you listened to nothing I've said?" Tollar snapped. "All that brutality and you just want to leave Sawulxo to it? And what about their numbers? Croves confirmed it for you. You really don't think that's a lot for a simple occupation? What are they here for? I can't fathom a scenario that keeps them in Sawulxo without roving the coast or trying to push inland, continuing to disrupt trade."

Before Saivyn responded one way or another, though Draminedes expected him to continue to argue, Draminedes was on his feet, surprising himself when he said, "She's right. But it's much worse than you think."

That got him some startled looks and everyone went quiet.

What the godsdamn hell do you think you're doing?

Draminedes's head swam and he wasn't quite sure if his legs were still under him, but he locked his focus on Tollar.

"I'm so sorry," he blurted, trying to keep a grip on his prime. "I didn't know. I'm sorry. Please forgive me. Please, have mercy. Because I think I can help you."

Now there were some grunts of alarm to go with the shock. He shook more, but couldn't stop now. He'd never get out of here alive, and where would he go? Back to Karthiry and her lies? They had to know the truth, he hoped they'd forgive him. That they'd understand.

"I was sent here—the woman responsible for this, she's a powerful aquamancer named Karthiry. I thought—she told me she was looking for new trade opportunities. That she wanted to help others the way she helped Biterna, where I'm from. She said there were negotiations going on and she was..." He gasped, eyes darting around as people leaned forward and others let their hands drift toward weapons. "Manipulation. To open trade routes. But she lied to me. I'm so sorry. She sent me here to spy on you, but I had no idea. I can't do this. Let me help you, please. Tollar's right, Karthiry means to control trade and resources, to push inland, and Upalint is her next target."

He paused, still watching Tollar, her silver gaze honed in on him. He was at her mercy. But there was no other way.

19

Tollar stared at the spy, or whatever he was, a pot-bellied young man with reddish brown skin and messy brown hair and the shadow of a beard on his face. A little shorter than Beenala and unassuming. Trembling. Fidgeting with his lenses. She tried to let his words sink in. Her heart raced. He didn't deny any of it. Said it was worse than they thought. Her body twanged. The room was the water rushing from the shore before a great wave.

It would break soon. She had to stop it.

"I appreciate your courage." She forced calm steps as she approached him. "How is it worse? It seems dire enough."

She cast a glance at Solia who flanked the spy. Was he still a spy if he revealed himself? No matter, Solia was grim-faced but hadn't gone for her weapons. Hopefully she was having the same thoughts Tollar was.

If this was really what it looked like, they needed him. Alive.

"I'm sorry." His whispered prime broke down. He trembled and clutched the strap of his satchel, muttering apologies as much to himself as to her, slipping out of prime and into a dialect close enough to Upalan that she mostly understood him.

"You're a civilian? From Biterna?" She switched to prime and slowed down.

He nodded, trying to watch her and stare at his shoes at the same time. She spread her hands out, away from her weapons, gliding slowly toward him. Tollar glanced at Beenala, sitting rigidly and gripping her cup. Tollar wished she could remind her to breathe.

"What didn't you know?" Tollar asked him. "Why are you sorry?"

"She lied. Karthiry." He clung to the strap of his bag. "She said we were coming here to help your people but that you didn't want help, no matter how much you needed it. I was sent here to get more information. I've been here two weeks and what I've seen doesn't add up with what Karthiry told me. I—she said we were helping Port Sawulxo. I don't know what's true anymore. I don't know what to do."

"Well, this is a step in the right direction," Solia said. She wasn't looking at this man, but at everyone else. No one had moved since he stood up, though there was plenty of whispering in angry tones.

"What's your name?" Tollar asked. "Your real one, not the name she gave you to lie."

His trembling eased. "I'm Draminedes, I worked the trade port on the big island in Biterna until the ships started hiring aquamancers and got faster, and they didn't need to stop with us anymore."

"And then this Karthiry showed up and made it all better?"

"She—no." He blinked, startled. "She made promises. There are others that command her, some king far to the north, I think. She makes promises from him. I don't think she's kept many. But she lies so much—I'm just seeing now."

"Aye, Biterna," Croves said, coming closer. "Loch took me and Shell after that, but the others were supposed to attack there after they left Lorinees, but turns out they didn't need that sort of persuasion. So they festered in pens in Meeri Bay for over a year until it was time to head for Port Sawulxo."

"I'm sorry," Draminedes whispered, staring at his own feet.

Tollar and Solia met gazes; Solia grunted and Tollar nodded.

"All right, Draminedes," Solia said. "You tell us what you know. Tell my friend Saivyn how much oxshit we're in, and then we'll see what kind of mercy we can offer you, if any."

Saivyn got half a shouted curse out before Tollar pulled the water out of his cup and shoved it down his throat. Beenala gasped. Chairs scraped the floor, though no one stood. When his coughing fit died down, he glared at her.

"That was a warning," she said. "This is bigger than how much I can't stand you. Shut up and listen."

Tollar and Solia stood on either side of Draminedes and brought him over to where Tollar had been standing, where everyone could see and hear him.

"I'm sorry," he repeated. "I didn't know. But I should have seen." He took a deep breath and continued in halting prime. "What Tollar describes rings true. Karthiry seeks to destabilize, though she told us it's easier to help you that way. Get rid of the dragons first—isolate them so they can't help you later, but you can't help them either. This makes it easier to capture them for her army. Then she uses weather to disrupt food, make the locals turn on each other. Then, so she reasons, she comes in with her people and cleans it all up. Shows you how to be civilized and intelligent."

"So she used these tactics to divide the locals in Port Sawulxo?" Tollar asked.

"Yes. And she has begun here. You have been more resistant to her efforts. The dragons are gone, but your weather-mancers are stronger than she expected. A setback, she called it. She sent me here to figure out how to get around that setback. You are next. She comes here next."

Tollar sucked in a breath. Her skin prickled with cold, like she'd sunk to the bottom of the ocean's deepest abyss. She exhaled slowly.

"But the Nishram are between here and the coast," Saivyn said.

"There are people in the lands between Sawulxo and here?" Draminedes sounded truly perplexed.

"She doesn't know there's a whole nation full of people in those valleys?" Tollar asked.

Draminedes shook his head.

"They wouldn't offer much resistance," Solia said. "Easy enough to pretend it's all empty jungle. They have hunters but no warriors. If your estimate of numbers on the northerners is correct, I don't think the Nishram stand much of a chance on their own."

Tollar grumbled and turned away. This was supposed to have been a quick trip home: hand off the dragon egg, find new residents for the farm, visit Auntie and Beenala for a season and then be off on the next adventure.

Instead this was a catastrophe. And coming here, straight here. There'd be no hiding Bale, and they'd definitely want her back. Her head felt light, her body too heavy, her heart pounding. Tollar had to leave, just pack up with Bale and go. Looking around, desperate for an exit, she caught Beenala's terrified expression. Tollar sighed.

Couldn't leave.

"Draminedes, you're certain this woman you serve is sending her forces to Upalint next?"

He nodded. "Served. I cannot serve her any longer. But yes, that's why she sent me here. There are spies here, many of them. Wizards hiding in the hills to ruin your weather and silver-tongued plants in your guilds to lay blame. To convince your wizards that the swibs are ungrateful and convince swibs that the wizards aren't even trying or, worse, hoarding supplies and lying about the disasters as a cover."

Solia gasped.

"This is what you were telling me about when I got back," Tollar said to her.

"Next they will try to convince the wizards that the leaders know about the problems and don't care," Draminedes said.

"All right." Tollar looked from face to face around the room, trying to will one of them to give her answers. "All right. We know what we're dealing with. Weeping ancestors, we know."

And there was only one thing they could do. Only one thing *she* could do.

"So we must be ready. We need to fight."

Draminedes sat on the stairs behind her, hanging his head toward his knees and gasping. Beenala crouched next to him while Solia remained watchful with a hand on the hilt of her sword. Tollar set to pacing. Her heart kicked at her chest, and it made her want to go kick Saivyn right in the face.

Murmurs ran through the gathered crowd, people shuffled, voices catching angry edges. That wave wanted to break.

The chief, Metar, sat in the corner, looking shocked and afraid and confused. Nearly as round as she was tall—not that she was especially tall—her ochre skin was ashy right now, her black eyes bright with fear as she stroked her fingers along the thick braid she wore over her shoulder. She wasn't the strongest chief they could have, and Tollar had no doubt she'd be voted out next year, and that was if she even wanted to run again.

"Chief Metar, what do we do with the traitor?" Tollar asked.

Metar blinked and recoiled like Tollar had slapped her, clutching her braid. The risk of asking the woman was that she wouldn't make a decision, that she'd ask them for advice and Saivyn would jump in with murderous intent. But Tollar had seen plenty of young fools like Draminedes in her travels, following the promise of riches to bad ends. She believed him that he hadn't known the harm he was causing.

If she was right about this Karthiry person, then she was a master manipulator and Draminedes never stood a chance.

Metar opened her mouth, and Tollar braced for the wrong answer. "This is terrible," Metar said slowly, bewildered. "I don't want to believe any of it. But the similarities in divisions here and in Sawulxo can't be ignored and we need every advantage we can find. Including loose-lipped traitors. Captain Solia, are you equipped to handle this man?"

"Now wait—"

"The chief has spoken, Sai," Tollar snapped.

"Yes, your excellency, I can manage the situation," Solia said.

Draminedes sat on the stairs, clutching his head and rocking. Beenala was encouraging him to breathe, and speaking in her slow, broken prime to make sure he knew what was going on.

"All right, we use what information he has for us," Tollar said. "I gathered you here tonight to help Port Sawulxo and those dragons. That we're dealing with invaders targeting us doesn't change that. Are we ready for this?"

"And who in the name of the ancestors put you in charge?" Saivyn snapped.

"I did," Metar said, warning in her tone. "She has first-hand experience with the problems in the north and that knowledge is an advantage."

"She's barely a rank two!"

Metar, unexpectedly defiant, met Tollar's gaze. "I'll send a Keeper to you in the next few days."

Tollar's heart kicked again.

"What?" Saivyn's face went a very interesting shade of purple-brown, and he managed to stand even straighter.

"I have made my decision, Commander Saivyn, and we all need calmer minds and cooperation if we hope to fare better than Port Sawulxo. Having the similarities between here and there pointed out makes them much clearer, the divisions more artificial."

"We must combat those divisions," Solia said. "I've begun, we have plenty of work left ahead of us though."

"We need agreement here first," Tollar said. "It's not an accident that I asked for leaders from across the city's guilds. We have time to ease tensions between swibs and wizards, especially now that we know how they've been manufactured. And we must. I expect this Karthiry means to push south in the spring. We can't let her."

Tollar glanced at Draminedes, who clutched his satchel against his stomach, but watched her. He shrugged.

"That doesn't give us much time," Solia said.

"We need to move quickly. We need to be united. The divisions are artificial, to weaken us, and we need to remember that. When we fight each other, we win the battle for our enemies."

"So we start with an agreement of facts?" Solia asked.

"Yes." Tollar swept her gaze across the room as she spoke. "Can we agree to what I've said, what Croves and Draminedes have said? That we are under attack from a cunning enemy that uses dragons to bad ends and that we must set aside grievances to mobilize."

Some positive murmuring, but a lot of sour faces too.

"Even if this is all a coincidence, it's in our best interest to treat this seriously," Drigoras, head of athletics, said. They were short, slender, lean, with bright blue eyes and long flaxen hair in a single thick braid. "Isn't it better to be prepared for enemies that never show than to be unprepared for the ones at our door?"

That got slightly more enthusiasm out of the others.

"I agree," Tollar said. "We must put an end to infiltrators trying to drive us apart, and we must repair the damage they've already done. We need to make sure everyone in Upalint knows what's coming and start preparing them. It will take many channels of communication. Balipar, do you think you can work with Shell and Croves and see if our situation with the dragons can be improved?"

"I'll see what I can do." They bowed slightly. Anything more and the massive green hat they wore would tip them right over.

"Even if the dragons don't want to help us directly, maybe they can help their kin in Port Sawulxo? We have a common enemy, and freeing those dragons will improve our chances of stopping the advance and maybe driving them from the continent altogether."

"Are we really enough on our own?" Beenala asked, rising slowly from where she'd been sitting next to Draminedes. "Even if the dragons free their kin on the coast, the sheer numbers coming out of the north make for impossible odds. We must have other allies. What if we appeal to the Wizards Guild? Surely this Karthiry is breaking convention and they can intervene?"

"The Guild has been useless," Croves spat. "They knew of this threat long before it reached the southern coast, and they've been cowards in the face of that golden king and his pet aquamancers, Loch and Karthiry."

Beenala pressed her lips together and sat down, but others also voiced similar concerns, suggestions of calling for aid.

"We can't rely on outside help," Solia said.

"We still reach out to everyone we can," Metar added. "I will begin with what contacts I have, and I will talk to our Guild representative about appealing to the wizards for aid."

"In the meantime, we need to extend our messaging among our groups and to the wider public. Especially if we don't get outside help, it will take every last one of us to defend what we love."

"This is a matter for the living," Toresona said from the side of the room, standing for the first time. Tollar hadn't noticed her and hadn't thought she'd come.

"Yes, Wise Mother, but are you not yet alive?"

"Don't insult me with your insolence, girl."

A hot spike burst down Tollar's spine, and she clenched her fists.

"Then don't be such a coward, Wise Mother," Tollar snapped, ignoring the gasps from the crowd. "You could raise an entire army of the dead to help us."

"The dead have earned their peace and that shall remain my focus." And with that she walked out, flanked by two acolytes.

Tollar's mouth fell open as she watched them go. Did they really not see the danger? The need for action? She spun to face Solia, glanced at the chief. While Metar's decision was final, she had no jurisdiction over the necromancers who were almost utterly separate from the rest of society.

"Well, that means we need everyone else even more," Tollar said. "So we must continue expanding our exchanges with circulars so we can halt the divisions between the elementals and everyone else."

"There are legitimate grievances between those groups," Saivyn said. "You can't just wish it away."

"We'll give them space to air grievances, but it needs to be a priority that we set those aside for now and work together."

"Swibs around here have been made to feel inferior."

"Based on lies playing on their fears."

"The shortages are real, no matter who's to blame."

"Yes, but everyone will have far graver concerns if we don't stop these northerners. I'll get Croves's and the traitor's help to paint a good picture for everyone of just what that will look like."

"She won't share power. She won't negotiate." Draminedes stood. "She won't try to understand your differences and will force you to conform to what she thinks is right. She thinks your farming practices are primitive, and she will convert your land."

"Is that why they're cutting down the jungle around Port Sawulxo?" Tollar asked, aghast.

"That was to make access for mining. There's something in the ground there that she wants—gold, I think."

Solia growled. "So she comes to plunder."

"The people I saw in Port Sawulxo are being stripped of dignity," Tollar said. "I don't think it's just the land she's coming for. She's already collected spoils of war along the way." She gestured to Croves.

"She believes you're all beneath her," Draminedes said. "That *we're* all beneath her."

"All right. So we start with disseminating information," Tollar said. "Everyone needs to know what we're up against. Solia can get word to the rest of the guard, Saivyn can brief his people, I'll help you with the athletics division," she said to Drigoras.

"I'll talk to the artist's collective," Beenala said.

A young woman sitting near the front stood. "I'm a teacher. I'll work with you to plan some new lessons I can teach the children about what's been going on. Sometimes that's how new information best spreads, from children up into their families and out into their neighbourhoods."

Tollar nodded. "Thank you. This is where we start."

"That's your plan then?" Saivyn snarled.

"It's the *start*. Most of this is as new to me as it is to you. We need a solid base if we hope to stop the invasion and help our neighbours. I can work with you on the specifics of that, but I think everyone's got enough to worry about for one night."

Saivyn scoffed.

"What?" she demanded. "After everything you've heard tonight, do you still believe this is more of my nonsense?"

"You're still on it about the port. Never focused on home."

She took a steadying breath. "We help our home by helping our neighbours. Saivyn, we can't leave them to this fate. To the northerners growing stronger at their expense."

"We expose ourselves to danger if we stretch too thin helping every last soul who falls on hard times. This is a matter for the military, not some greedy thug with no loyalties."

"Do you think I'm rolling in gold?" Tollar let threat edge her words. "That I'm like some bloated northern king lounging on a dragon's worth of jewels?"

Saivyn's scowl deepened.

"No one is paying me to be here right now." She took an angry step his way. "If I had no loyalty, I'd be gone already."

"Oh yes, let's give Tollar an icee for not turning tail and running this time. But she sure is quick to sacrifice our homeland for others and side with a confessed traitor!"

Saivyn shouldered through the crowd toward her, flipping from a gripping tool to a blade for a hand, and she dropped her hand to the blade on her hip.

"If you used your pebble brain for a minute, you'd put together that the man confessed at all because he wishes to do the right thing. What does he gain from this?"

Saivyn drew so close she smelled the pickled fish he'd had for dinner and saw the vein throbbing at his temple.

"A fool like you would believe such a ridiculous story. He's a traitor to us or to them. Or both. These people are slipperier than you'll ever know. He's probably telling you exactly what he was supposed to say. Probably giving you information that sounds right but sets us up for a waiting trap. You would take the bait. Metar can give you all the rank stripes she wants. Cover your whole damn head with them. You still haven't got a lick of sense and it will be our undoing."

"You speak ill of my stripes but it's beyond me how a frogging coward like you got any at all!"

Saivyn threw a punch at her head, but Tollar's only surprise was that he hadn't tried to hit her sooner. She caught his wrist, pivoted and used his momentum to throw him into a forward roll. Voices roared around her and, while keeping her focus on Saivyn, she extended her senses out into the room.

Solia had Metar at the stairs with Beenala and Draminedes, a couple of city guards with her. The rest dealing with the few warriors who'd come with Saivyn, and keeping people back. Croves had moved to the edge of the fight.

Saivyn rolled to his feet and charged at her, and it really was too bad he always let his rage cloud his judgment like this. She ducked under his arms and kicked his legs out from under him.

"Saivyn, stop it! This is exactly what they want."

He roared to his feet and kicked at her gut. She pivoted to catch his leg, tipping it up and driving him into the floor.

She backed away, not even getting her pulse up while he lay on his back, panting. Hoping he would see the folly in starting a fistfight with her was asking too much, even after she'd learned from world-class warriors all over the planet since the last time she'd kicked his ass.

But he was too proud, never having forgiven her for not letting him beat her, even once, in training when she was a teen.

"You're playing right into their hands, Sai. I'm not the one whose actions will doom us all. Where's your sense!"

"I'm not the one aligning myself with a Pit-damned traitor!"

"Who *are* you aligning yourself with exactly?"

"Upalint, not that I expect you to understand loyalty."

On his feet again, he rotated the blade perpendicular to his arm. She left her dagger where it was and put on a bored expression, because an angry Saivyn was a careless—and easily beaten—Saivyn.

The attack was a sloppy, wide open overhead stab, metal wrist easily caught. He'd learned something about fighting her because he got his hand around her throat before she threw him again. She slammed the heel of her free hand into his elbow, knocking the prosthetic loose. Releasing his wrist, she slammed the other hand into his other bicep so he let go of her. Her first hand was already on the move, slamming into his nose.

Not trusting that a broken face was enough to stop him, she kicked out the inside of his knee. Not enough to break it, but enough to have him on the floor.

"We need to be united," she said, her tone plaintive.

"I'm not listening to another word of this."

Saivyn staggered to his feet, adjusting his arm, and limped for the door, somehow still achieving ramrod posture.

"We can't stop them without you."

"I can't stop them *with* you!"

Then he was gone, the door slamming behind him and the group of warriors he'd come in with. The room fell into silence, taut and waiting, too many eyes on Draminedes.

"Well, that went better than expected." Tollar waved dismissively and looked at Solia. She pressed her mouth to a thin line. Beenala was on the stairs, her hands covering her face.

"I'll talk to this one," Solia gestured to Draminedes. "Then I'll talk to Sai. It'll go over better coming from me. It was a good effort, but he was never going to listen to you, Tollar."

"What do we do without warriors?" Drizoras asked, panic in their tone.

"The warriors won't leave us defenseless," Solia said. "This is a shock for everyone. Saivyn needs more time to let it sink in."

"What if Saivyn is right about this traitor?" Metar asked.

"I will evaluate him further, your excellency. We'll give him opportunity to prove himself, and keep close watch of him."

"I can give you some of the plants in your midst," Draminedes said.

"I leave it in your hands, Solia. You know the consequences of failure."

Solia bowed respectfully.

"There aren't enough of us, even if Solia convinces Saivyn," Drigoras said.

"We'll make it enough. And Beenala's right, we should appeal for outside aid. We shouldn't count on it, but we talk to the Guild and we talk to the dragons, and once Solia gets Saivyn on board, he can talk to his people in the Nishram. They may not be warriors, but they know their land better than anyone. And if that one is what he says he is," she gestured to Draminedes, "we can use him to send false information back to this woman Karthiry. Maybe we can lure her into a trap."

"All right, very good. That's enough for one night. Break out the casks. I'm taking this one upstairs for a few words." Solia gripped Draminedes's shoulder and ushered him up the stairs. "Your excellency, would you like to join us?"

"I trust your work, Captain. It's late and I've got an early start if I hope to begin addressing this in the morning."

Many people slipped out the door with Metar when she left, but the guards who were off duty pushed the tables into a more social arrangement and opened casks of wine and barrels of rum. Tollar was ready to drink herself into oblivion.

Or run and never look back.

But Upalint needed her. It needed her straight through until the spring. Straight through until they were all dead or the threat turned away. She'd fight for them. She couldn't not. She'd helped so many other places, this wasn't that different. But it ran the risk of her people really seeing her for who she was. For *what* she was. She might not be able to hold her magic back the way she liked, or let it run free the way she sometimes needed and not have to live with any judgement that came with it.

She'd never be able to return if they did.

But it was home, even if it wasn't always. Beenala was here, precarious on her lonely farm. What would happen to her if this got worse? If they couldn't stop the northerners at the port? She'd never leave, even to keep herself safe.

Tollar doubted there was enough rum in the world to get her through this.

She felt the approach a moment before a warm hand slipped into hers. Tollar smiled when she turned to Beenala and gently touched her dear friend's cheek. Some of the tension melted from Beenala's expression, but she was definitely holding her breath.

"Let it out." Tollar's smile spread. "And then take another one. Deeper than the last."

This earned a smile. And at least Beenala remembered to breathe. But her hand gripped Tollar's, the other hand tugging at the hem of her shirt.

"Did he hurt you?" She glanced at Tollar's neck.

"He's never come close in all the times he's tried."

"You're right, though. We need him."

"We'll be okay, Bee. I promise. It looks bad now, but we've got time. And you've got me, best aquamancer in the world. Probably."

Beenala rolled her eyes. But it was probably true. If anyone else had Tollar's kind of power, the Guild didn't know about them. And the Guild liked to know about any wizard with her kind of power. Now that they knew demon-hybrids like Tollar existed, they were looking for them.

"I'm glad you told me about that," Beenala said. "You should tell Solia. I doubt she'd mind knowing what kind of power she has on her side."

Tollar shook her head.

"You don't give yourself or the people around you enough credit."

"Home doesn't always mean much to me, but this is the only one that I've got. What am I supposed to do if everyone turns on me? Join those pyromancers in exile?"

"Saivyn may not see the worth in your knowledge and your power, but Solia does. She values your experience and your connections. Why do you think she let you take the lead on this?"

"So that if it all goes mango-shaped, she gets to keep her job and her rank lines."

"Those can be taken away?" Beenala's eyes widened, mouth hanging open.

"I understand it's not a fun ritual and I think involves some blood magic, but yes. A disastrously foolish decision can lose a warrior their rank."

"Blood magic?"

"Most of a human body is water. An aquamancer with the right training can do all sorts of things, including pull ink out of my skin."

Beenala's eyes widened. "Then you can do that sort of thing too."

"I wouldn't. Never tried. Don't want to."

"Even if it meant frog marching Saivyn around like the stiff arsehole he is?"

"Beenala!" Tollar closed her eyes and bit her lips to keep from laughing. "Yes, I could probably pull the blood around inside his body to make him do cartwheels." She shuddered. "I don't think I hate him enough to ever try though."

"Tollar, why does he think you do what you do for the pay?"

"You think I don't?"

"As you said, no one's paying you to be here. Well, I suppose Solia does when you let her put you on the guard roster. But that's not the same."

"Saivyn, and a lot of warriors, have certain ideas about warriors who don't stay home. It's ridiculous. I was always going to travel, why not do some good while I'm at it?"

Beenala gave her an appraising look. "You told me you take the most interesting jobs, not the highest paying ones."

"I got nothing but an accidental dragon egg out of my first trip to Port Sawulxo." Tollar sighed. Solia knew the truth about Tollar's travels, and that was okay. But did Tollar really need everyone else to know? Then again, only Beenala knew about Tollar being part demon.

"There's a reason Solia calls me a bleeding heart all the time."

Beenala gave her a sly look. "Tollar, are you in the business of being a hero?"

Tollar coughed. "Well, it's interesting. Cursed ancestors, Bee, that's enough. I need a drink. I need ten."

Beenala laughed as she walked off to get Tollar a drink. To see the way Beenala's face lit up, Tollar knew she had to find the middle ground. Maybe even find a way to stay like Beenala wanted. But for now Tollar wasn't going anywhere except to a war that might end them all.

Club leaders wanted to talk to her, gathering around now that she and Beenala were done having their moment, and she'd at least had time to put a new circular together, one with the basic facts. It would have to be updated. And she'd send them all a new one with more in a few days' time.

They didn't have enough to beat the invaders, not yet. But with luck, they would. And until then, she'd make do.

20

Beenala sat with her hands on the table and stared while Tollar chugged another mug of wine. At some point after seven mugs, Beenala stopped counting. She'd only had one cup herself.

"Tollar, are you going to be able to walk?"

"Mebbe not." She squinted at the mugs littering the table. "Can still make a wave."

"It'll be made out of wine at this rate."

"Pfft, we drink like this ev'ry night in the caravans."

"You're not in a caravan, Toll."

"Pfft."

"Are you okay?"

"Bit scared." Tollar bit her lips and scowled like she did when she'd gone and said more than she meant to.

"Why don't we go home? I've got more wine at the cottage. You can drink all you like where it doesn't matter where you pass out. I'm not carrying you home."

"Slept on the floor here b'fore."

"That might not be the best idea tonight. And Bale will worry if you're not home. In fact, she's probably starting to worry already. We really should get back."

"Shit," Tollar muttered. "Yes, fine, all right, let's go home."

Tollar pushed her chair back suddenly and sprang to her feet, swaying, and Beenala rushed to her side, ready to brace her if she tipped over. But Tollar adjusted her stance and got her bearing.

"Oh shit." Tollar's expression cleared. Beenala hated it when Tollar said those two particular words together in that particular tone because it always led to something she simply did not want to deal with. She followed Tollar's gaze. Solia came down the stairs with an ashy looking Draminedes, still clutching his bag.

"They'll eat him alive." Tollar gestured to a table full of off-duty guards. They glared at Draminedes, all of them slowly reaching for weapons.

Tollar was on the move, faster than someone who was probably ninety percent wine at this point had any right to move, and heading for Solia and Draminedes. Beenala hurried to catch up.

"Solia, where you keeping him?"

"Plenty of room here." Solia stuffed a fresh cigar in her mouth and hunted around for her flint.

"Oh really?" Tollar jerked her thumb at the table full of hostiles.

"Oh shit."

"You gonna stay here all night to watch him? Only way he'll live to see another sunrise. Unless you don't want him to see another sunrise?"

"I would especially like to see another sunrise."

At least, Beenala was pretty sure that was what he said, though between his accent and her poor grip on prime, she couldn't always understand him.

"I'm not letting them gut him," Solia growled. "Cursed ancestors!" Solia glanced around, the cigar disappearing into her pocket. The off-duty guards remained at their table, deep in their cups but hands on weapons.

"So I was right about him?" Tollar asked.

"Probably, shut up." Solia scowled around the room like the solution was hidden on one of the walls.

"Look, I'm far enough out of town to barely make it worth the trip for them, and I've got a dragon lurking around."

"You do?" Draminedes gasped.

Did Tollar just...? Beenala's eyes widened before she clenched her jaw.

"You let anyone else know that and no more sunrises for you." Tollar's voice was edged with threat. "I don't know where he's been staying, but he can't stay there anymore, and he can't stay here with you. And I've been thinking that if there are more like him—but better at what they do, no offense—then we should probably let him continue on like nothing's changed."

"He gave me some names," Solia said.

"I don't know who they all are," he said.

"We'll worry about that later, I'm sure. Bee needs sleep. I need another drink. You need to live to see tomorrow. We can all do those things out at my farm where my dragon will eat anyone who disagrees. Can we then?"

"Toll, no!" Beenala blurted. "I don't want him around!"

"Well, you stay in your cottage, then. We need him alive. He might need to keep playing a certain role, so he can't go with Solia. Do you have any other suggestions?"

"What about the chief?"

"That's not any better than bringing him to my house," Solia said. She looked at Draminedes. "You want to go with them? At least for the night, until I can get my people settled down."

"Whatever you think gets me more sunrises."

Tollar chuckled.

Beenala couldn't believe what she was hearing, that Tollar had told this possible traitor about their secret dragon and wanted him at her farm. How drunk was she?

"I'll bring him to the edge of town after we get the rest of his things," Solia said. "Near Salty's?"

Tollar saluted and did a clumsy about-face that almost knocked Beenala right over.

"I'm not waiting for him, and I'm not carrying you home," Beenala snapped, finding the door and heading for it.

Tollar was right behind her, and the four of them spilled out into the night, parting ways outside the guard house.

"What was that? Inviting a strange man to your house?"

Tollar shrugged. "There's lots of space as long as he doesn't mind the floor. And he'd probably sleep in goat shit right now if it meant no one kills him in his sleep. We'll need every last pair of hands if we're going to avoid ending up like Sawulxo."

Tollar seemed sure-footed out in the fresh air, but Beenala couldn't ignore how much she drank tonight. They walked in silence until the glow of Salty's inn lit up the lane, little lights hanging from the limbs of the banobi tree Salty and his inn called home.

Tollar slipped into the shadows around the side of the tree, right next to one of the windows and leaned against the bark. Beenala stepped in next to her, though she really wanted to keep walking.

"Have you really got more wine at home?" Tollar asked. "Or were you trying to trick me into making good life choices?"

"Yes."

Tollar sighed theatrically.

Beenala crossed her arms and leaned closer, her face only inches from Tollar's so she could meet her gaze in the darkness.

"What is this? What are you trying to bury?"

Tollar took a deep breath and let it all out in a groan, rubbing her hands over her face and leaning her head back. She closed her eyes, and Beenala half thought she would ignore the question and pass out on her feet.

"I've seen this before, Bee. Nothing quite to this scale, but I've seen neighbours in spats—one has something the other wants and the other is bigger and stronger and stops playing nice. It's bad. It's ugly. No one wins this sort of thing." She sighed. "It's hard enough seeing it happen to strange people in faraway lands."

"Oh." Cold spread across Beenala's limbs. "You don't think we can stop them?"

"I don't know yet. I thought we would just go free some dragons and call it a day. Now? If Dram is right, this woman he's been answering to has plowed over half the world."

"All the more reason to stop her."

"Yes. But it's more the challenge too."

"But she doesn't have a half-demon elemental." Beenala rubbed her arms and tried to breathe evenly. "Say, do you think the Guild would send that family of pyromancers? We should ask them."

Tollar snorted and pushed away from the tree.

"No really. Pyromancers as strong as you with a few dragons? That would be something!"

"I suppose so. I guess we'll see what the Guild says. But they've failed to stop whatever this was from leaving their primary lands in the first place. They barely think of us here at the *bottom* of the world."

"Bottom, hmpf." Beenala crossed her arms.

"Yes, well."

Tollar stepped into the road, startling Solia and Draminedes who were approaching the inn. Solia had been able to enjoy her cigar, barely a nub left of it while smoke curled languidly around her head.

"How many of those you had tonight?" Tollar asked, gesturing to the cigar.

"Third one," Solia grumbled. "Might not be enough of these in the world to get me through this mess."

"Any trouble getting here?" Tollar asked.

"Couple of the lads tried to follow us," Solia said. "I set them right. Don't think anyone knows where he's headed now. Keep him out there a few days. One or the other of you keep an eye on him. I don't want him leaving until I get some of this sorted out."

"Eh, no problem! If he gets out of line we'll feed him to Bale. She's getting tired of fish and monkeys."

Draminedes stammered in his language, a couple of words in prime jumbled in.

"She's got a terrible sense of humour," Beenala said to him. "No one will feed you to the dragon."

"As long as he is what he says he is," Tollar added. "Come along then, Dram. Before someone spots you and gets the wrong idea. I want to drink, not fight. Let's go."

Tollar kept her pace steady but slower than usual, and Beenala walked close beside her, wishing they didn't have Draminedes trailing behind them. She wanted to talk candidly. Wanted to know that they would be okay. That Tollar wouldn't go frogging off again if it got hard—Beenala had seen the caged look in her eyes as she realized what they were up against. Wanted to know that the things she'd said out in the wilderness held.

Was this really home for Tollar? Since they returned, she hadn't said anything about finding new caretakers for her farm, but it had only been a few days, and there'd been this meeting to plan.

And Beenala had just been too relieved to be home, to where her ancestors lingered and where she knew what day it was, to think much about the port or what they'd seen there.

Beenala had wanted more from that journey, to give Tollar the help she needed. And it had seemed so possible at first, lighting fires and finding food. Lurking around to find Chalky had been easy, and the trip had given her her first view of the ocean, sparkling and vast and endless. She'd thought she could be brave for Tollar. Instead she'd screamed like a child and jumped off the dragon the first chance she got to distract Tollar from her mission of freeing other dragons and then had frozen when she probably could have done something with the fire to distract those five other dragons. It was hard to admit, but Tollar probably would have gotten another dragon or two freed if Beenala had handled herself better.

She had *wanted* to do so much more. To protect Bale. To help Tollar.

When it came right down to it, she wanted to impress Tollar. It was ridiculous.

They rounded the bend in the road, at last, and came up the gentle slope to their pair of farms, the warm glow of a bonfire behind the house and the dark, glistening shape of Bale sleeping in the middle of it.

The little dragon hadn't slept in fire the whole time they were away, but came home exhausted, awake only to eat and then sleeping in fire the rest of the time. Croves, who left Shell with Bale through the day so he could spend time with Balipar and figure out his next course of action, said it was normal for Bale to sleep so much after the trying journey they'd had.

It was a lot, he said, for a dragon who'd recently learned to fly.

He and Shell were likely up somewhere near the top of Mount Acrintaga or somewhere deeper in the Naldes, where they stayed through the night. A few people noticed Shell flying low over the mountaintops, but he came down to hunt gezars and to go with Croves to the city to meet with Balipar and some of the wizards, and to care for the dragon egg they had hidden in the dragon hall of the chief's manor.

From what Beenala overheard, Balipar and Croves were trying to get a couple of other dragons to come out and help Croves and Shell bring the egg north to the dragon city.

"Bale! We've got a new friend?"

"Friend?" she said in her soft, hissing voice. She rolled to her feet and stretched her neck forward as they approached.

"It talks?" Draminedes stammered.

"*She* talks," Beenala said.

"Many of them do," Tollar added. "Shell doesn't, that's the one you maybe saw flying around earlier? He sticks with Croves. But he comes out here sometimes to teach Bale how to be a dragon. Which is a relief because I'm a shit mother."

"You raised her?"

"I stole her egg from your people in Port Sawulxo. Karthiry probably stole the egg after she killed Bale's parents. Bale went and hatched before I could return her to her kin. She wants to stay with us and, well, who argues with dragons?"

Tollar turned to Bale. "Come say hello! This is Draminedes. He's not for eating. Yet."

"Yet!" Bale chirped, showing teeth in her terrible grin.

"Ugh," Beenala said. Bale's sense of humour was every bit as bad as Tollar's. "You're a terrible influence on her."

"Yet?" Draminedes protested.

"No one's feeding you to dragons," Beenala said. Again.

"We'll see," Tollar said. "Just making sure he understands the situation and what the consequences are if he somehow snuck a few lies past Solia. Come on, then, Dram, let me show you around."

Beenala scowled some more.

Tollar waved into the dark. "Beenala's cottage is just over that way. My house is this one. Not much, you'll have to sleep on the floor and eat rations or whatever you can grab from the forest."

"Well," he said slowly. "I'm sure it's better than being fed to dragons."

Tollar gave him a wicked grin. "You understand what our forests are? I've seen what people like Karthiry call farms. Disgraceful."

"Yes... I've noticed the differences. It makes me wonder if, perhaps, Karthiry is driven by fear? If it was simply greed, she would adopt some of your practices. Your forests clearly have better yields than I've seen anywhere else."

"Ach, I don't want to talk about her. Bee, didn't you promise me some wine?"

Beenala rolled her eyes. "Tollar, it's the middle of the night. Shouldn't we just all go to sleep?"

"I'm not drunk enough for sleep."

Beenala lit the lanterns as they all came through the door.

"None of those magic lamps here?" Draminedes asked.

"Magic lamps?" Beenala said.

"Oh, the lights? No, most of the farms don't have those," Tollar said. "I forget most people haven't figured out how that works yet. Anyway, the power goes into the city, though I heard one of the inventors has something that might solve things out here."

Beenala had heard vaguely of an invention that would bring the lights out to the farms, but she was quite content with her fire lamps. Tollar showed Draminedes around, mostly by way of explaining what all the empty rooms used to be. She also made a show of rummaging through his things to make sure he didn't have secret weapons he planned to kill her with in the night.

"Look, I'm keeping you alive because it's the right thing to do, not because we're friends or I trust you or anything."

Draminedes looked pale again, but nodded. Beenala was relieved to hear Tollar talking some sense and taking even the smallest of precautions.

"All right, yes. I think I'd like rest," he said. "If that one used to be a bedroom," he pointed, "then I'm sure it will do."

"Eh, stay wherever. I sleep out here." She gestured around the main room that had once been the family's main living quarter, just off the kitchen. Some of Tollar's things hung from the beams but mostly it was neatly packed in her kit leaning against the far wall, her sleeping mat spread out next to it, near the hammock.

Draminedes picked up one of the lanterns and went into the nearest bedroom.

"I don't like this," Beenala said. Draminedes seemed terrified enough, but it was reasonable to suspect that was an act.

And Beenala's thoughts were overtaken by Tollar's story about the pretty man she'd kissed. Tollar's auntie, more like Beenala than Tollar, had never bothered with it and had done well on her own most of her life. A few special people came and went. It worked perfectly for her. Beenala assumed she was like Auntie, more inclined to be solitary. Tollar, though, was special. There had been an emptiness in Beenala's life on the farm that she hadn't felt even once since Tollar's return.

And it wasn't even that Beenala wanted Tollar kissing her or anything foolish like that, but she didn't like the thought of Tollar kissing *anyone*. Which she knew was ridiculous. But here she was. If she was being honest with herself, this jealous streak had started when Tollar told her when they got home that Croves had initially been aggressively flirting with her. Beenala hadn't seen it and Tollar insisted she'd turned him down.

"It'll be all right, Bee. You're tired. We're all tired. Just go get some rest. You don't have to bring me more wine. I'll come get it in the morning."

"Toll!"

"Fine, I should probably go to the market and buy more supplies anyway. I'll pick up adequate drink while I'm at it."

Beenala rolled her eyes and stayed rooted in the doorway.

"What's gotten into you?" Tollar asked.

Draminedes cleared his throat from the bedroom doorway. "I don't mean to be out of line, but I understand the two of you are more than friends?"

Beenala's face grew so hot she nearly checked for fire.

"It's complicated at the moment," Tollar said, "but you could say that, yes."

"Beenala, if it will set you at ease, Tollar is not the type of person I tend to find attractive. She's too... *she*."

"I see," Beenala said, her voice small and strangled, her limbs cold and jangly. She stared at the space between her feet and Tollar's.

Draminedes disappeared back into the bedroom.

"See? Nothing to worry about." Tollar bent to meet Beenala's gaze. Took both her hands. "All these years and you're going to stop trusting me now?"

Beenala cleared her throat but didn't have any words, glancing around the room so she wouldn't have to look Tollar in the eyes. Wanting to run, but also wanting to stay rooted where she was, with her hands in Tollar's all night long. The one thing she didn't like about being home was not sleeping under a dragon wing with Tollar, hand in hand well into the night.

"It doesn't matter what he is or what he wants—only one person I'm interested in that sort of thing with these days." She gave Beenala a significant look, and the heat in Beenala's cheeks spread all the way to her toes.

"But not right now," Beenala squeaked out, meeting Tollar's gaze with wide eyes.

Tollar's silver irises glittered with amusement and fondness. Beenala lost herself in Tollar's eyes, bottomless like the ocean.

She cupped Beenala's cheek in her hand.

"No, now's not the time," Tollar agreed. Her smile faltered. "I almost left. You saw it, I know you did. But you won't leave here and I won't leave you. Promise."

Beenala swallowed, the hot feeling spread right up into the tips of her ears.

"I'll see you in the morning?"

Beenala wanted to stay rooted to the spot, but Tollar's hand on her face was too warm, and her heart buzzed like a cicada in her chest. "Yes, of course." She took a step back. "Good night, Toll."

Tollar bid her goodnight in return, but to Beenala's fleeing back. She'd already broken away, stumbling down the ramp and across the yard lit only by Bale's distant, fiery bed. Once she was well hidden by the dark, Beenala stopped and turned. Tollar remained in her doorway, watching out into the night, that same amused and fond smile on her face.

It made Beenala feel better and flustered her even more. She lit a tiny fire in the lantern on her belt, only bright enough not to trip or run straight into the hedge, and then she continued home.

She'd been plenty foolish enough for one evening, and there would be so much work to do tomorrow.

Beenala checked the door but Ash didn't want in, and it was early yet for her to return. There was no sign of Tollar or Bale or even Draminedes. Maybe she'd gone hunting with the dragon? Beenala thought she'd heard Shell come and go, but her bedroom didn't face Tollar's house so she couldn't be sure. Beenala looked around her kitchen, couldn't decide what to eat and went back to her room and lay down. She hadn't been able to get dressed because she couldn't decide what to wear, so she was still in her night robe.

Cold tension sat in the pit of her stomach, dragging her into a dark abyss. It had been like this after each of her siblings left.

Well, except that this was much worse.

She actually missed, for the first time in her life, the way her mother used to come in her room on days like this and snap out some kind of command. Someone else making the decisions made it easier.

But it was just her. And she'd been up far too late last night, even after finally getting home, so she only got out of bed in the first place because someone had to open the door for Ash. But the dog was no longer around to make decisions for her. And it shouldn't be this hard. She didn't know anyone else so bad at making simple decisions like what to wear. It wasn't like she had that many options. Most of her things were linen shorts and shirts in the same colour.

But there was that one dress. She probably wouldn't be wearing that today, but how would she know?

Someone knocked on the door.

Finally, a decision she couldn't ignore. Beenala pushed herself out of bed and toddled through the kitchen to the front door.

It was Tollar, neat and clean in a sleeveless, knee-length dress, loose and flowing, that was a stunning sky blue with blocky trim in fuchsia and marigold, her hair rippling in the breeze and not looking like she'd drank her weight in wine last night. Beenala forgot how to breathe again. The bright smile on Tollar's face vanished the instant she saw Beenala.

"Bee! What's going on? Are you feeling unwell?"

"I don't know what to do."

"Oh. ...oh! Well, I came to see if you want to come with me into town. Bale will keep an eye on Draminedes, and I've got to put together my next circular. Figure I should talk to Solia about that."

"Should I come?"

"Well, do you need to have some kind of farming day? Per Graza's boys and your sisters were quite thorough. There isn't anything that needs planting or pruning or harvesting or mulching, is there?"

"No, I suppose there isn't. I suppose I could come with you into town."

Tollar's smile returned. "So you think you can get dressed now? I'll tidy your kitchen and make you something to eat. You didn't eat, did you."

Beenala's cheeks grew hot, and that was answer enough for Tollar, who began knocking around in the pantry. Beenala retreated to her room. A day in town. Going to see Solia and possibly other clubs.

Beenala pulled on her clothes, washed her face and picked up her comb. Took one look at her hair in the mirror and put the comb back down. By now she smelled fried peppers and followed it into the kitchen. Ash was back, trotting along behind Tollar, who spooned some beans into the skillet with the peppers and eggs.

"I hope you don't mind that I made enough for two."

"What about Draminedes?"

"Pfft. I told him to go with Bale into the forest and forage what he could. I'll give him a safe place to sleep, but he's not eating my food when I've barely got any of it myself."

"You live on a farm."

"Yes, well, I have to pick my breakfast, he can do the same. Oh, by the way, I picked some extra this morning since my nami berries are finally ripe." Tollar pointed to a bowl on the table and got back to work.

"Thank you, Toll."

"Do you think it would be easier for you if I made you a list of what sort of days I'm expecting to have? Like, today's a talk to Solia forever day and tomorrow will probably be a writing day and the day after will be a visit every club until my eyes bleed day. Does that help you?"

"I... don't know?" Beenala caught herself twisting up the hem of her shirt and stopped.

"Well, anyway, that's my next few days. You're welcome to join me if you're having trouble deciding what kind of day it is for you."

"Thank you."

Tollar picked up one of the large corn wraps and laid it over the egg in the skillet, like a big edible lid, pressing it down.

"Have some berries! I had my fill while I was picking them."

Beenala sat in front of the bowl of berries and nibbled at them. Ash sat next to her, forlornly watching each berry disappear without dropping to the floor. They were tart, but big and juicy. Another day or two of ripening and they'd be irresistible. She scritched the dog's ears, ate berries and watched Tollar glide between the stove and the sink, tidying up as she promised she would, and the cold, tight feeling in Beenala's gut loosened.

"You always put everything away so precisely," Beenala said.

"Easier to find things again if everything's got a place. And I'm in the business of needing to find things in a hurry, so..."

"And that works for where you live, too? Not just for how you pack your kit or whatever when you're travelling?"

Tollar stopped with a stack of clean plates in her hands and faced Beenala.

"I've never really lived anywhere before. Not since I was a kid sharing a room with my sister who was probably even messier than you are." Tollar's grin was not unkind. "Anyway, I haven't got enough stuff to test the rule at my place, but it seems to be working fine on your cottage. Didn't even notice did you?"

Tollar gave her a sly grin.

Beenala noted that things seemed generally tidier since Tollar began visiting her regularly, but didn't realize there was any sort of logic to it.

"Well... all right. But if you touch my paints I might have to light you on fire."

Tollar laughed, put the stack of plates away, and got back to their breakfast. Though it was probably nearer to lunch for Tollar. Beenala had no idea how the woman could so consistently be up with or before the sun no matter what hour she went to bed.

By the time they finished eating, Beenala had a hard time remembering why getting out of bed had been so difficult in the first place. Packing her bag to head into the city, she felt nothing but relief at how good Tollar was at managing, well, everything.

Hopefully she stays this time.

The bright fabric on Beenala's bedside table caught her attention as she stuffed the last of a day's worth of needs into her bag. She'd been up so late finishing it... She might as well. Before she lost her nerve, she swiped up the bracelet and strode out into the kitchen where Tollar waited, *still* putting away dishes.

"Ready?"

"Just about." Beenala thrust out her hand, palm up. "I made this for you. The last one's gotten a bit... travel worn."

Tollar leaned over, looking down so Beenala couldn't see her expression, but she reverently picked up the bracelet, turning it over to look. Ash sat next to her, intent on the trinket, hoping it was a snack Tollar might drop.

"It's got that vine pattern from my sword... and your machete and Mammi's necklace."

Beenala went very still. Weaving together the scraps of bright fabric hadn't take long at all, but she'd spent hours painstakingly stitching the vines over the weave. "Is that okay?"

The design had been created by Beenala's great-grandfather and meant for his kin. Beenala had used it in her work, had made the necklace for Mammi—and similar jewellery for all of her siblings and her father.

And Abilerit had agreed to let her help when she found out he was crafting a blade for Tollar. He'd been showing her a bit of metalwork for years, not that she'd ever be able to do what he did. But before he'd put on the final treatment, he'd let Beenala put the braided vine pattern at the base of the blade where it joined the hilt.

But she couldn't tell Tollar that.

Tollar had her mouth drawn down to repress a smile, though her eyes shone.

"Thank you, Bee. It's perfect." Tollar held it out to her. "You'll have to help me get it on."

Beenala's fingers shook as she tightened the fiddly little ends together, Tollar choosing to wear it on the same wrist as the dingier original. Beenala half expected Tollar to wear both until they disintegrated.

"You really are a softy," Beenala said before her brain realized what her mouth was doing.

"Hush now." Tollar's grin spread and she patted Ash's head. "What will I do if people find out."

Beenala went with her out to the hedge and spotted Draminedes coming out of the trees, eating a banana and holding a basket filled with mangoes, nuts and berries, and a fish dangling from a line.

"Well, he's not so useless after all," Tollar said, heading over. Bale wasn't far behind him. "Did he behave himself?" she called.

"Didn't have to eat him," Bale said.

Draminedes stopped and stared wide-eyed between the two of them. Beenala rolled her eyes.

"He teaches me prime," Bale said, in prime. Beenala tried not to be jealous of the fact that the dragon was already better at the language than she was.

"Fantastic!" Tollar said. "Teach her your home language too. Balipar says that dragons can learn to speak all the languages of the world. Wouldn't that be something, Bale? Speak to people everywhere you go?"

"What about prime?" Beenala asked. "Isn't that good enough?"

"Not everyone speaks prime. You barely do and you live somewhere thick with trade. Isolated places, like where I got your fiery pigment, haven't even heard prime before."

"More language," Bale said, still in prime.

"She's going to speak it all day now, isn't she?" Beenala said.

"Maybe she can help you with it when we get back. Or you can work with Dram and learn to speak Biternan? It's not that much different from Upalan."

Beenala shot Draminedes a look. "Why? Is he staying here long?"

"I can't see how it's safe for him to go home while the northerners are still there. He might be out here a while."

Beenala didn't know why she'd liked him better when he was fully Solia's responsibility, and she should be more welcoming when it looked like the poor man, practically a boy, didn't have a home anymore. She still didn't like the idea of Tollar's house becoming his home.

Beenala felt cold. What if he kept Tollar's farm and she left, back to her nomadic lifestyle? Something would catch her fancy, and she'd be off to some place Beenala could never hope to follow her.

"It will be safe for him in the city, won't it?"

Tollar shrugged. "Depends on how people feel about him and whether those names he gave Solia amount to anything. It will take time to prove he's not a threat, and he needs somewhere safe until then."

"Safe, yes," Draminedes muttered. "Very safe with a dragon over my shoulder all the time."

"If you don't give her a reason to eat you, there's no safer place to be, really."

Draminedes went still and Beenala sighed.

"Anyway, we're going into town for a while," Tollar said. "You're better off out here for now. Both of you stay put so we don't have any trouble, all right?"

"I've got notes to arrange," Draminedes said. "Or burn."

"Keep them for now. Is there anything I can bring you from the market?"

He shook his head. "I can go back for more." He held up the basket. "Fill your pantry."

"That would be excellent." Tollar smiled. "Keep us from eating all of Beenala's stores. And anyway, Croves should be back with Shell before long, so they can keep you company."

Bale's flying had gotten truly impressive on the way home from Port Sawulxo, with Croves and his wind magic to help stabilize her and Shell to show her how to do it properly. Having the extra dragon around made Beenala nervous, but it was doing wonders for Bale. Shell was like a proper parent for her.

Shell wasn't hostile the way Minty had been, making him easier to tolerate. So here she was, getting uneasily used to having dragons around. Maybe she'd adjust to it all yet.

And maybe she could do more for Tollar, even if she didn't have to. She could contact her mentor, practice new things with fire magic, maybe practice getting more used to chaos. And she could keep trusting Tollar, safe in the knowledge that Tollar understood. That she knew what she was doing.

21

Beenala followed Tollar through the empty guard house, her stomach twisting to see it again so soon, and up to Solia's office, surprised when Tollar stopped to knock on the closed door.

"What?" Tollar said. "She hates to be interrupted."

Solia opened the door, a thin cloud of smoke hovering near the ceiling, and gestured them both in. Beenala took the chair and let Tollar pace.

"Your new guest behaving himself?"

"He's practically a baby," Tollar said. "Did you notice? Anyway, he's remained polite and tries to be useful, and while I don't quite trust him, it's hard not to believe he's sincere."

Solia nodded and sat with her hands folded on her desk. "I've got my best out tracking down the names he gave us. Till something comes of that, we'll keep quiet about him. We need a wider report of what happened in Sawulxo to go out though. People need to know what you saw."

Tollar leaned on Solia's desk. "Yes, but I think we need to do this carefully. Need to get the facts to the heads of the guilds, but I think the circulars that go public will need to be different for now. I think we'll need to ease them into it if we don't want to terrify them into inaction."

Solia stared ahead of her, expression grim. "We can't take too long. I have to convince Saivyn to call up his reserves and then to get more reserves. People who don't normally fight need to be ready."

"Um." Beenala forced her hands flat against her knees and let out the breath she held. "I can talk to the artist collective. They're not all daydreamers."

"You think they'll fight?" Tollar wandered off across the room.

"Some, yes. But art has its own kind of power, like the stories you wield in your circulars. They teach people—hermits like me who never leave home, never see much farther than the hills around the city—it shows us what's out there, gives us a view of life in strange lands. It's... illuminating. Everyone likes a good story. And the best stories tell you things you didn't know you needed to know. We can get the storytellers who perform in the square to tell some new stories. Get the poets writing something different."

Solia nodded. "The message doesn't have to be obvious to be understood."

"You're sure you can get enough of them working on this?" Tollar asked.

"We have our own internal communication." Beenala looked down at her hands. "We don't advertise it quite like some of the other guilds."

Tollar stopped pacing. "Wait, just how big is your collective?"

"It's a collective of guilds," Solia said. "I thought you knew? The weavers, the painters, the sculptors, the writers—so many different kinds of writers... To say nothing of the musicians. There's got to be a dozen guilds and they all communicate through the collective."

Tollar stared.

"We use our art for a lot." Beenala smiled.

"And that's what you should do with your wider circular," Solia said to Tollar, leaning forward. "A tall tale with the usual embellishments. Just show them what happened, what it was like. No message, not yet."

"So we don't let them know about this woman Dram's been answering to?"

"I'm not sure they'd believe it. Show what she's done, but don't connect her to it yet. Let your story sink in, then give it the villain. Give me some time to verify more of what we learned last night. Not just from Draminedes, but from Croves too."

Tollar paced with an angry swiftness to her steps that Beenala didn't like.

"We have to do this right," Beenala said gently.

"We don't have enough time," Tollar snapped, throwing her hands in the air.

"I know you want—"

The door burst open, the guard from downstairs rushing in, "Captain! Just got a runner with a message about trouble down at the elementals compound. A whole throng of swibs has the place surrounded."

"Shit!" She snuffed out her cigar. "Send the word back that I'm coming, and mobilize everyone left in the building."

Beenala stood up and stared from Solia to Tollar as the guard rushed out the door.

"I didn't think it was this bad," Tollar said. "Swibs attacking elementals? Is this really where we are?"

Solia shook her head and grabbed her sword belt from her desk.

Beenala rose slowly from the chair, every part of her body feeling electrified and like she might vomit.

"We deal with this quickly. I'll get Saivyn watching who's coming and going from the city. There's no way this is a coincidence. Someone must have said something about Draminedes, or maybe one of the other spies was there last night. I don't know how they got it escalate like this but—"

"Captain!" A new guard rushed down the hall. "It's the market! Been flooded half the morning, looks like the drainage backed up and..."

This new guard stopped in the doorway when he saw Solia already geared up and on her way out.

"Well," Tollar said. "There it is. They manufactured a new crisis. Dammit."

"Can you manage it?"

"Of course I can." Tollar looked at Beenala. "You staying here or coming with me?"

"With you," she squeaked, feeling small and out of her element. "Just don't ask me to help with it... I don't think—"

"It's fine, Bee. Fire magic won't help here anyway."

The two of them rushed downstairs and, as soon as they hit the stones outside the building, Tollar pulled water out of the drains, enough for a lift, and propelled them down the city streets on a sheet of water, weaving in and out between carts, cyclists, and pedestrians.

Halfway down the block, Beenala gripped onto Tollar's arm and closed her eyes. It made the rush of wind and the lurch of them tilting around obstacles worse, but at least it eased the sensation they were about to slam into something.

When Tollar stopped and Beenala opened her eyes, they were at the edge of the market square. They stayed up on Tollar's watery perch, though it was indistinguishable from the rest of the market and half the street. A group of elementals argued with each other and a group of vendors, all of them hip deep in water.

"Shit."

"Tollar, what are you going to do?"

"Fix it. It will make that lot look bad, but the swibs need to see something flashy or this will only get worse."

Tollar growled in wordless frustration, glaring at the scene, her brow furrowed and silver eyes darkening to slate.

"This is bad," she said quietly to Beenala. Then loud enough to carry over the din, "Eh! Whose mess is this, anyway? I can't leave you lot for one day without you destroying half the city."

As she spoke, she raised her arms, bringing herself forward on a pillar of water, leaving Beenala safe and dry in the side lane. Once she had everyone's attention, Tollar set the water swirling around them, gathering it to her pillar as it grew fatter and taller until the market was dry.

Beenala thought it took longer than it should have, but Tollar had been careful to put things back and dry out items to reduce the amount of damage left behind by the deluge.

"Why couldn't you do that?" one of the vendors shouted at the red-faced group of elementals.

"Eh, that's no way to talk to your neighbours!" Tollar snapped from her watery pedestal. "They did their best, but someone stronger than them manufactured this flood. Good thing someone stronger yet was on hand to help. What do you do when I'm away? Ha! And I know just what to do with this. And that's enough arguing out of you lot or I'll put all this frogging water back!"

The column rushed away and swept up Beenala with it as it went, funnelling her up to the top with Tollar, high up over many of the rooftops. She held her breath and squeezed her eyes shut.

"Tollar... Put me down."

"I'll set you somewhere safe near the compound. This is bad. I don't know who the aquamancers are who did that, but they were good. I'm better, obviously, but I don't like any of this."

"Why are we going to the compound?"

"Solia will need some help. And maybe a distraction."

"Well, you're good at one if not the other."

"Hey! I can leave you in a puddle you know."

Beenala smiled and tried not to be sick over the way the ground rushed by so far below.

And when she thought it couldn't get any worse, she spotted the size of the angry crowd outside the elementals compound.

"Oh no," she said.

"Oh shit," Tollar said.

She went and made it worse yet by leaving Beenala on a sturdy, fat branch, flat as a tabletop, on a nearby banobi tree and then sank down to the ground pushing the floodwater out ahead of her. It caught up everyone, guard and elemental and swib alike, even Solia.

"That's quite enough!" Tollar shouted, the water carrying her voice over the cries of anger and surprise by those getting swept up by the flood.

Swept up, but not sunk or swept away. Everyone floating. No, encased? The water was solid. Like ice but still water. And Tollar stormed across the top of it like she walked along the stone street, shouting at everyone much as she had in the market.

"You want your water? Here it is. Mess all cleaned up, no need to thank me! Except maybe to leave my colleagues alone!"

She repeated what she'd said in the market, that it was some kind of bad prank and she expected better of everyone and how dare they treat their neighbours like this and what ever would they do without her.

"At this rate I might not leave again! And then where will that get us? You keep me here long enough with this nonsense and someone's going to pull my name for chief and nobody wants that."

There was some nervous laughter, from swibs and elementals alike, though Beenala was certain Solia would have a lot of work cut out for her making sure this didn't blow up into something worse. Tollar was joking, being as non-threatening as possible considering she had over fifty people trapped in water.

And she got points for trapping everyone, not just the swibs causing the real problems. Levelling everyone would help. For now.

As Beenala watched from above, the water spread out, seeping away and carrying people with it, dispersing the crowd before letting them go, each one as dry as if they'd stepped out of a desert.

Finally, Tollar pulled Beenala out of the tree on another one of her water columns, and she joined the conversation in progress with Solia and a few of the head elementals.

"...had to, and I'm sorry about that. But we've got to keep a closer eye on the magic going on around here. It was a sophisticated spell that flooded the market," Tollar said.

"You made us look like fools!"

"Well, I guess next time I'll just let the swibs burn the place down. How's that?"

"Tollar," Solia warned. To the gathered elementals she said, "Look, the information is new, but someone is trying to cause trouble between swibs and wizards, especially elementals. As insufferable as she is, Tollar is the best aquamancer we've got. So anything weird happens with water, send for her immediately. Tollar, I want a report on that spell in the market. Best analysis you can give, and maybe we can get ahead of this before things get worse."

"Right, fine." Tollar turned to the gathered group of elementals with a sweeping gesture. "Which one of you wants credit for the report?"

Beenala smiled and stayed in the background. Leave it to Tollar to not take credit where she deserved it, but also, Beenala recognized the wisdom in it. Tensions wouldn't be eased if Tollar was perceived as the only elemental doing anything about the local water problems and food shortages. Not that anyone was starving. Just noticing things missing from the market, the variety beginning to drop.

It looked like Tollar and Solia had this one under control. But how long could that last? Her mind often drifted to what Chalky said about the violence between swibs and elementals.

How far was Nytaltek from looking like Port Sawulxo? And could they really do anything in the face of it, even with some warning? It was already bad. It would likely get worse.

But Tollar's jokes had people laughing. Maybe there was still hope. And still time.

22

Tollar hefted one end of the borrowed bed, Croves at the head of it, carting yet more furniture through the hedge from Beenala's house to Tollar's. Ash had been trotting along beside her, but Beenala and Draminedes had recently started preparing dinner and Tollar suspected the dog was waiting for snacks to fall to her.

They were halfway up the ramp when Tollar spotted Solia walking her bike up the lane toward the house.

"Eh, I'll get Dram to help me get this into the room," Croves said, having seen Solia too.

Tollar didn't go down the ramp, but took a seat in one of the hammock chairs on the veranda—the chairs borrowed from Beenala recently, along with two beds, a table, some chairs, pots, pans, dishes, and an assortment of cushions.

"You planning on living here then?" Solia said, making her slow way up the ramp and watching all the activity through one of the open windows.

"For now, at least." Tollar was still sleeping in the front room, but had the hammock across the back corner now, her kit and clothing moved to the side so that the front room could be a proper gathering place. There were still unoccupied bedrooms, but using one felt too permanent.

Solia shook her head, opened her mouth like she meant to say something, and took out a cigar instead.

"I read your report."

"Ah, is that what brings you out here?"

"You know how to counter that?"

Tollar shrugged. She should have seen it sooner, after the flooded valley she'd unflooded, since there were only a couple of ways to achieve spells of that magnitude. Really, it came down to using demons or to wizards harnessing each other. Or being demonborn like Tollar was, but that really just amounted to using demons in a way that apparently only four people in the world could.

So Karthiry's people were harnessing each other's magic. It was easy enough with a group of wizards, though the Guild only taught it to their most elite. Looked like Karthiry had taught it to a good number more than that.

"If we're going to counter it, we need a lot more people here who know how to do the same thing," Tollar said.

Solia sagged into the seat next to her and exhaled noisily, smoke pluming around her head.

"You need Guild approval for that?" she asked.

"I doubt Karthiry got Guild approval for it."

Solia sighed. "I'll talk to Cerro."

"Because he's been so helpful." Tollar bit out the words a little more harshly than she meant to. But with the last few days listening to Croves describe exactly all the times the Guild could have stopped Karthiry sooner and didn't, Tollar's opinion of the Guild got even worse.

Solia swung gently next to Tollar, staring out into the lengthening shadows, the warm air growing more humid.

"I think we need to be prepared for a lot of unconventional tactics if we hope to win," Solia said.

"They're certainly using plenty to overrun everyone."

"Can you teach our people this magic?"

"I don't know."

Solia gave her a hard look, the cigar held still on its way to Solia's mouth. "Your report made it sound like you knew how to do this."

"Well, yes, I've been taught to harness magic. I just don't know if I can teach anyone else how to do it."

"Figure it out." Solia took an angry drag from her cigar.

"I do have access to two talented wizards," Tollar said.

"Is the northerner staying long enough for it to make a difference?"

"Even if he doesn't, Bee will patiently sit through my experiments."

Solia grunted in agreement.

"But Croves isn't going until after the northern dragons come for that egg, and apparently that'll be weeks yet."

"It's not going to hatch on us, is it?" Solia gave her a startled glance.

"I expect if it was, they'd be in a bigger hurry to collect it. So Shell and Bale are going to stay up in the mountains, more dragon time for Bale to learn how to properly be a dragon. And Croves is going to hang around and help us as much as he can. Though he's about as eager as I am to figure out how to help the dragons and their riders still stuck in Port Sawulxo."

"One problem at a time."

"I don't think we've got that long."

"Right." Solia chuckled mirthlessly. "Seven problems at a time then."

They swayed in their chairs in heavy silence until Tollar finally asked, "Are you okay?"

"No one's okay. Nothing's okay."

Tollar nodded slowly. "Looks bleak right now. But if we can bring Saivyn and Toresona around, and I get a good number of our wizards harnessing..." Tollar shrugged. "We've got a chance."

"I don't like leaving it to chance."

"Yeah." Tollar sighed. "But there's still too much we don't know. We just need to prepare the best we can, and enjoy life while that's still possible. You want to stay for dinner?"

Solia glanced at her, puffed out some smoke. "Nah, Nolly's expecting me home."

"I picked up some excellent wine at the market," Tollar said. "Bring Nolly."

Solia gave her a tight smile, patted her arm and stood. "Thank you for the invitation."

Croves came out as Solia reached the bottom of the ramp. He gave her a polite wave as she got back on her bike and headed out, trailing smoke from the last stub of her cigar as she went.

"Well, that was pleasant," Tollar said. "You hear much of that?"

"Just the last bit." Croves plopped into the hammock chair Solia had just vacated. "I don't intend to be caught again." His voice had a hard edge to it.

Tollar nodded. "We'll all do what we need to. And for now, we've got some magic to work on."

"Harnessing?"

Croves and Beenala knew the contents of her report. She'd spoken about it with both of them before turning it in to Solia. Beenala had been utterly lost, but Croves knew the basics, he'd just never done it.

"I'll need your help with it. You and Bee. Does Bee need any help with dinner?"

"Nah, Dram's got it covered. It'll get a touch crowded with all of us in there."

Tollar smiled. Crowding had never stopped her siblings from meddling in preparations. That was before Zarro though.

"Solia only ever talks about her wife," Croves said, watching down the lane where Solia had vanished. "She's got a husband though too, don't she?"

"It's more like Nolly's got a husband and a wife. Solia doesn't have a whole lot to do with Arvanin."

"Huh."

"I know your people do it differently," Tollar said.

Croves snorted. "My people are idiots."

Tollar laughed. "It's not that bad. Bee's parents are like that. Just the two of them together their whole lives, no one else."

"Oh, aye, there's nothing wrong with havin' yer one special person. It's the part that that's the only thing we're allowed." Croves shook his head. "Just ain't enough for everyone. Wasn't for my pa. But goin' out and lookin' for what's gonna be enough is taboo. Him having a mistress was a huge shame on the whole lot of us—him, my ma, Raia's ma, even us kids." Croves shook his head.

"Ah, right. You'd mentioned having a sister."

"Half-sister. And a brother. Well, had a brother. Vik. Older than me. More reckless. It caught up with him six years ago."

"Sorry to hear that."

Croves shrugged. "It's just the way it is sometimes. My pa outlived my brother by three months, though I don't think news of Vik's death reached him before he went. I'm not even sure where he was. Raia's ma kept track. He left us all after the whole thing came out—when Raia's ma was pregnant, she came to us and he left us all. So she stayed with us so she and my ma could help each other raise us kids. It worked out, but we never got out from under that shame till us kids were adults and up and left too."

"That's the part that especially doesn't make sense to me," Tollar said. "That your father's actions affected the rest of you. Especially children with no control of the situation."

"I told ye my people are idiots." Croves had been staring out toward the river but he looked at her now. "I was married for a time, when I was younger."

Tollar met his gaze but he looked away again. She searched his arms and there was one scar on the back of his wrist, one among many, that she supposed could have been a northern marriage tattoo that had been crudely removed. She didn't know how those worked, but she'd thought there was a mark to indicate divorce. She supposed it made sense that Croves had opted out of the foolishness entirely instead.

"She was a fine lass, but one person ain't enough for me. When I realized it, I let her go. Couldn't bear causing the same pain my pa had. Least we hadn't gotten around to having babies."

"Ah, yes." Tollar nodded and glanced toward the mountains. "Children do have a way of complicating things, especially if you'd rather they not get hurt. My mother didn't have that particular concern."

"And that's why ye hate this place?" Croves jerked a thumb at the house behind them.

"Mostly, yes."

Tollar was still watching the mountains, thinking of Bale—her unlikely daughter. She knew Bale was safe with Shell, and likely the other two dragons were with them, but Tollar worried. Wondered where Bale was. Hoped she was happy. The dragons didn't check in often, now that they'd settled on primarily staying in the mountains.

She caught Croves watching her, a sparkle in his eye and a grin on his face.

"What?"

"Ye really are her ma, ain't ye?"

"I was there when she hatched! I fetched monkeys for her because she couldn't even walk yet. Of course I'm her mother. That green dragoness cannot stand it." Tollar smiled.

"Ye ever think ye might have some human kids?"

Tollar pressed her lips together, glancing at Beenala's cottage before letting her gaze focus on the river.

"I'd have to learn how to stay put. And, well, the clock is running out on that one."

Croves laughed. "Ye ain't that old yet. And ye got lots of help if ye ask for it. Having two mas worked out just fine for me."

"I think we need to get through whatever Karthiry has in store for us before I can put anymore thought into that."

"Aye. It'll be a rough year." He let out a long breath, touched her arm and turned to her. "I know ye got Bee and I'm happy that's working out for ye, but do ye got room for one more in that equation?"

Tollar stared. His flirting had been persistent but mild since their conversation after the port, so she hadn't realized he'd still had his eye on her in a serious capacity. She'd have to choose her next words carefully.

"Even if Beenala was fine with it—and I'm not even going to ask her—the things you want in a partner are not things I have to give." He opened his mouth to argue, and she pressed on before he could. "I value your companionship, and I'll stand at your side when battle comes our way, but Beenala is everything I need beyond friendship. Please don't ask again."

She cupped his cheek affectionately and then stood to go in. It had to be just about dinnertime. Croves, thankfully, did not argue and stayed outside until Draminedes fetched him once food was ready.

He and Beenala had prepared quite the spread, and Tollar wasn't sure how they'd possibly eat it all without help from one of the dragons. Ash trotted merrily around the table, her eyes gleaming. There was a tall stack of flatbread and five kinds of sauces for dipping, fried bread pockets filled with meat and vegetables—some kind of Biternan specialty Draminedes had made—fish wraps and bean salad and fruit salad and sliced cheeses and rice balls and stuffed mushrooms and tucked away on the counter for later were halved coconuts filled with Tollar's favourite sweet rice.

If Croves had been wounded by Tollar's response to his advances, he hid it well. Patted her shoulder as he passed her to take his seat. None of them spoke much while they ate, except several compliments to Dram for his bread pocket things, which were rich and well-spiced.

It turned out they didn't need a dragon to help them, as Croves ate at least as much as newly hatched Bale had. Draminedes teased him for it and blushed when Croves responded well to the joke.

"Good thing we've got two entire farms!" Tollar said.

The scraps that didn't get eaten by Croves got dropped to the dog. Once they'd finished their rice, Tollar pulled out the crate of wine from the back of a cupboard and set it in the middle of the table.

"Tollar, an entire crate? Really?" Beenala said.

Tollar pulled out one of the bottles and pointed it at Croves. "If he drinks the way he eats, I should have got three crates!"

That got another round of laughter, and Croves took the bottle from her, popping out the cork. He didn't bother with a glass.

"This one's mine." He grinned.

Tollar rolled her eyes and got another bottle out. Beenala got three glasses and they headed into the main room to sit on the expanse of cushions—Tollar between Croves and Beenala, Ash tucked in next to Beenala, and Draminedes off to the side.

"So what's your sister like?" Tollar asked Croves.

"Oh gods, she's a beast. About yer height and twice yer size and can probably drink us all into oblivion."

"I like her already."

His sister was a dragon rider too, it turned out. The stories he had about her and the other two in their group sounded like the wild adventures of pirates. Tollar told her favourite story about her and Jarku jumping off the house until he'd landed wrong and broke his arm. Beenala listened politely, all her siblings were very tame by comparison. Draminedes had a brother and a sister, both of them little monsters as children. His sister had routinely found all manner of awful critters to leave as surprises for her brothers. Beetles in shoes, lizards in sleeves, and one stunned mouse trapped in their brother's pillowcase that had left him screaming and refusing to sleep in his own bed for a week.

Croves let out a hearty laugh and draped his arm over Tollar's shoulder, the action tucking her in a little closer at his side. His big arm and huge embrace enveloped her in a way she hadn't thought possible. It was nice? She glanced up and met his eye for a moment, and something tugged inside her. She gave him a quick smile and turned back to Dram's story, which was about his brother now. She was trying to follow as he spoke quickly and excitedly, his prime slipping a little.

A moment later, when Croves removed his arm, Tollar managed to feel both relieved and disappointed. She stuffed that away to examine later. Much later. And squeezed Beenala's hand.

"And then he fell right out of the boat!" Draminedes said. "And scared away all the fish for a league, so our mother made him eat seaweed for days!"

Tollar toasted him and fetched another pair of bottles of wine—one for Croves and one for the rest of them as laughter filled the house.

"Come on, Bee, your siblings must have done *something* foolworthy," Tollar said.

Beenala fidgeted and pressed her lips together, while Ash plopped her head in Beenala's lap. "Well, there was the time Prixi, as a toddler, overheard Ballow cursing..." Beenala paused. "I don't know the word in prime, but—" and she used the Upalan vulgarity for fornicating.

Croves immediately provided the translation.

Beenala blushed and everyone else laughed.

"Anyway," Beenala continued, red-faced. "Prixi went around using that word at every opportunity for a week."

"Aye, Raia did the same when she was a wee lass. Vik taught her that same word in Prairiean." Croves gave them all the translation.

"Of course you'd know the word for sex in every language," Draminedes teased.

Croves winked. "Aye. Three words you need to know in every language. That one, the loo and the pub."

Tollar rolled her eyes.

Draminedes, for all his teasing, was more than happy to teach them all the Biternan curses that involved fornicating with inappropriate people and things. He even had one that involved a boat.

"Is... Is that even possible?" Beenala squeaked, her face pale.

She was answered with uproarious laughter that made the dog bark, while Tollar, as gently as possible, explained to Beenala that it was not possible. Croves provided the translations of Dram's pet curses in both prime and Prairiean. Tollar gave the two of them the Upalan translations. Beenala sat with her face hidden behind her hands. It didn't get any better for her when Croves started translating all the ways you could tell someone to eat shit.

"Come on, Bee, you must have one!" Tollar nudged Beenala's shoulder with her own.

Beenala had her face buried in her hands again but peeked contemplatively between her fingers.

"Well..." Beenala took a long drink of wine. "I only know it in Upalan and it was Ballow's favourite when Erxo's best friend was being a toad. He used to tell him his mother found him in the cabbages." She was blushing furiously. "It's because it implies the whole family is cabbage-brained."

Tollar translated it to prime.

"I don't usually go for subtlety," Croves admitted, "but I'll have to remember that one."

"Oh, we've got one like that," Draminedes said. "But it's about having shit for brains instead of cabbage."

Beenala groaned and returned her face to her hands. Tollar patted her on the back and wasn't surprised when Bee started yawning not long afterward. The moons were both hanging low in the sky.

"I guess I should head home," Beenala said. "Even the dog has gone to sleep."

"One more bottle?" Croves said.

Tollar cut him a glare. "We've got practice in the morning!"

"All right, fine."

Croves started tidying up, Draminedes quickly joining him and blushing when Croves gave him another wink. Tollar walked Beenala and Ash back to the cottage, just in case the dragons hadn't frightened off all the gezars.

"This was a good night," Beenala said. "Like when my family still lived here."

"Ah, is this how it is having a family you actually like?"

Beenala gave her a longsuffering shake of the head. She glanced over the hedge back toward the house.

"What is it?" Tollar put a hand on Beenala's shoulder.

"Croves has been... flirting aggressively. With both of you, honestly. Is something going on?"

"He'd like there to be, but no."

Beenala opened her front door and met Tollar's gaze in the moonlight. "But you like him well enough."

Tollar touched Beenala's cheek briefly and smiled affectionately. "You're all I need, Bee. And we've all got enough to think about right now without complicating everything more than it already is. Where did this jealous streak of yours come from?"

Tollar had been teasing with that last comment, and had expected Beenala to bristle and sputter, but instead she sagged.

"I don't know. Tollar, you make me crazy."

Tollar laughed and wrapped Beenala up in her arms. "I'm sorry, Bee. I'm sorry I haven't been here and I'm sorry if I've made you doubt. But I'm here now and I'm yours."

"I'm glad you're here." Beenala surprised her by taking Tollar's face in her hands and drawing her down to kiss the top of her head. "Good night, Toll."

"Sleep well, Bee."

Tollar gave Ash one last pat on the head and waited until Beenala had a lantern in the cottage lit before heading back to her own house, quieter now, but not in the hollow aching way it had been for so long. Draminedes was already passed out in his bed, Croves shuffling around in his own room.

Tollar didn't know what the coming months would hold, but she cherished that right now there was room enough for some joy.

23

The misty edge of the market square loomed out of the autumn fog, and Tollar approached the open space in the centre where the caravan would leave at any moment. Likely the last one out before the rains made the mountains impassable until spring. It was hard not to be sour about that. She'd wanted everyone mobilized and marching on Port Sawulxo by now, but instead Saivyn still had his head firmly lodged in his arse and Tollar was still chasing down Draminedes's former colleagues.

"I don't see why you needed me for this," Beenala grumbled.

Like Tollar hadn't made her breakfast and shrouded the pair of them in a dry bubble through all this damp gloom. It had been a long time since Tollar had stayed in Nytaltek through a winter and now she remembered why.

"Yes, you need to be here. I didn't want to have to go all the way back for you before the match started."

Tollar worried Beenala would complain about the match too, but she stuffed her hands into her pockets and kept walking. It was Beenala's idea to come see what Tollar did volunteering at the athletics guild. Of course, it wasn't all scatterball matches, and Tollar's arm hurt from all the writing. And Beenala often worked with the collective, turning Tollar's missives into works of art, helping the writers craft new stories and guide the other artists toward visions of unity.

All the names that Draminedes gave to Solia had panned out, and some of those resulted in yet more names. There had been dozens of interconnected cells of elementals working in tangent, but Tollar doubted she'd found them all. At least the larger group had been disrupted, if not dismantled. It had garnered enough goodwill for Draminedes to take up lodging in the city again. Aside from Solia and Tollar's plan for his return to the north, he'd been kept out of resistance efforts, though he'd commented recently on noticing some of the results.

People were talking about Port Sawulxo. Starting to worry more about invaders with dragons than what their neighbours were up to. Tollar worried it was too little, too late, but at least with the impending rains closing the passes, invasion wasn't something they had worry about for a season. Catching traitors helped make the threat seem more real and point to something external, though little was being said about Karthiry just yet.

Too slow.

They should be meeting the threat head on, not cowering in the jungle, waiting for the inevitable. Tollar had done what she could. Hoped they were ready by spring.

And they'd managed to keep Bale a secret so far. Shell had stayed in the mountains with Bale, teaching her more about their ways. And Bale was big enough that she often spent her time up in the mountains. The bigger she got, the more she liked the cold. She'd been doing some night flying, too. Miraculously, with Shell gone—two of his kin coming and helping him cart the egg away—most people thought that Nytaltek was free of dragons again.

The snorts of oxen and stamping of llama feet carried through the quiet morning, and Tollar walked along the caravan until she found Draminedes, sitting in one of the carts, wrapped up in some skins and looking about as miserable as anyone on their way home possibly could.

"You came!" he said.

"Of course we'd see you off," Beenala said.

Tollar approached and gave him a quick embrace, making sure to dry him off before she did. He huddled deeper into the skins afterward and lamented she couldn't come with him all the way to the coast to keep him dry.

"Should we really be seen with him like this?" Beenala asked.

"Befriending key resisters to infiltrate deeper was my master plan all along," he said drily.

"Are you sure you have to go?" Beenala asked.

"It will go much worse if she sends someone looking for me. And I can do more at home. Like we talked about."

Beenala didn't like the deception involved in the plan. But infiltration went both ways, and maybe his information could throw Karthiry off enough to give them an advantage. Beenala herself had collected all that "information" from the storytellers she knew.

The caravan lead, Kraua, went by, checking to make sure everyone was ready to leave. She was Tollar's friend and stopped with them.

"You sure you don't want to come this time, Toll?" she asked.

Tollar absolutely wanted to go, but knew where she was needed. She grinned through her doubts. "You're already getting the second best aquamancer in Nytaltek to get you through the soggy passes! What more do you want?"

Kraua chuckled and moved on, checking the last of the train before getting them ready to move out.

"You trust her?" Draminedes asked once she was gone. His voice was shriller than normal.

"She'll see you get to Port Sawulxo safely."

"There's nothing safe about going there," Beenala said.

"They're his people there. Or at least they think they're his people. He'll be fine as long as he sticks to the story like we talked about."

Beenala had expressed concern about Draminedes's ability to lie, since he hadn't been in Nytaltek long before he'd betrayed his original mission. But Tollar didn't think it was fair to call that a betrayal. He'd come to his senses. She suspected there might always be a small corner of her mind that thought his was the cleverest of ruses, pulling one over on her, which was why he'd been kept out of the wider plans. But if he was going to betray Upalint, it seemed more likely he'd do it accidently, or give up out of cowardice and allow himself to be swallowed up by Karthiry's machinations.

Draminedes sat up straighter, lifting his chin. "I know where my loyalties belong now."

"Yes, but please remember what I said about trying to save anyone around you," Tollar said. "This is bigger than any one of us."

He sighed but nodded slowly, staring forward with a steely gaze. He'd tried to fit getting his family off the island into the plans they'd made, but

Tollar eventually convinced him that campaign would have to wait. One thing at a time. Stop Karthiry from taking over Upalint. Push her out of Sawulxo. Get some more allies and then take back the archipelago, not that pushing Karthiry off the islands would help Biterna's woes.

"Help us now and we'll see what kind of trade or aid we can send," Beenala added.

"Yes, yes. And I'll watch for new opportunities to turn the islands around."

Tollar had suggested making it a haven for pirates, but that hadn't gone over well. Still, the archipelago made excellent rum, and maybe they could get some real export power from it once they got rid of the northerners mucking up the place.

"And I know you want to tell me to be careful, but it's *my* island yet, not hers. And there are lots of ways back to the mainland. But I want *you* to remember to be careful. I know you don't like it, but you're the one people associate with resistance to what's coming."

Tollar nodded gravely and didn't even roll her eyes. He was right. She didn't like it.

Word got around quickly about how Tollar had saved a dragon in the north, how she'd called that meeting afterward, and how she'd saved the market from flooding and stopped the attack on the elementals.

Rank lines be damned, everyone assumed she was in charge. Which made it easier for her to manipulate the narrative and calm tensions over what had been happening. Having traitors to show for it—to be able to point at them and say, "See, people are trying to ruin us but we're catching them and doing something about it," had helped ease tensions.

But not all of them.

"We'll all do what we need to," Tollar said. "And hopefully be well met again in the spring."

The whistle went down the line that it was time to go, and Draminedes settled grimly into the cart, among the baskets of goods heading to the port for trade. It was the best Solia could get for him under the circumstances.

Tollar and Beenala stood side by side and waved. As the caravan vanished into the mist, Beenala slipped her hand into Tollar's and they stood there for a moment.

Oh sure, Beenala liked to act gruff like Draminedes hadn't grown on her at all, but the fact was she'd been like a mother hen around him about a week into his stay. When Draminedes moved back to a room in the city, Beenala had done a poor job hiding how it upset her. She'd always kept her cottage shut to everyone but her family and Tollar, but she'd spent so much of her spare time with the three of them at Tollar's house.

She smiled at the thought.

And she hadn't failed to notice the glances the two men often shared or how they always found ways to be alone together. Not that that stopped Croves from incessantly flirting with her. But Croves and Shell had left two weeks ago, and it had been nearly a season since Draminedes came back to the city, even if he visited her frequently.

Now the house would be empty again.

Was this what it was like for Beenala every time Tollar left? She swallowed the tightness in her throat and squeezed Beenala's hand. Bale was around more without dragons to keep her company in the mountains, but even then, she came and went while it was dark. It was back to Tollar and Beenala again.

"Ready for scatterball?" Tollar grinned.

Beenala rolled her eyes. She'd been mentally preparing herself all week to come see the match with Tollar. But she was getting better at adjusting her days, especially since Tollar had painted a schedule on one wall of the kitchen, using chalk to list major chores and activities for the week, as well as lists for "today" and "tomorrow" to get her friend thinking further out. Tollar remembered the way Beenala's mother used to do something similar—keeping everyone's schedules in her head like some kind of organizational wizard—and giving Beenala regular reminders. It wasn't so much that Tollar couldn't keep a mental schedule, it was that she was so unused to having to remind anyone. So a written schedule had to do.

So far it was working.

"I just want to stop at the collective's studio quickly on the way," Beenala said. "We have time?"

"Sure, a bit."

Tollar waited outside in the gloom, wanting to part the clouds and let some sun in but not wanting the attention that kind of magic would gain.

At least Beenala wasn't long, her bag bulkier as the two of them headed on toward the arena attached to the athletics guild.

While the athletics guild oversaw plenty of sports for both swibs and wizards, scatterball was the only one that integrated both. It was the only sport Tollar ever played anymore, though she tended to stick to volunteering as a safety enforcer—using pockets of water to protect players from harm. She was a little too good at the game to play without people asking the wrong sorts of questions about her skill, but she liked being able to keep participating.

It was a noisy sport with noisy fans, but this was a practice match, and during the same time the inventors guild was doing some preliminary trials in lead up to the winter solstice fair and competition, so most people would be there instead. She hoped it would be calm enough not to overwhelm Beenala.

As the arena came into view, Beenala gripped Tollar's elbow. "Okay, tell me again w—"

"Tollar!" One of Solia's guards rushed toward them. "Urgent request from Captain Solia. You're needed at headquarters immediately."

"Oh shit."

Tollar jogged after the guard, heading toward the compound and startled when she realized Beenala was trying to keep up.

"Why don't you head home?" Tollar asked when Beenala caught up with her and the guard. "This could take a while, and I know you've got painting you want to get done."

"I want to stay with you. It's a spend time with Tollar day."

Tollar nodded and didn't push. Since the near disaster of Port Sawulxo, Tollar had had some frank but gentle conversations with Beenala about her limits and how to express when she was nearing them. And the importance that she do so. And reassurance that Tollar didn't mind. But it was also important to allow Beenala the space to push boundaries on her own.

Tollar was certain Beenala understood how much Tollar could handle, and often effortlessly. But she was also certain that Beenala saw a lot of the hidden costs Tollar barely acknowledged.

They were halfway to the guard house when they met Solia and a retinue.

"Change of plans, Tollar, we're heading to the Wizards Guild." Solia's voice was sharp as dragon talons and far too calm and measured.

"What is it?"

"A farmer on the northern slopes caught another one of them in her flooded field, trying to make a break for it. Lucky for us the farmer was a better aquamancer and the enemy was alone. She dragged him into town. Brought him to the Guild, filing it as a personal grievance."

"About time someone did, too."

"Maybe this will be what it takes for the Guild to stop ignoring this?" Beenala asked hopefully.

"This is a big one," Solia said. "This one had a case full of documents. Had some more names in it too, I've got teams headed out to pick those ones up. But it had reports back. Clear evidence of the interference Dram alluded to."

Tollar chewed on this new information and the best way to use it.

"Maybe it's time to start telling the truth about Karthiry?" Tollar asked. "People must be asking where all these meddling elementals are coming from."

"It might be. Let's see how things go in the Guild first."

24

Tollar slipped into the back row of the chamber room, Beenala fast at her side, and watched Solia stride down the aisle of the tiered seating to the dais at the bottom. Two figures in clothing so mud-splattered it was impossible to tell the original colour were in the centre of the room. They were surrounded by wizards in their official guild robes, which Tollar never got used to seeing. Northerners liked robes, thought it made them look godly or some nonsense.

Where even are your wizard robes?

She shook her head. One of the muddied individuals knelt on the floor, looking about as miserable as a human could, and she assumed that must be the freshly caught spy.

"All right then, let's hear it," Solia said. Perpetually exhausted by Nolly's newborn, Solia was even less interested in preamble these days.

"We're waiting on Metar," Cerro said. He was the Guild representative in Upalint, always in pale blue wizard robes that matched his blue eyes, set in a round pink face with greying blonde hair. He was a smidge shorter than Beenala and had a build similar to Dram's. Tollar hadn't interacted with him a whole lot and didn't particularly like the spectacle this was turning into. But at least Solia was here to make sure things went as they should.

They had to get this right because they were unlikely to get another opportunity like this.

Metar came in with her assistant but also with one of the writers from the city-wide circular. That could be very good or very bad.

"What's he doing here?" Beenala whispered, her worried tone matching Tollar's mood.

"It's probably time to make things more official than the tall tales I've been spreading. Put a proper face to this."

"It's not too soon?"

Tollar shrugged.

Something this big, with this much evidence, they couldn't ignore it. It was weird for Metar to be the last one here though, when the Guild chamber was in Metar's compound along with a few other guilds that had global networks, like the merchants. Balipar had the dragon chamber off on the other end of the compound where they could meet with dragon blazes from nearby or delegations from the city in the north. Given the proximity to the action, it wasn't a surprise when they slipped into the room, somehow going unnoticed in a moss-green silk robe with a wide yellow belt and their hair pulled up into two puffball ponytails like bear ears.

Tollar crossed her arms and leaned against the wall, Beenala standing stock straight next to her, twisting the hem of her shirt.

The discussion in the middle of the room was in hushed and urgent tones, not loud enough for Tollar to hear much, giving her time to brood over the latest turn of events. Draminedes was right that she was seen as the face of whatever this resistance was they were building, but she'd been slowly trying to change the narrative to give Saivyn more credit—not that he deserved a lick of it.

But moving forward with this, probably with some vaguely public trial of this spy, would solidify things as they stood, with Tollar in charge and Saivyn a distant support.

Of course, if the stupid arse had put his colossal ego aside sooner and listened to her—sent some of his people with her to Sawulxo—things would be going so much better. They'd have absolutely been able to free more dragons in that campaign, and then it would be Saivyn leading things, not Tollar. She was too much of an outsider.

Much as she hated to acknowledge it, Saivyn would have the necromancers on board already if he were at the helm.

But he's an arsehole and it's his own ancestors-cursed fault he's playing second flute.

Okay, Tollar probably could have done more when she first got back, but Saivyn had always hated her. Right from the first time she'd knocked a weapon from his hand while sparring. Not her fault he was sloppy.

Arsehole.

He probably didn't care about people being sell-swords and only used it as an excuse to keep being such a rancid toad toward her specifically.

"Look, the evidence against you is overwhelming and my people are already rounding up your friends," Solia said. Finally something loud enough to hear. "You're not getting out of here, and I don't give one good cursed ancestor what Cerro here says."

"Eh, wait! Are they trying to move jurisdiction?" Tollar asked, standing straight.

"Tollar, please," Cerro said. "This doesn't concern you—"

"It absolutely frogging does! This is my home, and I'm the one who figured out what they're up to." She slipped passed Beenala and marched down the aisle, driven by blood like magma pounding in her ears. It was a very good thing she wasn't a pyromancer. "This one's been caught trespassing and that one's filed complaint. You've got wizards—Guild or not doesn't matter—using their talents to harm others, to harm others in the Guild. What the bollocks is the point of me joining your ranks if this is how you're treating us?"

Cerro sputtered. "Now look, it's not that simple."

"No, actually, it is." Beenala trailed along behind Tollar. "I've been petitioning you for two months. And I have absolutely been going through your dusty old files on the conditions of Guild membership. You make it damned hard for us to get in, even with the new tiers for one-talent specialists, and from what I've read it looks bloody easy to have our arses booted if we're using our talents to harm."

"I know this looks like a few bad seeds to you," he said, "but the problem expands all the way north and—"

"All the more reason to deal with it before it gets worse!" Tollar snapped.

"I daresay it's much worse than you know."

Tollar glared at him and paced the length of the dais. She gave the spy one angry glance as she walked past him and stormed back up to Cerro who actually flinched as she neared.

"I pull rank," she said. Blessed ancestors, she wished people would stop making her be the adult. "You people wanted me in your foolish Guild for a reason. The entrance exams changed and the tiers were created exactly because of people like me. Well, you do this right, or I walk."

The colour drained from Cerro's face. "I—you can't just—"

"Yes, she can," Beenala said. "Any of us are free to leave whenever we wish. So, do you want to keep the best aquamancer you've got or lose her over some spy?"

Tollar cast Beenala a quick look, wishing at once she'd shut up but also that she'd never stop. Cerro knew what Tollar was, but Tollar really didn't need anyone else in this room knowing. But the threat stood. They'd recruited Tollar, whole new tiers of the Guild with a separate set of exams, to allow people like Tollar to gain entry. Not only other half-demons, but other wizards with exceptional skills in only one area. Most wizards in the Guild had to be proficient in a wide range of skills, including the elements.

But after that family of pyromancers, and some troublemaker—another northerner—and then learning about Tollar, the Guild had been forced to change their centuries-long practices or risk some very powerful wizards becoming very powerful problems.

"I..." Cerro sighed and stared.

"What's this about, Toll?" Solia asked.

Tollar bunched her hands into fists and stared directly at Cerro. "The Guild changed how they rank wizards, changing who they let in and why. I'm the second highest ranking specialist they've got."

Cerro coughed and stared at her like a goat before a gezar.

"Way it was explained to me when they invited me to take the entrance exams—I wasn't interested, but went anyway just to see. Anyway, I guess they've had some mighty powerful wizards with only one skill. One element or maybe only healing, but so powerful at it they can cause trouble without the right kind of guidance."

Tollar leaned in closer to Cerro, sneering. "That what happened with this Karthiry woman? We know she's a powerful aquamancer. She get lost in the shuffle before you came to your senses about it?"

Cerro shook his head. "No, in fact. There's someone much worse than her, and someone much better than you, that led to the change."

Tollar rolled her eyes and stalked across the room. "Well, you want to keep me where you can guide me and keep my skills from becoming a problem, I guess it's time you do something about this lot." She gestured to the spy kneeling on the floor.

"Seems like you've got a lot of problems on your hands," Solia said to Cerro. "Lots of wrongs to right. Might be time to start?"

Cerro shook himself and turned to Solia. "Look, you deal with this one how you need to, I'll bring the petition, with Tollar's addendum—"

"And mine!" Beenala said. "And everyone on that frogging list we gave you months ago!"

"I'll bring this to the head of the Guild. You understand it will take some time."

Tollar dropped into a seat and waved dismissively. "Well, this problem you've let run wild for so long has already invaded Sawulxo, and from what we understand, we're next."

"Yes, we've given you the evidence of that," Solia said to him, gesturing to the spy. "Even if he won't confess, his reports, the ones he didn't destroy before Ilexi overpowered him, prove everything we need."

"I'll—" He closed his eyes and took a deep breath. "Look, if a few of your people will help me, I'll send a rapid message to Grand Chancellor Dira and see if we can get some kind of decision made faster. It'll take a fortnight before Dira can gather a quorum to decide."

"Better than us getting run into the ground by someone using *dragons* while you debate the merits of letting us continue to exist," Tollar snapped. "I can handle these aquamancers they have, but a dragon army? Who thought it was a good idea to let that continue unchecked?"

"Believe me, Tollar, we've been trying—"

The door slammed open, and Saivyn stormed in with an armed escort. "Leave the man alone, Tollar, you've done enough."

"You make it sound like *I'm* the frogging spy getting sloppy trying to rush off before the rains." Tollar reached for water from a cup on the table at the side of the room.

"It's amazing you haven't rushed off somewhere. If you're staying, you can at least make yourself useful."

She launched to her feet and the entire contents of the cup of water splashed across his face. She'd pitched it at him hard enough to sting, too.

"Cursed ancestors, Toll, none of this helps!" Solia snapped, getting between them. "Sai, what is it? And can you possibly ignore her for once in your frogging life?"

Saivyn glared at Solia for a moment before assessing the group gathered in the room. He pointed his blade-hand at the spy on the ground.

"That one's friends are giving us grief. More than aquamancers. They've got strong aeromancers and at least one dangerous terramancer with them. They're in two groups in the city and they're becoming a hazard. We need more elementals to counter them so we can bring them in."

Cerro looked equal measures horrified and relieved. "Well," he said. "I guess we'll put this aside for now, I trust Captain Solia can accommodate the prisoner in the meantime. I'll gather as many wizards as I can find to help you."

"I'll come," Tollar said to Saivyn, staring at a point next to his head because she knew she'd throw more water at him if she had to look in his stupid square face.

"We don't need your help."

"We absolutely do," Solia snapped. "With me, Tollar. Cerro, be out front in five minutes."

Saivyn grumbled the locations to Solia and marched himself right back out.

Tollar gave Solia a quick glance.

"You and him need to fight this out and come to some kind of truce or it's going to be the end of us."

Tollar gestured angrily toward the door. "He hates me. Can't even ignore me! I'll ignore him to the end of my days if he'd stop shouting directly at me every time we're in the same room."

"I'll lock you both in a room myself."

"Only one of us'll come out of it alive," Tollar growled. "And it won't be him."

Saivyn was a powerful man, but he was still a swib. If there was so much as a drop of water in that room, she'd drown him with it, marks on her forearm be damned.

She followed Solia outside, Beenala trailing her like Ash did when she had fish scraps, though looking far more lost.

"That one wasn't only a spy," Solia said. "From what I saw of his papers, he's been another one directing things. A proper instigator. He destroyed half his report, but it paints a very clear picture of what they've been doing here, and how." Solia stopped and looked at the two of them. "They've got impressive terramancers working in teams with aquamancers that've been hiding in the ground, where it's harder for us to detect, and then working the ground water for floods. Or hidden in pockets in the rocks of the mountains to drive the weather."

Tollar stared. "Where are they getting all these people? And how has the Guild not done anything about them sooner?"

"Cerro is being sly about it, but they're on a knife's edge in the north. These divisions between people and dragons and different factions of wizards run deep down there, and they're having a hard time getting control of the situation. I guess it started with the dragons and got worse from there. Whoever's pulling the strings from the north has much more power and influence than Karthiry."

"So we're up against half the world?"

"I can't see if they're connected or not. She might be capitalizing on the instability someone else is causing. Either way, we have to stop her. But first we stop this lot she's sent our way."

Beenala put her warm hand on Tollar's elbow, and Tollar turned to her.

"Bee, you should get home. Unless you want to stay here? You might be safer here."

"I heard where they are, I'll go around, go visit my parents until it calms down enough to get back out to the farm."

Tollar was both disappointed and relieved to hear Beenala say she was going. She wanted her to be safe, and her parents lived in a quiet neighbourhood far from the worst danger, but Tollar also wished she could handle what it would take to go with Tollar when she left. Beenala wanted Tollar to stay.

Tollar couldn't stay anymore than Beenala could go.

But now wasn't the time to think of that, leaving was a distant dream. Tollar had a city to keep safe, and Beenala had her own well-being to consider.

"Before I go…" She reached into her bag and pulled out a leather-bound volume. "I was going to give it to you when we got home, but… you'll probably be a while."

"I'm sorry—"

"No, no, you need to do this. They need you out there, Tollar. But I just wanted you to know." She held out the volume to Tollar and she took it, mystified. "Open it." Beenala's voice had almost disappeared entirely, and she blushed furiously while staring down at her hands trying to twist her hem into knots.

Tollar flipped the pages open, and her own words stared back at her. She blinked, went to the beginning and flipped slowly. Her own face grew hot and her feet barely touched the ground.

"Is this…?"

"It's every one of them. I kept them all."

"But… The collective?"

"I got one of my friends at the press to put it together for me. I know you don't have anywhere to keep books, but it can stay with me until you do."

Tollar stared at the pages without seeing. Every single pamphlet and circular she'd ever written, right here in one place. Bound professionally too. Sturdy.

"I don't… Thank you, Bee. I think this is the nicest thing anyone's ever done for me."

"Well then, you need better people." There was a sly spark in her brown eyes.

Tollar handed the volume to her. "Best you keep this safe until I get back. Let Bale know I might be late?"

"I will. Be careful, Tollar."

Tollar flashed her a winning grin. "You know me."

Beenala gave her a longsuffering look, and Tollar touched her hand briefly before she put the book away and left. Tollar took a deep breath, steadying herself, and turned to Solia who had very politely found something else in the courtyard to keep her attention.

"I don't know who it'll be harder on the next time you go," Solia said offhand. "You need to learn to stay."

"Don't think that I can. But I'm here for now, and that has to be enough."

"Well, I don't care what Saivyn thinks, I'm certainly glad to have you. What do you think about this mess?"

"I can flush out terramancers. Even stone eventually gives way to water."

"What was that Cerro said about your power? I know you're good, Tollar, but the best aquamancer out of everyone in the world who can specialize?"

"It's complicated, Sol. Maybe one day I'll tell you about it. But it's a bargaining chip we can use, so I will."

"I've always trusted your power. Are you sure you don't want to tell me about this?"

"Just keep trusting my power, all right? Now, these elementals we face... Do you want them alive?"

"That's up to you. Do what you need to, for yourself as much as for the city."

Cerro came out a moment later, and Tollar was glad to be moving. Solia sent Tollar with the best terramancer they had to the biggest group of spies dug in in some apartments not far from the university. Tollar kept glancing at the river as they went.

She stopped the terramancer and the other two elementals they travelled with and introduced herself.

"Yes, we know who you are."

"Okay, but who are you? If we're fighting together, I'd at least like to know your names."

The terramancer, who was built blocky like Saivyn but with darker skin and hair in long black braids, relaxed. "I'm Macana."

"Well met, Macana. So you know what I can do? I think we need to get this over with quickly if we want to keep from ending up with a repeat of the attack on the compound over the summer."

"You going to try to drown us again?" Macana asked bitterly, glaring right at her. "Make us all look like fools?"

"I can't help being as powerful as I am, but I can help what use I put it to. This has to be about protecting the city and not about egos. If we've got some time to prepare, I can make it look like you're helping. If we've got even more time, we can work together properly. Whatever we do, it's best everyone sees as many elementals working on solutions as possible if we want to stop seeing this happen. But we're close enough to the river, I can pull it along with us and you two can use it," she said to the elementals.

"What, and just drown everything in your path to do it?" Macana snarled.

"No, nothing needs to be in its path. But I'd rather we work together, since we'll have to eventually. Might as well start now."

Macana grumbled, but the two elementals interrupted.

"I'll work with you," said a lanky elemental with warm ochre skin who introduced himself as Eratona.

"I'm Tavalu," said the other, a tall, broad-shouldered woman with a strong jaw and light brown skin much like Beenala's, but blue eyes and long brown hair. "What's your plan?"

"All right, have you fought before? Properly, I mean. With your magic?"

Tavalu hadn't outside of sparring, but the other two had been reservists for Saivyn.

"All right, good. Tavalu, did you get the chance to read the analysis on the work done by those aquamancers that flooded the market?"

"Yes. You want to do that?" She was wary.

"If you're okay with it. All you'll need to do is stand nearby and stay as calm and still as you can. It will keep you from having to actually fight. No worrying about hurting anyone or fumbling over something."

"And you use my power?" Tavalu crossed her arms.

"Yes. If you can keep your focus, I can not only make myself stronger, but channel your elemental energy and use any elements you can." Tollar glanced at the terramancer, Macana. "I'll need you the most for this."

Macana was warming to the idea now that Tollar sought her input, so she told them her plan and they all stood blinking at her.

"Just a yes or no. I'm doing it, unless someone has a better idea."

"Ugh, all right," Macana said.

Tollar grinned and faced the river. It was near enough she could call to it without much difficulty. She made what looked like a wave, but kept rising and rising until it separated from the rest of the river, a whole river above the river. Shouts echoed from the wharf.

It wasn't enough to actually upset the flow of the river and barely skimmed any of its depth, but it came rushing through the air toward where she stood all the same.

"Stand closer to me, it'll be easier to get us there."

And then they were up on top of the water, which dipped down to collect them and bore them along on one of Tollar's solid sheets, drifting up over the rooftops.

Even without the directions Solia had given her, Tollar easily found their target. The dark cloud bearing lightning down on a neighbourhood next to the university was a bit of a giveaway. Tollar nudged Eratona and instructed him to handle it.

"I'll do what I can."

"If you can stop the lightning, that will be a help." Then the river crested over a final banobi crown, and Tollar steered it down toward the ground, straight into the middle of the fighting.

With Tavalu at her side, she pushed Macana and Eratona out in front, wanting someone other than her to be prominent. Too much attention led to questions about her power that she absolutely did not want to answer. And it really was critical that people see more wizards than just her fixing things. Eratona deflected the lightning aimed right at them, and Tollar let the river flow on without her group, keeping them on a stationary sheet while the water broke around them and flowed down into the fight.

She caught sight of Saivyn a moment before the water washed over everything. No time to be smug about the look on his face because she had to keep that face from filling with water.

She singled out all the people and let the water flow around them, giving them an air pocket.

This was meant to shock them. It was all right if it stopped Saivyn's people. His aquamancers would be able to keep going, and Tollar was certain that the three with her were enough to put an end to this.

"All right," she said to Tavalu. "Are you sure about this?"

"We have to stop them."

"I'm going to take your hand. If it's easier for you, close your eyes. Focus on your terramancy, it's what I need most."

She nodded and Tollar gripped her hand and waited for her to close her eyes. Tollar kept Tavalu stable on the wave and pulled energy out of her, focusing on the terramancy while she did. The influx of energy cleared the sludge from her thoughts, eased the headache she'd barely noticed forming. Terramancy was a strange feeling, clunky and slow magic, but infusing it with her water magic helped her to see with more clarity than she ever had before.

She sensed the earth like she'd always been able to see with water.

And the enemy terramancers stood out like bright light, too solid, her water flowing around them and the ground not moving as it should in their midst.

There were only two of them.

She tugged harder on Tavalu's energy and dissolved the solid rock around the terramancers, breaking it down with water even as she softened it with the counter-magic she syphoned.

This startled the terramancers long enough for her to push more water into their hold and flush them out, geysering them straight out into the air where Eratona waited for them with a whirlwind to keep them from gathering more soil to use.

Macana threw clumps of mud at the two elementals responsible for the worst of the weather, distracting them as they dodged and giving Tollar an opening to wash them out of the building they'd holed up in.

Tollar used the river to wrap the pyromancer on the roof in water. She pulled more out of Tavalu, careful not to take too much, knowing Tavalu would be near her limit, and ferreted out the last three wizards hiding in there. With more water pouring in through the window, she washed them out and released Saivyn and his people in enough time for them to spring on the wizards when they hit the street.

No more rushes of magic came from the apartments, and the storm in the sky dissipated. Tollar brought the wash of water down to street level, leaving her and her three companions behind as she sent it up into the air, curling back the way it had come to join up with the main flow of the Arazow.

"What the bleeding moons is wrong with you?" Saivyn snapped. "Are you trying to drown us all?"

Tollar released Tavalu and made sure Eratona was there to help her, as she was unsteady on her feet from the exertion, and then she stalked straight up to Saivyn.

"You're welcome," she snarled, gesturing to the wizards his people rounded up, all of them soggy and disoriented. "But I can always let them go, if you'd prefer to keep doing it your way."

She gave a pointed look to all of his injured soldiers lying in a doorway across the street before turning to the wizards who had come with her.

"If we're quick, we can provide back up for Solia. I don't know if she'll need us, but it's better than leaving her on her own."

"She's not doing anything else today, this took too much out of her," Eratona said, helping Tavalu sit down.

"I'm sorry." Tollar crouched in front of Tavalu. "It's harder until you get the hang of it."

"You should teach us," she said.

Tollar nodded and stood. "First, this needs dealing with."

"I'm staying with her," Eratona said.

Saivyn was trying to shout over her, but at least Macana agreed to help. Tollar wished Beenala had stuck around, a pyromancer would come in handy. Nothing for it. She pulled some of the retreating water back to them and rushed off down the street.

She didn't know what it would take to convince Saivyn to pull his head out of his arse. Was he going to make her win an entire war on her own? He'd find fault with her somewhere. Frog him. She'd keep doing what she could and it would have to be enough.

For now, Solia needed her.

25

Despite the heat of the building, Draminedes felt winter deep in his bones as he walked through the familiarly alien hallways of the chief's manor. Back in the long robes that felt both tent-like and constricting, wrapping around his ankles when he moved too quickly. Everything seemed the same as when he'd left, like he could easily fall back into his role of taking notes for a monster. He hadn't seen Karthiry yet, and he wanted nothing more than to get back on a boat to the mainland.

His father's house felt warm and inviting, like he belonged, but it was a small refuge in a sea of despair.

For now, he followed one of Karthiry's aides, some man he'd never interacted with before but saw around the manor frequently enough. He was being given some space to get his notes in order before he faced Karthiry for the first time in two seasons.

The aide pushed open a small door and ushered Draminedes into what was essentially a broom closet with a desk in it. It was small and stifling and barely enough room to stand between the desk and the door without getting hit by it when it closed. But it was space enough for what he needed, and it was private enough he didn't have to keep putting on an act.

Beenala had worried about this part. And it concerned him the most as well. But he held to Tollar's instructions and pulled out all of his notes from his satchel, which was more worn than it had been even before he left Nytaltek.

He wished he'd never left.

Fraught as it had been, he felt safer there. Everyone was pleasant and kind, though it was a guarded kindness from those who knew what he was. He missed the comfortable chaos of Tollar and Beenala. He especially missed the warmth of Croves. Part of him missed the security of having dragons around that didn't want to eat him.

Port Sawulxo had been everything Tollar said and, knowing what to look for, having his eyes opened, he didn't know how he'd missed it the first time. The hushed conversations and empty streets, the still-flooded neighbourhood, the downcast expressions, the northerners with weapons on every corner scrutinizing it all.

Probably because he hadn't wanted to see.

But there was no going back, and he had to do this. He held onto Tollar's words as he began carefully decoding his notes and writing up the report. Tell Karthiry what she wanted to hear. Tell her most of the truth.

He sighed.

Draminedes couldn't get his hands to stop shaking, so he set his pen down, amazed he didn't drop it seeing as how he barely felt his fingers. He scowled down at the pages and took a deep breath. And nearly jumped out of his skin when someone knocked on his door.

Hollen poked her head in. "Welcome back, Dram! I hear you had a fruitful mission."

"Yes, er. Just finishing up my report."

Hollen smiled and nodded and dipped her head out into the hallway to look around before coming all the way in and closing the door. Her expression grew serious.

"You saw it, then."

"I'm sorry?"

"How much she lies. Karthiry."

"Um."

"You don't have to play dumb to save your hide, Dram. I haven't been further south than this island, but I used to hear about Upalint from traders. Karthiry's words never sat right with me."

Draminedes nodded carefully. He'd known Hollen came with Karthiry from a mainland port in the north, but hadn't heard which one. One of the trading hubs, it would seem.

"So you came with her to... What?"

"Try to get her to see reason. When she came here she wanted to just plow over everyone here like she has in Sawulxo. I pushed for cooperation, let her know how desperate everyone here was with the trading dried up." Hollen shook her head and let out a frustrated breath. "Well, she at least made it look like she was cooperating with your people. Dram, she's not hiding the chief or letting him get much-needed rest. She killed him as soon as people stopped really looking for him as a leader."

Draminedes trembled and his whole body joined his fingers in numbness. He kept his mouth shut. No matter how much he agreed with Hollen, no matter what she had planned, Tollar had at least drilled into him the need for being discreet. She'd hidden an entire dragon for months. He could keep his mouth shut. For all he knew, Hollen was testing his loyalty.

"If she didn't see fit to keep the chief alive, she won't see the rest of us as any less expendable. She wants the resources in the south. That's it. Biterna is a staging point for her. She'll grind your people into dust and turn this into a fort. It's what she did to my people. This island is nothing more than a stepping stone for further expansion from the north."

Draminedes swallowed hard but kept quiet, and Hollen sighed and nodded.

"All right, you don't have to trust me. Probably smarter if you don't. But heed my words and be careful. I don't know what you've got in your reports, but it would help me protect people if you joined me in trying to convince her to actually trade with these people. I know what kind of technologies they have in Upalint. We could learn so much from each other. I just want her to see that. She doesn't have to wipe everyone out to benefit."

"Thank you for the warning." It was all he managed to say. How desperate was Hollen to speak so freely in Karthiry's very own halls?

Hollen went to the door and stopped in the hall. "And that's why you need to get there early this time. Way earlier than normal, all right?" Her tone was bright and cheery, free of the previous moment's warning. "I look forward to your report. I know m'lady is eager to hear what you've discovered."

"Yes, of course. Thank you, Hollen."

She closed the door and Draminedes practically deflated and sagged deeper in his chair until his forehead touched the desk. Hollen's plan was tempting, but did she really know what she was doing? Was there some way to bridge what Hollen wanted to do with what Tollar intended?

Maybe. But he would stick to his report and see how it was received first, then consider recommendations along the lines of what Hollen wanted to try.

Letting out a long, slow breath, he got back to it, keeping careful watch of the time. He didn't want to go to the meeting, wanted to run all the way back to Upalint, but even if he got off the island and to the coast, the mountains were impassable without the right kind of aquamancer or terramancer. Even then, Tollar might be the only one in the world with the power to get through that weather.

He shook his head. He needed to shove those kinds of thoughts way to the back of his mind lest they escape during the meeting. It would be catastrophic to let Karthiry know how powerful Tollar and some of the others were.

So he gathered up his papers, shuffled them into his satchel and pushed out into the hall. Karthiry's courtroom was on the other side of the manor, but now he wished it was across the hall. The long walk only worsened his trembling. But he kept his head held high when he pushed into the room and took a seat near the back. The room was nearly full and had been rearranged to accommodate them all. Some people were advisors he recognized—Hollen was up near the front at a long table facing rows of chairs—but there were many others he didn't know. More and more people from the north and fewer and fewer of his own people here than the last time he'd been in this room so many months ago.

Karthiry came bustling in from the far entrance not long afterward, surrounded by her usual inner circle and accompanied by a new dark-skinned young man carrying a satchel full of paper. A dark-skinned man who sat off to the side, present but not part of the whole. But sharing a lingering glance with Karthiry before settling into his work.

An abyss opened beneath Draminedes, and it was everything he could do not to pitch himself headlong into it.

And then another man came through the far entrance, another pale northerner who was possibly taller than Croves though a fraction his width, with watery blue eyes and stringy blonde hair and beard, in deep blue robes and glittering with jewels, walking with the bearing of a god.

He sat off to the side in a large, throne-like chair that hadn't been there the last time Draminedes had been in this room. He made brief eye contact with Karthiry, but otherwise watched on like this entire court was his entertainment.

"Master Loch." Karthiry bowed to him. He smiled and nodded. She glared out over the assembly and snapped out, "Call to order."

Draminedes swallowed and squeezed his hands into fists to try to get some feeling back into them. This level of formality was never a good sign. And the way Karthiry's thin lips pressed into a bloodless line did not bode well.

Oh shit oh shit oh shit they've found me out.

Should he run? Could he?

He forced himself not to look around, not to search for exits and see whether they were guarded. He faced forward, staring at a spot on the wall above Karthiry's head.

"Hollen, you've requested first order of business. Make this quick."

Hollen stood from her seat at the long table at the head of the room, near the end from where Karthiry sat, much farther away than she had been. So many dynamics had shifted in ways Draminedes barely comprehended.

"Yes, m'lady, thank you. Before we hear from Draminedes, I wanted to press for caution in our next moves. I'm sure Dram will have some illumination on the matter of the dragon, but I feel that anyone with the ability to challenge the port the way these people did should be treated with a measure of caution and perhaps even respect."

"Respect." The word fell from Karthiry's mouth like a stone dropping into the ocean. She exchanged a glance with the new northerner, Master Loch, who raised his eyebrows, finding something here amusing.

"They appear to have a level of sophistication we did not expect, m'lady. Perhaps we should investigate the possibility of making them allies. It would certainly be cost effective in the—"

"I've heard enough." Karthiry's words were crisp, glacial. Master Loch chuckled and Karthiry stood even straighter. "Hollen, I tried to be understanding, but you have pushed too far. This insubordination has gone on long enough, to the point I regret having plucked you, undeserving, from the gutter and given you such a glorious station on my counsel."

Draminedes swallowed. *Plucked from the gutter. Underserving.* Like Hollen was some stray dog and not the capable daughter of merchants poised to take over the family business. What could Karthiry possibly think of *him*?

But Karthiry was not done, pointing angrily at Hollen, while Master Loch murmured something in Prairiean, and the rest of the northerners at the head table smirked.

"I won't stand for these treasonous notions for an instant longer."

Draminedes bunched his fists around the fabric of his robes.

"Treason? No, m'lady! I have only your interests at—"

"That's enough, Hollen. It's quite clear where your interests lie, though I can only speculate at motivation. I'll not allow you to delay me a moment longer." She nodded toward one of her guards near the side door. "Take her."

"What? M'lady, no! Please, I'm trying to help!"

"Indeed."

Draminedes tried to drown out Hollen's pleas, growing increasingly shrill and desperate, devolving into screams as she was dragged out the side door.

"Well, that was unpleasant," Karthiry said.

"We must keep our house clean of this vermin." Master Loch spoke in prime for the first time.

Draminedes clutched the underside of his seat to keep himself from jumping up and trying to dissuade Karthiry from taking such drastic action against Hollen. But the hard gleam remained in Karthiry's eyes, and it was very clear how most of the rest of the room felt.

"All right, Draminedes, let's hear what you've got."

Draminedes did his best to stand calmly and stride purposefully across the room to leave his report in front of Karthiry, giving Master Loch a slight, respectful bow, even though he wasn't sure who or what the man was. Then he stood respectfully in front of Karthiry, staring at the tabletop while she skimmed through his notes.

"I see."

"Is m'lady displeased?"

"I had hoped... for something more definitive. Something damning we could use for leverage."

"They are quite divided," Draminedes said. "Your efforts have been going much better than initially reported. I witnessed several attacks on elementals myself, as well as a brawl between warriors and city guards."

Tell her what she wants to hear, Tollar had said. Just the right amount of truth.

This was the moment to see if it was working or if he would join Hollen at the executioner's block.

"Yes, other reports have indicated a sufficient level of disarray, but also that there is still a more organized resistance growing. I understand you were able to attend some meetings."

"Yes, m'lady."

There was still time, he could come clean and beg forgiveness...? But no, Hollen hadn't betrayed Karthiry half as much. There was no way out but through. It was too late for anything but the right thing—it was his only hope of survival. He stood tall, chin up, and pressed on.

"There were several meetings, mostly trying to deal with the weather disturbances and food shortages. But as you've said, they are unsophisticated. Their reliance on the land, living hand to mouth in the forests, will be their undoing. Each group had their own leaders and their own factions insisting that they alone had the solutions."

"So their leaders are in disarray?"

Well, that much was practically true, though Karthiry didn't need to know how hard they were working to achieve unity.

"Yes, m'lady. These brutes are too divided to oppose you in any meaningful sense."

"And yet they're organized enough to pose a threat to Port Sawulxo. They took three of my dragons, Draminedes. Did you know about that?"

"Yes, m'lady. Tales of a dragon caper reached me in Nytaltek."

"A caper." She nearly skewered him with her hard, green gaze. "How precious. Some of my sources on the ground there have tied that caper, as you put it, to a particularly troublesome aquamancer. Do you know anything about this?"

He swallowed but kept his voice calm and even. "Yes, m'lady. I was at a meeting she called, but it devolved into chaos almost immediately. Most of their leaders walked out and the rest got sloppily drunk. They sang old war songs, and I left after the third time one of them spilt beer on me."

"You don't think she's a threat?"

"She's a rogue, m'lady. A loose cannon and a drunkard. From what I understand, she is practically nomadic and seldom in the city. In fact, she was planning to head downriver to the east coast because she heard there were pirates looking for good aquamancers to advance their ships."

Karthiry narrowed her eyes at him, and it was paralyzing fear alone that held him steady when she asked, "So you know her?"

"I know *of* her, m'lady," he corrected with the politest bow he was capable of. "Her name is Tollar. I saw her a time or two at social clubs, always loud and drunk. A simple mercenary who gets bored easily and moves on quickly."

"Well she certainly had help in Port Sawulxo."

"Yes, m'lady. While I'm not entirely clear on the details, she seems charismatic, always drawing people to her whim of the day, but lacking the loyalty or competence to cement any kind of movement. Frankly, the stories I heard made her sound reckless. No sensible person would get mixed up with her twice."

Draminedes kept himself standing tall, forced his chin up before it could think to droop, even while he swallowed down the bile rising. How could he so easily say such things about someone who saved his life? Call people who had embraced him incompetent brutes? They didn't fully trust him, but treated him well.

But it was what Karthiry wanted to hear. That there was resistance, but not enough. Make her think she could walk right in and take what she wanted without a fight, like in Port Sawulxo.

"So you don't foresee any issues?"

"There will be some bumps," he said. "Some of the elementals started catching on, nosing around. They found Norli and I noticed others disappearing not long afterward."

"And you don't believe this is cause for concern?"

"No, m'lady. It seemed to be dividing them even more, many of the swibs believed the elementals were looking for scapegoats. We may have lost some people to it, but they are still just as divided."

"All right, thank you, Draminedes. Your service has been invaluable. I'm sure you must be tired from your long journey and from living in such conditions."

"Thank you, m'lady. I am pleased to serve you and to be back in civilization."

Karthiry smiled her shark smile and Master Loch watched him closely as he retreated to his seat while they continued discussing the issue. But it was clear that she was set on a spring invasion, as Tollar had predicted. He didn't like losing Hollen but couldn't see how to help her without jeopardizing the plan.

He could only help himself and keep moving forward, hoping Tollar's plan worked.

BEFORE

Tollar had had about enough of Zarro for one day, no matter if it was barely after breakfast, and she turned away and walked straight out of the house.

"Hey! I'm still talking to you," he snapped.

"Okay. But I'm done listening."

He muttered something to her mother, all of it lost to the noise of a pair of dragons passing overhead, and then Janda was at the door calling down the lane.

"Toll, you get back in here and show your father some respect."

"Subfather," Tollar corrected, turning. "And he doesn't get respect just for living in the same house as me."

"Maybe it's time we didn't live in the same house," he said.

"Sounds lovely. When are you leaving?"

She didn't wait for him or her mother to respond and turned away, calling a sheet of groundwater to carry her beyond where their shouts reached. When she first walked out the door, she'd wanted to go into the city to Auntie and maybe sneak another lesson down at the barracks, but now spotted Beenala heading into the forest with a large tool.

Tollar caught up to her easily enough.

"G'morning, Bee." Tollar stepped off the water onto solid ground. She held her hands out in greeting, and Beenala hesitated the way she sometimes did before propping the tool under her arm and taking Tollar's hands briefly.

"Hello, Tollar. Beautiful morning, isn't it? I was hoping for some nice weather, it's time to trim the canopy."

Tollar fell in step beside Beenala as she headed deeper into the forest, along the wide rows filled with crops. Beenala's family grew entirely different things from Tollar's, aside from the bananas, but everyone had some bananas, didn't they? And Tollar had noticed that the taller trees between the crop rows were mostly the same height, not staggered like on Tollar's farm.

"You don't cut any of the trees down?" she asked.

"Not until they die. Ours are for oil, not for building."

"What do you trim for?"

"To keep the canopy from stealing light from the crops. Just need to trim on this side." Beenala pointed. "Unless it looks like any branches are dead. Don't want those to fall and crush the plants."

"But you're just walking, not trimming anything."

"I'm starting at the farthest end and working my way home. My brothers will come along behind me after they're done fishing in the western canal and collect the branches for drying so we can use them to cook later."

"Oh, I can dry them for you, if you need to use them soon."

Beenala smiled. "Thank you, but we've got plenty for now."

"Can I help at all?"

"I guess you can pull any weeds you see, especially if you notice any chokevines."

Beenala stopped when they reached the far corner of the farm and took out the tool she'd had bundled under one arm. It was a series of poles she snapped together with shears on one end.

"Good morning, just a bit of pruning," she called to the trees. Then Beenala hoisted it up into the air, snipping off all the green shoots.

"You talk to the trees?"

"Everything on the farm. Don't you?"

Tollar knew abstractly that this was a thing her family must do as well, but maintaining adequate moisture levels was the only thing she'd ever done on her farm. And harvesting. Everyone had to help with the big harvests. But that was just picking things that looked ready to eat.

She knew more about Beenala's farm than she did about her own. Like the kinds of fish they kept in their canals, and all the different fruit their trees produced, and that there were nut trees too, though she wasn't certain which ones.

"It's just about time to plant the pumpkins, isn't it?" Tollar asked.

"Next week, I think. Squash and melons too."

"Can I help with that?"

Beenala smiled while staying focused on her work. "I'd like that. You don't have any squash on your farm, do you?"

Tollar shrugged. Beenala, still smiling, went on cutting down new growth while talking about the squash, relaying everything there was to know, and how she was trying to figure out how to make them bigger without losing the flavour.

Tollar let her talk, watching her lips, unable to look away.

Until Beenala caught her staring and they both blushed, and Tollar, staring at the ground, found some weeds to pull. Not with her hands, but by using her magic to yank at the water inside them and pull them straight out, roots and all. She left the weeds in the middle of the path.

"Looks like we'll need to heap the mulch thicker on these edges," Beenala said.

All the weeds Tollar pulled up came from the outer edge of the ground crops.

She went to pull a plant that looked like it might be a weed, but that also had really lovely, wide yellow flowers with deep purple edges.

"Uh, what are these? They're pretty, but do I pull them?"

"Oh, leave those. They're delicious!"

"Can I try one?"

"Sure, but only one for now. See how they're just starting to bloom? The bees haven't had much time at them yet, so it's not fair to them if we eat them all right away."

Tollar shrugged and popped a flower in her mouth. It was silky on her tongue with a savoury, heady flavour, only a touch of sweetness. The pair of dragons circled noisily overhead again, and Beenala's shoulders tensed until they passed. But she grinned at Tollar.

"See? Really good! Come back in a few days and we'll have some more. Need to leave a few to go to seed and propagate next year's crop, of course. Leave some to the bees."

No one in Tollar's family was half as interested in talking to her the way Beenala was. None of them, except Auntie of course, but she was a city lady and didn't know anything about growing food. Tollar didn't really want to be a farmer, but she was curious about the process. And Beenala, it seemed, could talk to Tollar all day.

As the sun arced overhead, beating down on them in the still air between rows, Tollar noticed Beenala sweating profusely despite the wide hat keeping the sun off her head and shoulders. Her face and thick arms glistened.

Sometimes Tollar forgot about sweat—years ago she'd figured out how to make it evaporate straight away and didn't even think about it anymore. So, focusing half her mind on pulling out the weeds, she extended her magic, pulling the moisture from Beenala's skin.

"Oh good, the breeze picked up," Beenala said, noticing the result but not the effect.

Tollar smiled, watching Beenala's lips and taking note of the smooth way her round body moved as she worked. Beenala was so often flitting disastrously from one thing to another like a distracted hummingbird, seeming almost clumsy. But out here in the forest, with her focus on one task, she had a certain grace Tollar hadn't seen in her before.

"It really is a lovely day," Tollar said. "Thank you for letting me keep you company."

Beenala rested the bottom of her tool on the ground and faced her, smiling again. "It's wonderful to have the company. I've got some extra lunch with me if you'd like to stick around and share."

"That would be perfect. I'll collect more water if you need any."

Tollar caught herself wishing that Beenala's family had room for one more. But they already filled their cottage to the brim. Tollar could at least spend her days on their farm where no one seemed in a hurry to get rid of her.

26

Beenala pulled her one and only dress over her head and smoothed down the wide skirt. It was sleeveless and high-waisted and flared out all around her and came to her knees. It had started out a brilliant orange, had faded over the years, and was back to a brilliant orange with a tinge of crimson after Beenala recently re-dyed it using the last of that wonderful pigment Tollar brought her from the top of the world. She'd embroidered the hem and neckline with her family's braided vine in black, white, and canary yellow.

It was the most vibrant piece of clothing she owned, and she wore it every year for the spring equinox festival.

She picked up her comb, immediately reconsidered, and glanced at the dog, curled up on the bed but watching her.

"What do you think?"

Ash closed her eyes.

"Fat lot of good you are."

She came out of her house to find Tollar leaning against the mango tree, wearing a sky blue... something... that looked like it might be one long piece of fabric strategically wrapped into a loose dress and around her torso to leave flashes of dark blue-brown skin between folds of soft fabric. Tollar's long hair hung loose over her shoulders and down to her hips in fat cascading curls, rippling in the breeze like the little stream feeding her farm down from the mountains.

Even Tollar's clothes were fluid, the blue running together with the brown of her skin like it did upriver where the Marrasayo, a powerful tributary, poured into the Arazow.

Tollar's dress looked softer than anything Beenala could imagine. Tollar had returned from some tiny little faraway island with a swatch of deep crimson silk that was like nothing Beenala had ever felt before or since. Beenala didn't know what the silk weavers in Upalint were doing wrong, but she'd begged Tollar to find out the secret.

It looked like whatever Tollar wore now was very likely more of that silk from faraway lands.

Beenala stopped short, appraising the effect. "You look like a bright spring day."

Tollar smiled. "And you look like a summer sunset. That dress is amazing!"

Tollar went to see Bale, who hadn't gone up into the mountains today. Bale was curled up in the dirt between the two houses and had been since she'd returned from her morning hunt in the jungle.

When Tollar reached her, the little dragon made the soft gurgling hiss sound that Balipar told them was the dragon word for mother. It warmed Beenala as much to hear her say it now as it had when Balipar first explained it. They also said Beenala and Tollar would have to let people know about Bale soon. She'd need to start flying more, not only at night. Though she *was* flying more, but farther away, leaving the farm before daybreak and flying through the dark until she was out of sight, hunting and swooping around in the distant mountains until nightfall when she returned.

She needed to be with her kin, though Beenala joined Tollar in not mentioning that. Bale insisted she stay with them. Nytaltek was as much her home as theirs.

Tollar held out her hands and Bale pressed her snout into them, nuzzling, until Tollar leaned forward and pressed her cheek to Bale's. She stayed like that, stroking the dragon's chin, as Beenala approached. Bale made that same mother sound in Beenala's direction and she smiled.

"Would you ever want to be the mother to a human?" Beenala asked Tollar.

Tollar kept stroking Bale's chin, though her hand had faltered for the briefest instant. "I've thought about it but I'm not sure how it would work when I'm away so much. I know a spell for it, but I'd still need a man involved to help things along."

Beenala wrinkled her nose and Tollar chuckled.

"Not like that," Tollar said. "I wouldn't even have to touch him. Just a bit of water magic at the right time. But even if I didn't bother with all that, raising someone else's child, kind of like Auntie did for me, is still too much when I'm gone so much."

"Couldn't you stick around more?"

Tollar stroked Bale's chin for a long moment. "I'm not sure. I don't think so."

"But this is the longest you've been home in one go, is it really so bad?"

"It's not bad, no. But I can't stop thinking about when this will all be out of the way and I can go. It's a little distressing to not be able to go when I want to."

"But why do you want to?"

"I just always have. There's just... so much out there." She gave Beenala a shy look. "I'd like to share it with you."

Beenala's cheeks warmed and she had to look away, stepping closer to Bale to pet her soft nose. "What are you doing in today? Thought you'd be lost to the mountains by now."

"I ate a gezar," Bale announced, clearly pleased with herself. "They're too big."

Beenala winced and Tollar laughed. "Got some regrets, eh? Give yourself a week, the way you're growing you'll be eating them daily before you know it."

Beenala tried not to notice the way Bale grew. She was bigger than Tollar's house and Beenala's cottage, but she wasn't quite as big as an adult male. She couldn't stop thinking that once Bale was full grown, she'd fly off into the world to find her kin and see what distant lands had to offer. She'd probably go when Tollar did. Maybe they'd go together. Tollar had her farm cleaned up, running at minimum capacity now, ready for a new family at a moment's notice.

Beenala pushed away the thoughts and the encroaching loneliness that tried to seep in. They would both likely remain for another season yet. Maybe it was enough time to convince them both that they didn't, in fact, need to stray so far for so long.

For today, at least, Bale would nap off her extra large feast, and Beenala would go into the city with Tollar for a feast of their own. The spring equinox was one of her favourite celebrations, and she couldn't remember the last time Tollar had been home for it.

She usually didn't come home until mid-spring or later.

"All right, then, Bale, you get some rest and we'll be back tonight," Tollar said, her voice full of amusement. "Shall I bring you a bauble to add to your pile?"

Bale snorted, a great warm gust that blew Beenala's wild fringe back.

"I'll get you something nice. Maybe something to match the purple on your wings."

Bale rumbled out her pleasure, almost like a massive purring cat, and then the two women set off down the lane toward town.

"I hope she'll be all right," Beenala said.

"It'll do her some good. Lessons learned and also a fresh source of food. She'd probably throw up if it was too much. She'll probably double in size by the time we get back."

"Do you think she'll leave? Go off and seek her kin?"

"At some point I'm sure she will—I know she wants to. But she'll probably always come back here, as long as there's a reason to." Tollar glanced at Beenala. "And she can get anywhere in the world in a matter of days. Lucky beast!"

"You want her to go so you can go with her, don't you?"

"That would be an incredible journey! I've not travelled by dragon before. Just that short jaunt home from Port Sawulxo and that was more fleeing than proper journeying. Listening to Croves talk about it though..." Tollar's expression got lost on some distant adventure. She shook her head and smiled at Beenala. "Wouldn't you go if you could travel by dragon? Take a quick trip to the coast, gone for a week and then straight back again before your trees even notice you've been away."

"I really don't know. It would mean a lot of sleeping on the ground. Or in my case, not sleeping."

Tollar grinned. "You were getting the hang of it before we got back."

"I was exhausted."

Tollar laughed. "Everyone's exhausted when they travel like that. It's rare to be as used to it as I am."

"I really don't know."

"But you got to see the ocean for the first time, what did you think of that?"

"Oh, it was beautiful when I wasn't utterly terrified. Beautiful and large. But looking down at it was like looking down into the sky and it was terrifying too."

"Hmm, never thought of it like that. I loved the ocean the first time I saw it. Was out on the east coast where it's all sandy. I ran straight out into it."

Beenala smiled, seeing it like she'd been there. And listening to Tollar recount the things she saw made Beenala want to see some of them with her. It was why she'd dreamed up that ridiculous trip to Port Sawulxo. But she hadn't accounted for all the danger that was apparently inherent in adventures. Or at least the sort Tollar went on.

Practice with her mentor, attending scatterball matches with Tollar, even watching on the fringes of little fights with more of Karthiry's infiltrators, none of it made her more comfortable with the danger. Tollar had started teaching a group of elementals how to harness each other's power, and Beenala joined them a couple of times but hadn't returned.

But there'd been little actual fighting since a week or so after Draminedes left. Tollar helped Solia and Saivyn track down the last of the infiltrators and things settled down. No more angry mobs of swibs going after wizards. Everyone leaving the elementals alone while they worked to repair some of the damage.

Tollar was out stirring the pot with her circulars, spreading them wide and starting to talk more about Karthiry, about what she'd done in Sawulxo and how. Started talking about some of what Draminedes said, about how the woman and her followers thought so little of the people of Upalint.

He'd given Tollar some direct quotes of things Karthiry had said, about how she thought their people were dirty, uncivilized barbarians who lived like pigs, unintelligent, every last one. How she would come and clean them up, cutting down the dirty forest to plant neat, sensible rows of wheat.

It was turning anger outward. Not all of it, but hopefully enough.

It was hard not to think about it all, especially when Tollar worried so much about what would happen when Karthiry came for them. The necromancers still insisted it was a matter for the living and refused to get involved. Cowards, the whole lot.

And Saivyn would rather spear Tollar than look at her. The feeling was certainly mutual.

Rather than win Saivyn over, Tollar's successes only made him angrier. And Solia still took the wrong approach, trying to get Tollar to meet him halfway. Even Beenala saw that his was an ego problem and there wasn't a concession in the world Tollar could make that would ever please him until he got over himself.

"No brooding," Tollar said, her tone light though her gaze was dark.

"Yes, sorry. Hard not to think about it, first day of spring and all. All we've worked for and talked about all winter is the spring, but not about how lovely it is, but about how trying it will be."

"It will be. But not today. Today, we eat goat spice pies and banana icees until we burst."

"But the market first."

Tollar jingled the coins in the pouch she had tucked away in some fold or pocket in her long skirt. There was so much fabric it was hard to say for sure. Beenala wanted to get hold of it, and maybe some of that silver threading she'd seen a while back, and stitch vines across it.

The market square was full of colour and sound and delicious smells. Half the city turned out to eat and sing and dance, and to celebrate the sun's return from its hiding place in the winter gloom.

Tollar found a vendor with all manner of brightly coloured baubles, including a large wheel of glass, meant to be added to a decorative window, that was the exact shade of Bale's wings. Beenala protested that giving a dragon glass was asking for trouble.

"Nonsense, Abilerit knows how to temper glass to make it sturdy enough even for a dragon."

And there was a book merchant not far off, and Beenala left Tollar there with her head full of dreams and other people's adventures while Beenala found a weaver selling spools of thread in every colour imaginable. Including one left of the silver.

But when Tollar joined her, she had more than the glass wheel tucked under her arm.

"You bought a book?"

"I thought I'd keep it at your place, on that shelf where you've got the volume you made me. Seems silly to have a whole shelf for one book."

Beenala stared and didn't remember to breathe until Tollar laughed and prompted her. To distract Tollar from the way her cheeks flushed, Beenala held open her bag so Tollar could deposit her latest treasures.

When Tollar held her hand out, Beenala took it, loosely twining her fingers with Tollar's. They strode through the market, buying pies and desserts and chocolates. They ate until nearly bursting—it was the only sensible thing to do on the first day of spring—and then sat near the centre of the market where the story songs were going on.

Neither woman could sing worth a damn, so they sat on one of the benches to listen to the old tale about the sun getting lost in the mist every winter. Of course, they knew enough about orbits and seasons to know better now, but it was still a fun story.

Keeping her hand folded in Tollar's, Beenala leaned against her, resting her head on Tollar's shoulder and enjoying the warmth of Tollar at her side. Tollar leaned in as well, resting her chin on top of Beenala's head, her breath rustling Beenala's hair.

It lasted a warm moment before Tollar kissed the top of Beenala's head and sat up to focus on the new song in the centre. Beenala felt like her stomach rippled with firelight.

Eventually, as the day wore on and they filled their bellies on new and delicious treats, the tables and benches and vendor stalls were pulled down the lanes and to the outside of the circle, and the drummers got set up in the centre around a bonfire. Beenala lingered near the edges of the crowd, hand in hand with Tollar, while the rhythm pounded out from the centre.

"Bee, do you dance?"

"I try not to make a habit of it."

"Come dance with me." Tollar faced her, her eyes bright silver in the firelight, and held out her other hand.

The flute accompaniment started, weaving in and out of the beating drums, more and more people transitioning from tapping their feet to dancing, and Beenala had never felt so self-conscious about her lack of grace. But she took Tollar's other hand and allowed the woman to sweep her up in wide, looping circles toward the centre of the crowd.

The spring dance had two versions—one for people with any sort of talent for it, and one for everyone else. Tollar knew both versions, because of course she did, but was gracious enough to lead Beenala through the easier steps, bobs and twirls.

And every time Beenala was certain she would trip, or crash into the other dancers, or step on someone's feet, one of Tollar's firm hands on her waist or shoulder or gripping her hand pulled her back to her centre of balance.

Night fell and the dancing gave way to the bouncing—dancers trying to out-jump each other while keeping on rhythm—when Beenala and Tollar bowed out. They watched while they caught their breath. Well, while Beenala caught her breath.

She'd spent so much of the day grinning that her face ached, so much time laughing her sides ached, and so much time dancing her legs ached. It was a delightful ache. When had she had so much fun on the equinox? In her entire life?

Beenala grinned up into Tollar's face, Tollar's silver irises alive with moonlight, and then she leaned in, resting her head on Tollar's chest and wrapping her arms around Tollar. Tollar's long arms encircled her, and she kissed the top of Beenala's head.

Beenala's chest swelled and the heat of the embrace became too much. But she held Tollar's hand as they threaded their way through the crowd under the unspoken agreement that it was time to head home.

Could she convince Tollar to come home for all the holidays? Better yet, could she convince her to stay? There didn't seem to be a good reason why Tollar left. Because she always had? Like some nonsense tradition kept around for the sake of it?

No, it was time to talk about this. Maybe she could get Tollar to come over for some wine. And to talk. Beenala needed a real, actual, not evasive or aloof—full of joking, snark and deflecting—avoidance of conversation about the real possibility of Tollar being able to stay put. To pull apart why Tollar thought she had to go, why she thought she needed so many layers of armour.

Tollar was off on another of her travel-tangents, talking about a festival she'd been to where all the young people were ritually coupled for the equinox.

"That sounds awful," Beenala said.

"I wouldn't do it, certainly, but they seemed to enjoy it. Huge feast. So much colour everywhere, bright ribbons on everyone and everything. Not much dancing though. You'd love the ribbons, Bee! If I go there again, I'll bring you some."

"Well, I've got wine at the house," Beenala said. "Why don't you come over and have some and tell me more about the ribbons."

Tollar chuckled and squeezed Beenala's hand. "I've never really noted the ribbons in the places I've been. They were noteworthy this time because there was just so frogging many ribbons everywhere!"

"Oh, well, you'll have to—"

"Wait, what's that?"

Beenala had been so lost in her thoughts and Tollar's wild tales that she didn't notice they were nearly home. Tollar pointed up the lane. Something glowing.

"It's fire." Beenala almost stopped in the lane but for Tollar holding her hand and tugging her forward. Beenala concentrated. "It's a lot of fire."

Tollar let go of her hand and ran ahead. Beenala tried to catch up, but her legs already ached, and Tollar had the longer stride, built for running.

"Oh no. Oh shit," Tollar said from up the road. Then she disappeared around the bend.

Beenala heard a despairing "No!" from Tollar just before Beenala came around the trees and stopped. She blinked and waited for her mind to process what her eyes saw.

The fire was Tollar's house. Just the entire house. And Tollar was inside?

As Beenala sucked in a breath and got her feet moving, Tollar pitched her kit out one of the windows—all of them smashed.

"No no no no no..."

Beenala was going to call for Tollar to be careful, when she realized Tollar was encased in water.

Should put that out.

But Beenala stared into the dirt patch between houses. Deep gouges marred the earth.

"Where's Bale?"

Beenala pulled a ball of fire from the house and pushed it out over the yard, illuminating it like midday and slowly cooling the night air around her. There was nothing but gashes in the earth, the side of the house nearest to where Bale normally slept dashed apart, listing precariously where the supports had been knocked away, with bits scattered through the dirt. Bale's little hoard of treasure also scattered from where it had been neatly piled next to the shed. Which was flattened and also on fire.

"Bale!"

Tollar's chorus of no's was checkered with curses, her tone growing more desperate. Beenala kept calling for Bale, pushing the fireball around above her to give her more light to see. Light all the way to the edge of the forest, but there was no further hint to the dragon's whereabouts than the disturbed earth closest to the house. Where Bale had been sleeping when they left.

Beenala startled after a creaking, timbery crash rattled through the night, nearly drowning out a panicky scream from Tollar. "Shit!"

The roof collapsed.

Beenala rushed back around the side of the house, letting the fireball dissipate behind her, finding Tollar standing in the yard, all life drained from her. Arms limp at her side, eyes staring but sightless, posture sagging.

Beenala had never seen her like this.

Reaching out tentatively, Beenala rested a hand on Tollar's shoulder. It infused her with life and she turned, folding into Beenala's arms, face buried against Beenala's shoulders, sobbing.

Beenala squeezed her and let her cry.

What do I do? her mind gibbered over and over.

Solving this kind of crisis was what Tollar did best, but Tollar had gone to absolute pieces. Beenala tried to understand. After Tollar refused to make the house into a proper home on her return, after she'd insisted she would find a new family to run things. This was not about four walls. But what?

And despair was not something Beenala expected. Tollar was always so snarling when things went wrong. But she'd skipped anger and even fear.

What is going on?

They both needed to think. Beenala really needed to think. She needed to get home and Tollar needed somewhere safe to sleep and they needed to find Bale. They needed help. Home first.

When Beenala turned for home, Tollar almost fell over. The strength gone out of her body, she was near to collapsing. Sobbing too hard to do anything but fall.

Beenala leaned in, getting her shoulder under Tollar's arm and checking her hip into Tollar's, half carrying her. She passed Tollar's kit and grabbed it by a strap with her free hand, then dragged both woman and gear across the yard.

Stopped short. Part of the hedge was on fire.

Need to put that out before it spreads.

And the house! She was a pyromancer, for pity's sake, standing here watching things burn. Beenala reached out with her magic to shut down both fires, like pinching a candle flame between damp fingertips.

And spared enough fire to hang over her and give her light back to her house.

Ash whimpered near the door when Beenala shouldered it open, depositing Tollar's kit on the floor and easing Tollar into one of the chairs. Tollar crumpled against the tabletop, still sobbing, while Ash paced a semi circle around the two of them, ears alert.

"Tollar?" Beenala laid her hand on Tollar's back and rubbed gently. "You can stay here. Long as you like. I've got plenty of space."

"It's gone."

"Four walls can be rebuilt. All the city's terramancers owe you, they can raise you something nice and solid, like the cottage."

"Granny's bone. It was on a shelf." Tollar gasped.

"Oh! Oh no."

"It's not just a house, Bee."

Beenala wasn't about to argue. She'd have been devastated if the cottage burned down. But it contained everything she owned. Aside from her grandmother's bone, everything Tollar owned was in the kit she'd saved. Spared because it had been on the floor.

It was blackened around the edges, but spared a real burning all the same.

"Bee, what am I going to do?"

"I don't know. This is a mess. But you can stay here and we'll sort it in the morning. It's late, come on, you need rest. And I need to feed Ash and go look for Bale."

"Bale?"

"Toll, she's not in the yard."

Tollar blinked and opened her mouth to respond. Closed it and shook her head. "Did she do this? But why would she? But why's she not here?"

"Excellent questions, I'll see what I can find out."

Beenala gripped Tollar's elbow and pulled her to her feet. She didn't quite have to carry her, but Tollar barely moved under her own power. She brought Tollar to her own bedroom, just off the kitchen. She'd clean out one of the other bedrooms later—all of them a mess of years of clutter and returned furniture from Draminedes and Croves departing that she hadn't bothered with yet—but she needed to get Tollar sorted first.

Tollar collapsed face first into the bed, weeping into the pillow. Ash jumped onto the foot of the bed and curled in against Tollar's legs.

"I'm going to have a quick look for Bale," Beenala said.

Tollar didn't respond.

Beenala went out into the yard, her lantern in one trembling damp hand, calling Bale's name. But Bale could be hunting. Or night flying. Or hurt. Regardless, she wasn't answering, and Beenala had no hope of finding a black dragon in night's bitter darkness. She tried summoning Bale, just in case, and waited far longer than she should have before conceding the dragon was not coming. She got all the way back into her house before she vomited. Ash came to her, a soft warm presence to ground her. And probably looking for her dinner.

Tollar stopped sobbing and made an attempt to wipe her face. She lay on her side, watching Beenala when she came into the room.

Beenala ached in a whole new, awful way to see her best friend like this. She sat on the edge of the bed and took Tollar's hands. Ash sat next to her, chin resting on the edge of the bed, watching Tollar solemnly.

"It'll be all right. You're safe here tonight and we'll figure out the rest in the morning. You can stay as long as you like. I wish you'd stay as long as *I'd* like." Beenala pressed her lips together and closed her eyes, wishing her mouth would behave itself just once.

But Tollar chuckled through her tears.

"Thank you, Bee. What would I do without you? You've always been there for me." But then Tollar's face scrunched up in a bitter, complicated way Beenala couldn't begin to understand.

"I'm always here," Beenala said, trying to comfort her. "It doesn't matter how many times you leave, I'll always be here."

Anger flashed in Tollar's silver eyes, and Ash booped her hands. "I didn't leave that first time, Bee."

"So you've said."

"He made me go. She *let* him do it."

"What, your subfather?"

"He hated me, Bee. *Hated* me." She shook her head furiously. "Because I was too much like my father, my mom doted on me because of it. He got jealous. Nothing I did was good enough. My magic was nothing but a threat. And because my mother was tired of losing men, she'd do whatever it took to keep him, including watch him throw me out for being *too much*."

Tollar collapsed into sobs, and Beenala squeezed her hands. Ash jumped up on the bed, curling on Tollar's feet again.

"Well, if you're too much of anything, it's wonderful things. Is that why you keep going? To surround yourself with better people?"

"To not be reminded I wasn't enough for even my family."

"They were wrong, Tollar. You're enough. You're more than enough." Beenala shifted and curled up facing Tollar, holding her hands. "We'll figure this out. It will be okay."

Tollar nodded but kept weeping. So Beenala stayed where she was to give Tollar the space and the safety she needed.

27

Tollar wasn't sure when she'd have woken up if not for Beenala rolling out of bed and disturbing her. Bright light streaked in through the windows, and Ash would need to be let out. Tollar's eyes stung and felt too large for her eyelids and her cheeks felt like she'd scrubbed them with broken glass. Her head weighed more than a moon, and she'd never be able to breathe through her nose again.

She rolled onto her back and draped her arm across her face, letting time pass until Beenala returned.

"I brought you some water."

A basin clanked on the bedside table before Beenala's footsteps retreated. Tollar didn't bother getting up, instead magicking the water onto her face, letting it sit there in a cool bubble, dealing with the worst of her hot blotchy skin. She scrubbed her hand through the water, left it in a dirty blob above her head and brought some more water over to drink.

Then she deposited the dirty water in the basin and brought the whole thing out to the kitchen and poured it in the sink.

Beenala stood next to the door, in front of the big wall schedule. She'd wiped off her plans for the week, moving them under the "this month" column, and she struggled to fill in today and tomorrow.

It was a mess of notes about finding Bale and fixing Tollar's house. And she was currently writing, erasing, and rewriting something, waffling between whether it was a today or tomorrow issue.

"Bale first," Tollar said. She glanced out the side window but couldn't see much beyond the hedge.

"Right, yes, that's what I thought. I'll get a message to Balipar. Do we need to tell Solia? Should I get Solia first?"

Tollar took a deep breath and resisted the urge to go back to bed. "We need to go look around first. In case she's hiding or somehow hurt. We can use a water platform, it'll go quicker."

Ignoring the ruin of her house, Tollar went toward the river, close enough to pull its water so she'd have enough to make a high column and went to the top of it to survey the farm's canopy. No damage, no smoke rising from the trees or the rows of crops in between. Then she and Beenala skimmed along to Bale's favourite hunting spots.

Nothing but monkeys.

Beenala was quiet and pale. "No sign of fire."

Beenala had mentioned over the winter that when she focused, she could sense Bale's fire the way she could sense any flame. Same way Tollar felt the water all around her.

No sign of Bale nearby. They went up Mount Acrintaga and around the other side where Tollar had stopped that flood. And nothing. Tollar stopped on the shoulder of the mountain and rubbed her hands over her face.

"We need help," Beenala said gently, her hand on Tollar's elbow.

Tollar wanted to lie down on the mountain and quit. But it was a long walk to the cottage, so she went back to save Beenala the trip by foot. It was harder to ignore the charred remains of her house from this angle. A cold block like ice settled into her stomach.

Back in the cottage, Beenala looked from Tollar to the mess of the schedule on the wall. Ash leaned into her legs, and she patted the dog absently.

Tollar collapsed into one of the kitchen chairs and grumbled, "Send a message to Solia, tell her to bring Balipar with her."

"Okay, yes. Should I go for her now? It'll be midday before there's a runner I can send."

"I guess you could go now."

Beenala pressed her lips together and grabbed her bag from the cluttered side table. Ash whined as Beenala headed out the door.

"Stay," she said firmly, giving Tollar a concerned look before leaving.

Ash immediately turned to Tollar, still whining.

"Don't look at me, I don't have any answers." Tollar scratched behind Ash's ears.

Tollar wasn't even sure what the questions were. Up until a few hours ago, she thought she'd be relieved to see the old place destroyed. The thought that Bale had burned her house down was not an especially pleasant one, but even that was overshadowed by the fact that Bale wasn't back yet. Did dragons vomit fire? Was that what happened?

"Ugh, no one tells me anything."

Ash leaned against Tollar's leg, and Tollar rubbed her chin. And felt so much of her tension release.

"Ash, are you made of magic? Are dogs happiness magic? You sneaky beasts."

Ash looked over her shoulder, doggy grin and tongue hanging out, the angle making one of her ears flop comically. Tollar laughed and kneaded her fingers into Ash's squishy cheeks.

But then Ash faced forward, ears alert, issuing one gentle little woof, before the door swung open, Beenala back already, and Ash trotted over to greet her.

"Unless you have some very interesting magic you've neglected to tell me about, there's no way you got to the city and back again already."

Beenala rolled her eyes and dropped her bag onto the table. "I ran into Per Lore near the end of the lane, and he agreed to take a message to Solia for me."

"All right." Tollar looked around the kitchen without really seeing it. She hated this waiting, the way it made her itch to walk out onto the road and keep going, never return.

"What do you think happened?" Beenala asked, standing next to the table, twisting up the hem of her shirt. It was a wonder she hadn't worn all her shirts ragged.

Tollar shook her head. "I have no idea. Best guess, Bale vomited up something flaming and accidently set the house on fire. Dunno where she could have gone though."

"I hope Bali will have some answers. But what are you going to do about the house?"

"I don't want the house, Bee. I never wanted the house. Or the farm. The next family can build whatever they want there."

"Oh." Beenala sat in the chair across from her. "What do you need? How can I help? Oh, I know, how about some breakfast."

Tollar managed to get half her mouth up in a smile. She sat watching Beenala break some eggs into the pan and follow it up with some tomatoes and beans. Ash also watched Beenala, far more closely. Beenala didn't know Tollar's trick with the corn wraps, but that was fine. She didn't really want anything to eat, but appreciated the gesture.

What *did* she want? Beenala had some pertinent questions. Need. What did she *need*? What was the difference between needing and wanting, anyway? She needed out of here, it was long past time. She needed Nytaltek to not need her as badly as it did.

She needed to go back in time and warn her mother away from Zarro in the first place.

She sighed. And rested her forehead on the table. She didn't lift it again until Beenala set a plate down in front of her. Tollar grunted her thanks and wordlessly shovelled food into her mouth, trying to ignore the way the dog watched every forkful hopefully.

Tollar collected up the dishes despite Beenala's protests that she should rest. Rest was the last thing she needed. If she couldn't run and never come back, she needed to move. So she washed and dried and put away the dishes and then tidied the side table while Beenala went to wash up. That was when Tollar realized she was still in her equinox party dress, stained and sooty and stinking, and considered her charred kit on the floor. It contained basic civvies and her uniform and travel gear. Everything nice she owned—except a couple of dresses in one of Bee's back rooms waiting for repairs—had been draped around the now-burned house to keep it from wrinkling. Had she left anything at Auntie's? Maybe a couple of nice things in the back of some cupboard?

She sighed and pulled the kit over to a chair so she could sit while looking through it.

Ash barked and Tollar noticed voices next door. Beenala joined her just as she headed outside. Solia and Balipar both stood in front of the ruin of her house, Solia inspecting the ruin in question while Balipar had their attention on the furrows in the ground, dressed in a simple, lemony short-suit today, their hair subdued in a single thick braid.

"Thank you for coming!" Beenala called, rushing through the hedge toward them, Ash trotting alongside her. "It's been awful."

Tollar hung back, staring at the ruin while her limbs felt cold and jangly, the cold block of ice still in her gut, as Beenala described what they'd returned home to last night and how their morning had panned out.

"No, dragons don't vomit fire," Balipar said. "And an adult made these marks."

"What?" Tollar came forward, that cold feeling electrified, tightening the muscles in her shoulders. "Are you sure?"

"They make all sorts of marks in the ground to communicate with me. These came from the talons of an adult."

"Did Croves come back with Shell or something?"

Balipar furrowed their brow and shook their head. "These marks are big enough they might be from a dragoness."

That block of ice in Tollar's stomach grew spikes and seized her very soul.

"What? But how—That doesn't—" She growled wordlessly and stalked away from them to watch the Arazow in the distance. Confusion gave way to dread. What business did a dragoness have here without coming during the day, or making some kind of noise?

"I'll get Cerro to help me put out a message to the Wizards Guild and see what we can find out," Balipar said.

Tollar bunched her hands into fists and couldn't stop pacing, still wanted to go forever. It didn't feel like any sort of misunderstanding or accident. She'd failed again, she wasn't enough again. They were doomed and Bale disappearing was only the beginning.

Solia gave her the usual platitudes, telling her she was welcome by the guard house any time and she'd find some people to help clean up the mess and she could take Tollar off the roster.

"No, I need something to do. Maybe extra shifts."

Solia gave her a pitying look, but there was nothing else she could do. Tollar didn't watch them leave, pacing into the cottage to change into the basic shorts and top she'd pulled out earlier.

"Tollar, will you be all right?"

"No. I need to leave."

Beenala gasped. "But what about—"

"I won't, but I need to. I need to get away from this place. From *that* place." She waved toward the burned-out husk.

"Walls can be rebuilt. I don't understand…"

"I hated what it was. What it should have been and wasn't. And I guess… I'm mourning not only that those walls were never a home, but now they never will be. And they *almost were*—with you and Croves and Dram there. I've never really known what it's like to have a home or to be part of something where I mattered. That's why I go, Bee. I don't want the reminder. Will I ever have what everyone else takes for granted? I'm like a ghost. Just doomed to wander forever."

Beenala pressed her lips together. "I have something I want to show you. Just a moment."

Beenala disappeared down the hall toward all those unused, cluttered bedrooms. She returned a moment later with a canvas wrapped in cloth, unwrapped it slowly and brushed away the dust.

"I was painting this the day you left—the day Zarro made you leave."

"You were the only one who cared." Tollar kept the anger out of her voice. It wasn't directed at Beenala, it wasn't Beenala's fault Tollar's family was awful. Except Auntie.

Except Granny, who she no longer had a connection to. She tensed against the rising emotions and focused on Beenala. Tollar swallowed the hot lump in her throat and took a steadying breath.

"It crept up on me slowly, knowing that I loved you, Bee. But that day made it clear."

Beenala smiled, blushing so deep even the tips of her ears went red. "It was a lovely day up to that point."

Beenala turned the canvas around so Tollar could see the painting. It was certainly older, the style different than anything Tollar had seen Beenala do. It showed the gentle, treelined slope from the farms down to the road that ran along the river, and the river off in the distance.

"I'd got it about half done when I heard the shouting and saw you go, and when you'd gone, I came back to it and the cheer I'd started with didn't feel right. The day was missing something."

Out of the corner of her eye, she saw faces in the plants in the foreground. When she looked directly at them, they faded into the greenery. The faces seemed vaguely familiar, all looking varying degrees of sad and hurt and defiant.

It was *her* face. A ghost of a memory of the girl she was half a lifetime ago.

Tollar's heart raced.

Despite the mournful foreground, the river in the distance glittered. Beenala had so clearly captured the sparkle and shine of it, of a perfect summer day. Tollar ached for that kind of calm perfection.

And ached that it wasn't her family but the girl next door who had cared enough about Tollar's absence to make note of it at all.

"Bee, this is magnificent."

"It's never been the same without you around. Until now I only ever saw you in the market, with a span of months or years in between, until you showed up right here again with a dragon egg. And that was certainly A Tollar Thing. At least it turned out all right. But the point is, you're here now, and it's wonderful."

"You say that now but my own mother got tired of me."

Beenala sucked in a breath and her expression fell, even her wild hair seemed to droop. And it twisted something in Tollar's gut to see Beenala sitting there, adrift and struggling amidst the upheaval of the day. And all because of Tollar and the chaos she brought everywhere she went.

It didn't matter how generous Beenala was about Tollar dropping a dragon into her lap, Tollar always dropped in out of nowhere and threw things into disarray. Her mother was right, she was too much.

She'd already been here too long, mucking things up, letting Beenala get too close like Tollar didn't know better. Was she inviting more pain?

"I'm not your mother, Toll. And I'm sorry that she failed you, but I wish you'd give me the chance."

Tollar shook her head and paced to the door. "You deserve better than someone coming and going on a whim and throwing your life into chaos."

"I don't care what you think I deserve, Tollar. What does anyone deserve? That doesn't matter. What I want is for you to stay here. With me."

"It's a lovely daydream, Bee, but I've done enough to burden you already." Tollar shouldered her pack and pushed out the door, despite Beenala's protests.

And she didn't look back, but knew Beenala would spend half the day standing in the door, watching.

28

K arthiry leaned over a table full of maps, and Draminedes had never seen her look so smug. He worried he'd somehow misstepped, that his usefulness had run out and he'd be joining Hollen on the chopping block by the end of the day. Well, he'd get a few days because Karthiry liked making a public spectacle of it when she executed traitors, and even she couldn't manufacture an audience in a day. Not yet.

Draminedes expected to have nightmares to the end of his days about the sound the axe made when it relieved Hollen of her head.

"Ah good," Karthiry said when she saw him. A couple of other advisors hovered around, Master Loch lurking in a corner, and Karthiry's new secretary—apparently a permanent replacement for Draminedes—seated off to the side. This one was a couple of years younger than Draminedes, with glowing brown skin and glossy black hair to his shoulders.

"Draminedes, my good fellow, can you explain more about these hill beasts you mentioned in your report?"

Draminedes hoped he didn't visibly sag upon discovering he was here for a legitimate reason, not to be trapped into exposing himself or to be thrown to the sharks.

"The locals call them gezars. They're a large hunting cat, size of an ox. Or so they say. They eat anything, and find humans fun to hunt."

"Yes, I saw that much. What's this about a rattling sound?"

"Ah, that's a bit of genius, I suppose." He smiled, not at the fact itself but about how Tollar had manufactured it. Scare tactics, she called it. "They're typically solitary creatures, but when they do hunt in packs they use the rattling sound to coordinate. Apparently they can oscillate their vocal chords to the point it rattles. The jungle echoes with it when they're stalking prey."

"I see. Do you expect this will be a significant hurdle in our efforts?"

"We won't be in the jungle, will we? The cats don't come into the city and rarely visit the roadways."

"Formidable creatures?"

"The locals relied on the dragons to keep the population in check. I think now they have the necromancers distract the gezars with animated corpses whenever anyone has business in the jungle."

Karthiry shuddered.

"M'lady, I suggest a squad of pyromancers on hand," Breon said. "Fire always scares away such beasts and it will clear the cursed jungle faster."

"You know what Master Loch thinks of that lot," Karthiry said testily, glancing at Loch in the corner.

"Of course, m'lady, m'lord."

"I've got a couple trustworthy ones stationed in Meeri Bay," Master Loch said, almost bored.

"Very good, your grace. I'll bring them in with this wave." Karthiry pointed at a clump of blocks on her map.

"What's that?" Draminedes asked, though he should know better. He recognized it as the area around Biterna, the mainlands to the north and the south. The water between was practically filled with the little blocks.

"My forces, Dram."

"Oh, I see." And he utterly failed to keep the horror off his face at the sheer numbers. He saw the little blip of them in Port Sawulxo, and that was bad enough. This couldn't be accurate, could it?

"Thank you, Dram."

He bowed politely and retreated, knowing better than to linger after a dismissal. And sticking around would be awkward—an icy feeling seized his insides, and his hands shook.

He'd been trying to prepare Tollar and her people for an invasion roughly twice the size of what they'd seen in Port Sawulxo. But this? It was five times that. Maybe more. Upalint on its own, no matter how powerful Tollar was, could never stop this advance.

And where would that leave him? On the right side. But the losing side.

Was this enough for the Wizards Guild to intervene? The Guild's numbers were certainly great enough, if they worked in concert, to put an end to Karthiry's expansion and exploitation.

It had always been a long shot, though. The administration of the Guild seemed like insufferable cowards.

He barely acknowledged Crendin, another of Karthiry's cronies, as they passed in the hall. Hoped his face hadn't given too much away. He went to the little office where he'd left his things, including his satchel of notes and paper and ink.

When he came out, intent on going home since it didn't appear Karthiry needed him for anything, one of the staff nearly collided with him.

"Master Dram!" Her tone was hushed but urgent. "Come with me, quickly."

She rushed down the hall, and Draminedes trailed behind, puzzled. She slid open a servants' access panel, cleverly camouflaged into the wall, and ushered him into the narrow hallway and staircase down to the kitchens.

"What—"

"Just come! I'll explain in a minute."

So he followed her down into the kitchen where the cooks were entirely too silent as they prepared the next meal.

"You found him!" Peniope shouted.

"Tell him what you heard."

"Dram, it's awful! What did you do in the south?"

"What do you mean?"

"I heard that awful man, Crendin, telling one of those other awful northerners that he heard you talking to Hollen before she was sent for execution, that she was a traitor and you were too."

Draminedes blanched.

"It's true then."

"I... what did you hear?"

"Crendin said he didn't like your answers to Hollen and went snooping—messages sent to some remaining spies in Upalint—and found out you'd been working with the locals."

"Absolutely not." He hoped he sounded more convincing than he felt. "I befriended a group of resisters to learn more about their plans."

Peniope gave him a pitying look.

He sighed.

"It's true then?"

"Yes... I couldn't... Hollen was right, Karthiry is..."

"She's a monster, Dram, and it's about time you saw it. Come on, you have to get out of here—he was heading straight to Karthiry to tell her what he found. Was telling everyone he saw on the way."

Draminedes leaned against a counter and giggled. High pitched, dreadful sounding, but he couldn't stop it, could barely breathe. All this for nothing. And it would probably destroy his entire family. Hollen had been a saboteur, but Draminedes was a complete traitor.

How could he get out of this alive?

"Come on, Dram. Out the laundry door, follow me!"

Someone else gave Draminedes a shove to get him going, and he followed Peniope down more narrow stairs and underground, through a labyrinth of hallways, past the steaming, smelly laundry room to a door. It opened onto the side of the hill the manor was built on. Out of sight of the main quarters.

Peniope pointed out the path. "Go that way, until you get to the bridge and then follow the stream up to the village. You won't be able to stay there long, but you know all the hiding places on the island as much as I do. Don't let them catch you. Go help your new friends in the south if you can."

Draminedes gave her a quick embrace and rushed down the path before the search for him began in earnest.

Draminedes sat stinking and filthy in the ferns outside his father's house, waiting and hoping. He came every evening to watch and always left before dawn. Karthiry's people couldn't watch his father forever, could they? There had to be a point where they gave up. Hopefully before he starved to death or they found him.

He was sick of eating stolen fruit and coconuts. But even if he caught fish, he couldn't risk a fire to cook it. He wasn't tired enough of fruit to try eating anything raw yet. And now he suffered a headache from the eye strain of dirty lenses, but his robes were such a mess all they did was smear the dirt around when he tried cleaning them.

He'd tried following his father to look for an opportunity to talk to him, but Karthiry's people watched his entire family too closely.

Did everyone know what Draminedes had done? How many of them cared if they did know the truth? Maybe Karthiry told some kind of lie about it. She certainly hadn't been entirely truthful about the charges against Hollen.

He wouldn't know until he spoke to someone he could trust. If there was anyone.

Would Father turn me in?

Draminedes had no idea what his family thought of the northerners. It had never come up before he left because there was no reason to suspect anything was wrong on the island. It seemed like everything was finally improving after so many years of loss.

But watching from the edges these last two weeks, it was clear that his people were losing even more, but in different ways.

Draminedes was about to give up on the night, when a runner came over and immediately left with the entire watch except one stationed at the road. He stood up straight and stared after them. Then realized what he was doing and ducked behind the ferns. Watched, but they didn't return.

Creeping through the ferns, he approached the back door. Then hesitated. Were there more of Karthiry's people inside? He hadn't seen anyone come or go, but that didn't mean anything.

Was this a trap?

He crept under a window to listen, but the house was quiet save for the rustling of his father moving around, the familiar sound of his footfalls.

Draminedes couldn't do this much longer. They would catch him one way or another if he didn't get help, so he may as well take what appeared to be the only opportunity he would get.

He knocked on the back door, softly so as to not alert any of the neighbours.

His father growled from inside.

"Haven't you people bothered an old man enough?" His father pushed open the door, mouth open and scowling, but then his eyes widened and his expression softened when he saw Draminedes.

"Hurry and get in here." He kept his voice low so the guard left on the road wouldn't hear. He ushered Draminedes through the door and into the kitchen. "Where have you been?" His father assessed him. "Living in the bush this whole time? Dram, what is happening?"

"I don't know what they told you, but it's probably true."

"You've been working with people to the south?"

"Yes. She's about to invade them and they're good people. She'll destroy them. She's got dragons, Father, I saw what she did to Port Sawulxo."

His father, Sariledes, gestured to a seat at the table and began brewing some tea. He moved slower than he used to, the weight of his years sitting heavy around his middle, less grace in his movements now that he had bad joints from too many years of the wrong kind of work since trade dried up. He had the same terracotta skin tone as Draminedes, but black hair like Draminedes's brother and sister, all of them about the same height, though the way Sariledes stooped made him seem shorter.

"I don't know what you expect to accomplish with this, son."

Draminedes sighed. "I don't know either. Helping them was the right thing to do. And it's clear to me now how Karthiry manipulated our people, took advantage of the state we've been in."

His father nodded slowly, getting a sack from near the door. "She seemed like a good opportunity, cloaked in her golden words, when she first arrived. But nothing has changed, has it? Some of our people have disappeared in the night and others have been publicly executed, and otherwise we're still right where we were."

"Do you think it will change? Can we get a rebel force together to overthrow her?"

"You, son, won't be doing anything on this island for quite some time."

"What do you mean?"

"You can't hide forever. Trying to organize the people who see through the lies will take more nuance than you can manage when half the island believes you're a traitor. Half the island is holding out hope that she'll keep her promises. They'll fight to the death in the hopes she'll turn things around."

Draminedes stared down at the tabletop, steadying his hands against its edge.

"What do I do?" His voice rose so that he had to take a deep breath.

"You need to go, son. Leave thoughts of rebellion for now. Taking it too fast will result in too much bloodshed. More people need to see the truth first. There are some of us trying to help that along."

He looked up at his father, rooting in the pantry, sack in hand. "You? How? Why didn't you say something to me sooner?"

"You weren't ready to hear it. You were too pleased to be contributing to the household, too focused on the chance of prestige. But I've been hearing whispers from the families of people working in the manor. I know what she did to the chief."

Draminedes gripped the table edge and tried not to be angry with his father. How much of this could have been avoided if he'd had some notion of what he was getting himself into? Though his father was right. He wouldn't have listened, would he?

It had taken him weeks to see the truth in Nytaltek even though it had been staring him in the face the moment he stepped into the market.

"Then what do I do?"

"You trust these people in the south?"

"Yes. They had no reason to believe me or take me in or help me. They had every reason to drown me in the river, but they didn't. They let me help them."

"They weren't just setting you up to come home and be destroyed? A useful tool, like Karthiry views you?"

His hands shook and his head spun. Could they have? He'd tried not to think it, needing to hope. He shook his head and sat straighter.

"No, Father. I believe them."

Sariledes nodded decisively and handed him the sack. "Go get cleaned up and grab a couple changes of clothes. I hope these people in the south are as true as you say."

Draminedes stared wide-eyed.

His father glanced out the window at the guard on the road. "You don't have a lot of time."

Draminedes snatched the bag and went down the hall to his room, his father speaking softly as Draminedes swiftly changed out of his foolish dirty robes and stuffed what he could into the sack full of supplies.

"I've got boats left, son. You take one and go. I'll—oh godsdamnit here they come. Out, now."

Draminedes scrambled for the back door while Sariledes pressed a note into his hand. "Bitoru, go. Give this to Nelen, she'll know what to do."

The door closed softly and Draminedes lunged into the ferns, lying flat until his heart stopped racing. Then crawled, slow and careful and constantly looking back as the watch took up posts around his father's house again.

Bile rose as he snuck away from the only real home he'd ever had, creeping like a thief in the night. But maybe there was a new home for him out there, if he survived. He hoped Tollar and her people would be as welcoming a second time.

29

Beenala let Ash out for the morning, and the dog bolted off into the ferns, hopefully not to disturb another den of tarantulas. Beenala didn't care how good they were roasted with some herbs in a banana leaf, pulling an entire colony of them off her dog was not something she ever wanted to do again.

This time of morning, Tollar should be coming over for breakfast with something fresh picked from her farm to share, brimming with tales, and wondering what mischief Bale was up to.

Bale.

Beenala swallowed the hot lump in her throat. It had been a week with no sign of Bale. Balipar had convinced Cerro to send out a message looking for the little dragon. But no one had seen her.

Beenala glanced at the schedule on the wall, which she'd wiped clean the day Tollar left and hadn't coherently filled in since. After using up all her dishes and nearly running out of food, she'd decided that first thing in the morning was for completing the most urgent chore. Today, it was dishes. Only washing them. Putting them away wasn't vital.

Beenala supposed she ought to head into the forest and collect eggs before she was overrun with chicks. She went to the board, picked up her chalk and stared. Did today feel like an egg day? Did it matter? She could just do it, couldn't she?

"No, not today."

But she resolutely scrawled Eggs in the column for tomorrow.

"Well, it's a start."

The matter remained of finding a way to fill today. Her first reaction was to go lie in bed. But she hadn't been able to sleep in her own bed since Tollar left because the pillow smelled sooty, but mostly like Tollar. Beenala had never put any thought into the way people smelled before. Tollar smelled like damp earth and sunlight.

The smell of Tollar reminded her of being in Tollar's arms after the dance. Beenala hadn't hugged anyone since the last time she saw her mother, but she very desperately wanted another hug. Specifically from Tollar.

She grabbed her walking stick and bag, wrote Bale in today's column, and stepped outside, whistling for the dog. Ash ran over, cheerful as ever and thankfully not covered in spiders, and Beenala patted her head before setting out into the jungle.

A hug from her mother wouldn't be terrible either, but going in to visit her parents would be a lot of effort. The inventor who won the winter competition had come up with a way to pass messages through wires like the ones that carried power from the dam to the lights. If it were a reality and not a dream for the future, a quick message over a wire to her mother was something she could handle.

But not the explanations.

Why had hugs suddenly gotten so complicated?

She had no idea what to do about the mess and tried imagining what Tollar would do.

Well, she didn't have to imagine, Solia came by a couple of days ago to see how Beenala was doing and told her all Tollar did was drink when she wasn't on duty and that if she didn't pass out under one of the club's tables, then she slept on a spare sleeping mat up in the locker room.

Solia couldn't figure out why Tollar wasn't staying with her aunt and why she insisted on living out of a locker and rarely leaving the guard house.

So okay, don't do what Tollar *was* doing. But what *should* Tollar be doing right now? What would she tell Beenala to do?

"She'd tell me to clean my frogging kitchen." Well, that was for later. "She'd tell me to frog later and do it now."

Beenala sighed, and stopped walking, leaning her stick against a tree and realizing her thoughts had brought her to the base of Mount Acrintaga.

She fished her notebook out of her bag, wrote This Week at the top of the page and Dishes Away under that.

Solia also despaired that Tollar had given up on trying to get everyone else ready for the inevitable invasion. Beenala wondered if it was because if Upalint lost the battle, it would be easier for Tollar to leave. Had she so thoroughly given up on everything here?

She put Talk to Cerro next on the list because maybe if she bothered him about it enough, he'd convince the rest of the Wizards Guild to help them. Oh, sure, the Guild hadn't outright refused to help, but it certainly wasn't in a hurry to decide. Beenala was certain they would stall until the northerners were unstoppable and then fret about how no one could have seen that coming.

She sighed.

And if she was nosing around the guilds, she might as well see how the new convince-everyone-to-fight play was coming along so she wrote Playwrights next.

And then she noticed Ash trotting merrily away with her walking stick. "Hey!"

She chased after the dog, who was entirely too pleased with herself, relishing in the game of chase and then in the tug of war they had when she eventually allowed Beenala to catch her.

"We're supposed to be looking for Bale."

Studying the jungle around her, she decided to go further east this time. It felt like she'd already scoured the entire jungle between the river and Mount Acrintaga. It was time to skirt north and east around the edge of the city and see what the mountains that way had to say.

She kept searching because if she stopped she'd have to admit to herself the likelihood that Bale was gone for good.

She swallowed the hot lump in her throat and picked a careful path eastward, always choosing to head uphill in the hopes of finding a good vantage point that would offer some clue. She walked until the sun was at her back, snacking on the wrap and fruit in her bag, tossing the occasional morsel to Ash.

Until Ash ran off barking, something ripping through the jungle at alarming rate up ahead. The noise stopped suddenly, the dog still barking.

"Ash?" a too familiar voice called.

Beenala gasped and ran after the dog.

"Tollar! What are you—?"

"Could ask you the same."

"I'm looking for Bale." She hadn't meant to sound so indignant, but didn't appreciate the shock.

Tollar smiled mournfully and couldn't meet her eyes.

"Wait, are you looking for her too?"

"Course I am."

"Well. I've searched everything from the river east to here and north to Sentinel Bend."

Tollar nodded, kept looking at the trees.

"I hear you're a legend now," Beenala said.

Tollar winced.

"Draminedes warned you about this." She crossed her arms.

"Doesn't mean I have to like it."

"But it's a good thing, isn't it? Solia said people are rallying around you to avenge you against the northerners."

Tollar rolled her eyes. "We don't know what happened. What if one of us actually finds Bale and brings her home? There goes the sob story everyone's painting around me. Like I need a sob story."

Beenala blinked and dropped her arms at her sides. "Tollar, if Bale is out here and we find her? You'll be even more the hero who thwarted the northerners to rescue your dragon. Hero dragon rider status level elevated! We can't unburn your house, they'll still rally."

Tollar sighed.

"It won't be long. I know you hate it but we need this."

Beenala pulled her reservoir out of her bag, still getting used to the warmer weather. It was already clear and dry out in the flats and starting to dry out on this side of the mountains. It wouldn't be much longer before the interior mountains were passable.

Two weeks at the most.

But when she tipped her reservoir up, no water came out.

"It's empty," Tollar said softly, holding out her hand. Groundwater already swirled up, waiting. Beenala held the reservoir right way up and Tollar filled it.

"Anyway, thank you. Now, I've got some daylight left to use."

"Yeah, okay." Tollar raised a water platform out of the ground and sped off further northeast.

Ash whined, taking a few uncertain steps in the direction Tollar had disappeared.

"Come on." Beenala headed straight north.

"Oh bugger, I should have asked her where she's looked." Beenala sighed.

Coordinating their efforts, and seeing if anyone else was looking, would save them from going over the same patches of jungle. It seemed hopeless, a fool's errand, but it didn't take long for the jungle to swallow whole cities. Part of the work of the necromancers was to cut it back from the old ruins of the Dead City.

Beenala stopped partway up the latest mountain with a terrible thought.

The necromancers. Tollar hadn't gone to talk to them. No one had tried since Solia's failed attempt right after Draminedes revealed himself.

Ash licked her hands, twisted up in the hem of her shirt, and Beenala let out a slow breath. It was easy enough to think the necromancers couldn't do much, but with enough willing dead for them to command...

Beenala sighed.

People were, in a general sense, ready to fight invaders, but there was a lot of training left if they were to have a chance. Once rumour went out that Tollar's home had been destroyed by northern spies, it had really galvanized the city. That didn't mean they had enough numbers. Or at least not enough numbers who knew what to do in a fight.

There was the army, and they could be relied upon, but it wasn't enough. But who could say what kind of numbers the necromancers could muster? How many ancestors were tucked away in those hills? And if what Draminedes said held truth, the northerners didn't know anything at all about the necromancers. Thought of them as monsters.

Well, they'd certainly be at their temple, or whatever it was. They lived there, in their little cluster of huts outside the main entrance to the Dead City. The dead didn't keep a schedule and so neither did the necromancers.

But that means talking to necromancers.

And the sun was getting low, by the time she got out to their hills, it would be dark. Beenala shuddered.

Well, Tollar wasn't doing it. And Solia hadn't been able to convince them yet. What chance did Beenala have? She wouldn't know until she tried.

Provided they didn't try to relieve her of her skeleton.

They didn't do that, did they? Kept the dead but didn't *make* the dead. Right?

Beenala smoothed out the front of her shirt and gripped the strap on her bag. She was certain the necromancers were kind of like terramancers, but that they used their magic on dead things. Since Sawulxo, she'd learned a thing or two about fighting with fire, and she could always turn and run. She could do this.

"Come on, Ash."

Beenala headed down the mountain, toward the city to stop at one of the markets to get rice balls for dinner and some jerky for Ash. Without her bike, it would be the middle of the night by the time she got home.

She picked up the pace before she talked herself out of it. So she walked briskly, the dog at her side, and at least it was mostly downhill, a gentle slope, from Nytaltek proper downriver to the old ruins and barrows. To the Dead City and the realm of the necromancers.

It was darker than it should have been, trees hanging over the path, and her little lantern seemed unable to penetrate the gloom. And why was it so quiet? Shouldn't there be screecher monkeys and night birds?

Beenala only remembered being out here once, when it was time to bring her grandparent's skeleton to its final resting place. No one from the family had been gifted a bone, but that was fine because none of them really strayed far anyway. They weren't like Tollar, always wandering off.

She expected bones everywhere, maybe some chanting, but it was still and quiet, only some gentle torchlight outside one of the huts at the end of the path. And the hills looming dark behind the little mini village.

Beenala couldn't focus her gaze on any one thing, and her heart raced, body buzzing. She wiped her hands on her shirt while Ash leaned against her leg.

"This is not a place for the living," a young man said, coming out of the one hut with lights on.

"But you're here and you're not dead."

He gave her a longsuffering look and stood in her path.

"Well, it's true. I don't want to be here long, and I don't come to disturb the dead, I just want to speak to the Wise Mother."

"The Wise Mother confers with her charges." He gestured toward the dark hill, the ruins of the old city buried under centuries of neglect, overgrown with vines and ferns and trees. Only the entrance was kept clear of growth, clean stone decorated with gold, though it was weathered and showing its age.

"Well, then I guess I *will* have to disturb the dead. I must speak with her. I didn't come all this way to argue with you."

"Who are these insolent children," Toresona said in her soft voice.

Ash barked. Beenala and the young man both looked to the entrance where the old necromancer slowly made her way out into the night.

"I'm sorry to disturb you, Wise Mother." Beenala bowed deeply and gave Ash the Lie Down hand signal. "But our need is great. And I know the living aren't your concern, but I fear this concerns the dead as well."

"Oh?"

Beenala knelt next to Ash, stroking the dog's silky ears and steeling herself.

"I've had time to think about it, and when we were in Port Sawulxo, where the northerners have done quite a lot of damage, it wasn't just the living that suffered. I saw temples stripped and destroyed. I saw long dead corpses left in floodwaters, the living not allowed to gather them. They did, of course, slowly and at night, they went out to collect their dead. But the indignity of it. Can you imagine that happening here?"

"We will continue to shepherd the dead as we always have, even if they require extra time reaching us." Toresona leaned on her bone cane.

"But there's no guarantee *you* will still be here. Any of you. I don't think Tollar put enough thought into it, but I heard Croves tell her about seeing the priests and necromancers of Sawulxo being given the same disrespect as everyone else."

"We can hide in the Dead City, child. They'll barely know we're in there."

"They will notice." Beenala gestured to the gold etched into the arch around the door. "They come for everything, regardless of source. They won't fear entering your hills and taking whatever treasures they find. Or where they find those treasures."

"They wouldn't dare steal from the dead!" Toresona stamped her cane against the ground.

Ash whined and Beenala draped an arm around her.

"Wouldn't they? Nothing else is sacred or safe. They've shown no respect for the dead in any other manner. If they're vulgar enough to steal from and destroy temples, I can't see why the dead cities and our ancestors would be any different. This is what Tollar has been trying to tell you, though she hasn't the patience to convey it. Please, Wise Mother. This is for the dead as much as it is for the living. It has everything to do with our way of life, which includes our ways of death."

Toresona scowled off into the dark.

"I will think on what you have said. I will discuss it with my people."

"Thank you, Wise Mother. I know whatever decision you come to will be the correct one." Toresona gave her a knowing grin. Beenala bowed her head and remained kneeling.

"And, Wise Mother, when Tollar's home burned, she lost the bone connecting her to her grandmother. One of yours came out to search for it but there was nothing but ash to find. Do you think, if her grandmother still speaks, that maybe it can be replaced?"

"Don't push your luck, child." But Toresona's eyes glittered.

Beenala bowed her head one more time, then stood and fled, Ash trotting at her side, the warmth returning to her limbs as she put the Dead City well out of sight. She wished she'd thought to go home first and get her bike. It was a long walk up the slope to the city of the living and beyond to her farm, where she was unlikely to get much rest before tomorrow's work began.

30

Tollar groaned herself awake and was careful sitting up, having slammed her head into tables too many times. Blinking away the sleep, she realized she hadn't passed out under a table this time. Well, that was a lovely change of pace. But it really was too bad she couldn't stay black out drunk all the time.

At least this time she'd had the sense to fall asleep on the wide bench in the locker room. It had some padding to it, almost like a bed.

"Where the bleeding moons did my mat end up?" she muttered.

She staggered to her locker, doing her best to ignore the way her stomach lurched and her head tried to split apart. The mat was rolled up in there, tucked in next to her kit. All right, she hadn't lost anything in the night, so that was also a win. Now to get some water.

There was a hand pump at one end of the room, meant for filling up reservoir bags for guards on duty, but Tollar shoved her entire head under the spout.

The water sluiced over her and she pulled it through her pores, a trick she didn't use when anyone else was around, but that she'd perfected over the years with guidance from caravan healers. Put water where her body needed it and filter out what ailed her. It put tremendous strain on her, forcing her body to work at impossible speeds, and she braced against the basin so the dizziness didn't take her off her feet.

But when she was done, she felt... Not refreshed, but not about to die anymore.

The sunlight slanting through the windows told her it was late afternoon, drifting into the evening, and she'd managed to sleep most of the day after drinking half the night. But she was training that group of elementals tonight, so she had to get cleaned up and ready. She should probably seek a meal while she was at it.

I'd like to seek a meal on the other side of the world. Where was that place with the juicy steaks?

Tollar groaned. This was much earlier in the day than she usually started thinking of leaving.

"Oh, there's the worthless toad, finally gracing us with her presence," Saivyn snapped from the open doorway to the hall and stairs.

"No thanks, Sai, I don't want to dance tonight." She headed for her locker.

"Sai, honestly, that's enough." Solia came in and went to her own locker.

"Shit, is it shift change already?"

"Oh, are we not paying you enough to keep track of the time? You gotten so used to coming and going when you please, you can't handle the duty here?"

"I'm not on duty tonight. Shut up, Saivyn."

"No, I don't think I will." He came in, standing a few paces away, arms crossed over his barrel chest. "Why are you still here? Can I pay you myself to get you to leave?"

"Sai, stop it." Solia again.

"Why in the name of the ancestors do you keep defending this thug? You think we don't have good enough aquamancers without her? Ones we don't have to bribe to stay here?"

"I don't take bribes," Tollar snarled, her voice low and edged like the blade she wanted to put through his damned throat.

"Oh really? What do you call it then?"

"Getting paid, Saivyn. I get paid. Solia pays me to keep the city safe. Caravans pay me to keep their stuff safe. Little villages surrounded by bandits pay to keep their homes safe. You get paid for the things you do, this isn't that much different."

"Don't you dare compare what I do to your thievery! I get paid to defend my home—to keep Upalint safe!"

Tollar slammed her locker door and faced him. "When Upalint needs me, I'm here. But how often do you really need me? I go where I'm needed, what's wrong with that?"

"You have no integrity!"

"Take it back or I'll kill you where you stand."

"No. Integrity."

Tollar snapped the dirty water from the basin in a tight coil around Saivyn, leaving him unable to move. When he tried to shout, she shoved some water into his mouth to gag him.

"Tollar—"

She glared at Solia's attempt to interrupt before focusing on Saivyn.

"No integrity?" Without looking, Tollar pointed at the biggest spiral on her shoulder. "No integrity when I saved this island nation, Latuva, from pirates looting everything they had? Oh, but they paid me! They paid me a pittance, barely enough to keep me fed until the next place." She pointed at a dot on her bicep. "No integrity when I fished this little boy out of a well and drained the water from his lungs before it killed him? They didn't even pay me for that one!" She pointed at another. "No integrity when I held a great wave back after a sea volcano erupted? Held wave after wave back *on my own* until pyromancers and terramancers calmed the volcano and erected a wave break in the sea. And again, they paid me only enough to get me to the next campaign."

Tollar pointed at another and another and another on her chest and arm and shoulder, naming them all, naming her price.

"Don't you dare tell me I have no integrity. I don't sit here on my rank lines and collect dust, Saivyn, I help people, and unless they're people with more money than sense, I only take what I need to get to the next place that needs me. Ancestors curse you and your line to its end!"

She let the water splash around his feet and turned away. He drew a breath and Solia stepped around her to intercept.

"Don't, Saivyn. Or I will let her drown you where you stand. You're out of line. Leave."

And miracle of miracles, he left. Without another word.

"Is it true?" asked a new voice from near the door.

Tollar looked up at the tall, broad-shouldered woman with blue eyes and light brown skin standing in the doorway, and it took her a moment to place Tavalu.

"Did you really do all those things?" she asked.

"Yes. The Keepers don't just hand these out," she gestured to her left side.

Tavalu came in, her eyes sweeping Tollar's chest and shoulder, down her arm. "You have so many."

Tollar took a deep breath and turned to her locker, pulling out her sword, not wanting to go through this. Tavalu's awe was too much like the look Beenala had given her when Tollar explained the tattoos to her. Weeping ancestors, that felt like a thousand years ago.

Things made sense then. She'd still known where Bale was.

If she was being honest with herself, she had a pretty good idea of where Bale was. But thinking about it contributed to the amount of rum she consumed. Even if there was some way to get Bale back from the northerners, had they broken her? Would she be the same dragon?

"I was on my way by and knew you'd be here," Tavalu said. "Thought maybe I'd walk with you to the training."

"You joining in?" Tollar remembered that Tavalu had been nearly drained when Tollar harnessed her energy and had been too nervous about it to join them since.

"Seems like a good time to get over the fear. Worse things are on their way."

Tollar nodded and started for the door, but Solia cleared her throat.

"Uh, I'll meet you on the street," Tollar said to Tavalu.

As soon as the elemental was gone, Solia got right to it. "You were drunk last night."

"Not a crime."

"You were drunk on shift."

"Nothing was happening."

"Tollar."

Tollar sighed. "I'm sorry, all right? I just... I'm not the only one drinking myself into oblivion. That doesn't make it right, but come on. How many boxes of cigars have you gone through this week?"

Solia crossed her arms and stood in front of Tollar. "You're not even hungover."

"Aquamancer trick."

"Before these invaders show up, you're going to tell me what the deal is with your power. If you don't, I'll tell everyone you're nothing but a soft-hearted hero."

Tollar glared.

"Tollar, I don't know why you think you need to hide. Is it because Saivyn can't spare you an ounce of empathy? You know he's an outlier."

Tollar turned away, wishing Solia wasn't between her and the exit.

"I turned myself into a target and it cost me. It cost Bale. It nearly cost Bee."

"There's no proof it was northerners. Running from it doesn't make it better."

Tollar rounded on her, nearly snarled out a line about her running from Nolly, but that wasn't fair. Solia's job was demanding, she couldn't be up all night helping Nolly and Arvanin play nursemaid, and other city leaders gave her a hard enough time for it already. None of them believed her that it was only until the baby settled and started sleeping through the night. Tollar doubted she'd be renting a room she barely used from Per Mora, who was only one street over from Arvanin's shop, if she didn't intend to return.

"The community is here for you, if you'll let us," Solia continued. "People think half of what you say is fiction. But even if the other half is true—even if it's all true—we see how powerful you are. And how much you care. You're one of us, Tollar, if you want to be. You don't have to keep suffering like this."

Tollar shook her head. "Sol, I've got to get a meal in me before I start training or I'll fall over. Don't make me barf on an empty stomach."

Solia grunted and seemed disappointed. "Get on with it then. But if I catch you drunk on shift again, you're off the roster for a season. And think about what I said."

Tollar slipped passed Solia, not wanting to think of much of anything and just do her job. Tavalu waited out on the street.

"You all right?"

Tollar grunted, too frustrated for anything else.

"I know everything is bad and none of us are really all right," Tavalu said, "but you look extra rough."

"Thanks."

She should say more but it was such a knotted mess to unravel she didn't know where to start.

"I think I'll feel better if I can get a few more of you learning to harness each other's energy."

"Well, then, I'm glad I—"

"Oh shit." Tollar spotted a face in the crowd. One she hadn't seen in years. And hadn't spotted that face until it spotted her first.

"What—" Tavalu started, and then Tollar's mother called, "Baby girl, is that you?"

"Um, I'll meet you at the compound." Tavalu quickened her pace.

Tollar tried not to feel betrayed as she looked for an exit. Wished she'd thought to pretend she didn't see her mother, Janda, and keep going with Tavalu. And then her mother was in front of her.

"Oh, pet, I didn't realize you were still home!"

"That's because I didn't tell you." Tollar watched the passing crowd.

"Still a bitter child, I see. Even after I left you everything?"

Tollar scowled. "You left me the scraps no one wanted. Typical. Leave the rubbish burden farm to your rubbish burden child?"

Janda bristled. "That's hardly accurate."

"Isn't it?" Tollar bunched her hands into fists, fire coursing through her veins. "You threw me away! And for what?" She made a show of looking at the empty place next to Janda, noting she was alone. "Was he worth it?"

Janda's expression hardened. "You've always been a terrible child."

"And you've always been a terrible parent." Tollar pushed passed her and continued down the street, ignoring her mother's protestations, thinking about finding the biggest cask of rum in the market. Didn't need to be sober to teach.

Why did she stay here? The likelihood of Tollar having anything but anger for her mother was low. Her siblings were scattered. She could write to Auntie.

Don't need to be here. It's not like they want my help anyway.

Didn't want it but they did *need* her help, didn't they? Even if they all started cooperating, their chances of success were low. Even if they were all cooperating *and* Tollar stayed and did her damnedest, it still looked bad. She wanted to run from the hopelessness as much as from her personal turmoil.

Tollar had never run from a fight before. If she started now, would she ever stop running? This place had started, very briefly, to feel like home. No. Not this place. It was Beenala. Tollar had thought she was just being soppy when she told Beenala that wherever Beenala was that was home for Tollar. Beenala wouldn't run. And even if Tollar could somehow convince Bee to abandon her family and her ancestors, what would Beenala think of Tollar for running from a fight, for leaving their loved ones to their doom?

The idea of seeing the same disappointed expression on Beenala's face as Tollar's mother constantly wore dropped a ball of spiky ice into Tollar's guts.

She groaned and scrubbed her hands over her face.

She had to stay. No matter how hopeless it was, she couldn't leave Beenala. But Tollar hated being on the losing side.

Time to do something about that.

31

Draminedes sat on the edge of a half-demolished wall in Port Sawulxo and stared out over the flooded section of the city. He'd seen it day in and day out, first when he'd been here to travel back to Biterna, and again in the three days since he landed. And it still horrified him.

They were leaving it. Not letting the locals drain it or rebuild. A reminder.

And no one in the port knew what to think of him. Any of Karthiry's people he ran into, he pretended to be one of them, on a vague mission from her ladyship. None of them dug too deep. They knew better than to pry. And any locals he ran into, he tried passing himself off as a lost traveller.

It wasn't too far off the truth. He'd never felt so lost despite knowing exactly where he was.

When he closed his eyes, he imagined he was on Biterna, sitting on his father's porch, drinking tea. But that home was gone, gods knew for how long, and the only other place he'd ever known was inaccessible at the moment.

With the interior valleys still underwater, he had no chance of getting back to Upalint before Karthiry's forces were upon them. But he had to warn Tollar. They had no idea the numbers they faced, even if there was any resistance to be had here in the port.

"Hey there, no loitering!"

Draminedes looked up the street to see a pair of patrolling northerners coming his way, speaking in prime. They both carried battleaxes, scowling

310

like they were looking for a fight. He should run, but the strength went out of his legs. He gripped his pack.

"Sorry, friend," he called back. "Just resting my legs after the journey." He indicated his pack.

"You need to move along," the first one said.

The second glared at Draminedes and spoke Prairiean to his companion, who stopped suddenly to listen.

"You're from Biterna?" he asked Draminedes.

"Um. Yes. Arrived recently on a mission from her ladyship."

"A mission." The second one kept glaring. Said something else to the first one and they picked up their pace.

"My friend here thinks you look familiar," the first one said. "Like a traitor they haven't seen on the island for some weeks."

"What? No. I don't know anything about that."

They rushed him and Draminedes tripped over his own feet trying to back away and landed on his ass, tangled in his pack.

"Stop! This is some kind of—"

The second guard, who was nearest to Draminedes, fell sideways, crying out in pain. The first halted and turned, and Draminedes gasped. Croves stood in the street, swinging some kind of giant club/hammer thing at the remaining guard. It hit the man in the knees, and he screamed, one leg bent at an angle that made Draminedes's stomach turn.

He fought with his pack to get up, but Croves was there, hauling him to his feet and wrapping him up in a big meaty hug.

"What the pale hell are ye doin' here?" Croves took Draminedes's face in his hands.

"I was about to ask you the same."

"Follow me. More of 'em will come."

Draminedes blinked. Of course, the screaming would draw attention. Croves ran and Draminedes did his best to follow, down streets and narrow alleys, a calm walk down a block of wide avenue, and then swiftly down another narrow alley until they reached the flooded street, where Croves turned again, heading parallel to the flood with water lapping gently at the stone roadway.

"Tollar send ye here on a mission?" Croves asked.

"I'm afraid no one's sent me here, but I need to get some news back to her. Where's Shell?"

"Hiding in the mountains till I need him. What do ye need to send to Tollar?"

Draminedes glanced around, the seemingly deserted streets felt too wide and exposed. "This is perhaps not the best place to talk about it. Is there somewhere safe with more trustworthy ears?"

Croves nodded grimly and kept walking along the flood zone.

"You and Shell came back for the other dragons, didn't you?"

"Aye. Can't leave 'em."

Draminedes smiled, finding the first bit of comfort since leaving Nytaltek. He reached out and gave the large man's hand a squeeze. Croves squeezed back, gave him a quick, amused look.

Croves turned from the flood and brought him through a residential neighbourhood, finally stopping at a plain house and knocked on the door. Dogs erupted in a cacophony that Croves patiently ignored. A woman leaning on a cane opened the door a moment later and squinted suspiciously out at the two men.

"Afternoon, Chalky. Got a friend of Toll's here, needs some help."

"How good a friend?" Chalky scrutinized Draminedes.

"I, uh, I'm helping her try to end all this." He gestured vaguely toward the drowned neighbourhood.

She looked to Croves. "You trust him?"

"Absolutely."

Chalky nodded once and opened the door. Another man, Brilly, her brother, fixed Draminedes a drink while he told the three of them about what had happened since Croves and Shell left Nytaltek.

"The invading force is much larger than Tollar anticipated, and I need to warn her. I don't know if she'll have time to gather the necessary allies to turn away Karthiry's army, but she needs to know all the same."

Chalky closed her eyes and tried to breathe steadily. "If anyone can find a way, it's Tollar. My brother can take you to Firinas. She can help you send a message. Hopefully it'll get there in time."

Brilly stood and Croves with him, and they gestured for Draminedes to follow. Back into the neighbourhood, but Croves paused on the street to say he'd see Draminedes later, turned down a different street and vanished.

"Something going to happen under the eastern ridge?" Draminedes asked.

"We're working on it," Brilly said.

"Maybe I can help? I can't go back to Upalint until the weather turns and the passes dry out. I know a little of what Karthiry has planned and what some of her key assets are."

Brilly nodded. "We can use all the help we can get."

They walked out of the city and down a winding path, away from the section of jungle that had been cut down to make way for the gold mine, until they reached a section of forest where the trees were absolutely black with birds sitting in their boughs. Draminedes's footfalls faltered and Brilly gave him a nudge to keep him moving.

"They're not as bad as they look," Brilly said.

"They're not making any sound."

"She's trained them to only make noise when they're in need. Firinas is one of the best aeromancers I've ever met, and she pours her talents into working with birds. And they wouldn't be stealth messengers if they went squawking along everywhere, would they?"

"Oh, you mean for me to send a message to Tollar via bird?"

"Yes, these particular birds are the least likely to be intercepted, and birds are the most reliable source of communication we have until we can safely gather large numbers of wizards or get messages out with caravans. Not that many are coming this way anymore. And we can't trust any of the aquamancers coming and going from here."

"Ah, yes. Karthiry does have quite a few of them."

"Odd element to have preference for."

"Yes, well, she's attracted the best of them, and water is a patient, powerful element."

Brilly shrugged and knocked on the door.

Firinas was much younger than Draminedes would have expected of someone with such mastery over an entire flock of birds like this. But she was quiet and solemn, while Draminedes had somehow expected her to be more birdlike. Well, that's what he got for making assumptions.

"How can I help you?" she asked.

"My friend here needs to get a message to our allies in Nytaltek."

Firinas gave them a shrewd smile. "That is currently my favourite place to send secret birds. Come in."

She set a scroll, inkwell and quill down in front of Draminedes while chatting idly with Brilly. Draminedes stared blankly for a moment.

"Go on, dear, start your message."

"What about payment? Or speaking passwords so you know I can be trusted?"

"If you weren't trustworthy, Brilly or Chalky would have gutted you and left you in the swamp. Helping to get rid of these cursed northerners is the only payment I need from you."

Draminedes set about writing the message.

numbers are 5x larger than anticipated, preparing but holding. Your assumption about timing is correct. I have connected with C&S and locals you know and will do what I can. -D

He worried it was too simple or maybe not cryptic enough, but Brilly glanced over his shoulder and nodded.

"It'll do."

Firinas set a small tube down in front of him. "Who's it for?"

"Tollar. I don't actually know her kin name." He felt himself blush. "But if you send it to Tollar via Captain Solia, that ought to do it."

"Oh, I know which Tollar you mean." Firinas's face lit up in a grin.

"Is she really so famous?"

"In certain circles. Especially after orchestrating that attack on the prison ship and freeing a couple of dragons. It was very inspirational in these parts. You a friend of hers?"

"I... Yes, I suppose. Nytaltek is the only place I have left where I know people."

"Well, you know people here, now," Brilly said. "You need a place to land until this business in Upalint is settled? My family has some room to spare if you're willing to work to help us overthrow these northerners."

"Nothing would make me happier."

And he had hope for the first time since Peniope warned him of his impending doom an age ago in Biterna. In addition to hope, he had a place and a purpose, and maybe, if the gods were willing, he'd make some new friends and reconnect with old ones.

BEFORE

Beenala sat at her table in the market square, watching an aeromancer put on a show pretending to be a swib juggler. He used a touch of magic here and there and acted comically shocked every time. The loose crowd gathered around laughed along. Beenala was damp and tired and having a hard time keeping her work dry in this miserable weather. Her mother had sent her down with the usual coconuts and bananas, and the first of the season's corn crop.

Beenala had worked hard with her middle brother, Ballow, who was a full elemental and a floramancer and had been hanging off Da's every word about corn for three years. Their efforts paid off and it was the best corn Beenala ever tried.

Too bad she would have to cart most of it home. Someone had at least taken most of the coconuts. Those were the worst to bring back, especially after a long, boring day of sitting.

Beenala hadn't sold a single bag or rug. She'd used some of the leftover strips of that lovely crimson silk Tollar brought her a year back, and the bags hadn't garnered any interest today. Too gloomy. Too damp. At least she'd have something to help hold all the corn when she carried it home.

It was almost time to go, but she feared closing time wouldn't come soon enough. A group of teens, not much younger than she was, really, were trying to prove to each other how brave and tough they were by being utter toads to everyone in the market today, as teens sometimes did. These ones, however, were meaner than most, and the ringleader, a greasy-haired girl Beenala didn't recognize, was bigger than most of the adults around.

So far the city guard hadn't done anything about them.

They were at the next table over, laughing and taunting, knocking things to the stones and driving away potential customers. Beenala focused on the mat she was weaving in her lap, willing the teens to pass her by.

"Aye, what's this rubbish then." The girl loomed over Beenala's table, knocking one of the baskets of corn onto the stone. "Oops."

Beenala flinched, stared at her trembling hands and forced them to keep weaving the bit of fabric.

Please go away, please go away, please go, please...

"You actually selling this nonsense? No, I guess you aren't, though."

Beenala held her breath and waited, hoping.

The girl slammed her hands on the table while her little gaggle of monsters laughed. "Answer me, you frog-faced goat-jumper!"

"Oi, you little toad!"

Beenala looked up, recognizing that voice. The greasy girl and her entire greasy gang turned as one, half-formed taunts and sneers frozen on their lips.

"Are you bothering my friend? Looks like you've been busy. Make you feel big picking on folks trying to provide for the rest of us? You need someone to pick on? Well, I'm here, so come on."

One of the boys ran off. Tollar strolled closer, the flat of her big longsword—a new acquisition from Abilerit two seasons ago—resting against her shoulder. She moved like the river, slow and powerful, tall like a sentinel. Bigger than the greasy girl by a handspan.

A smile bloomed across Beenala's face as Tollar swaggered closer, tapping the blade against her shoulder, her armour plating bright in the dull light. It warmed her against the cold damp day.

"What's the matter, frog-face?" Tollar shouted. She took two swift strides to close the distance and stand directly in front of Greasy, glaring down on her. "Not so big anymore?"

Another of the grease gang peeled off the edge and bolted down a side row and out of sight.

"Got nothing to say, now, do you, goat-jumper?"

The girl trembled and sputtered, no actual words coming out.

"That's what I thought. Apologize to my friend."

The girl glanced wide-eyed over her shoulder at Beenala and then at Tollar.

"Apologize!"

"Uh, ah, sorry."

"You little monsters have no respect anymore. Sorry, *Per Beenala*."

"Sorry, Per Beenala," Greasy wheezed.

"Sorry you were a frog-face," Tollar prompted. "And you won't do it again, will you?"

"SorryIwasafrogface." She gasped a ragged breath. "Iwontdoitagain."

"Now clean up your mess." Tollar loomed over the girl's shoulder, her silver eyes flashing as the evening sun peeked between clouds for the first time all day.

The girl crouched down and hastily grabbed all the corn and its basket and dumped it on the table. She started like she was going to run, but Tollar got a handful of the back of her coat.

"Oh-ho, you're not done." Tollar pointed the girl at the table next to Beenala's. "You're going to repeat it to every single vendor here." Tollar gave her a shove and stared as the girl stumbled through her apologies, the last of her gang fleeing.

Tollar sheathed the sword and stood next to Beenala's table, arms crossed, watching Greasy's fumbling progress.

"You didn't have to be so mean to her," Beenala said.

"Oh, I really did. Been some complaints about that one. This is just the first time any of us have caught her at it."

"How long have you been back?" Beenala blushed and focused on her weaving.

"Oh, maybe a week?"

"This is the first I've seen you." The embarrassment was nearly enough to end her, but then she noticed how warm and dry she was. Even the stones beneath her feet were dry while dampness reigned in the rest of the market.

"I don't go to the farm anymore. Been staying with Auntie."

"You could still come out and visit me." She held her breath, waiting for Tollar's response.

"You're right, I suppose I could. And if I don't make it out there, now I know to look for you here."

Beenala grinned and looked up through her eyelashes at Tollar. "Thank you for helping with those kids. It's good to have you home."

"Good to be home."

Greasy finished with her apologies and cleaning up, cast Tollar one final, wounded look, and ran off down one of the rows and out into the streets.

"All right then, what have you got here?"

"Oh, the usual fare. But the corn is really good! Ballow and I have been working on it, manipulating the soil."

"Excellent." Tollar watched a pair of dragons glide silently overhead, toward the chief's compound where they visited the dragon whisperer in the dragon chamber.

"And what about the rest. You make all this?"

"Yes, Mammi said it was finally good enough to sell."

"And she's right!"

Beenala felt like she floated in a warm pool and clutched her hands to her chest.

Tollar put the spilled corn in one of Beenala's bags and piled the last of the coconuts on top. "What do you want for all this?"

"Oh, you came to trade?"

"Coin okay? It's really all I've got. But Auntie makes the best coconut pie and corn wraps I've ever had, and she loves these bright colours. And you used the silk I brought you! It's beautiful. I wish I could bring more of what you make with me when I go. That's the problem, though, isn't it? Can only take what I can carry. Can't even bring books with me!" Tollar's expression grew wistful.

Beenala looked down at the scraps she was weaving into the mat.

"I could make you something smaller. Maybe a wristband?"

Tollar smiled, half her mouth turning up and her silver eyes dancing so that Beenala could barely catch her breath.

"Thank you, Bee. I'd love that."

32

Tollar stifled a yawn with the back of her hand and waited outside the chief's compound for Solia to join her. She'd changed into her uniform early, though she had hours yet until her shift, but she needed to look more respectable than normal for this.

She'd only just returned from the Wizards Guild and teaching the elementals there. They'd gotten the hang of harnessing each other's power, but she was getting them used to weaponizing it, to doing it quickly. She simulated battle situations, hoping they'd act and not freeze when the time came.

Today she'd made all of them battle her. They'd lost, but Tollar wanted nothing more than to sleep until tomorrow's shift.

"What's going on, Toll?"

"I hate losing. Time to stop messing around."

Tollar felt Solia's eyes on her but went into the building for their meeting with Balipar. They didn't go to Balipar's office, though, and Solia grew alarmed when Tollar led her toward the dragon chamber instead.

"It's all right, I ran this by Balipar first. It's just the one dragon and nothing will get set on fire as long as everyone minds their manners."

"Including you! That's the part I'm worried about."

Tollar wouldn't even justify that with a response.

Balipar waited in the doorway, today's outfit didn't disappoint—bright orange turquoise-jewelled vest and matching long shorts under voluminous black cloak with canary yellow lining, and corkscrew hair gathered into a loose, wide ponytail erupting from the top of their head and held together with a turquoise-jewelled scarlet wrap. Tollar smiled and envied them the pretty wardrobe.

She only had the one dress she couldn't yet bring herself to wear again. She had all sorts of things at Auntie's, but hadn't seen her since the house burned. Auntie must know the truth, including about Granny's bone, but that didn't mean Tollar had to go there and talk about it. Or pointedly not talk about it.

"Is she here?" Tollar asked.

"She has come."

"And you gave her the basics of my request?"

"I did. Croves and Shell have been in contact with her, and have softened her opinion. She's willing to hear more."

Balipar pushed open the door, their cloak swishing with each movement, inviting Tollar and Solia in. They gave Solia a curious look since Tollar hadn't mentioned she'd be along, but they didn't say anything.

The emerald dragoness with delicate yellow scale patterns sat in the large, glittering chamber. Typically, the leaders of a local dragon blaze spoke only to the leaders of human countries, always through a dragon whisperer. The dragon chamber was designed for this purpose. It was also beautifully decorated, this one with a sparkling glass tile mosaic of the surrounding jungle's most beautiful blooms.

Has Beenala ever seen this? She'd love it.

Tollar brushed the thought aside and waited for Balipar to go through the formal introductions. Dragons rarely spoke to humans who weren't designated dragon whisperers or who weren't humans they had somehow become friends with, like Croves and Shell. This dragoness liked Balipar well enough. She agreed to speak to Tollar directly. Or, more accurately, let Tollar speak to her.

Balipar was translating.

"Why doesn't she talk?" Tollar whispered, before approaching. "I saw Shell speak to Croves a few times and Bale wouldn't shut up."

Balipar shrugged. "That's her business."

"You sure this'll work?"

"Just go talk to her. Use your manners." Balipar made a shooing gesture with their hands. Tollar was surprised they could even lift them with all those thick glittery rings they wore.

"Solia, stay here with them. I only need you to listen for this."

Solia crossed her arms and leaned against the wall.

Tollar bowed deeply to the dragoness. "Greetings, Mistress. Thank you for coming all this way after I was so rude to you."

She snorted but otherwise didn't move. Good sign? Well, Balipar wasn't shouting at her to run, so it must be okay.

"I would like your help in finishing what I started in Sawulxo, first with that egg and then with Shell. None of those dragons belong in that port or in cages. We have allies on the ground there, and I can help you."

"I relayed that part to her," Balipar said softly from behind her.

"I have no doubt you want to free your kin. I've learned more about the troubles in the north and how they've spread, and I think if we work together here, we can undo some of that damage."

The dragoness looked to Balipar. "She wants to know what you think you have to offer that the dragons don't already have."

"Well, I bring allies in the port with intimate knowledge of the pens where your kin are being kept, for a start. And also, I don't think any of your dragons are aquamancers."

The dragoness growled.

"There's some bad history between a few key aquamancers and the dragons," Balipar said. "She's barely tolerating you right now."

"Aquamancers like that Karthiry who's taken over Biterna? She's the one conquering half the land between here and your dragon city, isn't she? I can guarantee you I'm a better aquamancer than she is. Not only in character, either. I know the Wizards Guild has been reluctant to give you the help you need. But I will help you. I'm a Guild member, and I've been training others here."

Tollar glanced at Solia and Balipar. Her insides felt sharp and cold, rough sea ice on a bitter winter day.

"I'm a member through the specialist tiers. I'm only an aquamancer, but Dira herself has said she knows not of a single aquamancer with more power than me. Not Karthiry, not anyone else she works with. And I'm on *your side*."

The dragoness stared at Tollar for a long, breathless moment before slowly curling up on the floor, her neck extended with her chin resting on the tiles, her face not far from Tollar.

"She's interested," Balipar said. "This means she wants to hear more."

"That's it. That's all I've got. I want to free the dragons in Port Sawulxo and I've got the power to back it up. There isn't an aquamancer stronger than me, not one the Guild knows of anyway. What more do you want?"

"Why are you so strong?" Solia asked.

"Someone's got to be the best. I can't help that's me."

Solia stared.

Tollar sighed. No point in being a coward. It hadn't been that bad telling Beenala, had it?

She glanced at Solia, at Balipar, then turned to the dragoness.

"I'm part water demon." The humans behind her gasped, the dragoness tilted her head to one side and stretched her neck out, scrutinizing Tollar.

"I know there are pyromancers like me. It's a good bet there are others, but power like this doesn't go unnoticed for long. All the same, the less people who know about this the better. We have common enemies, known to the Guild and confirmed not to be what I am. I can help you stop them. We can free your kin."

She tried not to think that if that's where Bale was, maybe they could free her too.

The silence stretched on, the dragoness staring at Tollar. Finally, she lifted her head and looked to Balipar. Tollar didn't understand what passed between dragon and whisperer, but Balipar picked up on some clue.

"Tollar, can you control water demons?"

"Yes. I can open doorways to their realm, too. Pour endless water out if it's needed."

The dragoness's expression darkened.

"But she's on your side," Balipar said. "I want to send note of this back to your city, back to Ondias. This might be the ally you've been looking for. An aquamancer with this kind of power? She might be able to smooth what's broken with the demons."

"I'll do whatever it takes to free your kin. I'll do what I can to help you through other troubles. I'll not have these rogue aquamancers sullying an entire element like this."

"But?" Balipar asked.

"Mostly, it's a point of pride. And the right thing to do."

Tollar sighed and looked at Solia. Guess it was a good thing, in more than one way, that she was here.

Solia grinned, glanced at Balipar but spoke to the dragoness. "Tollar is in the hero business, though she'd prefer you didn't tell anyone. Appearances to keep up, you understand."

Tollar rolled her eyes. "And if you can see fit to help our people against this common enemy, I would be indebted to you."

"But freeing those dragons in Port Sawulxo will be a tremendous leveller," Solia said. "We'd stand a chance against the northerners if we face them human to human."

Another look passed between Balipar and the dragoness.

"All right, thank you, Tollar." Balipar stepped between her and the dragoness, cloak billowing as they spread their arms to usher her toward the door.

"What, that's it?"

"I'll advise her and she'll go back to her kin, and I'll let you know what they decide, all right?"

Tollar wanted to argue, but Solia had her by the arm, dragging her out the door. "Thank you, Balipar, Mistress." Solia bowed at the doorway, Tollar did the same, and then the door closed.

"Water demon?" Solia asked.

Tollar almost couldn't look at her, the ice in her guts twisting, except Solia sounded... impressed? Tollar met her gaze, and while her mouth remained pressed in a line, her eyes shone.

"Yes. Water demon."

"Huh. Well, that explains some things. You should have said something sooner."

Tollar explained about the pyromancers like her. Solia frowned.

"But this isn't the north, Toll. And I've always defended you, even when you didn't deserve it."

"Eh, when have I not deserved it?"

"How about both times I've seen you half drown Saivyn this year alone?"

"Pfft, he wasn't in danger and he deserved it anyway."

Solia shook her head and opened her mouth, but Tollar cut her off.

"I'm not telling him I'm part demon. He doesn't need anymore ammunition or anymore reasons to hate me."

"He might finally see your worth."

"More likely he'll see me as a freak. I can't trust him with this, Solia. That's why you're here and he's not. Beenala knows too—my family and the Guild, obviously—but I'm not telling anyone else until I can be certain I won't get permanently exiled for it."

Solia crossed her arms. "I thought you couldn't wait to leave?"

"That doesn't mean I never want to come back. I don't feel like I belong anywhere, but the closest I've ever come to it is here. Especially in the last season."

Solia gave her a half smile. "You know, part of belonging involves being around?"

"Ach, you sound like Bee."

"You should stop being a fool and go see her."

Just when Tollar's icy guts eased, Solia had to go and say something like that. Solia gave her a hard look.

"You don't give her enough credit, especially if you love her the way I think you do." Solia patted her shoulder and headed for the exit. "But she's stronger than you think—than she thinks, though maybe she's starting to realize it. And you should stop babying her over the danger—we're *all* in danger, Toll—and go home."

"Home, right." Easy enough for Solia to say when home was a concept she understood well enough to have taken it for granted her whole life. And maybe there'd be time soon enough to head out to the farm and check on Beenala. But Tollar had more to do if she had any hope of keeping anything at all in Upalint intact beyond next season.

Her gut got colder and her chest tighter as she thought about her final errand for the day before her guard shift began.

Tollar's pace slowed as she approached the barracks and her stomach clenched. It was a good thing she hadn't eaten in a while. She wasn't much of a puker, but today was a good day for it.

Sloppy ancestors, I need a drink.

Instead, she rested her hand on her hilt and walked straight in. Everyone knew her, many of them people she'd trained with so long ago, when she was practically still a child, swapping sword-fighting lessons for water-related chores. And those that didn't know her recognized the city guard uniform and didn't think twice about her being there.

It was the middle of the evening meal, which was exactly what she'd planned for if this was going to work.

And it really needed to work.

She strode right in, her feet remembering the way for her, and easily found Saivyn at the head table. He didn't notice her with all the commotion in the place, all the soldiers coming and going with meals or drink or finished already and heading back to work.

He didn't see her until she was right in front of him, drawing her longsword.

"What the—"

She drove the point right down into the table an inch from his plate and the hall went silent.

Good.

"What's about to happen to Upalint is much bigger than how much we hate each other," she said quickly. And then, through gritted teeth, "If you will join me in protecting our home from those northern monsters, I will swear my sword and full allegiance to your army to the end of my days."

Saivyn sat there, opening and closing his mouth, random grunts coming out of him, while he turned a very interesting shade of purple. And while he continued sitting ramrod straight in his seat, with all the other high-rankers flanking him, losing his temper on her the way he liked to when only Solia was around wasn't an option here.

He had no space to be petty.

It was the only way. She hoped.

But he sputtered, gripping his fork, tapping his tool-hand on the table, and looking like his entire head was about to explode. Some of the soldiers whispered.

Oh shit, did I miscalculate this?

"I've convinced the dragons to help us." It wasn't a total lie. They would probably do *something* that would benefit Upalint.

Saivyn's eyebrows went up, his expression clearing. He coughed once.

"Tollar, why is your sword in my table?"

"Er..." She gripped it in both hands and yanked it out. "Just wanted to make sure I had your attention. Probably not the best way to ask for a truce."

"The dragons will help us?" He sounded somewhat baffled but less furious.

"Yes. And if you can bear to work with me, I'll even stop trying to drown you in your cups."

It happened so fast that Tollar nearly missed it, but Saivyn's mouth twitched, ever so briefly, in a manner that could almost be interpreted as an aborted attempt at a smile.

"Anyway, I've been training some of the elementals up at the Guild, and if you've got any wizards here who want to learn a neat new trick to make their magic stronger, let me know. You know where to find me."

Then she sheathed her sword and walked out without another word. If she was quick, she'd have enough time to grab some rice balls and fish bites from a street cart before she had to start guard duty.

33

Beenala finished a light dinner in the collective's social club and headed out into the street. She hadn't been able to eat all afternoon, too worried about what would happen in this meeting she'd learned about only that morning—Cromba having let her know about the invite when she got in and suggesting she be the one to represent them.

Because she was friends with Tollar and this was another of Tollar's big meetings.

And if Tollar was putting out the call to everyone, it was probably time. Maybe Karthiry was on their borders already. And the very idea set Beenala's stomach trying to collapse in on itself so that she almost regretted dinner. But she'd been too lightheaded to keep not eating.

Thinking about Tollar, about seeing her, made Beenala want to head straight home and hide. Maybe the invaders wouldn't notice her one little farm.

Beenala sighed.

If she could face the necromancers in their Dead City in the middle of the night, she could face Tollar now. And much worse things later.

A crowd gathered outside the guard house, the main doors closed tight. Beenala noted Metar and her retinue were there, and Saivyn and his top command, and Drigoras and Balipar and dozens of others. Many of them the same ones who had been there when Draminedes had come forward. No sign of Toresona. Had Tollar not bothered sending an invite?

You should have told her!

Beenala adjusted the strap of her bag and tried not to think of what ifs and should haves.

The doors pushed open, bright light spilling out into the street.

"All right, then, come on in," Tollar said.

From her place at the back of the crowd, Beenala barely made out the top of Tollar's head as she held one of the doors open to welcome everyone. Beenala sucked in a breath and barely moved as everyone else in the crowd shuffled forward. Until it was only Beenala standing on the street like a fool.

Tollar looked up and spotted her.

She came out the door and let it close behind her. Solia had been holding the other side open, gave Tollar a significant look, nodded, and closed the other door.

"Bee! I'm so glad you came!" But Tollar kept looking down the street or back at the closed doors.

Beenala took a few steps in her direction and stopped.

"Oh, seared ancestors, this is ridiculous," Beenala muttered and closed the gap between the two of them, Tollar looking like a hare before a hawk.

Beenala held out her hands in formal greeting, not sure what else to do when Tollar was so hard to read. But a smile touched Tollar's lips, and her stance softened as she leaned forward and quickly took Beenala's hands. Only to let them go immediately and pull Beenala into an embrace.

Beenala squeezed her and let out a long breath. And then stood in the lane, letting Tollar hold her, like when her mother comforted her after night terrors as a child. The chaos of the world fell away until it was only her and Tollar, both where they belonged.

When Tollar released her, she kept her hands draped over Beenala's shoulders.

"I'm sorry, Bee." She shook her head and looked down the street. "I shouldn't project my family's behaviour onto everyone else, especially not you, when you've been there for me, over and over again. It's always been you, Beenala, even when everyone else abandons me."

Beenala squeezed one of the hands on her shoulder. "I shouldn't have pushed you. I saw the trauma whenever you spoke of your family, and I refused to connect the dots. You don't have to stay, Tollar. It's enough that you always come back."

Tollar smiled and her other hand cupped Beenala's cheek. "I probably don't have to leave quite as much as I do. And I was so busy trying to get out of here, that I failed to notice the courage you have. Beenala, you took on an angry dragon! I'm an absolute toad for ever doubting you."

"Will you come home, then? Stop sleeping under tables and living out of a locker."

Tollar pinched her mouth closed. "Solia told you."

Beenala opened her mouth to respond, but footsteps drew near, and she shyly stepped back, still holding Tollar's hand.

"What the soggy moons..." Tollar muttered.

Toresona approached with half a dozen necromancers in her wake. While the rest of them passed by without acknowledgement and entered the guard house, Toresona paused for a moment, assessing the two women. She nodded, a knowing smile touching her lips, and then she went inside.

"What—How—Why is she here?"

"I haven't just been sitting in my cottage all this time. Well, maybe for a few days. But I've been busy."

Tollar let out a noisy breath. "You talked to the necromancers?"

"In the Dead City. In the middle of the night! It was dreadful."

"Bee! You got the necromancers to come?"

"I spoke their language, was all. Made them understand exactly how much is at risk."

Tollar stepped closer, taking Beenala's shoulders and smiling, mystified. Then she leaned forward and kissed Beenala's forehead.

A shiver danced down Beenala's back, while warmth bloomed in her chest. She took Tollar's hands and gazed up into her shining silver eyes.

"We might get through this yet." Tollar explained how she'd called a truce with Saivyn, and told Solia, Balipar, and Minty about being half demon.

"Ah, and since you have not been exiled, that also appears to have gone all right."

"Yes, okay, you're not the only one I underestimated and I need to quit that, but Saivyn doesn't know. No one else does. I'm not sure they really need to. But let's get in there before they get bored and go home."

Beenala gripped Tollar's hand, numbness buzzing through her body. She took a deep breath against it. "You still didn't say if you'd come home."

"If you really want to have me putting order to your perfectly good mess…" Tollar winked and Beenala rolled her eyes. "All right, yes. Someone has to help with mulch day."

Beenala smiled.

"But you've got a proper room for me?"

Heat rose to her face and she pressed her lips together. "I cleaned out my old room, the one I used to share with Prixi until she went off to school. I put a little shelf with your books in it too, I hope you don't mind."

Tollar wrapped an arm around Beenala's shoulders and squeezed. "That sounds perfect." She released Beenala and gestured for the door. "Shall we?"

Beenala sat between Solia and Balipar at the table on the edge of the open space where Tollar paced. Solia was in uniform while Balipar wore a sleeveless fuchsia dress made of a single panel with slits up to their hips and twists of their hair hanging in fat loops.

Tollar recapped what they'd done so far, how she'd been teaching local wizards how to harness each other's power, how she had a tentative agreement with the area's former dragon blaze, though Balipar confirmed only that they would help free the other dragons in Port Sawulxo, but otherwise wouldn't involve themselves in human affairs.

"Do they think they might like to at least burn some of the northerners' ships on their way out?"

Balipar smiled. "I'll mention it to them."

Beenala wondered about Croves and Shell and whether they would break rank or stay with their blaze.

"And I got a note from Draminedes, he's in Port Sawulxo with Croves."

"How come you get a bird and I get nothing?" Saivyn asked. His tone made Beenala clench, wondering if maybe Tollar was being optimistic about that truce.

"I'm sorry, Sai, but your contacts could've been taken or killed. Until we can get more of our people in, I just don't know."

Tollar stopped pacing and stood in the middle of the room, surveying the gathered faces, some confused, some irritated, some afraid. Well, that all tracked, didn't it?

"He confirmed a spring invasion and also let me know that while the northerners haven't advanced inland yet—we've still got time—we face numbers five times greater than we anticipated."

Beenala didn't think she'd ever breathe again, not until Solia briefly touched her shoulder. Several people groaned about the news.

"Yes, that's how I felt about it too," Tollar said.

"Can we really trust his intel?" Saivyn asked.

Tollar shrugged. "I've tried to account for the possibility he'd betray us. With this, I don't see why he would lie. Unless to discourage us? But we've got hope yet. Tell them about the plan we've been working on, Sai."

Saivyn stood up and Tollar paced to the opposite side of the room and leaned against a table. They barely looked at each other, never occupied the same space, but he hadn't called her a toad and she hadn't tried to drown him so it was certainly an improvement.

"I've been corresponding with my contacts in Nishram, first warning them of the danger to their lands, and then to discuss the possibility of resistance. One of their elders, Kehnopa, has suggested that we ally our forces and prepare defences along the northern edge of their territory. They had a particular valley in mind."

"What, they want to fight the northerners there instead of here?"

"It seems a better strategy to combine our forces and throw everything we've got at the invaders as soon as possible. I'm vaguely familiar with the valley they suggested. It will give us the advantage of higher ground while also being unpopulated this time of year. I'm told it's part of the Nishram's autumn hunting grounds."

"I expect it will be pretty soggy right about now," Tollar said.

"Yes, which isn't necessarily to anyone's advantage, given the number of aquamancers they have."

"But they don't have aquamancers who can do what I can, and I can clear the way for us to get out there and be ready before enemy aquamancers can make much headway inland."

Saivyn's expression darkened but he sat down and didn't challenge the point. Beenala wondered at the small miracle. And that he'd been convinced they couldn't hide within their own borders. Would the wonders never cease?

Tollar resumed pacing, tapping her tented fingers against her chin.

"We spoke with Draminedes somewhat about our enemies' expectations, and I think we should lean into that—"

"What, that we're all a bunch of stupid brutes?" Drigoras cut in.

"Yes. I sent Dram back with some rumours to spread, playing on their superstitions and fears. They're afraid of us, that's why they don't want to try negotiating. They know we're more advanced. Soggy moons, they don't even have the buzz bulbs we do! And who knows what they do with their wastewater. They don't want to see that. Don't want to think that we might turn the tables on them. So they build us up to be monsters to justify their means."

"Are you thinking of the western badlands campaign?" Solia asked.

"Yes. It worked well enough for them, didn't it?"

"For the rest of us," Beenala said. "What does that mean?"

"I was on a western continent, a bit south of here, with forests made of spiky trees, like cacti but massive almost like the sentinels. Anyway, the locals had a disagreement with their neighbours and I was there to help settle it, and they did this, lean into the worst expectations. Except not actually. They only made themselves seem like monsters."

"But why? Doesn't that make people more likely to fight?"

"Oh they keep wanting to fight, but they're so terrified that we'll do whatever awful thing we've made them believe that they panic and can't fight worth a tarantula's arse."

Toresona stood up and Tollar stopped pacing and bowed deeply before backing over to stand next to Beenala.

"I think this is where our skills will be most useful," she said.

"Yes, of course, Wise Mother. We are indebted to you for any aid you give."

Toresona gave Tollar a shrewd look and came into the centre of the room.

"We have willing dead whose bones we can march, ready to disrupt their peace and risk an early trip through the Door of the Beyond. We only need our ancestors for the opening salvo. Then we can use our fallen enemies."

Tollar winced. "Yes, Wise Mother. I hate your plan, and we should absolutely do it."

"Tollar!" Beenala gasped.

"No really, it's terrible. Just trust me." She sighed. "War isn't supposed to be fun."

"We shall, of course, release their dead once the invaders have been turned away," Toresona said.

Tollar bowed respectfully as Toresona returned to her seat. Tollar asked Saivyn questions about the Nishram's role, but Beenala tuned it out, staring at the tabletop and thinking about what Toresona had said. Tollar was right that it would be terrible, and Beenala's mind kept skittering away from the idea, but there might be a way to make the walking dead worse yet.

She jotted in her notebook.

Tollar rubbed her hands over her face and looked around at everyone. "Is that it then?"

"We've still got Firinas's raven," Solia said. "Shall we send it back with a message?"

"They should know we're coming, yes."

"We can send them specific instructions, can't we?" Saivyn said. "Let them know not just that we're coming, but to what end."

"All right, I'll go back, since I said I would. And Dram said he'd connected with Croves and locals. I assume that means Chalky and probably the other dragon riders. I've worked with them once, I can do it again."

"No," Saivyn said. "We need you here."

"I promised—"

"You promised that the dragons in Port Sawulxo would be freed," Balipar said. "You didn't promise *how*."

"I'll go." Beenala stood suddenly. Sweet ancestors, Tollar's impulsiveness was wearing off on her.

"Bee, no!"

Beenala gave her a hard look, bracing her hands against the table so they didn't shake. "Saivyn's right, you need to be here. I've been there before, I know Chalky and Croves. And now I also know my own limits in that sort of situation, so I won't overextend. I think if I stay on the edge of the fight, maybe hidden but near enough to use pyromancy, that I can be far more effective than I was before."

Tollar opened her mouth to argue, snapped it shut again. Balled her hands into fists and took a deep breath. Beenala held Tollar's gaze, neither of them speaking. Beenala stood straighter, far more certain in her decision than she had been the first time she'd volunteered to go to Port Sawulxo.

"We'll need some good aquamancers to counter theirs," Tavalu said. "And definitely more pyromancers to help Beenala. I can go with them and oversee some of the power-harnessing you taught us."

Tollar sagged and turned away. "Fine."

Solia went up to her office to prepare the message and send the raven back to Port Sawulxo.

"All right, so we've all got our roles sorted then?" Tollar glanced around. "Go back to your respective people and get them ready. I'll call you back as needed. Let's have a drink first, eh?"

Some of those gathered started leaving, including Abilerit, but Tollar stopped him near the door. Beenala remained in her seat next to Balipar, so she didn't hear what Tollar needed of the blacksmith, but whatever it was put a wicked gleam in his eye. He nodded and left.

Tollar kept talking to others on their way out, so Beenala got up to fetch a drink. She could certainly use some wine after all she'd learned tonight. Dread sat like an ember in the pit of her stomach. She grabbed a cup for Tollar while she was at it.

Tollar was at the table, having a hushed conversation with Balipar when Beenala returned.

"I will relay the message to them that if they can spare any aid our way after those dragons are freed, that your more specific talents will be available to them," Balipar said.

"What, the thing about me controlling water demons?"

"Yes, that thing precisely. They may have a different kind of hero's quest for you." Balipar's tone was grave but their grey eyes shone.

"Ack, one battle at a time. Let's get through this first."

Balipar smiled and went to get a drink.

"Do I want to know?" Beenala offered Tollar a cup.

"Eh, probably not."

"And... Tollar, do you really think we *can* get through this?"

"No." Tollar's voice shook. "But we're going make them regret crossing the ocean all the same." She took the offered drink. "Just the one."

Beenala tilted her head, having fully expected Tollar to drink half a cask on her own. Tollar's eyes crinkled when she smiled over Beenala's surprise.

"You've got wine at home, don't you? I could use some peace and quiet and maybe even a real bed."

Beenala took a gulp from her cup to hide how warm her cheeks were. Her heart raced. And then the cup slipped out of her shaky hands, clattered against the table and splashed wine everywhere.

"Oh no—!"

Tollar leaned across the table to right the cup and gestured with the other hand, washing the wine back into the cup, pulling out the little splashes on Beenala's shirt.

"Maybe we've both had enough to drink," Tollar said. "Want to just go?"

Beenala brought their cups to the kitchen while Tollar went upstairs to grab her kit, which, Beenala noted when Tollar returned, had been replaced and was no longer charred. She took Tollar's hand as they strode through the door, grinning.

"Tollar," a man's voice called.

Tollar's grip on Beenala's hand tightened and they both turned. At first, Beenala didn't recognize the tall, lean, dark-skinned man standing outside the guardhouse door.

"Jarku." Tollar's voice was strained and cautious. Her oldest brother came closer, and Tollar tensed, gripping Beenala's hand even tighter.

"Should I leave you—"

"No." Tollar tugged her closer. "What is it?" she asked her brother.

"I heard about your fight with Ma."

Beenala hadn't heard about this and watched Tollar, whose face became politely uninterested.

"I'm not here to argue with you, Toll. I didn't know you were still here until Ma told me what you said. She came to me looking for sympathy, but she didn't find any. I never liked Zarro either, and I wish I'd said something."

Tollar's grip on Beenala's hand hurt and Jarku glanced her way. Tollar stared straight ahead. Silent.

Jarku sighed. "I realized he was the problem and not you months before he drove you out for good. And that's on me. I was an arrogant young coward. I'm sorry for what happened and my role in it."

Tollar's grip loosened and she took a shaky breath, though whatever emotions she felt didn't reach her face.

"I appreciate that, thank you," she said.

Jarku glanced at Beenala again, though she couldn't fathom he expected her to help at all.

"You don't have to accept my apology," he said. "I just wanted you to know. But maybe we can meet for lunch or have dinner together with Auntie sometime?"

"I'm not here that much, just getting the farm squared away."

Jarku's smile was sad when he said, "That's okay. Whenever you want to talk, I'd like to see you."

Tollar nodded and Jarku thankfully turned away then.

"Well, that was interesting," Tollar muttered.

"And maybe not terrible? You don't have to forgive him, but wouldn't it be nice having some more family to talk to? I'm sure his children would love to hear their auntie's stories."

Tollar stopped and met her gaze, a smile blooming on her face. "Maybe. But Bee, you're all the family I need." She kissed the top of Beenala's head.

Heat rushed to Beenala's cheeks, and she leaned closer to Tollar as they headed for the cottage. She hoped Tollar made amends with her brother, though they certainly had enough to worry about for now. And then her thoughts slammed back into focus, and she remembered what she'd volunteered for. At least holding onto Tollar's hand meant she wouldn't fall over.

There was so much to plan.

34

Beenala crouched with Tavalu in the shadow of a burned-out building near Port Sawulxo's eastern ridge and waited for the signal. It would be impossible to miss. The entire city would see it.

At least Tavalu gently nudged her every time she forgot to breathe.

And she didn't have to be in the first wave going into the compound. She barely remembered what the inside of it looked like or where anything had been. The dragon riders were all familiar with it and would be leading the rest of her team in this mission.

It wasn't *her* team. It was Macana's team, Beenala had just been the first one to volunteer. And Croves and Chalky had taken over, Croves coming out with Shell to find them in the forest when they'd been a day out. Shell had flown them the rest of the way.

The northerners had already landed the bulk of their force and started moving inland when Draminedes got Solia's message and sent Croves out to find them and learn more. The northerners were still moving people and supplies inland. The dragons would go last, but there was no guarantee they'd be held in these pens after tonight.

So Beenala waited while everyone else got into position—which she understood to mean they were stealthily taking care of any guards on duty. *Taking care* of them probably meant killing them, but Beenala tried not to think about that part and hoped she wouldn't have to kill anyone. She didn't think she could.

Tollar said it was awful.

Tavalu nudged her and she took a slow, deep breath. And held it again. Because breathing made her want to talk and talking was very likely to expose them.

Tavalu gripped Beenala's shoulder, digging her fingers in painfully, and pointed up.

Beenala thought that another dragon diving off that ridge would be too obvious, but it was the most difficult attack to defend against and the easiest to keep concealed until the last moment. It probably also helped that Shell and Croves were far better at this than little Bale and Beenala could ever have hoped to be.

Shell came diving off the cliff, silent as a shadow, and Beenala would have missed it entirely if Tavalu hadn't pointed it out. Croves rode in what looked like a small pocket, but that he called a harness, strapped to Shell's great arm and secured between spikes. Beenala would have loved the harness for the trip here from the middle of nowhere, instead of being carried in one of Shell's large hands.

Now Tavalu was holding her breath too.

The great gout of fire came, far more impressive than what Bale had managed months ago. The screaming began. Dragons shrieking too.

"Let's go!"

Tavalu tugged on Beenala's sleeve as she sprang to her feet. Beenala did her best to keep up, both of them running low and sticking to the shadows as much as they could on their dash into the compound. But fire lit up the whole world.

Enemy-controlled dragons already rose up in their pens, and this was where Beenala was to focus her attention for as long as she could. Tavalu would stay with her and focus on boosting Shell's fire until the other riders freed their dragons.

Now that they knew what to expect, they'd come with the right tools—pyromancers and terramancers who could break the locks, and bolt cutters for the pairs who didn't have an elemental with them.

Beenala didn't worry about what was going on behind her. Tavalu watched that direction. Beenala only had to suppress the fire of the dragons leading the counterattack.

They shrieked their rage as their flames sputtered and their cruel masters whipped them. Chains enchanted to pierce their tough skin.

Croves said they would free those dragons and bring them to the dragon city where they would be rehabilitated. They'd done it already with a few dragons who had been freed from similar conditions in the north. Beenala hoped he was right and that they were successful.

Can't fail.

And they couldn't, not really. Not when they were outnumbered. Beenala had seen the endless armada from the air when Croves and Shell brought them in. Just endless lights like the night sky twinkling out in the middle of the ocean.

Two of the captive dragons and their riders burst from their pens and joined Shell and Croves in throwing fire at northern guards.

The enemy dragons screamed and two of them launched into the air, teeth and talons out, raking at the newly freed dragons until they were far enough away to be beyond Beenala's influence. And then they attacked with fire.

Her hands felt cold and she wrapped them up in the hem of her shirt, probably holding her breath again as she poured her entire focus into the last three enemy dragons, the air getting colder around her from the effort. But they came out of their enclosures too. Still no fire, but pounding along the ground, tearing at potential hiding places.

Moving toward where she and Tavalu hid.

"Oh no."

She faltered and the fire poured out of the three dragons, one of them getting frightfully close.

"It's okay, I've got this." Tavalu gently took Beenala's hand as they'd agreed upon and practiced before. "Calm and still."

Beenala closed her eyes, held her breath and bore down on Tavalu's hand, every part of her taut. Maybe not as calm as she could be, but utterly still. She'd hoped to play her role without help, but success was more important.

And the weird sensation of emptiness washed over her. Cold and buzzing and scattered, like her awareness had become a startled flock of birds rushing in every direction at once.

That was her magic going places she had no control of. Going into Tavalu who sent it where it needed to be. And going with the force of two wizards combined. All Beenala had to do was be still and let Tavalu take what she needed. Stay quiet until she neared the end of her power.

Tollar discovered that wizards could drain each other into unconsciousness if they took too much too quickly.

Beenala felt lightheaded, but not weak. She hoped that was normal. But she'd stand here until she collapsed if that was what it took for Tavalu to keep those dragons from tearing them to pieces. Her head got heavier and her body lighter, the air colder with all the pyromancy and the solid ground shifting like beach sand as Tavalu used more terramancy.

Tavalu let go of her hand and she opened her eyes, startled as her power came flooding back in, hitting her like a strong cup of chocolate in the morning.

She gasped.

"Bee!" Croves flew overhead, Shell swooping low. "To the pens!"

"What...?"

"Oh my." Tavalu tugged on Beenala's sleeve, turning her around.

"Baby dragon!" someone shouted.

"It's Bale!" Croves called on his newest pass overhead, before he swooped up into the sky, Shell shrieking with his talons bared, digging into the side of one of the enemy dragons.

Beenala had a moment of confusion, wondering why he would try to gut these dragons they'd claimed to want saved, and then a human shape went flying through the air, landing not far away. Not gouging the dragon, but ripping its human masters off of it.

And then it registered what Croves said.

"Bale is here?"

"Go!" Tavalu nudged her in the right direction.

Beenala ran, staying in the shadows to avoid the northerners. More elementals waved for her from outside one of the pens. As she reached the door she heard Bale's little teakettle voice. Her heart nearly stopped.

"Bee!"

"She's been fighting us," Macana said.

"Bale, these are my friends! We're here to save you! Hold still, we'll get you out."

Bale settled against the ground, making the gentle sound for mother that Beenala thought she'd never hear again. She wept silently as she wrapped her arms around the end of Bale's snout.

When the elementals snapped the last of the chains holding Bale down, the little dragon, who was very nearly the size of Shell, plucked Beenala from the ground and deposited her between the same two spikes she'd nestled into once before.

And then they were airborne.

This was not part of the plan.

Beenala went cold, gasping for air, trying to breathe against the dry heaves. Not eating had absolutely been the right choice.

Now what?

Don't fall off!

Beenala clung to the dragon, crouching in as close as she could to Bale's body, and squeezing her eyes shut. It took half her concentration to keep from falling off and the rest of her concentration to keep from screaming herself hoarse. But Bale was much better at it this time, climbing fast and banking at speed, swooping with control Beenala didn't know she had.

But she opened her eyes and did start screaming when Bale shuddered and lost momentum.

She'd collided with one of the enemy dragons.

And right in front of Beenala was one of the northerners, whipping the dragon behind the head with a chain. The same chains they'd very likely used on Bale. Beenala's blood roared.

"Bale, knock him off!"

Bale tilted and dropped away, but swooped back around and got behind the enemy dragon. Smaller than the rest, but old enough to have proper control of her flight, Bale was faster and more manoeuvrable than the other dragons.

She came in low over the other dragon's wings and whipped one of her talons out, knocking the enemy rider off.

Beenala was grateful for the noise of battle covering over the man's screams. She couldn't hear anything but the sizzle of fire and the shriek of dragons. But there were more and more dragons in the air, and when Bale banked to follow Shell, Beenala got a dizzying look down. Only one dragon left in the pens. The four remaining eggs already scooped up.

Free them all, Tollar had said.

"Bale, down! Let's help them!"

She had no idea how Bale heard her over the din, but Bale rolled into a dive, streaking toward the ground.

"Fire!" Beenala shouted.

It was too far from the ground for Bale to reach on her own, but Beenala pulled the fire in two streams to rake the ground around the pen and chase off the northerners closing in. Whatever pocket of cold air the magic created was lost behind her as Bale zipped forward.

Beenala spotted Tavalu running toward the final pen, flinging dirt and shooting fire to keep a path clear through the northerners. It was fierce now as the northerners risked losing all of the dragons in their power.

"There, Bale! Do you see her? Pick her up!"

Beenala used a wave of fire to point out Tavalu, and then Bale banked hard and dropped suddenly, Beenala's stomach lurching, her back pressed against the spike behind her, the only thing keeping her from flying off. It felt like all of her insides were trying to crawl out through her eyes.

And then Bale levelled out and scooped up Tavalu.

Circling the pen, Bale directed more fire at the northerners on the ground. Tavalu helped her. Cold and gasping despite Bale's heat, Beenala glanced up, watching for any of the enemy dragons to swoop down. She'd lost Bale once, she wouldn't lose her again. They were bringing everyone home. The twelve other dragons they'd freed, plus Shell, kept their enemies occupied.

And people rained down almost as much as fire did.

Shaking, she dug her knees into Bale's soft flesh, and closed her eyes, huddling down and letting the others do their work.

The dragons and their riders focused on pulling the northerners off of the slave dragons. Beenala wondered if it would be enough to free them. She'd gotten the impression over the last few hours, in preparation for this battle, that the beasts had been broken and might not respond well to freedom.

They had to try. And at least get them further away where they couldn't interfere in what was to come next for Port Sawulxo and for Upalint.

"Go, go! Up!" Tavalu cried.

Beenala looked down. The final dragon headed skyward, the last of their people clinging to it or gripped in its large hands. This was a massive dragoness even as far as dragonesses went and the gale from her wings almost knocked Bale off course as she rushed past.

Bale climbed quickly as well, following this last dragon up into the air, far above the edge of the ridge and climbing. And moving farther inland and away from the city.

They're corralling these dragons away from where the northerners' elementals can reach them with magic.

Beenala couldn't remember if that had been part of the plan or not. She'd been too focused on her specific role.

And was too shocked to discover that Bale had been here all along.

At last, Croves's people overwhelmed the last of the enemy dragons, all of them free of their brutal masters. Each surrounded by a pair of the other dragons. They moved slowly into formation, with an escort dragon at the head, the rear and above.

Shell had been flying beneath but came up to where Bale easily glided, keeping pace with the rest.

"We'll get you to that Nishram valley," Croves called over the rush of wind around them, "and then we go. These lot have a long journey north to get these dragons to safety and healing. But I think we can burn a few ships on our way."

"And Bale?"

"She's her own dragon."

Beenala smiled and patted the side of Bale's neck. Then she latched on as best she could and pressed her face against Bale's hot skin and squeezed her eyes shut to let her racing heart catch up with them. Despite that, she felt a strange and elated sense of peace.

They'd found Bale.

Tollar would be so pleased to see her again. Even if she chose to go with her kin, at least they'd have that small reunion.

35

Tollar stood on a column of water jutting from the valley's southern slope where she was close enough to intervene when necessary but far enough away to see almost the entirety of the battle. The bottleneck was working, so far. The first wave of northerners—what was left of them—had reached the pass just after dawn. So far none of them had made it *through* the pass.

Mostly on account of all the walking corpses in the way. Battle had started with ancestor volunteers from Upalint, all of them dressed up in terrifying monster costumes—that had been Beenala's idea, inspired by some play called Broken Fathers. The northerners had charged through the pass straight into a wall of undead horrors.

Unable to harm the reanimated corpses and unable to push forward, the northerners had ended up trapped in the pass, and the ones who hadn't fled in terror had been easy prey for the archers. Once Tollar's forces had taken down enough of the northerners, the necromancers had sent the ancestors to the back of the valley, near Tollar, and were using northern corpses instead.

It was horrifyingly effective.

She couldn't tell which of the shapes on the ground were reanimated northerners and which were those still alive, but her enemies fought poorly, so the necromancers still had an effect. And there were enough of them to reanimate thousands of corpses.

Right now, Toresona was on the western edge of battle with half of her group, the other half on the eastern side. One acolyte had stayed in the Dead

City to tend to the remaining dead and all the rest were here. The team that had gone ahead to pick off approaching northerners had trailed in behind them, though Tollar still wasn't sure where the team was now.

The Nishram and that small team of necromancers had been spread out in the jungle on the other side of the pass, whittling down the numbers of the northerners over the last two days as they approached, the scare tactics having been largely successful.

And groups of her least-talented fighters roved the jungle in clusters, with rattles to replicate the sound Draminedes hopefully reported as belonging to gezar hunting parties. These fighters carried obsidian-tipped clubs and wore the paint designs the Nishram hunters did to scare animals. They had Nishram guides among them so they wouldn't get lost, and permission both to be on the land and to use their paint designs. In return, Upalintan elementals would help rebuild the valley after battle.

Assuming they all survived. Tollar was very diligently ignoring their odds.

But it didn't help the invaders' cause that Tollar had found a stream to divert and manipulate so she flushed them through the pass and right back out the other end of the valley, off to ancestors knew where. All the way to the ocean, maybe?

None of her concern.

She tried to avoid killing any of them, remembering how Draminedes had been so confused and the way Karthiry had manipulated him. How many of these people were the same?

It wasn't her job to judge, it was her job to turn them away.

She let a fresh wave from the stream wash down the mountainside and push more northerners right back out the way they'd come. A great amount of earth went with it, and she assumed a group of her terramancers must be at work as well.

Tollar was trying her damnedest to not utterly destroy the valley. Teams of elementals had narrowed the pass in preparation, and the diverted stream was both clogging up the gap that remained and uprooting vegetation, carving new gorges and leaving boulders everywhere. So far Tollar hadn't had to do anything huge like open a water portal and flood the valley. They were making an awful mess though.

It was war.

So messy. So unnecessary. So much work to rebuild afterward. If there *was* an afterward.

But she turned her mind away from that and called her arrowheads back to her. Abilerit had done a superb job, as usual. He'd crafted them to have hollow centres filled with water. The water inside worked exactly as she'd hoped it would, allowing her to manipulate the blades the way she could any bit of water. Like she could the blood in those people down there if she really put her mind to it.

But she knew what the price of that sort of magic was. It had to be a last resort.

This was enough. They were pushing the northerners back. It was an endless stream of them, but Saivyn and the Nishram elders had chosen the perfect location to bottleneck the enemy.

If Beenala and the others hadn't been successful with the dragons, that back up would bear down on them in another day or so. It was possible that the dragons alone were enough to take Upalint.

No point worrying about that. She'd have her answers soon enough. All she could do now was keep flushing the northerners back out through the pass and using targeted geysers to keep her people from being ambushed by anyone who got past Tollar's floods and the necromancers' corpses.

Toresona's group split up, only a couple of them staying with their leader, while the rest headed deeper into the pass and out of sight.

"What the...?"

A fresh wave of northerners came roaring in, and Tollar's latest flood missed enough of them that she couldn't worry about the necromancers. She flung her blades out in front of her, spiking them one at a time into the melee, putting them through the legs of as many northerners as she could.

Her sword was strapped to her back along with the pair of bigger spears Abilerit had made her. These ones he'd tempered to pierce dragon skin, and she was saving them, just in case.

If only she'd considered it sooner, she'd have had him make more.

But time had always been against them.

Saivyn jogged up to the base of Tollar's pillar, and she split it, funnelling water under him and bringing him up to where she stood. He wobbled, arms out like he expected to be sucked into it at any moment. She rolled her eyes.

"If I was going to drown you I'd have done it by now."

Saivyn pointedly ignored that. "My scouts came back from the borders and it's mixed news."

"It always is."

Saivyn stared. "There have been a good number of defectors, perhaps a quarter of their forces turning back from the terror tactics alone. But their numbers are endless. Toresona has sent a group in deeper, bringing a legion of their dead. I've advised them on a formation that I think will be most effective."

"But?"

"We're vastly outnumbered."

"How are we on losses so far?"

"A few. Only seven dead, but dozens of significant injuries. Toresona is staying to walk our dead to the back of the valley toward the road so they're out of the way, and we can get them home again when it's over."

"The injuries, severe?"

"Some. The healers are doing what they can, and the elder Kehnopa has brought her best medicine weavers to the valley to help, but—"

The screech of dragons rang out over the valley. Tollar's blood ran cold.

"Oh no."

Saivyn's big brown face grew ashen, tinged with green.

The cry repeated and Tollar recognized it as a battle cry. She pulled out her spears, half her attention on the battle below where both sides stopped to watch for the approach. The other half of her attention was on the sky, looking for the dragons.

She spotted two shapes coming in.

"Only two?"

"That's good, isn't it?" Saivyn asked.

"Depends which two and who controls them."

Tollar gripped her spears and watched, and the whole valley stilled with waiting. The dragons drew near enough that their colours resolved and her heart nearly stopped. There was the familiar green of Shell, but a smaller shape with the black and amethyst pattern Tollar had given up on ever seeing again.

"Bale!"

"That's good?" Saivyn said. "That's your dragon, isn't it?"

"Yes! And Shell!"

"Can you see who's with them?"

Saivyn strained to see, and Tollar's excitement drained away as she realized his concern. As delighted as she was to see Bale, if it wasn't Beenala with her...

She stood frozen atop her waterspout, staring at the approaching shapes and trying to breathe through tightness in her chest. Saivyn laid a hand on her shoulder, and she gave him an acknowledging nod. She'd have preferred Solia out here with her, though someone had to stay in the city as a last defense. But she'd sent two-thirds of the city guard with them, and Saivyn remained professional, so that helped.

A familiar pale face peeked around from behind Bale's horns, and Tollar made the most undignified sound in her entire life.

"It's Bee!"

Without thinking, she turned and hugged Saivyn, who made an equally undignified sound, and she let his half of the column sink to the ground while she pushed hers up higher.

Bale screeched and swooped down toward her.

"Bee! Praise the ancestors!"

She kissed thumb to forehead and watched the approach, all the other shapes on the two dragons. Bale clutched Tavalu and had two other wizards on her back along with Beenala, while Shell had several more on his back and one each in his hands, including Macana.

Both dragons circled around to land behind Tollar on the slope, and she dropped down to the ground to join them. Beenala scrambled from Bale's back and rushed to Tollar, the pair of them crashing into an embrace.

"You did it!"

Beenala squeezed Tollar tighter and buried her face in Tollar's shoulder.

"And you found Bale! Bee, this is incredible!"

"Tollar, it's awful."

Tollar hadn't thought Beenala's hair could look more dishevelled, but parts of it flopped over in every direction imaginable while other parts stood haphazardly on end. She ran her fingers through Beenala's hair and held her tighter until she stopped trembling, while Tavalu and Croves came over to give her a quick report of how it went.

Tollar kept one arm wrapped firmly around Beenala's shoulders, but stretched out the other to drape around Croves's neck and pull him closer, planting a kiss on his cheek.

"I'm glad to see your big bear of a face again."

Croves chuckled and wrapped both Tollar and Beenala in his treetrunk arms, giving them a quick squeeze. While briefly in the circle of his arms, Tollar felt that same tug from the winter. One she still didn't have time to examine.

"We're here for ye," Croves said. "The others have gone, but Bale wanted to come home and we had to return yer people. We'll stay until the battle's won or lost."

Tollar let out a long breath. "Thank you, Croves. You don't have to stay, but we appreciate you being here. That we've freed the dragons and taken that advantage away from them is all I hoped for. And then you found Bale!"

With Beenala calmer, Tollar let her go and went to Bale, so much bigger now, but she craned her neck down so Tollar could stroke her nose. Bale nuzzled her.

"I'm so happy to see you again."

"Time to fight," Bale said.

"Yes, I'm afraid so. But only if you want to."

"I burned ships!"

Tollar chuckled. "Did you now?" She looked to Croves.

"Aye, we regrouped after the rescue and made a few passes of fire at their armada on the way out."

"Then you've done more than I could have hoped for. I can't express what it means for me that you stay. That you brought Bale home."

"Fight," Bale repeated.

"I can't," Beenala said. "I'm sorry, Tollar."

Tollar touched her cheek and smiled. "You've done more than I imagined, Bee. Stay back here. Help if you can, but rest. You've done enough."

Croves climbed into his harness, and he and Shell sprang into the air, followed by Bale. Tollar braced against the wind and watched them go.

"This is only the beginning," Tavalu said. "There were so many boats left in the port with more invaders pouring in. Even after we burned out half the armada." She shook her head in dismay. "This is the tip of the spear."

Tollar sighed. "Any resistance building with the Sawulxans?"

"Some. Freeing Shell and the riders started something, and your friend Chalky thought if we succeeded in freeing all the dragons and burning some ships that it would galvanize her efforts. We didn't stick around long enough to see if it worked."

"Chalky knows her people. But even if she's wrong, we've got dragons and they don't. We've got necromancers and they don't. And you've all got me and I can do things no other aquamancer can."

"Let's get back to it," Saivyn said.

Tollar nodded and he went down the hill. She turned to Beenala, a hand on her shoulder. Beenala squeezed the hand. Flinched when Bale and Shell swooped overhead, shrieking their battle cry.

"Go, Tollar, I'll be fine."

Tollar kissed Beenala's hand and pushed herself back up to the top of the water column and washed another wave of northerners back out of the valley.

36

A warm hand on her shoulder woke Tollar up, and she blinked into the bright morning sun, instantly regretting both being awake already and that anyone had thought it a good idea to let her sleep so late. It was Beenala crouched beside her, a fond smile trying to break through the worry on her face.

"I'm okay." It came out as a groan.

"We can wait another day, can't we?"

"If we're going to chase them, we can't relent. Can't let them regroup. If we don't keep going, we have to turn back and hold the valley. Who knows what they'll do to the rest of Sawulxo while we sit."

The worry lines on Beenala's face deepened, and she ran her fingers over a lock of Tollar's hair that had escaped her braid. Tollar breathed deeply and smiled.

"No matter how this all ends, I'm grateful we had this time together."

Beenala grinned, filling Tollar with light. "Toll, are you going soft on me?"

Tollar's smile went lopsided. "I've always been soft on you, Bee."

Beenala laughed and it was balm to Tollar's weary bones.

Tollar sat up and stared blankly around her. The camp was empty and everyone was gone, only some trampled foliage as any trace that half of Upalint and most of the Nishram had even been here.

"What—Where—?"

"They packed up before dawn, like you told them to, and when the noise of that didn't rouse you, Saivyn and I agreed you needed more rest. He's brought them all onward, and Bale went too so she could set some fires, but she should be back for us soon."

Tollar opened her mouth to object, realized the wisdom in the plan and wished they'd thought of it days ago. She rubbed her hands over her face, drank some water and considered if she was hungry enough for rations.

"Oh, I found a berry patch." Beenala produced a small sack. "Kehnopa said they're not poison. They're a bit sour."

"Anything's better than rations."

"Should we let you sleep tomorrow morning as well?"

"If Bale doesn't mind coming back for me, then that's probably an excellent idea."

"Tollar, you can't keep this up much longer."

"Good thing we're almost there." Tollar thought she did a good job keeping the strain out of her voice. It was not, in fact, a good thing they were almost there because she still had no idea how they could stop the northerners. She was powerful and had the advantage of a dragon, yes, but there were just so godsdamn *many* northerners.

They'd passed the edge of Nishram territory, into Sawulxo, and would be in the port in two days, maybe three. It depended on whether the northerners turned to fight or fled the entire way. Though Tollar agreed with Saivyn that this was likely not fleeing, but luring. And if Tollar couldn't do the things with water that she could, and if they hadn't had a pair of dragons to aid them, she'd have never suggested chasing them.

She'd given up the high ground and a perfect bottleneck and led her people to a much bigger fight. She expected to find the entirety of the northern army waiting for them when they reached the port.

In any other circumstance, it would be a terrible idea. But from Port Sawulxo, Tollar would have one mighty river and the entire ocean at her command. She didn't know if it was enough, but everyone else thought it was worth a try.

Shell and Croves had gone ahead, scouting for her before going directly into Port Sawulxo to make contact with Draminedes and Chalky to let them know what was coming. The hope was that it would unite the fledgling resistance there and give Tollar more of an edge.

The usual jungle chatter, subdued as two armies went through, silenced entirely and Tollar's skin prickled. A shadow fell across them, making her animal brain scream at her to run.

It was Bale, of course, returning for them. But it was always terrifying to see such a large predator move so silently.

"Ready?" She lowered her giant head to the ground.

Beenala helped Tollar pack up her kit before they both climbed up to sit between the spikes on Bale's back. Beenala sat in front of Tollar, her pack tucked in front of her so Tollar could sit behind her and wedge her own pack in behind, cushioning them both.

There weren't many places to hold on, so squeezing in was the safest option. It was that, or have Bale carry them, but she needed her talons free for extra defense.

"We should see about getting a harness like Croves has," Tollar said.

"I have no interest in making a habit of riding dragons."

Tollar chuckled.

Bale flapped her wings and Beenala leaned forward scrunching herself up against the spiny bit in front of her, face pressed to pack and eyes closed. Tollar's stomach lurched as the dragon lifted from the ground and picked up speed.

The jungle raced away below them, warm air lashing them and making it hard to breathe. Tollar crouched low, letting the spike in front of her act as a windbreak, and trying to keep sense of where they were. The ribbon of road between trees was barely visible through the canopy, but it was obvious when Bale caught up with the long column of Upalintan soldiers. She passed silently overhead, some of their people looking up to wave or cheer, and sped along the road until the column of retreating northerners appeared, half a day's march ahead.

Bale became decidedly less quiet, startling Tollar.

The little dragoness swooped in close, shrieking all the while and raining fire down on their enemies, with little care for who or what she hit.

Tollar was also startled by the wanton destruction.

"Bale! Perhaps we can use some precision?" Tollar called.

Bale pitched skyward, circling high above the canopy, but twisting her head so that one glittering eye watched Tollar.

"She knows these are the people who stole her from us," Beenala said over her shoulder. "Kept her in a cage and beat her with chains when she refused to do the terrible things they wanted her to. She's understandably angry."

"These aren't actually the people who hurt her. *Those* ones will still be in the port. Most of these people are probably just as manipulated and disposable as Dram ever was. I wouldn't be surprised if many of them are beaten down human versions of the dragons they steal."

Beenala gave her a dark look. "You think Bale should go easy on them?"

Tollar glanced at the army below. "I think she should be targeted with her attack and give them a chance to reconsider their choices. Some things are worse than death. No reason we can't make them utterly miserable all the way back to the port."

Bale snorted and kept circling.

"What do you have in mind?" Beenala asked.

"Help guide her fire to destroy their supply carts rather than the people—target the wheels, no reason our own people can't use the supplies. Try to put out the forest she's burning. No need for that. And if we can swoop past a stream or—there, I see a river to the east—then I think I can make their trip a living nightmare. Leave them too exhausted to help their friends when we get to the coast."

Beenala leaned forward and called, "What do you think?"

Bale angled higher, up into the clouds.

"I want to destroy them," Bale said.

"I know, and hate is a natural reaction," Tollar said. "But if you let your hate burn too hot, you burn only yourself. Causing hurt to others won't undo the pain they caused you, Bale. And escalation runs the risk of making this worse. There are other ways to stop them. Let's wear them down."

Bale flew wide circles high above the retreating northerners, high enough that Tollar could almost make out both armies. The air was cold and crisp and hard to breathe.

"You have rank," Bale said. "I will try it your way."

Then she dived back toward the jungle. Beenala groaned and nestled against her pack. Tollar squeezed her legs tighter around Bale and leaned forward. Bale headed east so that Tollar could gather a large portion of the river and make it chase them back to the road.

"Approach them from the front, let me put this water to good use first."

Bale flew in closer and Tollar turned the road into an impassable bog. Well, nearly impassable. Didn't want to stop them, only give them something to think about while her people stayed at a menacing distance.

Bale swung around and came down the road straight toward the retreating army.

"Up, Bale! Away from where their magic can reach you."

She tilted her wings and brought them slightly higher, then let loose with more fire. Beenala did her work this time, pulling the fire away from trees and focusing the stream on carts of supplies. When Bale got to the end of the line, she doubled back, taking aim for what they'd missed. She swung back and forth along their line, aiming for supplies until no more wagons were visible.

"Well done, Bale!"

"I want to burn more."

"I'm sure you do. And once we get to the port, you might get that chance. But for now, what if you circle above where they can't reach and screech until you need rest? Swoop down at them now and then, just to scare them."

Bale barrel rolled down to the column, the momentum pressing Tollar against the spike behind her and Beenala against Tollar. Bale screeched all the while, and then drew her wings in so she fit between the trees and screamed, talons out, plowing over everything in her path before spiralling into the air.

Tollar and Beenala braced against the spin, and Tollar had to close her eyes.

"Did Shell teach you fly like that?" Beenala sounded ready to vomit.

Bale screeched in return and circled for a while. She swooped in now and then to knock over northerners. She kept it up all day, only depositing Beenala and Tollar with the rest of their people once they'd begun to set up camp.

Then went deeper into the mountains to hunt gezars.

"How many do you think you'll eat tonight?" Tollar called.

"Four!"

Tollar blinked and looked at Beenala. "Has she really grown that much?"

"Yes, honestly. And she's still growing, I might add. And she's spending her days on revenge. I'm sure it's all quite tiring for her."

Tollar shrugged and lay out her sleep mat. It had been a much-needed restful day, though she'd had to use some energy making that bog and making sure it kept pace with the northerners, drying out the land behind them for easy passage for her people.

"I've got to have a word with Saivyn," Tollar said. "But today was a good day."

"A good day, really?" Beenala looked at her askance.

"Well, best kind of day we can hope for under the circumstances."

Tollar sought out Saivyn to see if he had any suggestions on improving those circumstances and getting them in and out of Port Sawulxo as quickly as possible. Preferably all in one piece.

37

Tollar watched from Bale's back while the glittering line on the horizon grew as the morning went on. They'd reach the port by midday. Their enemies likely arrived there sometime in the night, though Tollar and Saivyn had halted their troops and insisted on rest. No sense in exhausting themselves chasing the enemy through the dark.

"I'm not ready for this," Beenala said.

She'd been watching the coast grow nearer too.

"You should stay near the back."

"No, I'm staying with Bale."

"You can't distract her. She can't bring you to the edges if you get overwhelmed. We need her out there the whole time."

Beenala sighed. "If it's too much, I can stay out of it while staying with her. I can hang on and try not to vomit on myself. I understand the dangers. I want to try."

Tollar smiled fondly and laid her hand on Beenala's shoulder.

"All right, Bale, land in that valley, and we'll wait for everyone to catch up with us."

Bale brought them down where the road came up alongside the main fork of the Black River that skimmed the west side of Port Sawulxo before draining into the ocean. Croves and Shell returned the previous evening to let her know that the northerners gathered the bulk of their forces in the long valley beyond the city that had been underwater until the port's dam was destroyed.

Where Bale landed was separated from the enemy by a single pass. She idly caught fish from the river while they waited, and Tollar got more rest.

She'd used very little aquamancy in the last two days, allowing herself some time to prepare. Given the numbers Croves reported, Tollar would have to do a lot of heavy lifting if they wanted any hope of success. Dread settled on her chest like a moon. Her mind wasn't as rested as she'd like, considering all the big decisions ahead, but her magic was strong. Endless like the sea.

She could do this. Right?

You have to.

She glanced at Beenala watching Bale and then at Bale still catching fish and stifled a sigh. Could she do this without losing everyone she loved?

She chewed on some of the awful fish jerky while she watched her army approach. Toresona, Saivyn, and Kehnopa were together near the front of the long column, the elder two on donkeys, and they came quickly to make final plans with Tollar.

"Wise Mother, are you ready to go in first?"

Toresona's dark eyes gleamed and she glanced at the rows upon rows of corpses obediently following her. "Croves and I discussed some key locations to position my people to keep the enemy dead marching along."

Tollar nodded grimly.

"They'll make a good shield for the rest of us," Saivyn said.

"The trees will make good shields for us," Kehnopa said.

Tollar bowed respectfully. The old woman had come with a force nearly ten thousand strong, mostly hunters wearing animal skins with heads attached or the large skulls worn like masks. Tollar preferred not to get a good look at them, the effect enough to give her nightmares.

"Remember, stay to the east. It's where most of the trees are anyway. We don't need to surround them, but I want them funnelled toward the river."

"You're sure the enemy aquamancers won't be able to keep them safe?" Saivyn said. "You really going to overpower the whole lot of them?"

"I'm not doing this alone," Tollar said. "Tavalu and her team have become excellent at spotting how the enemy hides elementals in the earth. She knows her role the same as the rest of you."

Toresona and Kehnopa continued on, the dead going ahead of the living now, while Tollar sat with Beenala, and Saivyn watched their people approach. The rest of the army stopped along the wide basin, artificially low on water to give them plenty of space to gather and re-form their lines.

"Sai, you're sure your people know what to expect? No one will start screaming or crying?"

"Give me some credit!"

"I need to be sure they'll remain calm or this is going to be a disaster."

"I don't see how you can make it work."

"Sai, she carried a dragon egg on a boiling wave for five days," Beenala said. "I think she can manage this."

Saivyn gave Beenala a sour look at the reproach but kept quiet. Good. Tollar didn't want to have to slap all the teeth out of his head when they'd been getting along so well.

Tollar kept working at the piece of awful jerky, not because she was hungry but because she needed to keep her energy up. She watched the Nishram and the necromancers with their army of dead make their way into the pass. Tried not to let the wait wear her down.

When the time came, she finished chewing the rations, and stood up, elevating herself on a pillar of water so everyone saw and heard her.

"All right then, this is it. We stay true, remember our roles, and ancestors willing we push these monsters straight off our land and liberate our neighbours. We have the society of necromancers, two dragons, and one extremely powerful aquamancer to our advantage. And should the battle cease to go our way, we can retreat and regroup and come at them again, or wait for them back in our own valley."

Tollar focused upriver where she'd been holding the water all morning. She brought the wave forward, trying to keep it slow and not let it drown out the valley, not let it scare her own people. The water in the stream next to the road rose up toward them.

"Remember your roles, and mine. Don't fight the water. Do your best to keep your balance so you can make a dignified entrance. You won't drown, either way."

The water reached the army and lifted them all with it. Many of them swayed and stumbled, but she didn't push the water yet, letting it rise and letting them adjust to standing on the surface.

A glance at the pass showed her the Nishram and necromancers were gone.

"All right, we move."

Beenala climbed up onto Bale's back, and she lifted up to glide in lazy circles low above the floating army.

Tollar stood at the head of the growing wave and pulled the whole lot of them on it downriver through this valley and the pass, sweeping into the next valley, Port Sawulxo barely visible between a gap in two hills far beyond.

The screams reached her.

She narrowed her eyes and smiled, hard and grim. The necromancers were already hard at work. The northerners scattered, their lines breaking, as they were confronted by legions of their dead comrades. The screaming intensified as the massive wave bearing her army swept into the basin, not constrained by the riverbank.

Tollar rode the wave farther into the valley, leaving her people behind the necromancers' dead shield and pulling the water around the front line to wash away anyone too close to her. The Nishram did an excellent job of driving the northerners toward the river with their arrows, or the sheer dread fright of their appearance.

Standing on a platform of water, the river breaking around her and rushing past, Tollar lashed wave after wave into the battle. She pushed the current, heavy with northerners, swiftly out of the valley and down toward Port Sawulxo.

And the sea.

If they had any sense, they'd swim straight to their ships and leave.

Of course, if they had any sense they wouldn't be here at all.

There were so many of them, her mind tried to retreat from it. An ocean of people. A vast lakebed filled with humanity. And there were some wizards in their midst and most of those were aquamancers and terramancers, but largely it was an army of swibs with blades and crossbows.

And none of the wizards had been able to do much to counter Tollar yet. Erect some levies, knock her waves off course, but there weren't enough of them.

Bale wasn't using fire, instead swooping into enemy ranks to snatch up soldiers and drop them into the river. Tollar couldn't be certain from this distance, but it looked like Beenala clung to Bale, probably face hidden and eyes closed.

The northerners caught on to Tollar's tactic and stayed closer to the eastern edge of the valley, though the spears and arrows of Kehnopa's forces kept them from retreating too far in that direction.

Tollar redirected the flow of the river, pulling it east beyond where her people clashed with the north. She focused on the wizards she could see, plus archers and any larger weapons like their catapults and that crossbow so big it was armed with a harpoon that they were trying to aim at Bale.

That one got her blood rushing, and she cut a large wave through the throngs of northerners to mow it down and wash it away.

The largest weapons were easiest to take out, big and clumsy to move, their handlers couldn't get them out of the way fast enough to avoid the river's onslaught. And they could only run so far. There didn't appear to be enough terramancers with them to move the eastern mountain out of their way.

And Tollar felt the river running up against resistance as she pushed it east. She had to pour more focus into directing the current. But every now and then a pair of elementals would pop up out of the earth, driven from their hiding place by Tavalu and her team.

Upalintan elementals had pushed ahead of the necromancers, following along the riverbank with bands of aquamancers redirecting Tollar's magic to keep them safe.

It was more work to flush out the enemy aquamancers, but they weren't coordinating with each other like Tavalu's team, and Tollar eventually overwhelmed their magic and swept them into the river. And there was no sign of any real leadership from the northerners. The wizards were scattered among the ranks, pockets of leadership, but no one like Tollar at the head of the battle.

"Where is she...?"

Draminedes had only given Tollar a brief description of Karthiry—pale older woman, always immaculate and wearing white—but Tollar didn't see anyone who fit. There were very few women to begin with. Any of them doing anything interesting immediately stood out.

Bale shrieked and Tollar looked up, spotted Shell and Croves coming up over the hills to the north, led by a gout of flame. Bale kept picking up northerners and dumping them into the river. But Croves and Shell had suffered far longer and had little restraint.

Wonder how long it would take to just sit here and let the dragons do it all?

Victory was likely to come in the ability of Saivyn and Toresona and Tavalu to keep Tollar from getting ambushed. They were similarly protecting Bale and would soon do what they could to keep Shell safe.

What they lacked in numbers, they made up for in strength and unity.

But the sooner Tollar found Karthiry and dealt with her, the sooner they could take apart the rest of the northerners' defenses and send them packing. Although, from what Draminedes said, Karthiry didn't seem to do any of her own dirty work.

Manipulate others into it, and sit back and watch.

Well, someone had to be in charge of all these people. Whoever it was, Tollar would draw them out. Attack the leadership and hope the rest devolved into chaos. Even better if they gave up and left.

It would take bigger scare tactics than some reanimated dead for that.

Tollar had resisted frightening water magic most of her life, even out in places she'd never been before and would never see again. Hadn't ever wanted people to fear her before.

But these people? They *needed* to fear her.

Her own people were well behind her, but she moved further downriver. With an endless supply of northerners to attack, no reason to needlessly risk her own.

She gathered the river around her, not a drop of it making it past where she rose on a column of it. Like a reverse waterfall. The river running straight up into the sky. It was even worse than a great wave, and then she set the whole thing spinning. Swirling around her, a towering vortex, moving toward the invaders' lines.

Shell and Bale both came closer, staying well above and circling counter to the water's spin. As Tollar's personal whirlpool grew, the dragons rained fire below them, aided by Beenala's power and reaching where it never could on its own.

Tollar wished she could see it from the ground.

Most of the northerners in her immediate vicinity had either stopped entirely or started running. Her people rushed in to fill the gaps. Beenala also drove the dragonfire at the northerners to herd them toward the dried-out riverbed.

Smiling, Tollar raised her hand where Beenala could see it and started a countdown. Closed her fist when she ran out of numbers and let all that water drop.

Bale was there to hold Tollar up where she'd been, giving her all the focus she needed to ensure that thundering wave of water went exactly where she wanted it to.

The crashing river carved a massive swathe through the northerners, perhaps reducing their numbers by half and washing them out of the valley.

What did it look like from the city? Could Chalky see her oppressors being washed past?

Well, if that didn't get the attention of the wrong people, nothing would.

"Thanks for the lift, Bale! Time for us both to get back at it!"

Tollar gently pried open Bale's talons and fell away from her friends, landing casually on her feet in the middle of the river she'd unleashed.

And ah yes, there it was, a flash of white water, something making a monstrous wake despite moving against the current and coming straight for her. Excellent.

Tollar pushed her senses through the water and found twenty wizards in a wedge pattern, all close together. Odd. She pushed the water, trying to make it a barrier, but they broke through.

"Ooh, a challenge!"

Tollar grinned, gripped the entirety of the river that spanned the length of the valley and gave it a mighty push, tearing it forward, accelerating it beyond reason. It slowed her new friends, but didn't stop them.

Well, that was new.

Had they found some other demon-hybrid aquamancer?

That would be a touch more of a challenge than she wanted, but she needed to know her new adversaries' abilities before she could plan to counter them. She surfed out to meet them head on. But nearly fell into the river as she drew near and realized it was one pale elemental at the head of the wedge dragging the rest of them, who were bound together in a forced magical harnessing that defied comprehension.

A wave came up out of nowhere and battered her down into the river's depths, jarring her out of her initial shock. Tollar propelled herself to the surface and came up in front of the advancing elemental and her... what? Those people were nothing but energy sources. Some of them had already passed out.

No wonder she'd tied them together.

"You must be Karthiry." No one else could be so monstrous, and this woman with her human cargo certainly matched the description Dram had given, right down to all the glittery ornamentation and the sneer. "Good, now I can get this over with."

Another wave came up out of nowhere and slammed down onto Tollar, but she was ready for it this time and let it pass harmlessly over her, holding her platform on top of the river.

"You know you'll drain them all to death before you can touch me?"

Karthiry roared and slammed Tollar between two waves. Tollar put on an exaggerated wince and didn't lose her footing for an instant.

"What are you!" Karthiry shouted.

Tollar smirked. "Not used to a challenge? Poor thing."

"Dram said you were a drunkard."

"Oh good!" Her grin widened. "Turns out I was never going to run off with pirates. Sorry to disappoint."

"Figures he was lying about that too. Good thing I had him executed."

Tollar kept control of her expression but swallowed the thickness in her throat. Could she have found him hiding in the port? Had Tollar sent him to his doom?

Shell dove toward them, all teeth and talons and fire, but Karthiry had some kind of shield—a thin veil of water or maybe an air vortex? Shell's fire bubbled out around it, and he skimmed sideways when trying to fly straight at her. Would it keep Tollar from washing the horrible woman out to the ocean?

Karthiry lashed her with water, but it sluiced off.

"Look at you, tied to twenty elementals and you're still thrashing at me like a toddler having a tantrum. Really, it would be in your best interest if you took all your people out of here and went back to wherever you came from to think about what you've done. I'll help your boats along, even. Just get off my lands and leave my people alone."

Karthiry laughed, brittle like rotten ice. "*Your* people? *Your* lands? Hardly! I can see with my own eyes you're not one of them. I don't know what you are or where you come from, but little people like these could never produce something with your kind of power. You don't belong here."

Tollar ignored the way her blood turned to ice and refrained from looking around to find Beenala.

"You see, there was a time I'd have agreed with you. But I was wrong and so are you."

"You'll never get the recognition you deserve here."

Tollar smiled thinly. "I have all the recognition I need."

"I can give you real power and a station worthy of your abilities."

Tollar laughed and shook her head. "More like you can *take* my power. Lash me to you like those poor fools." She nodded toward the line of elementals, another of them falling unconscious. "I have everything I need right where I am, and I'm not letting you take it."

"I've already taken half the north!"

"Why isn't that enough?"

Karthiry shook her head and stared like Tollar had suddenly turned into a dung heap. "Unless I have it all, someone else might have more than me."

Tollar did lose control of her expression this time and could only stare.

"I *will* have it all," Karthiry said. "You can't stop me."

"Oh, but I can."

Tollar clenched her fists, done talking to this fool of a woman, and brought the water up around Karthiry and her unfortunate power supply, solidifying it, sealing them in a great block of ice and propelling them further downriver. Cracks appeared and it wouldn't be long before Karthiry broke free.

She really meant to drain all the life right out of those elementals. Tollar needed to change tactics. She hadn't wanted to resort to demons.

"Bale, Shell! To me!"

She rose on a column of water to meet the dragons halfway and called instructions to their riders. "Croves, get everyone in the port away from the river; Bee, get all our people to retreat. Fast as you can, go now!"

The dragons sped away. Tollar felt the ice casing around Karthiry shatter, felt through the water as she gathered power and took up the charge. Tollar braced herself and pushed giant waves into Karthiry's path, making her slam through them.

Needed more time. Croves hadn't even reached the city yet.

But not too much time or this woman would kill every last one of these elementals while trying to defeat Tollar.

She tried to pull the woman down into a whirlpool, but she resisted Tollar's magic and surfed around the edge of it. Karthiry blasted Tollar with a sharp gust of wind. Tollar's limbs buzzed, her heartrate pounding in her ears. Skidding across the top of the river, almost out of control, Tollar bunched her hands into fists and grit her teeth, pulling a ball of water around herself to let it take the brunt of the wind.

Karthiry lifted boulders out of the river and dropped them at Tollar, who had to be quick to avoid them. She tried to catch Karthiry in another block of ice, but only encased a couple of the elementals, doing nothing to slow Karthiry down.

She already dragged a row of wizards from each arm, most of them passed out and floating on the surface of the river. One of them didn't look like he was breathing anymore.

Tollar was out of time.

She ducked under a boulder aimed for her head, retreating further upriver to give herself some space. She hadn't done this trick in a while.

Putting all her focus on the water, concentrating and digging deeper into the element, she pulled it apart, opening a passage directly to the water realm. She opened it wide and high, an impossible torrent ripping through the valley, sweeping away every last soldier in front of her.

She hoped Beenala got their people out of the way.

This kind of magic was difficult to control, and it took all her focus to hold the portal steady. She held it until her mind couldn't focus on the effort anymore and closed it.

But Karthiry, soggy and with only one of her power sources left conscious, still stood on the river's surface, her bright eyes gleaming. Tollar gasped. It shouldn't have been possible.

"I know what you are," Karthiry snarled. "Thought there were only pyromancers like you."

Tollar stared, cold as the bottom of the ocean. What would it take to stop her?

Tollar slammed a wall of water between them and retreated further, paralyzed by the vision of being strapped to Karthiry, that horrible woman sapping her endless power to drown anyone who stood before her.

Karthiry pushed forward against the current, coming straight for her, that sick gleam in her eye. "I know *exactly* what to do with you."

38

Draminedes rushed through the ranks, stumbling over the smooth river rocks covering the ground, hoping he looked courageous and not like an even worse traitor. At least the helmet obscured enough of his face that no one recognized him yet.

So what if they recognize you?

Well, they might kill him, for a start. And if he was going to die here today, it had better godsdamn mean something. But it was a long way up the valley to where all the water was happening, where Tollar would be.

He had to warn her. She had no idea.

Of course, he hadn't had any idea until yesterday. The information had come in pieces until Loch landed on the coast. How could anyone have anticipated someone worse than Karthiry? Draminedes knew Loch was the real mastermind behind the invasion, but his power? Draminedes shuddered.

He struggled up the slope, wishing Karthiry hadn't brought the battle out into the valley. But the port was no use as a strategic point if they destroyed it entirely. It had the benefit of keeping Tollar far enough from the ocean she couldn't use it.

But she'd need to. Was there enough water in the world? Was Tollar's power enough?

It wouldn't be if he didn't get to her.

Karthiry went skimming past, helpless wizards tied to her in a gruesome line. Draminedes had never been happier to be a swib in his entire life.

Karthiry could do a lot of awful things to him, but she could never drain him of power he didn't have.

Draminedes hoped, briefly, that even as she sucked away the power of all those wizards, Karthiry would be no match for Tollar. And when she initially went flying downstream encased in ice, his hopes soared.

But he was near enough to hear the ice crack, and he watched in horror as she broke free. Some captain shouted at him to hold the line, but Draminedes ignored him and resumed running as Karthiry zipped up the current.

"No, no, no...!"

When she started throwing boulders at Tollar, Draminedes thought he'd just about die. It wasn't bad enough Karthiry was a really good aquamancer, she was a full elemental and had good command of all four elements. And now she had a big energy boost to go with all that malevolent will.

But the Upalintans were retreating.

And he was close enough to see that Tollar didn't look terribly concerned.

"Oh no."

He stopped and looked around. No high ground in sight. Only northerners as far as he could see, and all of them rushing toward Tollar. Who was definitely about to do something big. She opened up space between her and Karthiry, put up a wall of water.

"Oh no."

A shadow passed overhead. It was Shell and Croves returning, and they were his only chance.

Everyone will know.

Yes, if he took off his helmet, if he let them see him with dragons, warning Tollar, it would confirm, without a doubt, where his loyalties lay. That what had happened on his mission wasn't one of Karthiry's manipulations.

But if he did nothing, his friends would die right along with him.

Ignoring the jostling northerners around him, he yanked off his helmet and shouted to both dragon and rider. He ignored the way everyone around him stopped. And stared.

"Shell! Hurry!"

At least the dragon spotted him and turned, but the river rose swiftly under whatever Tollar was doing.

He thought he heard someone call him a traitor, but it was lost to the roar of water. Draminedes kept his focus on Shell, even as the ground was swept out from under him.

Coughing, sputtering, doing his best to stay afloat, while struggling northerners screamed all around him, he watched Shell with his arms outstretched.

Shell plucked him from the torrent and pulled him up into the air.

"I need to get to Tollar!" he shouted. "Drop me down there!"

"Ye sure about this?" Croves asked.

"Someone's got to help her—she doesn't know! I know I promised—"

"Ach, get down there. We'll come back around for ye. If it goes wrong, let the water take ye. Toll has control of it and we'll be swift to find ye."

Shell circled around and glided in low, letting go of Draminedes far higher up than he would have liked, even with the river down there to catch him.

And he slammed into Karthiry, taking her shoulder in the hip, flipping over the line of wizards and dropping into the water with one foot tangled up on... something. Pain exploded through his body and he cried out, filling his lungs with water. There was an arm in front of his face and he pulled on it, bringing his head above the surface so he could scream over what felt like a broken hip. Maybe his leg was gone entirely?

Well, at least there were no sharks in the river for it to summon.

He clung to one of the unconscious wizards, about three from the end of the line, though he'd lost his lenses in the collision, probably at the bottom of the river now, and the line was mostly a blur. If Karthiry didn't have their power, she wouldn't stand a chance against Tollar. So he yanked his knife from his belt, screaming at the pain stabbing through his hip and into his gut as he did. And sliced the ropes binding the wizards.

Three of them floated away and he turned to cut free another.

Tollar watched him from beyond where Karthiry staggered on top of the river while the water rushed past. At least he wasn't the only one in pain from that collision.

"Toll! Reinforcements in the port! There's an aquamancer worse—"

Karthiry screamed at him. The air crackled, wisps of electricity rippling over Karthiry's arms before it streaked down the line of wizards toward him.

The pain in his hip had been nothing compared to what came next.

39

Lightning. That horrible woman used frogging lightning. On Draminedes. Tollar had had a brief moment of relief at his reappearance—and annoyance at herself for entertaining Karthiry's incessant lies—but now her insides seized as he floated away, bringing one more of the bound elementals with him. She focused on the water around him to keep him afloat, but then Croves and Shell returned, scooping him up and collecting the unconscious wizards.

Good.

She didn't realize she'd had lingering doubts about his loyalty until he dropped spectacularly from the sky and slammed into Karthiry. Tollar had no idea what he'd tried warning her about, but he'd interrupted her panic and shown her what she should have thought of the instant Karthiry arrived with all those people strapped to her. Like things.

Tollar pulled out her spears and flung them across the distance, aiming for the ropes over Karthiry's arms.

The woman screamed, her forearms torn with the rope, and the remaining wizards floated away. Karthiry got a grip on the nearest one, the only one still conscious. So Tollar reached into the pouch on her belt for her little arrowheads and flung them, even as she brought the spears back around.

All of Tollar's weapons pierced Karthiry's arms from both directions, one of the arrowheads going clean through her wrist, breaking her grip. The wizards floated away.

But Tollar couldn't pay attention to them. Karthiry figured out the spears and tried to wrest them out of Tollar's control. Bale swooped in somewhere behind Karthiry, hopefully for the drained wizards. Maybe she'd use some fire in parting.

One by one, Tollar brought the spears and arrowheads back, strapping them down. Secured again, they couldn't be used against her, but she needed something else to bring Karthiry down.

Karthiry came closer, struggling against the current now that she had only her own power to propel her. One of her arms hung limp, the shoulder dislocated by Dram's dramatic appearance, but the other hand grasped at Tollar. Grabbing for her power. Tollar needed to do something to stop her or she'd end up like the dragons, caged until it was time to sap her power for ancestors only knew what terrible ends.

What could someone like Karthiry do with power like Tollar's?

Can't let her.

Tollar reached for her sword, but more of that lightning crackled over Karthiry's skin. Tollar got an ice shield up between them.

Ice fragments exploded in a blizzard around the two of them, but Tollar didn't give it time to settle or time for Karthiry to prepare another attack. She drove the ice around the other woman, packing her in glacier tight with that one grasping hand sticking out in front of her.

A length of rope still knotted at the bleeding forearm.

Tollar grabbed the rope, careful to avoid Karthiry's skin. It had never once crossed Tollar's mind that she would need to protect against someone siphoning her power against her will. There had to be a way, but this wasn't the time to experiment.

Moving the ice where she needed it, Tollar wrapped the rope behind Karthiry's back and trapped her other arm in it, pulling both tight against Karthiry's body.

The air sizzled around them as Karthiry tried to summon more lightning, but Tollar seized her by the front of her robes and plunged them both into the water.

Karthiry brought a bubble of air around her face, and Tollar swatted it away. Snarling and struggling, Karthiry put another air pocket around her face, only for Tollar to pull that away too.

The pair of them plunged all the way to the river bottom, pressed against the side of a boulder, with Tollar pinning Karthiry to the smooth gravel. She inhaled deeply, letting the water in, letting Karthiry see what she could do. And then held on, pushing the other woman into the ground.

Karthiry's eyes bulged. She thrashed, screaming out the last of her air.

Tollar didn't know what it was like to drown. She would never know. Her bile rose and her arms trembled as she held Karthiry in place, batting away all of the woman's attempts to bring an air pocket to her face.

But every time Karthiry tried, she got little sips of air.

"You're only making this worse."

For both of them.

Tollar had never watched someone die like this. Never been so close. Never had it drag on. Panic rose as Tollar remembered Draminedes's warning. There was something else. Someone bringing reinforcements. Did Karthiry think someone could save her?

Tollar pressed her tighter to the riverbed and swatted away her newest attempt at air.

Striking like a snake, Karthiry lashed her head so that her cheek grazed Tollar's forearm. Tollar yanked her arm away before Karthiry got any of her power, but Karthiry kept twisting, trying to get any part of her against Tollar's skin.

Fury raged like all the world's rivers. Tollar was nothing but a power source to this woman.

Snarling, Tollar twisted her body so that she could pin Karthiry's shoulders with her feet, sitting on the awful woman's legs. And she'd given her more than enough opportunities. She had to end this before Karthiry got hold of her.

Tollar closed her eyes and focused. Swallowed bile and reached for the water inside Karthiry. The water that made up her blood.

It was harder to breathe, like the water in her lungs had turned to ice and her vision blurred with tears before the river washed them away. But she was out of options.

Tollar reached her magic into the struggling woman and pushed it at her wounded arms. The water around Karthiry grew pink, then red. Karthiry thrashed anew, but Tollar kept pulling. Draining her, even as she managed another air bubble.

Draining until her pale skin went white, and her tense body went limp.

Tollar glanced at her right forearm as she let Karthiry's body drift away on the current. She let out a sob and curled in on herself against the stone. But something shifted down current. She felt it through her own horror and shame.

Something big was coming.

Exhaling the water, Tollar pushed herself up to the surface and out onto the riverbank, where her people gathered. Staring into the water upstream where she'd been struggling with Karthiry at the surface.

Bale came to her first, able to track her from above.

"Tollar!" Beenala cried.

It caught other people's attention, more of them drawing near. Too close to the river's edge and danger none of them understood.

"It's not over!" Tollar shouted. "Get back!"

But they cheered her safe reappearance and likely what they thought was a victory. The roar of a great wave entering the valley from the north drowned out all sound, and Tollar barely heard Beenala cry out beside her.

Tollar gestured Beenala back to Bale, signalled for the little dragoness to get into the air where they'd be safer. Tollar put her hand in the river and concentrated on the wave bearing down on them. She'd stopped bigger waves. But never one driven by a powerful aquamancer before.

She slowed the wave. Couldn't stop it.

Whoever was coming had opened a water portal. And was letting water demons out. She couldn't see their shimmering humanoid shape from here, but felt them as bright points in the water.

"Oh shit."

Tollar didn't have time to think of what that meant; all her concentration went into battling whatever this new threat was. Everything she had left amounted to stopping this wave, a mountain of water sitting over half the valley and far too close to sweeping away all of her people.

Would Saivyn know to get everyone out? Was there anything Tavalu's team could do?

Tollar had never thought to ask if they knew what to do with elemental demons. How to control them or how to send them back to their realm. She'd never heard of anyone but her using elemental demons in battle before—they were too unpredictable, too dangerous.

What is this madness?

"Tollar!" Beenala called from above.

"Bale, that's a human you're allowed to eat!" She pointed at the aquamancer at the head of the wave she held.

Beenala screamed wordlessly as Bale headed for the wave. Dragonfire lashed out, enhanced and pushed beyond capacity.

"Tollar, what do we do?" Tavalu shouted.

"Get rid of the demons."

Tavalu didn't ask any nonsense questions and ran off with her team along the riverbank. Tollar let herself move with the current, keeping her focus on the mountain of water. She'd stopped it. Now, could she push it back?

Whatever this new aquamancer was—another demon hybrid like her?—the two of them were likely to lay waste to everything within several leagues before this was over. Her thoughts skittered across the memory of all those dead husks of fish. She needed to take this out into the ocean, away from her people and away from Port Sawulxo, and to where Tollar would have more water to work with. Where mistakes wouldn't kill every bit of life for leagues around.

But it was like pushing an actual mountain, like she was trying to work earth instead of water.

She should have asked Tavalu to leave someone behind to give her a boost. Her mind flitted to Karthiry with all those drained wizards tied to her, and Tollar worried she'd never again be able to harness another wizard's energy.

She spared a look in Tavalu's direction, saw her gripping hands with another aquamancer, and the two of them driving demons back into the water realm.

Tollar submerged her will deep into the water, making it an extension of herself, and pushing it further. The new aquamancer opened water portals and pulled demons through almost faster than Tollar could track, but gave up ground.

She'd pushed the wall of water to the edge of the valley, watching as the water beneath her passed over the destroyed dam.

A dragon screeched, and another. And another?

Tollar held the water where it was and looked around. Was Bale hurt? Croves and Shell in trouble?

And then she saw her, the green and yellow dragoness who led the local dragon blaze. She had the overcast male dragon with her, Shell taking up position at the dragoness's other wing so the trio came over the mountains from the west and aimed all their fire at the new aquamancer.

The newcomer countered with water shields and lashed coiling loops of water out at the dragons. But gave up more focus, so Tollar kept pushing them back. Halfway between the dam and the city.

While she pushed the water downriver, she dispersed it as well, making it smaller and less of a threat should she lose control of it.

Now there was a thought she wasn't fond of. Had she ever lost control of water before? Maybe as a child but those were such distant hazy memories. There'd been all sorts of missteps in using the *magic* but had she ever lost control of the outcome with the *water*? Well, now certainly wasn't the time to start. Tollar grit her teeth, dug into the water and got back to work while the dragons swooped and circled, trying to burn down the new threat.

40

Beenala clung to Bale's back and kept her eyes open only so that she could watch Tollar. The other dragons flew a pattern Bale had never trained for, so Bale left them to it and instead circled above Tollar.

Bale growled at the aquamancer on top of his wave, some pale, greasy looking northerner. She couldn't tell if he was part demon like Tollar, but so far he wasn't overpowering her. Did that mean anything? He was making little swirling patches of water that demons came out of. Water portals? Was that what Tollar had meant about that?

The creatures slid down into the valley after the others, where Tavalu and her team... melted them. Or something. Beenala had worked to summon and then banish a fire demon exactly twice—once under the careful supervision of her mentor and once to prove she could during her Guild entrance exam.

It had... looked something like what Tavalu was doing to the water demons. Maybe?

"Keep focused on Tollar!" she called to Bale.

The newest batch of water demons trickled down the side of the stalled wave toward Tollar. Could they hurt her? Would they recognize her as partially one of their own?

Beenala held her breath and watched as the wave stopped its slow progression downriver and little portals opened up under the demons so that they disappeared.

Well. Why hadn't she done that in the first place if she could?

But the wave had stopped moving. Did she not have the power to do both? That seemed ridiculous.

But she'd been at it all day, hadn't she. Hadn't let up since they left Nytaltek an eternity ago.

"She's tired. Bale, we need to help her. Let's get down there."

Beenala clenched her whole body against the way her stomach rose when Bale dived. But she didn't throw up. Maybe she'd get used to this yet?

Tollar looked up as they came toward her and locked gazes with Beenala. Her grim expression relaxed, and she reached up one hand while Beenala leaned over and stretched out her own. She clasped hold of Tollar, straining to haul her up as Bale glided past.

"The dragons can't get close enough," Beenala said. "Do the demons listen to you? You're like a little sister, aren't you?"

"When did you ever listen to your little sisters, Bee? They're always hard to work with, and I can't keep my focus on everything and speak their language with enough conviction to do anything but send them away again."

"Tavalu had that under control."

"She's too far away to do anything about the ones coming upriver at me."

"He's powerful, Toll. I don't know what we're going to do."

"I don't either."

Beenala went cold at Tollar's admission.

Bale circled up and around so that they got a good look at him.

"He's too good to be a normal aquamancer," Tollar said. "But I'm not sure he's good enough to be part demon. Unless he's holding back?"

Beenala's skin prickled. She looked at Tollar, who rubbed her hands over her tired face. She looked terrible. Worse than exhausted. And the sun was getting low. They had to beat him now or retreat until Tollar had rest. And he'd only get stronger with the wait.

"We need to do something now," Beenala said.

"Can you reach him with fire magic?"

Beenala shook her head. "Even with my magic, we can't get close enough. He almost pulled that green dragoness right out of the sky with one of those water whips of his."

"Ancestors keep us. How is he so strong?"

The cold prickle bit deeper, Beenala struggled for a deep breath.

"Analyze the how after we stop him."

"I don't know if I *can* stop him." It came out in a horrified whisper that made Beenala numb.

But movement from behind them caught her attention, and she felt Bale moving under her and the pressure of Tollar next to her.

"Well, I guess it's a good thing you don't have to stop him alone." Beenala pointed to the slope next to the dam where Shell set down Tavalu and her team of elementals. "Look, Croves went back for the others."

Tollar pressed her lips together and stared blankly forward.

"What if you do the boiling wave thing? Do you think that would get him?"

Tollar opened her mouth to respond, snapped it shut and sat up straighter. "I have a better idea. Bale, get us down to Tavalu for a minute."

The little dragoness banked around the wave, held stationary by Tollar while the other three dragons kept distracting that awful man.

"Tollar, what madness is this?" Tavalu asked.

"I don't know, but we need to stop him. Has Saivyn taken the swibs to safety?"

"Yes, they're retreating. The necromancers and the Nishram too. What do we do?"

"I might let go of that wave here in a minute when Bee and I get back up there to do something. Can you catch it, or at least keep it from taking out all of Port Sawulxo?"

Tavalu bit her lip and looked at the elementals gathered with her. Cerro gave her an encouraging nod.

"We can contain it, at the very least."

"All right. Watch it closely, but keep working on the demons. Don't let any of them get away to cause mayhem down in the city."

Tollar put a hand on Beenala's shoulder. "You ready for this? We'll combine our magic."

Beenala tensed but nodded.

"All right, Bale, take us back up and approach him from the south. Try not to let him see you coming."

"What are we going to do?" Beenala asked.

"Do you remember when I told you about geysers?"

Beenala gasped. Her shoulders itched like electricity ran across them, but her hands were so numb she barely gripped Bale's spikes.

"We drive him out to the ocean where he can't hurt anyone and I get rid of him for good."

"Toll, are you sure?"

"Dram said he was worse... I assume he meant worse than Karthiry. I can't even fathom that. We can't let this go on. And I can't stop him here without destroying us or what's left of the port."

Tollar turned her attention to the water, a funnel of it spiralling out and away from the rest of the wave, growing and extending and stretching up. When she extended her hand to Beenala, she didn't hesitate.

"Lots of fire, Bee, hot as we can make it."

Beenala took a deep breath and squeezed Tollar's hand, focusing on the heat and fire of the dragons, pulling Bale's dragonfire away and channelling it into that new vortex of water. Tollar gripped her hand tighter and pulled on Beenala's magic, forcing the water and fire together.

The sizzling roar echoed across the mountainside as Bale crested the wall of water. The northern aquamancer turned toward the sound, but his focus was on Bale rather than what Tollar was doing.

And she kept pulling energy—fire from Beenala and water from that wave—and slammed that supercharged waterspout right into him.

It blasted him like from a cannon, and he shot away toward the city.

And the mountain of water he'd been wielding collapsed.

Beenala felt the tug on her energy as Tollar tried to catch the whole thing at once. She couldn't see what was happening, blinked her eyes to clear them. Felt lightheaded, like she was floating.

"Bee!"

An influx of energy cleared her head. Tollar gripped her hand. Beenala hung off Bale's side. More energy, Tollar transferring it back to her. Beenala tried pulling herself up and her legs swung off the side of Bale, the shift in weight tearing her from Tollar's grasp.

"Bee, no!"

Beenala held her breath, eyes wide, holding Tollar's horrified gaze, all of it suspended for an eternal instant.

Then Beenala plunged.

"Bale, help!"

Bale banked into a dive and caught Beenala before she fell very far. Clutching Beenala to her chest, Bale pitched herself up, gaining altitude. Tollar fell past.

"Toll! What!"

Eyes closed and limbs limp, Tollar plummeted.

"Bale! Get her!"

Bale banked, the lurch of the sudden directional shift made Beenala's head spin. She lost sight of Tollar! Bale rolled into a dive, putting Tollar back in view.

Just as she slammed into the surface of the river. And sank out of sight.

"No! Tollar!"

Bale screeched and pulled out of the dive, skimming the top of the water, talons dragging through it, but it was so murky, full of silt and battle debris, and she came up with only a snarl of branches. Beenala couldn't see more than a finger's width down into the water.

"Tollar!"

Beenala's eyes felt packed with sand, and she resisted the urge to rub them. It wouldn't make a difference, and she needed to keep looking. Needed to focus on sustaining the firelight, keep it on the water.

"Bee," Tavalu said behind her. "Not much longer."

Her voice sounded far away and slurred, like she was drunk at the bottom of a well. They'd been at it all night. Tavalu didn't sound like she had much energy left, and Beenala felt guilty for continuing to syphon her. But this was the part of the cityside riverbank where Chalky said they'd found a bunch of others after the first battle wave. Something about the current... There was more debris here than anywhere else, that was for sure.

There were little twinkle lights of locals on the ground with lanterns, wading through the flood zone and looking.

Beenala wasn't the only one refusing to give up, she was just the only one left on a dragon to skim over the water. Croves with Shell, plus Minty and

Cloudy had helped her search well into the night, but rested now. Bale was silent and focused. She might not take rest at dawn even if Beenala did.

Beenala knew how it looked to everyone else. None of them believing her when she said Tollar could breathe water. The pitying looks they gave her. But even if Tollar hadn't survived the fall and the river, they couldn't leave her out here. Toresona knew that better than anyone, and had been the first to volunteer to come with Beenala, letting Beenala harness her energy until the old woman couldn't sit up anymore.

And now Tavalu didn't have much strength left in her.

"We can't give up," Beenala whispered, her voice thick with tears she refused to let fall.

Tavalu squeezed her shoulder.

"It's almost dawn," Tavalu said. "Just a few more minutes, and then you need to rest. We can keep looking in the daylight."

Beenala swallowed unkind words. They were unfair words, too. Tavalu was right, but Beenala couldn't bear the thought of Tollar out here alone.

"Wait, what's that!" Beenala focused the light on where she thought she'd seen a glint of metal. "Bale, go back!"

The pair of wizards gripped tightly as Bale banked hard and swooped back around.

"There, by that fence-thing!"

Bale came in close, her wings extended straight out and stiff as mountains, not causing the barest ripple to obscure Beenala's view.

It was the hilt of a sword on what looked like a pile of rags. But Beenala had helped make that sword, and she'd recognize that vine pattern anywhere. She leapt from Bale's back, landing in hip-deep water and slimy silt over stone. Sloshing, she half swam half ran and gripped the strap.

And pulled. Too heavy to be a sword attached to rags.

Beenala pulled Tollar, her insides seizing over how cold Tollar felt, like death. The gentle current buffeted them both against the snarl of fencing half secured to the ground and catching all manner of debris.

"Tollar, please..."

Beenala hauled on Tollar's uniform and got her face out of the river, got her onto her back, and dirty water poured out of her mouth in the dim light of Beenala's little fireball. And then Tollar made a noise like sucking mud through a bamboo shoot. More water sputtered out of her mouth.

At last, she inhaled cleanly.

Beenala sobbed. All those tears and all that air she'd been holding in all day, exhaled out in shocked relief. She clutched Tollar against her like the river would reach out and snatch her away.

"Bale! Over here! Tavalu, she's alive! Come quickly!"

Bale called out for the first time all night and banked around.

Alive, but Tollar's eyes remained closed. She didn't move at all but to breathe. And breathe poorly. Beenala had never been on anyone's deathbed, had only heard talk of a death rattle before. But she was sure this was what it sounded like.

"Bale, hurry!"

41

Tollar opened her eyes to dim light, short of breath and her limbs pulling her down like lead. Everything ached. She was warmer than she'd ever been, all swaddled up in blankets that didn't make moving any easier. And wrapped in Beenala's arms. Beenala pillowy soft and warm beside her. Tollar wheezed in an aching breath and tried to roll over.

Beenala came awake with a start, the little lantern on the bedside table flaring with light.

They were in a tiny room stacked with crates all around the bed so that Tollar couldn't even see the walls.

"Tollar!" Beenala whisper shouted. "You're okay! Praise the ancestors!"

Tollar coughed, struggled for another wheezing breath. Not okay. Her lungs were full of... something. What had even happened?

"Basin," Tollar croaked.

Beenala unwrapped the blankets and shoved Tollar up so she was sitting. Then she placed the basin where Tollar could reach it. Tollar gripped the edges of it and plunged her entire face into the cool, clean water. And inhaled. Deep as she could.

When she exhaled, the water came out of her mouth black and muddy.

"Oh my," Beenala gasped.

Tollar patiently sifted the water out of the bowl into a blob floating in the air and dusted the remaining dry silt into the cup standing on the table. She let the water back into the bowl and submerged her face, inhaling water and exhaling sludge. She repeated the process until she'd expelled every last grain of silt from her lungs.

They still ached.

She stretched her mind back, trying to understand how her lungs had nearly filled with mud. She'd been fighting Karthiry on the river and then... oh.

"Dram?"

"He's with the healers. They've handled his burns, most of them minor, but he dislocated his hip and..." Beenala winced.

"And those harnessed wizards?"

Beenala cringed and ushered Tollar back into bed, swaddling her up in the blankets so that she rested with her head in Beenala's lap. Beenala leaned down to kiss Tollar's temple and then sat stroking her hair.

"I'm sorry, Toll. One of them died. There was nothing you could have done. The others are recovering. They all had broken arms and dislocated shoulders."

"She strapped them together like cargo," Tollar snarled. "Dragged them around like supplies. Not people, just things. And she found out what I am and wanted to do the same to me."

Silence stretched on for longer than Tollar liked. When Beenala spoke, her voice was soft.

"Is that why you killed her?"

Tollar balled her hands into fists and squeezed her eyes shut, trying to unsee the life go out of the woman's eyes and the way she'd gone limp under Tollar's hands.

Beenala rested her hand gently on the back of Tollar's neck. "It was probably the only way to stop her," Beenala said carefully. "Those wizards she tied up... Half of them were like Dram, manipulated and lied to. The others, kidnapped and held..."

"Like the dragons. She wanted to do that to me, Bee. She wanted my power. Who would stop her then? And what about that other one? What was he?"

Beenala rubbed her back and made a soft, comforting sound.

"His name is Loch. We didn't find him and the northerners are gone, the last of their boats left after sunset."

"How long has it been?"

"You were in the river for a full night. Bale and I found you early yesterday morning. You slept all day and it's probably a couple more hours until dawn. But you should rest. Chalky's people have things under control. Chalky and the dragons and Saivyn. You can rest, Toll."

Victory of a sort. But Tollar felt no joy in it, not with all the loss and destruction and that aquamancer, Loch, still out there.

"No, we need to—" A coughing fit seized Tollar, setting her lungs on fire.

"Toll! Do you need more water?"

Tollar did her best to shake her head while the coughing wracked her body, making every bump and bruise from her time in the river sing out in agony. When it died down, Beenala made her sip water.

"Who knows what you were breathing all that time," Beenala said, a worried mother hen. "I'll see if Chalky has any lizard weed I can make into tea."

Tollar nodded slowly and let her go. It might be too late for lizard weed to do any good, and Tollar didn't want to think about what she may have been inhaling at the bottom of the river. She glanced at the cup of dirt that had come out of her. A full day was a long time for things to fester.

She sighed. There were excellent healers here, probably with access to green sprout mushrooms. And there was Beenala, whose hidden talents and capacity for both bravery and kindness were not to be underestimated.

Tollar settled deeper into the blankets, safe and comforted, and fell asleep before Beenala returned.

After

Tollar popped a fish out of the canal and caught it in Beenala's basket, which was now utterly full. She pressed the lid down over top and got some water under it so she wouldn't have to carry it. She considered a water platform for herself but decided it was a fine day to walk.

The hot summer sun beat down on the corn between the nearest row of trees and palms provided shade to the canal. Tollar stayed on the path in the shade as she made her way down the row, inspecting the squash acting as a buffer between the corn rows and the path. Everything was getting big. She elevated the ground water as she went, so the plants didn't have to work quite so hard.

"Tollar, would it kill you to carry it?" Beenala teased, coming down the intersecting path with a long bundle of bananas over her shoulder and Ash trotting merrily along beside her. The dog had been ecstatic when they returned, bouncing off the two of them and barking. She rarely left Beenala's side.

"I could use the water trick on yours, too, and then neither of us has to carry anything."

Beenala rolled her eyes.

"Come now, do you want me to get this dirty?" She gestured to her dress, a simple design similar to Beenala's orange dress, but the once-white fabric had been dyed the same turquoise as the sea around Port Sawulxo. Or, at least the turquoise it became once all the sediments Tollar's magic stirred up had settled.

Beenala surprised her with the dress as a summer solstice gift, and Tollar had no idea how she'd dyed the fabric and stitched the little silver vines around the neckline without Tollar noticing what she was doing. Especially since they hadn't been home from Sawulxo for very long before the solstice.

"You know," Beenala said with jovial reproach, "I did make you some nice work clothes."

"Yes, but if I wore them, I'd have to work."

"Oh, just come on. Per Graza will be here soon, and I don't want to be the reason she's late delivering these to the market for us."

Tollar almost reiterated her offer to float the supplies downriver to the market and not bother Per Graza who did enough for them already, but Beenala was very set on the arrangement. Besides, they both knew Per Graza would keep the best fish and bananas for herself.

When the two of them reached their cottage, Per Graza hadn't arrived yet to collect the supplies, but Draminedes was in the side yard, puttering around on a crutch as best he could while his hip took the time it needed. At least he was walking now.

Ash yipped and bounded over to see him, nearly knocking the poor man down.

It was a good thing Croves and Shell came back with them after they'd done as much as they could to help clean up Port Sawulxo. Croves and Shell left four days ago, heading north to settle some affairs before returning to join Draminedes for good. Croves had made an excellent nursemaid for him. But Tollar had no idea how the bear of a man had been able to live in the tiny mud hut some local terramancers had hastily put together for Draminedes when he first limped back into Nytaltek with Tollar and the rest of the army.

Tollar was a little disappointed not to have Croves around, even if he was coming back eventually. While he'd respected her request and had stopped asking her for more than friendship, he still flirted relentlessly, if mildly. And she really hadn't minded.

Shell was gone, but hadn't left Bale lonely for company. Minty and Cloudy—Beenala's secret names for them, though Balipar warned her from ever letting them know that—came regularly to see Bale, off with her right now. The green and grey dragons had little to do with most Upalintans, but Tollar hoped in time Bale could help repair the bond. At any rate, it was good for her to have her kin around to teach her the things Beenala and Tollar never could.

Tollar stood at the hedge, under the shade of the mango tree, and watched Draminedes work in his slow, swib fashion, stopping occasionally to throw a stick for Ash or scratch behind her ears. He was rebuilding the house out of stones, slab by slab. At least he'd let Beenala bring in some other terramancers to help her get the support columns and foundation of it laid solid. He'd wanted to build it out of wood and palm fronds.

Beenala had gently reminded him of what happened to the structure the first time around, and he'd gone with something more dragon-proof.

It wasn't very big yet, but the new design allowed for it to be built upon. It would be plenty big enough for Croves and Draminedes to start. But he hoped to attract other strays and build out a nice little compound. He'd need the help if he was really going to take over the Lipraxo farm and make it his own.

Tollar and Beenala couldn't really help him. They had their hands full with their own farm, even with Per Graza and her boys lending a hand.

At least he'd stopped talking about returning to Biterna. He'd learned not long before they left Port Sawulxo for Nytaltek that while the northerners had been driven from the mainland, many of them were on his home islands, still using Biterna as a staging ground.

It was hard to say when Biterna would be safe for him. Not until the northerners had been neutralized. But for now, Upalint focused on supporting Port Sawulxo as it rebuilt and fortified against future attack.

There would be no liberating Biterna before that.

Tollar had her mind bent toward it. And to finding Loch. Especially once she learned from Grand Chancellor Dira that Loch was exceedingly powerful, able to use demons in unique ways, but not a demon hybrid like Tollar. He was the reason the Guild had instated the specialist tiers.

But if he wasn't part demon, Tollar could beat him. Eventually. Turned out, spending a night submerged in a war-polluted river had not been beneficial to her health. Tollar had developed both blight fever *and* swamp lung, which really didn't seem fair. The healers had plenty of green sprout mushrooms to deal with the blight fever, but they'd also needed an infusion of sunny shores mushrooms for the swamp lung. Then she'd pushed too hard before recovering fully, wanting to help restore Port Sawulxo. And now she got tired faster. Breathing water was difficult when clean and impossible when not.

So she needed to heal. And then to train before she took on Loch again.

But ancestors willing, that was exactly what she planned to do. The local dragon blaze, acting on behalf of the wider dragon population, had asked Tollar to help them counter him. Hopefully it would go better than it had with Karthiry.

Tollar didn't realize she'd been scratching at the new butterfly tattoo on her forearm until Beenala laid a hand over hers. The two met gazes and Beenala gave her a sympathetic smile. At least Tollar had gotten three new spirals down her left arm and a fresh set of rank lines.

Not that she'd caught up to Solia or Saivyn at all. Both of them had ranked up as well.

"You sure you don't want to come with me?" Tollar asked Beenala.

"You sure you don't want to stay?"

Tollar smiled. "I'm going to swing around to the north and visit Chalky before I come home. You don't want to visit Chalky again?"

"I've seen enough of Port Sawulxo to last me my entire lifetime." Beenala straightened the hem of her shirt. "Are you sure you'll be home for the winter solstice?"

"I promised, didn't I?"

"It's just... Nearly half a year. Why so long?"

"That's how long it'll take to help get Kraua's caravan where it's headed and get home again."

"I suppose it's a nice start to hear you call this place home."

Tollar smiled. "I've never had a home before. For you, like most people, home is a place, but for me, home is the right people. Home is wherever you are, Bee."

Beenala's cheeks flushed and she squeezed Tollar's hand. She didn't like the idea of Tollar leaving anymore than she liked the idea of going anywhere herself. But Tollar had promised to escort Kraua's caravan long before she had any sort of notion she'd ever want to stay in Upalint.

"There will be real beds this time," Tollar said. "You don't have to sleep on the ground under a dragon."

Beenala gave her a look. "Even if I did come, I can't keep asking Per Graza to do everything."

"Well, hurry and get this boy trained up." Tollar gestured to Draminedes.

Draminedes hobbled over and looked at the large bunch of bananas Beenala had hauled in.

"Even if I knew what in the name of the moons I was doing, there's no way I can do all the physical labour," he said. "Not without Croves around to be my muscle."

Tollar nodded slowly and looked out over the river, glittering in the distance. They wouldn't know for months yet if Draminedes would get his full mobility back. He was determined to be a farmer anyway. Good thing he would have a bear-man and a dragon for help.

Then she spotted Toresona coming up the lane, not noticing her on the other side of the hedge until she passed one of the gaps.

"Wise Mother," Tollar called. "What brings you out to these humble gardens."

"I heard talk of you getting ready to leave again," Toresona said reproachfully. "Thought you'd sworn your sword to Saivyn's army."

"Saivyn saw the wisdom in keeping me in the reserves." Tollar's cheeks grew warm.

"Indeed." Toresona stopped right in front of Tollar, planted the end of her bone staff in the ground and looked up at her, staring hard. She nodded once and reached into her long black robe, etched in silver and gold.

When Toresona held her hand out, palm up, Tollar blinked at the bone she held and gave the old woman an expectant look.

"From your grandmother."

"Wait, what? I thought these could only be gifted *before* death!"

"She saw how deeply it upset you to lose the connection. Not that you ever really could. You know she volunteered her bones to the war? She was one of the first, convinced many others."

Tollar's mouth fell open, though she guessed she really shouldn't have been surprised.

"She told me to take this, second knuckle from the same finger you had to start with. Take it and don't give me a fuss. You know it would insult her to refuse."

Tollar gripped the bone and held it against her chest. "Thank you, Wise Mother. I'll take better care of this one."

"I can weave it into your bracelet," Beenala said.

"Yes, well. Your granny also has a message: talk to your brother."

Tollar bristled, but knew better than to argue.

"*Only* your brother." Toresona's expression softened. "Not all wounds can be healed."

Tollar bowed, thought about Jarku's suggestion of a meal with Auntie. Maybe it wouldn't be so bad?

Toresona winked at Beenala and left as abruptly as she'd appeared.

"Bee. Did you have something to do with this?"

Beenala looked down at her hands, her cheeks reddening.

Tollar leaned forward and kissed the top of her head.

"Thank you, Bee."

"I know how much it meant to you." Beenala rubbed her palms on her shorts and met Tollar's gaze. "And I know how much it means to you when I go with you. But give me, oh, about two years to get over the last adventure."

The jungle around them quieted abruptly, the hair on Tollar's arms standing up. Bale spiralled overhead before looping out over the city and back into the mountains. She liked to remind everyone that maybe having a dragon around wasn't such a bad idea after all.

Tollar grinned, but Beenala fixed her with a stern look. "Now, if Dram doesn't mind waiting with the supplies until Per Graza can come pick these up, we've got work to do before my parents arrive for dinner. It's mulch day."

Tollar laughed as Beenala turned on her heel, picking up her tools as she went. She gave Draminedes a wave as she followed after Beenala, feeling light on her feet like the sparkle of sunlight on the ocean.

Scan here or visit thodestool.ca/news to learn more about Vanessa's work
or to sign up for her newsletter.

FAVOUR FIRE: FIREBORN SERIES BOOK FIVE

A Sneak Peek

CHAPTER ONE

The ground beneath Neesha's feet shook, and she wondered if she should be more concerned than she was to be standing on an actively erupting volcano? Nandara had been taken aback when Neesha told her what she and Spark intended to do, so Neesha hadn't even bothered to mention it to her mother and especially not Ondias before she and Spark had set out through a fire portal. She knew exactly the look Dionelle would give her, and Ondias would give her an agonizingly boring lecture about being a responsible adult and blah blah blah.

Besides, Neesha *was* being responsible by coming with Spark instead of letting the girl come alone. Only a fool would believe that forbidding Spark from coming at all would actually work.

Spark was nattering on the way she did, up to her knees in one of the gentler lava flows—they'd both agreed not to mention to anyone else how the fire portal they'd opened had brought them out into a much less gentle flow, not that they hadn't been able to get control of the situation quickly. It was mostly fire, and the rest was very hot earth, and both of them could work with those elements, so what was the problem? They'd made themselves little stone rafts to float to more solid ground.

The ground shook again and Neesha glanced to the summit. The flow was getting heavier, the fountaining fire at the top spouting higher.

Nandara, at least, had given her some useful warnings, primarily about how unpredictable an erupting volcano was. But they lived with dragons. How much worse could this be?

Spark was dragging her fingers through the magma before scooping it up and cooling it into dark shapes that looked a lot like the sort of work she was doing to help repair the dragon city. Neesha hadn't been able to master fusing the obsidian and diamond the way her daughter had, so she didn't get to go up to the city nearly as often as Spark did. Especially now that Abyss had left with her family, back to the mountains near Pasdale.

That was fine. Didn't bother Neesha. No, not at all.

She went to the... riverbank? Lavabank? Whatever. And knelt at the edge, running her own hands through it and watching the bright glowing shapes. Her white skin stood out even more against the dark orange flow. She and Spark both were white like fresh snow, hair and skin both. But where Neesha had blue eyes with a fiery amber ring at the outside of her irises, Spark's eyes were fire, flickering to reflect the lava right now. And while Neesha was on the short side and tended toward daintiness, Spark was like a dragon, tall and broad and strong.

Neesha scooped up some lava, sifting it between thumb and fingers. It was neat, but she didn't find it nearly as academically interesting as Spark, who was still muttering to herself about composition and compounds and replication and...

Neesha had no doubt the girl would figure out how to make fireproof notes and come back out here to study the lava flow in more detail.

And Neesha really needed to stop thinking of her as a girl. She was coming up on nineteen now. It was one of the things that had made Neesha's relationship with Dionelle nearly unbearable back... Before. Even now, Dionelle often treated Neesha like she was still a teen.

Of course, Spark had been terribly sheltered most of her life, right up until that terrible year where she'd been exposed to the worst traumas the world had to offer. And now she was back to being insulated. Safe in the bubble of the dragon city. There'd been a time it was necessary, for all of them, to get over what had happened and to figure out how to be a family.

Well, as best as they were ever going to figure that part out.

Neesha didn't think Spark needed quite so much insulating these days. Since they could both go anywhere in the world where there was some fire burning, Neesha had started doing just that—taking Spark on mini adventures.

This particular volcano wasn't even that far away. If Abyss had been around she could have brought them here within a day. Somewhere northwest of the dragon city. Spark had heard about the eruption from one of the returning scouts and had been immediately fascinated, badgering Neesha to go with her to see it firsthand.

Neesha sat on the bank with her chin in her hand, elbow on knee, feet in lava, watching Spark have a fantastic time. Probably with that dopey dumbstruck mom look Ember had discreetly informed her she had whenever Spark was deeply enjoying something. Neesha didn't think she'd ever get over the bitterness at missing so much of this clever human's life, but that didn't mean she couldn't enjoy it now that they were together again.

And then she realized that the cute little fireproof boots Ember had made her were filling up with lava.

"Ah, shit." One nearly came off when Neesha pulled her feet up. She stood on the bank to dump them out.

Spark looked up at her. "Oh! Oh no..." Standing on one leg, Spark lifted a foot up out of the lava to discover that she was missing her boot. Lifted the other leg to find the same.

Neesha laughed.

"Ember's going to kill me." Spark went hunting around with her hands, trying to find her boots, but they'd probably been washed down the slope out onto the distant plateau where the lava had begun to pool.

"Ember will delight in making you a new pair, this one a snugger fit."

Ember loved the challenge of working with what limited dragonskin they had to make fireproof clothing out of. Neesha was wearing the suit she'd made out of Neesha's old purple wizarding robes, one with a lot of straps and buckles to tuck in the looser fitting parts when they were flying with Abyss. Spark's suit was a patchy grey and white, mostly the darker grey patches, a little more utilitarian, but still with some straps and buckles for her flying harness and glider attachment.

Neesha laced her boots a little tighter but didn't put her feet back in the flow. Spark went back to mucking around in magma, and Neesha went back to watching her. She'd hoped there'd be something a little more magically exciting to do, something new to practice. But fire portals were routine and everything else they'd been doing didn't even involve active magic. Fire couldn't harm them.

Nandara had warned that the volcano was more than fire, which was why they'd come in boots. The liquid earth did feel different than walking on the ground of the fire realm, and the bits where Neesha had been walking were sharper, but it was a smoother bed under the flow where Spark focused all her attention.

Neesha hadn't done much magic at all since late-winter when she and Spark had finally completed their full Guild entrance exams, trading in their specialist tokens for Guild badges made of some kind of charmed iridescent gemstone. Neesha had initially been ecstatic to finally be a full Guild member and sincerely hoped someone told Loch about it. But with nothing to actually *do* with her magic out in the middle of nowhere, the excitement had worn off.

The ground shook again, continuous now and the roar from the summit was all she could hear. Like all the dragons going to battle at once. Wincing against the sound and trying not to let it crumple her, Neesha looked up to the fountaining fire above them to see a horror of fire and smoke and debris. A dark plume raced downhill toward them and fiery chunks burst from the cloud to land nearby.

"Shit!" she gasped, drawing from the fire all around them and pulling open a fire portal between her and Spark. "Let's go!"

The fire couldn't hurt them. But flying chunks of rock and whatever gases that plume held sure could.

Spark was frozen to the spot, her eyes wide as she watched the plume consume everything before her. Neesha pulled up a little fireball and threw it at Spark's shoulder. Spark shrieked and nearly fell over into the lavaflow—getting swept away was the last thing they needed right now.

Neesha stumbled across the shuddering ground and caught Spark's shoulder near the lavabank, tugging her to the portal. No easy feat when Neesha still had noodle arms and Spark was possibly twice her size.

Neesha wouldn't have expected it, but the roar of the fire realm was somehow a quiet reprieve from the roar of the exploding volcano. Spark staggered to a stop next to her, closing the portal behind her.

"What in all the hells was that!"

Neesha gave her a wry smile. "That, my dear, was a volcano."

Acknowledgements

I am truly glad that I wrote the first draft of this book even before the pandemic started because otherwise I may have never finished it. Revising it has been a slog, not only because so many parts of it hit me right in the gut as I anxiously await to see if our neighbour is going to invade and destroy us, but because the way everything is on fire makes it extremely difficult to be creative or productive or even upright and not crying. I perpetually feel like I have a scream trapped in my chest. Like I'm chained to people sleepwalking off a cliff.

And I want to make it perfectly clear, written here in words that will get printed on paper and possibly outlast those trying to destroy us: Canadians **do not** want to be Americans. We like you just fine, but we are *Canadian*. We are not America Lite. We have our own cultures and ways of being that are different. We want to hold onto those. Our sovereignty is important and something we will viciously fight for. And under our polite, apologetic veneer, we are extremely furious and deeply unhinged. This is profoundly existential in a way I wish more Americans understood.

I am very very tired of living in interesting times—and I don't even have it that bad! I hope that this book gives you a spot of joy, a bit of a distraction, and maybe the drive to keep fighting. I don't know about you, but I ran out of hope sometime in 2021 and spite is what I have left.

The fight is always worth fighting, even if all it does is slow our enemies down. Deny them the easy victory they expect. Your joy and your existence is a thorn in their side. Dig in and twist! You're stronger than you think and have more courage than you know, and I hope you discover both when the need arises.

I had so much fun writing this book, and I'm just so excited that it's out into the world for other people to enjoy. And after the year I've had, struggling so hard with burnout and being unable to write for months, with the usual background chatter of ideas utterly silenced, getting back into writing and publishing with this book is something of a triumph. I thought I'd gotten over the burnout, but putting out 4 books in a year was perhaps a bit more task than I was up to. After my last book came out, my brain went into hibernation for several months. I worried about my ability to finish this book or the final book in the series.

But the writing came back, and it was a joy to return to this world and this series. Writing still goes slower than I'd like, but at least it goes.

Time for thanks! Thank you again to my family, and in particular my dad this time, for all the support. Thank you to the amazing team that helped me put this together: Kris for continuing to track the lore, Sydnee for the sensitivity read, Kaya for stepping in at the eleventh hour to make sure copy edits got done, Ursula for the excellent scene break design and some perfect character art, and Leesha for the absolutely amazing cover. OMG that cover—I'm in love!

And once again thank you to all my Kickstarter supporters, without whom this book wouldn't be possible.

ABOUT THE AUTHOR

photo by Mike Thode

Vanessa is a word sorceress and Nebula Award-winning fantasy author whose life seldom strays from the world of books, especially during winter hibernation. Even her volunteer work revolves around the literary world, currently as co-founder and events director of KW Writers Alliance and as a coordinator for the SFWA volunteer team.

When she's not being bookish, she's into astronomy, hiking, gardening, and has a personal goal to visit all the national parks. Don't ask her about her love of trees unless you've got some time. She loves Halloween and hates to be cold. Vanessa lives in Waterloo (no, the other one) with her spouse, daughter, and dogs, where she can be found in her butterfly garden, achieving her final form as a garden witch.

To learn more, visit thodestool.ca or follow her on social media @VRicciThode